STAR TREK™
DISCOVERY

SOMEWHERE TO BELONG

DAYTON WARD

Based upon *Star Trek*
created by Gene Roddenberry
and
Star Trek: Discovery
created by Bryan Fuller & Alex Kurtzman

GALLERY BOOKS

New York   London   Toronto   Syd

G

Gallery Books
An Imprint of Simon & Schuster, Inc.
1230 Avenue of the Americas
New York, NY 10020

First Gallery Books trade paperback edition May 2023

GALLERY BOOKS and colophon are registered trademarks of Simon & Schuster, Inc.

For information about special discounts for bulk purchases, please contact Simon & Schuster Special Sales at 1-866-506-1949 or business@simonandschuster.com.

The Simon & Schuster Speakers Bureau can bring authors to your live event. For more information or to book an event, contact the Simon & Schuster Speakers Bureau at 1-866-248-3049 or visit our website at www.simonspeakers.com.

Interior design by Kathryn A. Kenney-Peterson

Manufactured in the United States of America

10 9 8 7 6 5 4 3 2 1

Library of Congress Cataloging-in-Publication Data
s been applied for.

N 978-1-6680-0229-2
  978-1-6680-0231-5 (ebook)

Dedicated to my wife and children.
They're where I belong.

HISTORIAN'S NOTE

The events of this story take place in 3189, several weeks after Michael Burnham and the crew of *U.S.S. Discovery* NCC-1031-A saved Federation Headquarters by defeating Minister Osyraa and the renegade "capitalist syndicate" known as the Emerald Chain (*Star Trek: Discovery*, "That Hope Is You, Part 2") and approximately four months prior to the destruction of Cleveland Booker's home planet, Kwejian, by a dark matter anomaly (*Star Trek: Discovery*, "Kobayashi Maru").

01

Planet Xahea – 2258

Sunrise.

Reclining in a chair on the balcony outside her private bedchambers, Me Hani Ika Hali Ka Po lifted a silver cup from its matching saucer and held it to her lips, blowing across the surface of the tea it held. Across the vast expanse of forest forming this portion of the grounds her family had owned for eleven generations, she watched as the first hints of pink began pushing against the darkness beyond the trees.

It was her favorite time of day. This brief interval between waking from slumber and facing whatever official task or duty awaited her arrival to her office was hers and hers alone. Even though she had awakened earlier than normal in anticipation of a crowded work and public appearance schedule, she insisted on reserving these few precious moments for herself.

"Good morning, Your Highness."

The quiet yet authoritative voice drifted through the doorway leading from the balcony into her private chambers, and Po turned from the lightening sky to see Lan Aki Ga Bomi Ren, her closest aide and advisor as well as a dear family friend, standing at the threshold. Like her, he had already dressed for the day's schedule and, as was his unfailing custom, he presented himself in a manner befitting professional decorum in a dark tunic that fell to midthigh over matching trousers and shoes polished to a fine sheen. His hair, silver and thinning with age, was slicked back against his skull, complementing the deep-blue lines and patterns of his ancestral facial markings.

"Good morning, Ren. Already hard at work, I see." Po smiled in greeting to her trusted mentor, the one person among all of those pledged to serve her who enjoyed unfettered access to her private chambers at any time of the day or night. It was a privilege Ren honored and respected to an exacting degree, never imposing upon his queen unless required by circumstance or the necessities of duty. If he was here at this early hour, it was with sufficient reason. Po suspected she already knew what had brought him.

"I apologize for interrupting your personal time, Your Highness," he said, offering a respectful nod. "As I am sure you are aware, today's schedule is rather demanding."

Rather than voice a reply, Po instead chose to call forth her personal shroud, rendering herself all but invisible. The genetic trait was one her people had possessed for as long as anyone could remember. There were those who believed it evolved as a biological protective response at some early point in her people's prehistory. Others were certain it was an attribute imparted by the planet itself, with which many if not most Xaheans believed they carried a special bond dating back to the world's creation and the birth of their civilization. While the ability normally manifested itself in response to perceived threat, some few people, such as Po herself, could call upon it at will. She tended to reserve it for moments like this, if only to elicit a laugh from Ren.

"I am afraid that will not shield you, Your Highness," said her aide. "There are a number of smaller matters requiring your attention in timely fashion, and I have already organized the bulk of those tasks for you to address."

Allowing her shroud to dissipate, Po asked, "Don't you ever just want to sleep in, forget work, and have some fun?"

Without a moment's hesitation, Ren replied, "If only such a fantasy could come true, Your Highness."

"Is that snark?" asked Po. "Didn't I outlaw that?"

Choosing to ignore the question, Ren produced from behind his back a personal tablet, which he held before him as he pressed a control and the device's embedded holographic interface came to life. Various pages of information coalesced into existence, arranged before him in a curved ribbon, which he inspected for a moment with practiced ease before offering the tablet to Po.

"As you can see, I have arranged the documents based on the priority established by the council, the members of which await your appearance with barely contained enthusiasm."

"You need to be in charge of the council," said Po. "Or maybe just their various staffs. Imagine what we might accomplish in a single day, let alone an entire legislative session, with you whipping them into shape. Just the thought of setting you loose to terrorize them with your organizational acumen makes me giddy." She offered a mischievous smile. "But I'm pretty sure you'd enjoy yourself entirely too much. Besides, do you know how loudly they'd balk at the audacity of a *mere commoner* in their midst, teaching them how to do their own jobs?" Her smile widened as she entertained the notion. "It's worth doing just for that. What do you think, Ren? Ready for the challenge?"

Drawing himself up and maintaining his impassive expression, her aide replied, "I serve at the queen's pleasure, Your Highness." Then his lips curled upward in measured amusement. "However, I would rather enjoy such an errand."

Ever the professional whenever Po presented herself to the Xahean Council and other representatives of the planetary government, and most especially whenever the queen appeared in public, Ren reserved his less restrained observations for moments like these, when it was just the two of them working together. Po welcomed his frank opinions without reservation. More than an assistant or even the teacher he had been when she was younger, Ren also served as her conscience. She trusted him to be absolutely truthful with her while still maintaining the respect he showed to all members of the royal family and elected government leaders. It was this dichotomy and his ability to shift between the two disparate facades that made him such an effective, welcome counselor. It also allowed for frequent bouts of much-needed humor and friendship that older members of "the establishment" would likely consider inappropriate for their queen. Po had learned from observing her parents, but especially her mother, that sitting atop the leadership caste of the Xahean people was very often a lonely, isolated platform.

"Every day since I took my place here," she said, gesturing for him to sit in the balcony's other chair, "I've been grateful for you. Not just your assistance or your guidance, but your simple presence." She had been reluctant to take on the role of queen following the deaths of her parents and her brother, even fleeing the planet for a time before she realized there was no avoiding her responsibilities. It was Ren who had stood by her side all those years, who once again pledged his unwavering support as she moved into this new phase of her life. "I couldn't do everything the crown demands of me without your friendship. You honor me and your family every day, Ren."

Now seated across from her, the older man bowed his head. As was normally the case, he was uncomfortable with such praise. "It is you who honor me, Your Highness. Serving your family is the privilege of my life, and it allows me to take care of my own family in a manner I never dreamed was possible, even with the opportunities you and your mother have created for all Xahean people."

One would never know from his appearance and speech that he represented the last generation of his family to work in Xahea's dilithium mines. Born of common stock, Ren had followed his parents' path into the mines where he and countless other Xahean citizens toiled to extract the rare, valuable mineral from the planet's depths. Given the quality of its dilithium deposits, Xahea had quickly become a prominent player in interstellar commerce.

During a visit by the queen, Po's mother, to inspect one of the mines as she sought to bring improvements to those whose contributions and sacrifices made it successful, Po had met Ren. His straightforward answers to her mother's questions, delivered with utmost respect and a genuine passion for matters of import to the labor force, had so impressed her that she invited him to a meeting at the royal home.

It was to be the first of many such discussions aimed at finding ways to improve not just the mining process but also the labor conditions, compensation, and other benefits for workers and their families. Growing out of those conversations was a hitherto unprecedented program of improvements the new queen would champion.

After reviewing and signing the documents Ren gave her, Po willed the tablet to rise from her hand and float across the table to her aide. Telekinesis was another gift imbued within each Xahean, for reasons that remained unknown. While it had obvious practical uses, she learned early on and much to her mother's chagrin that it could also be a tool for mischief.

"Those should keep the council busy for a portion of the day," she said as the tablet landed in Ren's hands.

Tapping a few controls on the device, Ren replied, "Your first meeting is with the leaders of the mining consortium. The next phase of automation enhancements is scheduled for installation soon, and they wish to outline expectations as far as production impacts during the upgrade period."

"Didn't we discuss all of this during the initial planning meetings?" asked Po.

Ren nodded. "Indeed we did, Your Highness, but the consortium leadership is worried even the reduced estimates are overly optimistic, and they wish to present alternative schedule estimates. According to the briefing I read, worker safety is the driving factor in these proposed revisions."

An alert tone from his tablet made him glance again at the device. He frowned as he read whatever was displayed upon it.

"Your Highness, I have just been alerted to an incoming subspace communications request." He tapped another control. "It is from the *Enterprise*."

Po's eyes widened in recognition. "The *Enterprise*? Captain Pike's ship?"

Nodding, Ren replied, "He is requesting to speak directly with you, alone and on a secure frequency."

"Really?" It had been some time since Po had heard from Pike or anyone else from Starfleet, and her last encounter with them had been anything but routine.

Moving from the patio and crossing from her private residence to the small office she maintained in the family mansion for state business, Po looked over her shoulder as Ren stood at the entrance to the workspace, his expression apprehensive. "What's wrong?"

"Captain Pike's request was to speak to you alone, Your Highness."

Po waved away the reply. "Don't worry about it. One of the benefits of being the queen is I don't have to follow rules or requests I don't like." She was not worried about Ren's discretion even with such a sensitive matter as the one she suspected was the reason for the *Enterprise* captain contacting her this morning. "Open the frequency, please."

Crossing the office to the oversized viewing screen set into the room's far wall, she positioned herself before the monitor and waited as Ren made whatever security and encryption arrangements were necessary to complete the subspace connection. A moment later, the screen flared to life, coalescing into the image of a human male, Christopher Pike. Dressed in the gold tunic and dark trousers and boots of a Starfleet captain, Pike was—Po presumed—quite handsome for a member of his species. What she had liked from her first encounter with him was the quiet, confident authority he projected. It was evident during that meeting, when he had commanded the crew of the *Discovery* including her good friend Sylvia Tilly.

With his hands clasped behind his back, Captain Pike said, *"Your Serene Highness, I bring you greetings from the United Federation of Planets. Thank you for speaking with me."*

"Are you kidding?" Po made no effort to hide a wide grin. "This might end up being the best part of my day."

Pike returned the smile. *"In that case, and since I know how busy you are, I'll get right to the point. I told you I'd make contact when a certain something happened. It has. All is well."*

He said nothing else, and neither did he have to, as Po knew without doubt what he meant. Commander Michael Burnham, after disappearing along with her ship, *Discovery*, through a temporal wormhole, had signaled their arrival at a point in the distant future. Her mind's eye filled with visions of her dear friend Sylvia Tilly. Po thought of her often, just as she had wondered these past months what might have become of her and her companions aboard their starship.

"That's wonderful news, Captain." Despite contacting her on an encrypted frequency, Pike would take no chances revealing too much information about what had transpired. She recalled her earlier conversation with him, soon after *Discovery*'s departure. There was of course no way to communicate with *Discovery*, but Pike explained Burnham would signal only if their transit was successful. Like the *Enterprise* captain, Po could only hope she and her crew were safe and able to find peace as well as a new home for themselves.

Pike's expression grew thoughtful. *"None of it would've been possible if not for you, Your Highness."* He offered a small, respectful nod. *"The Federation owes you a tremendous debt, and so do I. Thank you again."*

Po smiled at the captain, recalling how even Ren had taken her to task upon her return to Xahea following *Discovery*'s visit to the planet and Pike and his crew's request for assistance. The device she had created as a tool to recrystallize dilithium had proven vital to the effort of keeping the ship and the valuable alien data repository it contained away from the machinations of Section 31, a rogue intelligence agency within Starfleet. She had then led a counteroffensive against a fleet of Section 31 drones sent to attack *Discovery*, helping to buy time for Burnham to open a wormhole that allowed her and her ship to escape into the future.

As for her "dilithium incubator," assisting *Discovery* was, she decided, the sole good purpose to which it could be put, at least for now. Her original goal for the invention—a means of reducing the environmental impacts of mining dilithium from Xahea—had always been to protect her planet from further harm. It was a solemn duty, she decided, to safeguard the world that was so much more than simply home to her people. Following *Discovery*'s departure for the future, she had destroyed her only working prototype. While Po could certainly rebuild the device if the mood struck her, she had no immediate plans to do so. There were those who would only seek to use such an invention for personal gain, or worse. At this point in the history of her world, it was an idea that caused more problems than it solved. Allowing that was beneath a queen pledged to lead her people on a path to a thriving future. She would just have to find another way to protect the precious world they all called home.

"This is wonderful news, Captain. Thank you for telling me. Safe journeys to you and your crew."

Pike smiled again. *"As my science officer is fond of saying: Live long and prosper, Your Highness."*

The captain's visage faded and the viewing screen deactivated, leaving Po once more alone with Ren.

"Well, how about that?"

"Most excellent news, Your Highness. I knew the fate of your friends was weighing on you." As her trusted confidant, Ren was the only person with whom Po had discussed her experiences with *Discovery* and its crew. Beyond that, she had promised to honor Starfleet's desire to classify the entire affair. Only a private journal, with entries written in her own hand and locked away in a secure vault along with other treasured family heirlooms, offered any insight into events Starfleet would forever deny even took place. The true fates of Tilly and her crewmates were forever consigned to an obscure corner of forgotten history.

Meanwhile, the thought of them finding a new home in a reality that was almost too distant to imagine filled Po's heart with joy. Sylvia Tilly had helped her at a point when she stood at a crossroads, deciding between ascending to her role in Xahean society or running away. Feeling lost amidst the stresses that came with her own life path, Tilly offered a sympathetic ear, and she and Po had supported each other to arrive at a place of realization and acceptance. It was one of the greatest gifts Po had ever received, and she hoped Tilly felt the same way. Po would miss her friend and suspected she would spend many a quiet moment contemplating the future Tilly and her crewmates might forge centuries from now, long after Po was gone.

"In a way, I envy them," said Po. "*Discovery*'s crew. Tilly. What will they see? What will they accomplish?" She shook her head. "Contemplating the possibilities is overwhelming, but I hope they're able to make a joyous life for themselves." Also, the thought of Tilly and her friends traveling to a point where they might observe whatever the future held for Xahea was an even greater motivation for Po to press forward with the work she knew lay ahead.

Drawing a deep breath, she offered Ren a knowing smile. "Meanwhile, my job is to help guide our people toward a similar goal, and I can't do any of that without you. We should probably get started."

Ren drew himself up, as always her prim and proper adherent ready to support her in any way he was able. "A laudable aspiration, Your Highness. I eagerly anticipate what our own future might bring."

02

Starship Discovery
Federation Headquarters – 3189

Movement, slow and deliberate against her body, roused Michael Burnham from sleep. A familiar weight and warmth slid along her shoulder. Soft and gentle, it progressed to her neck and she felt it coming to rest along the side of her face. Freeing her right hand from the tangle of sheets, Burnham slid it across the bed until she found the other body lying next to her. It took her a moment to realize Book was lying on his side and facing away from her, the smooth skin of his back warm beneath her fingers.

Wait.

The single word tugged at her consciousness, goading her from slumber. Now fully awake, Burnham opened her eyes and turned toward Book only to find her vision filled with dark hair. It did not belong to Book, and for damned sure it most certainly was not hers.

"Grudge." Dry from sleep, her voice was a croak as she spoke. "What are you doing?"

In response, the cat began to purr. Her green eyes narrowed as she settled against Burnham's head and neck. Without thinking, Burnham reached up to stroke Grudge's flank, which elicited still louder purring. It was that special time of day, before the hustle and demands of duty carried her away from her quarters, when the cat solicited a precious few moments of companionship. While Grudge still deferred to Book when allowing physical contact from inferior bipedal life-forms, her acceptance of Burnham was a work in progress. This was not yet a common occurrence, but now it happened with enough frequency that

Burnham could almost believe the cat liked her. Grudge leaned into Burnham's fingers as they massaged her neck, the purring growing more intense and now laced with an unmistakable air of transitory satisfaction.

"You're in her spot, you know."

His voice low and thick with sleep, Cleveland Booker rolled onto his back, turning to face Burnham and Grudge. With a smile, he reached up to run his hand along the cat's back. For her part, the feline accepted the increased attention with her normal stoicism.

"Her spot?" Burnham regarded Book with narrowed eyes. "She's in *my* spot. *You're* in my spot. *This whole bed is my spot.*"

Book chuckled before clearing his throat. "Deny it all you want, but it's inevitable. I thought you would've learned that after a year of sharing my ship with her."

"That was different." Burnham smiled, enjoying this latest iteration of their little verbal sparring matches that provided momentary amusement at times like these. "That's your home, and hers. I was an intruder."

Shifting himself to a sitting position, Book adjusted the sheets around his waist and propped a pillow behind his back. "It's her ship and she lets me fly it, but your point is still valid as far as it goes." He smiled, gesturing around Burnham's quarters. "In fact, the way she sees it, all of this is hers now too. You might want to start getting yourself aligned with that reality."

Burnham rested her hand on Grudge's back. "Is this your way of telling me you're planning to stick around?"

"I'm not in a hurry to be anywhere, if that's what you're asking." Book regarded her with a cocked eyebrow. "Why? Are you looking to get rid of me?"

"Not just yet." Burnham studied Grudge, whose eyes now were closed as she endured the soft stroking. "Besides, it's been a long time since my life was anything resembling routine. I'm still getting used to the whole idea."

Book rolled his eyes. "Michael, I've known you for over a

year now. 'Routine' isn't a word I'd use to describe you. Obsessively compulsive? Absolutely, but routine? Never."

"That's because the version of me you know was busy adapting to a whole new universe." She waved her hand in the air. "This ship and crew? This is the real me. This is what was missing from my life for a long time, even before I showed up here."

It was only in the past few weeks that the reality of her present circumstances along with those of *Discovery*'s crew had finally begun to assert itself in Burnham's mind. With no looming threats or larger issues weighing on her attention, life aboard ship had settled—

Into a routine. She smiled at the admission.

The change had come with almost as much abruptness as her arrival in the thirty-second century, well over nine hundred years after the era in which she had been born and come of age. An entire lifetime of successes and failures, hopes and dreams, triumphs and tragedies, was but the smallest footnote in the annals of a history that from her point of view had expanded by nearly a millennium in the blink of an eye. The future into which they had emerged—the one for which she and *Discovery*'s crew believed they had sacrificed so much to safeguard—bore little more than a passing resemblance to what she had imagined they might find.

Hardship had fallen upon the Federation and the entire galaxy over the centuries they had bypassed. Countless lives along with entire worlds endured radical changes if not outright annihilation. Epicenters of power once thought to be guiding lights of inspiration on an interstellar stage had seen their influence wane and even crumble. This was the reality into which she and her crew had been thrust, and within which they were still seeking a measure of equilibrium. While her people had comported themselves with distinction, she knew that beneath the veneer of duty and obligation lay the beating hearts of living beings separated from everything they had known and loved.

"I know that look," said Book as their gazes met. "It's the one you get when you start thinking you're the mother to everyone on this ship."

Unable to suppress a smile, Burnham nodded. "It's true, in its own way. I am responsible for them, their welfare and their safety. I'm not here to wipe their noses or help them with their homework or cheer them on when they play sports, but what they do reflects on me, and what I do absolutely impacts them. That's the job."

It was a job for which she had spent the majority of her early adult life training, guided by Philippa Georgiou, her commanding officer aboard the *Shenzhou*. Georgiou had been the ideal role model, both as a person and as a Starfleet captain, and it was she Burnham endeavored to emulate.

Right up until the moment you betrayed her.

The silent rebuke sprang unbidden from the depths of her memories. Burnham knew on an intellectual level it was a simplistic distillation of what had been a very nuanced and complex situation. The steps she had taken during the tense first contact with the Klingon sarcophagus ship were intended to prevent a war rather than start one, despite putting her at odds with Georgiou. After failing to convince her captain that firing on the enemy vessel before it could attack was the prudent action, Burnham subdued Georgiou and assumed command of the *Shenzhou*. Only later was it revealed that the Klingon Empire had been spoiling for a fight, intentionally destroying a Starfleet communications relay in hopes of luring a ship to its location. The resulting conflict between the Federation and the Empire had been costly, not the least of which when calculating the lives lost. Despite being sentenced to life in prison for her mutinous acts, fate and circumstances saw her path cross with *Discovery*.

She had worked hard to re-earn the trust of Starfleet and her shipmates, an effort that ultimately saw her guiding *Discovery* through that wormhole and more than nine hundred years across space and time. There was a time following her arrival here in the thirty-second century and her reunion with the ship and its crew that Burnham considered leaving Starfleet, at least the version that existed in this still largely unfamiliar future. The year she spent with Cleveland Booker, working as a courier without the rigors of protocol and duty, had come to define her; it had also given her cause to question her choices and that commitment. Despite the challenges presented by a post-Burn galaxy and its effects on the Federation, it still offered an opportunity for a fresh start. It was a tempting proposition, with the allure of it all enhanced by the unlikely yet enticing relationship she had forged with Book. In the year following her exit from the wormhole, Burnham had been forced to adapt to a new reality. The situation required her to compartmentalize and even abandon ways of thinking that at one time were second nature to her. She liked to think these changes had not altered her at the most fundamental levels, but even now there remained a lingering uncertainty. Facing those challenges had almost been enough to make her shed her uniform, figuratively and literally. If she had never reunited with *Discovery* and her friends, that might well have been her choice.

Fate, of course, had other ideas.

Book rested his left hand on Burnham's arm. "You're right about one thing. This *is* the real you. From the moment we saw Saru and the others on the screen, I knew you'd never abandon them. It was etched on your face." Before she could respond, he held up his other hand as if to stave off protest. "You just said it yourself: this is the part of you that was missing. I know, you and Saru didn't see eye to eye at first, and maybe you really did consider walking away from all of it, but once you started actually working together, the writing was on the wall." He offered a small, knowing smile. "It suits you."

With nothing else to add to the conversation, Grudge had fallen limp against Burnham's shoulder, her eyes closed and her breathing slow and steady.

Burnham studied Book. "We were doing all right. I admit

it was hard, but I was starting to settle in." She saw the expression on his face, knowing that it now was her turn to forestall his reply. "I know, I never gave up looking for *Discovery*." To do anything less was unthinkable. A significant number of the ship's crew had chosen to accompany her on the insane, one-way journey to the future, leaving behind everything and everyone they had ever loved. Their commitment to her was as overt an act of devotion as any she had ever witnessed. Burnham owed those people—every single one of them—nothing less. Further, she had felt that same level of responsibility to the Federation and Starfleet in which she found herself.

"I never stopped trying to figure out what caused the Burn. After all those months of waiting and hoping with nothing to show for it, in the back of my mind I started considering the possibility I'd never accomplish either of those things. It was difficult to even entertain those thoughts, let alone try to put myself in a place to accept them, but little by little, I let them try to take root."

"I know you did," said Book. "At least, I think you did, and maybe—just maybe—you let a bit of that get past your defenses. Still, I'd already gotten to know you well enough by then to understand you'd never completely give up. You'd always have your eyes on the stars, waiting for your friends and trying to figure out the Burn. I was right there when your communicator signaled their arrival, remember? Nothing was going to stop you from getting to them, and after that? Nothing was going to stop you from finding Starfleet, and then everything that came with it." He gestured around her quarters. "And now here we are. This is your home, Michael. As it should be. As it was *meant* to be."

The ship's intercom chose that moment to ping for attention, followed by the voice of Zora—the artificial intelligence residing within *Discovery*'s main computer system—speaking with her unfailingly pleasant demeanor. *"Good morning, Captain Burnham. It is now zero seven hundred hours, Federation*

Standard Time. Your meeting with Admiral Vance at Federation Headquarters remains scheduled for zero eight hundred hours."

As if sensing a pending shift in the status quo that involved humans disrupting her slumber, Grudge opted to remove herself from her resting place next to Burnham. She sauntered toward the foot of the bed before dropping to the floor and out of sight. With the cat no longer separating them, Burnham turned onto her side and reached out to rest her hand on Book's thigh. Still propped against his pillow, he shifted so that he now lounged beside her, facing her with his nose nearly touching hers.

"Duty calls again," he said.

Burnham let her hand roam. "Seems that way."

"The burdens of command."

"It's a thankless task."

In truth, she had no idea why Vance even wanted a meeting with her this morning. She and the rest of *Discovery*'s crew had been ordered by the admiral to stand down for a few days of shore leave following their last assignment. As the break had been a long time coming and, in her opinion, sorely needed, she had encouraged her people to take full advantage of the opportunity. However, given the unpredictable nature of Starfleet missions and current needs, she suspected Vance had an assignment for *Discovery*, which was fine with her. Shore leave was nice and the downtime welcomed, but she was ready to get back to work.

Sliding his left arm beneath her, Book pulled her closer. "Maybe you could call in sick."

"I don't think the admiral would appreciate that. Or believe it."

"That's not the rebellious Michael Burnham I know."

"Good morning, Captain Burnham," said Zora. *"It is now zero seven zero one, Federation Standard Time. Your meeting with Admiral Vance at Federation Headquarters remains scheduled for zero eight hundred hours."*

Burnham shifted in the bed, giving her hands more room

to maneuver. "Thank you, Zora. No further reminders are needed."

"A database incorporating more than one hundred thousand years of accumulated information," said Book. "Perhaps the most sophisticated and comprehensive computer system in existence, and you've got it set up as your personal alarm clock." He smiled. "Being the captain certainly has its privileges."

Burnham responded with a playful slap. "I didn't set it up. It did that all on its own." The action, innocuous though it may be, was just one small component of a much larger, far-ranging effort on the computer's part to conduct what it perceived as its primary function: caring for the ship's crew.

She, Burnham reminded herself. *Not "it."*

Further, safeguarding *Discovery*'s crew seemed to be a mission Zora had assigned to herself, the personification of the Sphere data residing within the computer system. Accumulated by a benign life-form encountered by *Discovery*, all of that information had been transferred into the ship's computer as the newly discovered being neared the end of its life. This made *Discovery* along with the Sphere life-form's data a prize sought by Control, a malevolent threat-assessment artificial intelligence created by the clandestine Starfleet agency Section 31. If Control were to gain access to the repository, it would achieve consciousness and be all but unstoppable. Indeed, at some point in the future, it had accomplished—or would accomplish—that very thing.

Enter Burnham's mother, Doctor Gabrielle Burnham, and the "Red Angel" suit she and Burnham's father had created for Section 31 to send a single individual through time. The suit was developed as a counter to Klingon efforts to escalate a "temporal arms race" between their Empire and the Federation. When Klingon agents launched an attack to capture the suit, Doctor Burnham used it to escape, jumping to a point nearly one thousand years into the future. There she learned Control had evolved to a point where it had destroyed all life in the galaxy. Her attempts to go back in time and prevent Control from seizing the Sphere data and achieving that level of sentience brought her and the suit to her daughter and *Discovery*. Her efforts were hampered by her being anchored to her arrival point in the far future, which yanked her back after the twenty-third-century version of Control succeeded in destroying the Red Angel suit.

With Control still a threat, *Discovery*'s crew constructed a new suit, which Burnham wore to guide the ship through a wormhole to the thirty-second century, far beyond Control's reach. It was now gone, and *Discovery* and her crew remained guardians of the Sphere's data and the unexpected identity it had adopted since merging with the ship's computer. Just as Burnham and her people had pledged to protect the information from corruption or exploitation, so too had the computer and its—*her*—evolved presence undertaken a similar role with respect to the ship and the organic beings dwelling within it.

Apparently, this included reminding Burnham of her schedule for the day.

Satisfied Zora would leave her alone, at least for the time being, Burnham moved closer to Book. "Don't tell her, but I don't really need an entire hour to get ready for a meeting."

Duty could wait a bit longer.

03

At precisely 0755 hours, Burnham materialized in the foyer outside Admiral Vance's office. Despite having received her uniform from the replicator in her quarters not fifteen minutes earlier, she found herself tugging at her collar and sleeves and making other adjustments. She had only just gotten used to the more subtle gray uniforms worn by the Starfleet officers who greeted *Discovery* upon its arrival at Federation Headquarters barely two months earlier. They were a far cry from the predominantly blue ones worn aboard starships in the 2250s, which Burnham admitted to herself she missed. This new variant—a deep red tunic with its prominent black stripe extending down from her right shoulder, along with black trousers and dark leather boots—was a much bolder choice. She decided she preferred the look, but she was still getting used to the fit.

"Good morning, Captain Burnham."

Turning toward the new voice, she found herself greeted by Eli, the medical hologram that also served as a multifaceted assistant to Admiral Vance. As always, the computer-generated avatar presented the appearance of a trim human male perhaps fifty years of age, with brown hair that was both graying and receding at his temples. Instead of a uniform, Eli wore a stark white ensemble with matching belt and bow tie. Only a standard-issue tricom badge above his left breast offered any hint as to his Starfleet affiliation. From her past interactions with him, Burnham knew his piercing hazel eyes missed nothing, and at this moment they were focused on her.

"Good morning, Eli. How are you today?"

The holo shrugged. "I've not received any significant modifications to my programming since our last meeting, so I am largely unchanged. And you?"

"About the same." Only as she replied did Burnham realize she was still fussing with the sleeves of her uniform, and she clasped her hands behind her back.

Her response seemed to satisfy Eli. "Yes, that mostly tracks with my current readings of your limbic system, and you do seem more relaxed this morning. I trust you're sleeping well?"

"Very well, thank you." It had taken some time to become accustomed to the holo's penchant for conducting its medical scans as a matter of course rather than as requested or if a situation demanded such action.

He doesn't like being called "it," Burnham reminded herself. *That's twice you've done that, and you haven't even had breakfast yet.*

"Excellent." Eli gestured to the entrance to Vance's office. "Of course you're right on time for your meeting with the admiral. He's on his way and asked me to direct you inside."

The holo turned and headed into a larger workspace, dominated by a free-floating situation table and a view of various starships docked at or holding station in proximity to Federation Headquarters. As she entered the room, she noted Fleet Admiral Charles Vance entering from an adjacent passageway.

"Captain Burnham," he said, extending his hand in greeting. "Thank you for joining me so early in the day."

As ever, Starfleet's top-ranked officer was a recruiting advertisement come to life. His gray uniform with its red and gold piping was immaculate and tailored to his trim, athletic frame. His black hair and beard were all but overrun with gray and the lines around his dark eyes bore mute testimony to a life of duty and responsibility and the challenges that come with a commitment to those ideals.

"Good morning, Admiral. What can I do for you, sir?"

As she spoke, she noticed movement to her left and turned to see the office's other occupant rising from a sofa positioned along the room's far bulkhead. It was Doctor Arbusala, a male

Denobulan of whom she and the rest of the crew had seen quite a bit during the past two weeks. As he was a civilian, his clothing was far more casual. A dark maroon shirt and jade-green trousers, all loose fitting and looking far more comfortable than any uniform, were accompanied by leather sandals on his feet. His hair, long and brown, was pulled back from his face and secured in a ponytail, accenting his high cranial ridges. His crystal-blue eyes seemed to sparkle, and the lower half of his face stretched into a wide smile as he acknowledged Burnham.

"Good day, Captain." Arbusala clasped his hands in front of him. "A pleasure to see you this morning. And I see you've wasted no time transitioning to the new uniforms Admiral Vance approved."

Before she could stop herself, Burnham ran her hands along her sides, smoothing her tunic. "I have to admit, I wasn't too thrilled with the gray ones." She tossed a meek glance toward Vance, who chuckled at her comment.

"It wouldn't be Starfleet if we didn't change things up every now and again." Looking down at himself, Vance tapped the front of his uniform top. "It goes in cycles, you know. I've done my share of reading about Starfleet history and one of the things I found interesting was how the chronology of uniform styles tends to remain in step with Starfleet's primary focus—or its perceived primary focus—during that point in time. Periods dominated by a heightened emphasis on exploration and discovery were underscored by bolder, more colorful uniform designs, whereas those times when we found ourselves facing far more ominous challenges such as war, disaster, or other struggles provoked darker, conventional styles."

Arbusala said, "It is an interesting connection."

"Agreed," replied Burnham. "The designs may change, but the colors seem to have remained consistent more often than not." She shrugged, touching her right hand to her midsection as she glanced at her own tunic. "At least, when they've opted for more color."

Vance said, "For whatever reason, fate has seen fit to bring you and your crew to us, Captain, and after giving it some further thought, I've come to believe your presence here signifies a turning point for us. I thought it warranted something to mark the occasion." He paused, offering a small grin. "As for the colors, well, I guess some things never go out of style."

"Like bow ties," said Eli, and for the first time Burnham realized the holo had not simply disappeared after leading her into Vance's office. Instead, he stood to one side, hands behind his back as he awaited instructions from the admiral. When she looked to him, he tilted his head to one side while gesturing to his own bow tie. "They're a universal constant."

Vance allowed himself a small laugh before saying, "That will be all, Eli." In response to his direction the holo dematerialized without another word, leaving Burnham alone with the admiral and Doctor Arbusala.

"I've been doing my own reading as well, sir," she said. "Call it ongoing 'homework' while catching up on the history we missed."

The centuries she and *Discovery*'s crew had skipped over as a consequence of their transit from their own time had brought tremendous change. In particular, the Federation had seen periods of unconstrained growth and prosperity, interspersed with periods of incredible challenges and strife. There was a lot of information to absorb, and that did not even begin to account for the histories of Federation allies and enemies, some of whom had moved from one grouping to the other and even back again in their absence. Worlds and civilizations unknown to her at the time of her departure had risen from humble beginnings to become influencers on an interstellar stage.

The pre-Burn Federation had experienced unprecedented exploration that only served to expand the boundaries of known space. This included forays into the farthest reaches of the distant Gamma and Delta Quadrants, feats accomplished without the use of spore drive or similar technology. Instead, perfecting the art of navigating wormholes—stable and otherwise—along with the development of quantum slipstream propulsion had allowed for the traversing of "transwarp" corridors, reducing by orders of magnitude the time required to cross vast interstellar distances. Given the uncertainties at the time of the Burn's origins, such efforts were curtailed in an effort to mitigate risk. Now that the disaster's cause had been solved, Burnham expected to see a return to those initiatives.

In so many ways, she mused, *we got here just in time.* The promise of what the future held for her, her crew, and the entire Federation was almost too much to comprehend and appreciate. Burnham decided she would enjoy the challenge.

Vance said, "While I'd love nothing but to talk about all of that history, Captain, I'm afraid that'll have to wait for another time." With a smile, he directed Burnham toward Arbusala. The Denobulan had once again taken his seat on the sofa, which was flanked by a pair of straight-backed chairs and a low-rise table to form an informal meeting area. Burnham waited for the admiral to select one of the chairs before sitting across from him.

"I know you and your crew are technically still enjoying some well-earned shore leave," he said, settling into his chair. "And I didn't want to call you back unless I thought it was absolutely necessary. So I left things casual. At least until I couldn't." His expression turned serious. "I'll be sending you out again very soon. It's not an emergency, but it's important. Word's starting to spread about the expanded availability of dilithium, and the threat of another Burn is now pretty much over. We've had several requests for assistance from former Federation worlds who hope to reestablish contact. Our initial efforts have been very successful, due in no small part to the efforts of you and your crew, but as the saying goes: no good deed goes unpunished." He punctuated the statement with an understanding smile. "What can I tell you, Captain? You've made yourselves indispensable."

Burnham nodded. "I've been keeping up with reports, sir. I'm excited to see the renewed outreach."

"It's a delicate balancing act right now," continued Vance. "Say what we will about the Emerald Chain, they filled a void we left behind following the Burn. For better or worse, in many cases they were there for people when Starfleet wasn't. While I certainly believe a post-Chain galaxy is a good thing, that will not feed people or provide them the resources and support they were promised by becoming Federation members. Plus, with the Chain now fractured into who knows how many splinter groups, I suspect our short-term headaches with them will remain for some time. There's a lot of fence mending to be done, and Starfleet's presence—its visible, proactive presence—will be critical in the coming months."

The admiral gestured toward her. "Of course, *Discovery* is an important part of that process. Your ship's spore drive is a godsend, and while I'm not eager to show it off too much lest it attract the attention of unsavory types in the mold of Minister Osyraa, it's our best option for accomplishing our short-term goals of renewing ties with many of our former member worlds, all of whom stand to once again be invaluable friends and allies."

"Understood, sir," said Burnham. "However we can help, my people and I are ready."

Vance's smile returned. "I never doubted that, Captain." Pausing, he indicated Arbusala with a slight nod. "Of course, the good doctor here reminds me that you and your crew continue to be a unique leadership challenge for me."

Here we go, Burnham thought. *This could be interesting.*

Leaning forward in his chair, Vance rested his forearms on his knees and clasped his hands before him before once more meeting Burnham's gaze. "The truth is your crew is still acclimating to our century. I know those who chose to accept the risk of coming with you to our century, which all by itself is an incredible gesture of trust and loyalty, have had a lot to deal with in what for them was a very short amount of time. You at least had a year to adapt, but your people hit the ground running and haven't stopped since they arrived. Then I barely gave you time to catch your breath following the Chain's collapse before I had you out there showing the flag. *Discovery* answered that call and exceeded our expectations, but I can't expect you to keep doing that if I'm not also looking out for your welfare."

He indicated Arbusala. "That's why I had *Discovery* stand down, and asked the good doctor here to make himself available to you and your crew these past few weeks. I know Doctor Culber has been doing a fine job acting as counselor for your people, but I also know it's not his field of specialty. Plus, I thought it might be beneficial to talk to someone 'outside the family,' as it were, even with the complications that entails."

There was the ongoing challenge of maintaining Starfleet's official cover story to explain *Discovery*'s sudden arrival at Federation Headquarters. With the "Temporal Accords" enacted long after the ship's departure from the twenty-third century, time travel or any other action that might cause a disruption to this or another timeline was prohibited. *Discovery*'s transit to this century was therefore a closely guarded secret, with only Vance and a handful of individuals entrusted with that knowledge. So far as the general public knew, the ship had been on a long-term deep-space assignment beyond the Alpha Quadrant's boundaries when the Burn occurred, and the crew's descendants had spent the intervening decades making their way home.

"I'll admit it hasn't been easy," said Burnham. "However, all things considered, I think we're doing all right."

Arbusala said, "For the most part, I agree with Captain Burnham's assessment. Having had the opportunity to speak with a considerable number of the crew, I'm not seeing anything I didn't expect to encounter. Stress, heightened emotional responses, bouts with depression, and so on. Their morale is certainly high, and I believe it's a wonderful coping mechanism, but I fear that without additional time and support for their transition, we'll eventually begin to see more signs they're struggling to adapt to their new status quo."

"Essentially," added Vance, "I'm worried your people, and

perhaps even you, are simply maintaining an even keel. Carrying out the assignments I give you, substituting duty and obligation for proper physical, mental, and emotional care, will ultimately prove detrimental to your crew's health and effectiveness. Even if I was the sort of cold-hearted bastard to do such a thing, I don't have the luxury of running *any* crew into the ground, let alone yours."

Burnham was actually relieved to hear both Vance and Arbusala offering their thoughts on this matter, which echoed her own concerns. During this brief period of downtime, she knew that nearly a third of *Discovery*'s complement had taken the time to speak with the counselor. The details of those conversations were privileged, but she was confident Arbusala or Vance would communicate to her anything of notable concern. So far, that had not happened, but she was aware that could change without warning.

"What do you propose we do?" she asked.

Vance replied, "What we've already been doing, but with a small twist. I'm returning *Discovery* to active status, but I'd like Doctor Arbusala to accompany you on your next mission. Your destination, the planet Evora, is four days away at warp eight. I've alerted the Evoran leadership you'll be arriving then. The situation doesn't call for using *Discovery*'s spore drive, and Doctor Arbusala's been looking for an opportunity to observe your people in action while continuing his interviews."

As if anticipating pushback, Arbusala said, "One of the innovations that occurred after your departure from the twenty-third century was an increased emphasis on assigning specialists to starships with the sole purpose of overseeing the crew's emotional well-being. These counselors have been a presence aboard ship for centuries. Often they're Starfleet officers, but civilians have also filled the role. They usually become key advisors to a ship's command staff, ensuring the crew functions at a high level both psychologically and emotionally."

"I can definitely see an advantage to having such an officer," said Burnham.

Arbusala replied, "My presence aboard your ship for this

mission is temporary, Captain, and it's not my intention to inspect or judge you or your crew. Indeed, I'm not even required to make a report or recommendations to Admiral Vance. My intention is to be available to your people just as I have been these past weeks, but with a change of scenery from which I believe we all might benefit." Then he smiled. "Also, I'm told your crew has a particular recreational activity that's taken hold during off-duty hours, where you present entries from ancient Earth entertainment media."

"You mean movie night." Now it was Burnham's turn to smile. "Yes, it's become quite popular." She extended her hands toward him. "You've done so much for us already, Doctor, and you're more than welcome to join us."

Arbusala's smile widened. "Excellent."

Appearing satisfied with the proceedings, Vance said, "I'm authorizing a dilithium consignment for you to take with you, Captain. You depart at zero nine hundred hours tomorrow, with an expected arrival at Evora ninety-eight hours after that. I expect you'll represent the Federation in your usual fine fashion."

Burnham nodded. "We'll do our best, sir."

As they rose from their seats, Arbusala said, "I'll make the necessary arrangements and have some of my personal effects transported aboard later today. I'm looking forward to our journey together, Captain."

"Likewise, Doctor." Burnham meant that. It would be good to get back out among the stars, where she had felt at home most of her life. She knew the return to normalcy was good for the crew, but she did not discount Arbusala's and Vance's concerns. If there was something going on beneath the surface of her people's calm veneer, she wanted to know about it so those issues could be addressed with the necessary haste and sensitivity. She harbored no illusions of her own capacity to recognize every warning sign. "I'm grateful you'll be with us for this mission, and I'm sure the crew will have no problems with you being aboard ship."

04

"I can't believe the captain's letting him aboard the ship."

Sitting at the edge of their bed, Paul Stamets watched Hugh Culber pace across the sleeping area of their shared quarters. Stamets had entered the room to find Culber in this state, his white medical officer's tunic strewn across a chair as he stalked back and forth, lost in his own thoughts. Stamets's arrival was enough to bring Culber out of his trancelike movements, but when he acknowledged his husband, it was with an obviously forced smile. The first moments of their strained conversation danced around vague reasons for Culber's foul mood, and Stamets waited for him to circle back to the root of his irritation in his own time. Several minutes had passed by this point, although Stamets already knew the real source of these feelings. Still, he remained silent, allowing Culber to decide on his own when and how best to open up. Finally, Culber stopped pacing and turned to regard Stamets with an expression of unfettered annoyance.

"Arbusala."

Stamets extended a hand. "Hugh, come on. Doctor Arbusala's been nothing but open and friendly since he started interacting with the crew."

"Of course he has." There was no sarcasm or cynicism in the reply. Indeed, Stamets heard the subtle shift in Culber's voice, moving away from such negativity and embracing the simple truth.

The Denobulan counselor had been the epitome of professionalism from the moment Captain Burnham informed the crew Arbusala was making himself available for anyone who wanted to talk. Transition to life in this new and unfamiliar reality that was the thirty-second century had been as abrupt as it was chaotic, with very little time to even acknowledge their surroundings, let alone make any attempt at adapting to them. From the moment Stamets and the crew arrived here, they had been pressed into action by circumstances they barely comprehended. Only now, weeks after the dissolution of the Emerald Chain and *Discovery*'s return to Starfleet's active roster, was reality beginning to assert itself with authority. To his credit, Admiral Vance had anticipated the difficulties the crew might face during this period and taken swift action to address any potential issues, in the form of counselors such as Doctor Arbusala.

As Culber took his hand, Stamets asked, "Have you talked to him? Not as a colleague, I mean. Have you—"

Culber sighed. "I know what you mean. And yes, I have talked to him. Both as a doctor and a . . . as a *patient*."

"I learned he doesn't like to use that word. He prefers terms like 'guest' or 'visitor' or even 'participant.'" Stamets offered a small smile. "That's what he told me the first time we talked."

"*You* went to his office?" Culber frowned.

Stamets replied, "No, nothing so formal, though I guess you could call our discussion a session. At least, after a fashion." He recalled how he happened across the doctor during one of his visits to Federation Headquarters. "I was taking a walk in the marketplace area they have, looking for interesting places to eat and checking out their recreational facilities, and I crossed paths with him. We exchanged pleasantries and he asked how I was doing. Arbusala said he didn't want to keep me, but we ended up just walking together along the esplanade." Smiling at the memory, he shook his head. "At the time it seemed like such a random encounter, but the next thing you know, we're sitting on the coffeehouse patio, and I just start . . . opening up to him about various things."

Culber released Stamets's hand before moving to sit next to him on the bed. "What did you talk about?"

Shrugging, Stamets replied, "This and that. How I'm still

adjusting to life in the here and now, that sort of thing." As he had for the past several weeks, he opted not to discuss his lingering resentment toward Captain Burnham. On an intellectual level, he understood her reasons for forcibly evacuating him from the ship when it was seized by Minister Osyraa and a boarding party of Emerald Chain agents. Burnham's actions kept him from being exploited by Osyraa as she came within a hairsbreadth of being able to control *Discovery*'s spore drive. She had threatened the lives of Culber and Adira Tal if Stamets did not surrender to her. Regardless of whatever mistreatment from which Burnham might have saved him, Stamets had wanted to make that decision for himself. The choice to remain with her, their crewmates, and their ship while working to rescue Culber, Adira, and the others should have been his to make. While he no longer felt the anger he experienced in that moment she launched him into space to be recovered by Starfleet, what lingered was the resentment at having his agency taken from him.

Instead of giving voice to those feelings, Stamets tapped Culber's forearm. "Being able to interface with the spore drive without the implants. I was a little embarrassed that I hadn't thought of that first, but then I checked myself. Along with the rest of us, I was still learning how to fit in here. That means getting up to speed with respect to all of the technological advances from the past nine hundred years. In case you're wondering, there's a *lot* of them."

"Tell me about it." Culber rolled his eyes. "The advances in medicine alone are incredible. Holographic doctors? On-demand organ regrowth and replacement? The ability to map an entire brain down to the smallest detail, including every memory a person's ever held in their mind? I didn't even bother trying to count the diseases and other ailments that have been cured." He paused, as though pondering what he had just said, before adding, "On the other hand, there's no shortage of new medical mysteries requiring study, so maybe I'm not completely useless just yet."

Stamets could not suppress a small laugh. "You and Arbusala are more aligned than you think. He reminded me technology is only as good and useful as its intended purpose, and a big part of that comes from the people employing it." He held up his arm again. "I'm perfectly okay not being stuck in the arms anymore, but I'm still necessary for the spore drive to work. Even after all this time, they never bothered to try or else they still can't replicate what we did *nine hundred years ago*. I swear, Hugh, talking to him didn't even feel like a counseling session. I don't know if that was his intention all along, or if he just rolled with it as we kept talking, but never once did I ever feel as though I was being psychoanalyzed. He's very disarming that way."

"Yes, he's very good at putting his patients . . . I mean his *guests* . . . at ease," said Culber. "I picked up on that during our first meeting, when he came to see me in sickbay."

Offering an encouraging smile, Stamets replied, "Again, I think you two are more alike than not. You both have a very comforting way about you that engenders trust. I know as much about psychiatry as I do any other field of health or medicine, but I'm guessing it's a quality you want in the person treating you. I know it's a big plus for me." He patted Culber's leg. "It's just one of the reasons you're my favorite doctor."

Culber smiled. "I'm not even sure why he came to see me. Captain Burnham had already told us we weren't under orders to see him, and to schedule a visit with him at our leisure if we wanted to take advantage of the offer. But with me he made the first move."

"Professional courtesy?" asked Stamets. "I didn't ask about it when I spoke with him, but I can't imagine he doesn't know what you've been doing since we got here. You've played a huge part in keeping the crew together and looking out for us. I doubt we'd be doing nearly as well as we are if not for you. I suspect Doctor Arbusala knows that, just as I'm betting he's also sensitive to the possibility his presence here might be interpreted as some kind of statement against you or anything you've done." Stamets put his arm around Culber's shoulders. "You're not feeling anything like that, are you?"

Culber grimaced. "I know I shouldn't be, but I can't help it." Shaking his head, he blew out his breath. "It seems silly, the more I think about it."

"It's not silly," replied Stamets, pulling Culber closer. "You're feeling sidelined, maybe even pushed aside. I know what that feels like, believe me. All I'm saying is you should give Arbusala a chance. Find a way to work with him. Compare notes, that sort of thing. You know the crew far better than he does. Chances are good you've picked up on something about someone he won't catch, at least not right away. I know there are ethical boundaries you each have to respect, but surely there's a way to navigate those while still looking out for the crew's best interests?"

He felt Culber lean into him, the way he did when he was down about something and needed a little support, but Stamets recognized tension beginning to ebb. The quiet moment and reassuring words were having their intended effect. Sensing a shift in Culber's mood, Stamets nudged him before pushing himself to his feet.

"Let's get out of here. It's movie night." Moving to the closet across from the bed, he began rummaging among his clothes for something to wear, something comfortable and not at all resembling a uniform. "Or, if you'd rather try something else, I have a couple of new favorite lounges I found along the Boulevard." His forays to Federation Headquarters' spacious entertainment district had seen him almost getting lost amid the broad cross section of restaurants, shops, holosuites, and other assorted sports, recreation, and leisure facilities. "Since the Emerald Chain disbanded, the station's had an influx of private merchants setting up shop. Before, it was just a Starfleet facility and felt like it, but the place is really starting to come alive."

Rising from the bed, Culber replied, "Sounds like fun. I like the idea of a night on the town, or whatever you call it when the town's stuffed inside a space station." As he selected a maroon shirt from his own wardrobe, he added, "But I'd still like to check out the movie. See how people are doing, that sort of thing."

Stamets could hear the change in Culber's voice, recognizing when he was beginning to relax, but he still sensed the underlying tension. There could be no complete hiding of any feelings of being watched and judged, particularly from a professional colleague. Stamets carried his own sense of being under scrutiny, and he suspected most of the crew did, as well. For Culber, that stress could only be magnified.

Just a night on the town, Stamets thought. *An evening among friends. This will be good, for both of us.*

05

"He's here."

There was no mistaking the irritation in Culber's voice, though the doctor spoke only loud enough for Stamets to hear. Stamets reached for his husband's hand and gave it a reassuring squeeze as he glanced around the hangar bay. There were thirty or so people scattered around the deck, some in folding chairs or sitting on cargo containers while others reclined on thick blankets, arranged before the oversized holographic representation of the film being displayed in the air above them. The visual playback hovered before the darkened bay's massive entry that looked out between *Discovery*'s pair of detached warp nacelles. Beyond the ship lay the interior of the immense space station that was Federation Headquarters.

It took Stamets only a moment to pick out Doctor Arbusala from the rest of the group. Though he was not sitting alone, to Stamets he also did not appear to actually be a part of the trio of *Discovery* crewmembers lounging atop blankets near the rear of the viewing area. The Denobulan sat atop a cargo container with legs crossed in a meditative style, ramrod straight as he ate popcorn from a bag.

"Why is he here?" asked Culber, perhaps more to himself than Stamets or anyone else.

Stamets replied, "So far as I know, it's his first extended stay aboard ship. He's probably just getting the lay of the land, checking us out in our native environment to see how people are doing in unguarded moments. It has to be easier introducing himself that way than taking sessions in his office on the station."

"Or wandering around the Boulevard."

Choosing to ignore what he thought might be a subtle dig, Stamets returned his attention to the Denobulan, who was staring transfixed at the holographic projection while sporting an enthusiastic smile. Before Stamets could look away, the doctor looked in his direction and both his eyes and his grin widened in recognition. He waved, and Stamets felt Culber squeeze his hand.

"Damn it."

Despite the comment, when Stamets looked to him he saw Culber's own smile. It was bright and welcoming, and to anyone else but Stamets likely appeared completely genuine.

"Now what do we do?" said Culber, his voice barely a whisper.

Stamets replied, "Roll with it." With a gentle tug on Culber's hand, he led the way across the hangar bay to where Arbusala was already uncrossing his legs and rising to his feet. His attire was a loose-fitting, dark-blue shirt with matching pants, along with his ubiquitous sandals. Stepping away from the adjacent group of crewmembers, he kept his voice low as he greeted Stamets and Culber.

"Good evening," he said, still holding his bag of popcorn. He gestured toward the projection. "I've heard about your movie nights from other members of the crew, and I've been looking forward to experiencing it for myself."

"This isn't a normal turnout," offered Culber. His voice was pleasant enough, but Stamets still detected the hint of apprehension. "I'm guessing a lot of people are enjoying one last night of shore leave before we ship out tomorrow."

If he detected any unease, Arbusala chose to ignore it. Instead, he nodded in apparent agreement. "I always find it interesting when Starfleet crews make port at a starbase or planet for shore leave, just how many crewmembers opt to stay aboard ship." He shrugged. "I know some of that can be explained by duty schedules and having to remain close by for one reason or another, but you'd be surprised just how many people never leave their ship when it's in port." Digging into his popcorn bag, he smiled. "The comforts of home, I suppose."

"We're heading out ourselves," replied Stamets, realizing as he spoke that Culber was saying the same thing. They exchanged awkward glances before Culber continued, "We just dropped by to see how things were going before heading out." He paused, glancing toward the projection. "I don't even know what Zora selected tonight."

Stamets realized he had no idea what had been scheduled either. Zora had curated an extensive list of films and other entertainment media from its database. As Culber described it, the collection was rather diverse, spanning centuries of such presentations, while focusing on various means of elevating or maintaining the crew's morale in keeping with the primary goal of movie night.

"It's from the end of Earth's twentieth century," replied Arbusala. "From what I've read, stories about your planet's people being visited by representatives from other worlds were quite common, across a number of different entertainment delivery platforms." The doctor gestured with his popcorn bag toward the projection. "I came late and from what I can tell, this presentation depicts sentient beings from a distant planet arriving at Earth and mistaking a group of actors for officers assigned to an advanced starship. The actors apparently once portrayed such characters for a serial entertainment program years earlier. Mistaking them for the genuine article, the visitors have gone to great lengths to re-create in remarkable detail the starship from the program, and have enlisted these performers to come to their defense against a tyrannical overlord of some sort." He smiled. "From what I've seen so far, the entire premise is as amusing as it is utterly charming."

"Seems a bit far-fetched," said Stamets. "Unless absurdity is the intent?"

That evoked an even broader smile from Arbusala. "Indeed, Commander. The absurdity is what makes it so delightful."

Leaning in closer, he added, "However, I must tell you that I find some of the character portrayals and even their depictions of advanced technology to be surprisingly reminiscent of early Starfleet efforts. Some of the comparisons are rather striking." He gestured to them. "Come. I do believe there's still quite a bit of story remaining."

"We should probably head over to the station," said Culber, and Stamets detected the barest hint of annoyance in his voice.

Taking the reply in stride, Arbusala offered a deferential nod. "Yes, of course. Enjoy your last night of shore leave. If you're interested in suggestions from the Boulevard, may I recommend the Bolian Pearl? It's a wonderful little fusion restaurant, family owned and with an amazingly diverse menu featuring dishes that combine the best elements of Bolian, Ni'Var, and human cuisine. It also has a wonderful atmosphere that makes you believe you're sitting on a moonlit beach."

Despite his earlier comment, Culber said, "That sounds nice." He looked to Stamets. "What do you think?"

"I think if we're getting one last meal before going back to replicator food, that's the place to go." To Arbusala, Stamets said, "Thanks for the recommendation."

"My pleasure." The doctor's smile returned. "I'm sure we'll be seeing each other soon."

He returned to his cargo container and resumed his cross-legged sitting position, attention once more on the film and his popcorn and leaving Stamets and Culber to exit the hangar bay. As they entered the adjacent corridor walking side by side, Stamets made a point to bump slightly into his husband.

"See? That wasn't so bad. Was it?"

All pretense of contentment vanishing, Culber shook his head. "This is going to be the longest week of my life."

06

The doors parted in response to her approach, and Burnham smiled at the welcoming sounds of camaraderie drifting into the corridor from *Discovery*'s crew lounge. Earlier in her career, she might have walked past such a setting without giving it a second thought, likely intent on proceeding to her destination to carry out some task she deemed of greater importance. Now, however, what she heard was cause for investigation.

"Good evening, Captain," said Lieutenant Linus, the tall, lithe Saurian who served as one of *Discovery*'s junior science officers, from where he stood next to one of the food replicators set into the adjacent bulkhead. A broad smile creased the gray-green skin of his reptilian features, which were accentuated by his large, dark eyes. Retrieving a large metal tankard from the replicator, he held up the vessel in greeting. "It is good to see you."

Pausing at the lounge's threshold as Linus walked past, Burnham took in the scene before her. A quick count told her nearly thirty members of the ship's complement occupied space at tables around the room as well as stools positioned before the bar occupying the room's center. Outside the viewing ports set into the opposite bulkhead, multihued streaks of light indicated stars slipping past as *Discovery* plunged through subspace at warp. A low buzz permeated the lounge, an amalgam of overlapping conversations and laughter along with tones and music from some game or playback from a holographic presentation. Burnham noted couples at a few of the tables, sitting close and engaged in quiet conversations while seemingly oblivious to the activity around them. She watched Linus move to join a group of younger officers who had taken over the lounge's far corner, pushing together a pair of tables and arranging chairs around them. Additional chairs were purloined from adjacent tables, and two crewmembers were in the midst of acquiring a third table while Burnham watched.

One of her regrets from that period of her nascent career aboard the *Shenzhou* was her focus on work to the near total exclusion of all else. She knew it was a holdover from childhood as a human living and being raised in Vulcan society. Still, her adoptive mother, Amanda Grayson, had frequently advocated for a more balanced approach to life.

"You're not Vulcan," Burnham could hear Amanda saying. *"Yes, you're expected to comport yourself in a manner consistent with Vulcan expectations, but do you see me meditating or studying a textbook when I want to relax? Of course you don't. I read, but I read things that bring me joy. I listen to music. I tend to my garden. I sneak away for a moonlit swim. Even your father will tell you it's not logical for a human to force themselves to live in a way that's dishonest to their nature."*

It was a sentiment later echoed by Captain Georgiou, who made a habit of walking the decks of the *Shenzhou* following her normal duty shift. Not seeking status updates or other official reports of her crew's activities, Georgiou instead asked the people under her command about their lives away from their shipboard responsibilities. She liked to hear about families, relationships, hobbies, anything that did not involve their work. While she had always been a demanding taskmaster, like any successful leader, Georgiou knew her people operated at a sustained high level of dedication when they felt like part of a team—of a *family*—where every member knew their contributions were as valued as they were necessary.

Still brimming with notions of Vulcan logic and efficiency, Burnham had understood Georgiou's approach, but it was not until the burdens—and the privileges—of command fell upon her own shoulders that she had truly come to comprehend the varied and occasionally contradictory subtleties of effective leadership. To that end, she had adopted Georgiou's practice of checking in on her crew outside of their scheduled assignments and work areas. It was but one of many enduring gifts bestowed upon Burnham by her beloved mentor, and each day she strived to be worthy of the example set by her friend. She was not yet there, but she liked to think she was making progress.

Stepping farther into the lounge, Burnham noted the hive of activity that seemed to be dominating the room's center. She noted two of her alpha-shift bridge officers, Lieutenant Commanders Keyla Detmer and Eva Nilsson, standing with six of their colleagues and watching whatever was happening at the table they surrounded. As she moved closer, Burnham caught flashes of green. She smiled, realizing that a poker felt top had been laid across the table, and now was littered with cards and chips.

"Captain," said Detmer, holding up her drink in greeting before using it to gesture to the table. "You're just in time. It's getting pretty interesting."

Other members of the crew shifted to allow Burnham to step closer, and she got her first look at the game in progress. On the table's far side sat Lieutenant Commander Ronald Bryce, who by the looks of things was the dealer for the current hand. Seated clockwise from the communications officer were Lieutenant Commander Joann Owosekun, Commander Jett Reno, and—to Burnham's mild surprise—Doctor Arbusala. Everyone's attention was focused on Reno, who appeared oblivious to her fellow players as well as their audience and perhaps everything else in the known universe. The engineer was not studying her cards, but instead the sizable pile of red, white, and blue chips amassed at the table's center. Varying stacks of chips sat before each player, and Burnham noted that Reno and Arbusala were doing very well for themselves and appeared to be evenly matched with respect to winnings. Although Bryce and Owosekun had each folded for the current hand, they were still in the game despite occupying more precarious positions based on their own dwindling collections of chips.

"What are you going to do, Commander?" asked Bryce, holding whatever remained of a deck of cards in his clasped hands.

Her eyes fixed on the pile of chips as though running calculations in her head, Reno replied, "Slow your roll, ace. What's your rush?"

"If this is you bluffing," said Owosekun, "it's the worst bluff I've ever seen."

Bryce grinned. "You had your chance, Joann, and you folded." He then turned his gaze to Reno, his expression one of mock seriousness. "Commander, the bridge called. We just skipped another nine hundred years waiting on you."

The comment earned various laughs and chuckles from most of the other players as well as onlookers, and Reno tipped a finger to her temple in mock salute. "I knew I liked you for a reason." She went silent again, eyeing the table for another moment before reaching for several of her blue chips and tossing them into the pile. "I'll see your forty credits and raise you another forty."

"They're playing for credits?" asked Burnham, whispering as she glanced at Detmer.

The flight control officer shook her head. "Not really, but Commander Reno said it was obscene to play poker without chips, and Doctor Arbusala agreed with her. This is more about bragging rights than anything else. Reno's good, but I think Arbusala might be better."

For his part, Arbusala betrayed nothing as he reacted to Reno raising the bet. Without hesitation, the Denobulan selected four of his own blue chips and placed them atop the pile. "I see your forty, Commander, and raise you forty more."

Nodding in that confident way she exuded, Reno matched the bet. "Call."

Arbusala laid his cards faceup on the table, and Burnham saw three jacks—spades, hearts, and clubs—accompanied by a pair of nines: hearts and aces.

"Full house," he said. "Jacks over nines, as they say."

The revelation drew a modicum of hushed whispers and other audible expressions of appreciation. Burnham looked to Reno, who maintained her relaxed posture in her seat, smiling at Arbusala's cards. In seemingly blasé fashion, the engineer reached for her cards and turned them faceup to reveal an ace of diamonds along with a quartet of queens. The audience and the other players reacted with assorted laughter and even some light applause.

Reno shrugged. "Sorry, Doc."

Smiling in good-natured defeat, Arbusala offered a conciliatory nod. "Very well played, Commander."

Leaning forward, Reno stretched her arms to the center of the table and began sweeping her winnings toward her. "Ten months on the *Hiawatha*, I had to find something to occupy those five or ten minutes every day when I wasn't working or passed out from exhaustion." She moved the chips into a neater pile. "So I started playing games with the computer. After I let it kick my ass at chess for a while, we moved on to things like Othello, Terrace, backgammon, that sort of thing. I'd never even played poker until the computer suggested it." She used both hands to gesture to her impressive stack of chips. "And look at me now." To the audience still loitering around the table, she directed, "My subjects, bring forth the finest black licorice in all the land."

With Bryce and Owosekun offering their good-humored surrenders, the game broke up. Remaining in her seat as the others rose to their feet, Reno eyed Burnham with a roguish grin.

"Care to dance with the devil, Captain?"

Burnham smiled. "Maybe next time. I just wanted to walk the decks a little before chaining myself to my desk." Her ready room and a litany of status and progress reports awaited her attention. It was one of the necessary yet far less glamorous facets of command. Despite her various attempts to prove otherwise, none of it, if left unattended, addressed itself on its own.

"And they wonder why I never wanted a command of my own." Reno stood, leaving her winnings on the table. "Actually, I'm sure exactly no one has ever wondered that." She nodded first to Arbusala, then Burnham. "If anyone needs me, I'll be teaching the bartender everything they're doing wrong. Have a good night, Captain."

Appearing to wait until the engineer moved out of earshot, Arbusala turned to Burnham. "A most remarkable individual."

"In so many ways," Burnham replied, watching Reno head toward the bar.

"Her record is extraordinary." Arbusala shook his head. "Nearly a year spent living aboard the crashed remains of her ship, improvising and adapting so many disparate and damaged systems in an incredible effort to keep wounded shipmates alive. She *volunteered* to place herself in that position. It's an incredible act of bravery and self-sacrifice."

Only after reading Reno's official report on the entire incident had Burnham come to understand and appreciate the engineer's actions, which had gone well beyond even the most demanding call to duty. During the earliest days of the Federation-Klingon War, the *U.S.S. Hiawatha*, a medical frigate transporting wounded personnel and supplies to Starbase 36, crashed on the surface of an asteroid. The ship lacked sufficient evacuation pods and other auxiliary craft to support the entire crew, in particular several critically wounded patients who likely would not survive such an ordeal. With the chief medical officer one of those killed in the crash and the rest of the medical staff needed to oversee those patients and crew who could be moved, Reno volunteered to stay behind and tend to those who faced the highest risks during any transport. With only the *Hiawatha*'s-compromised systems and supplies to assist her, she set to work stabilizing the remaining patients, jury-rigging all manner of medical equipment along with anything else she thought could be repurposed. She used the computer to supplement her existing medical knowledge, which—while limited to the duties of a field medic—had received a natural enhancement by virtue of assignment to a hospital ship.

Expecting rescue within days at most, Reno eventually accepted Starfleet had likely deemed the *Hiawatha* lost thanks to the violent gravimetric waves permeating the region the asteroid called home. That, or the war with the Klingons had taken a turn for the worse. Both of those explanations proved to be true, and more than ten months passed before *Discovery*, at the time under the temporary command of Captain Christopher Pike, found the *Hiawatha* wreckage while pursuing the Red Angel mystery. Reno and her patients were rescued, with the engineer remaining with the ship as the investigation continued, ultimately choosing to stay with *Discovery* when it was decided the ship would travel to the future.

"She barely had time to process being rescued before being thrown into your fight to protect the Sphere data," said Arbusala. "And yet, she played an integral part in your crew's success. I'd call her adaptable, but that seems like a criminal understatement."

Pondering the doctor's candid assessment, Burnham glanced around the lounge to ensure they were not being overheard by other crewmembers before returning her attention to Arbusala. "You've been here long enough to get at least a surface evaluation of the crew. What's your take on her? *Is* she adapting, or just doing a good job masking her true feelings?"

She stopped herself, knowing she was treading a line between a captain's concern for a subordinate and that individual's right to privacy. Burnham knew Reno was one of several people who had accepted Arbusala's invitation to speak in private, but she had no knowledge about the substance of any resulting conversations.

Gesturing to a nearby unoccupied table, Burnham waited for Arbusala to seat himself before settling into the chair across from him. She was aware of a few crewmembers in proximity who were doing their best to appear they were uninterested in their captain's conversation with a Starfleet counselor. She leaned across the table toward Arbusala.

"When we found her, she'd been working her ass off for nearly a year. She lost her wife in the war, with no real chance to grieve before getting wrapped up with us. It's obvious she's good at compartmentalizing her emotions, but I still have to wonder. I'm not asking you to betray a confidence, Doctor, but—"

Arbusala offered a comforting smile. "I understand your concerns, Captain, and rest assured I would not withhold any information I felt you needed to know with respect to the safety of your ship and crew. While I cannot divulge specific topics of my various discussions, I have indeed developed preliminary appraisals of several members of your crew. While there are some issues I believe require additional consultation and assistance, your people demonstrate an uncommon resiliency in the face of everything they have endured over an extended period of time. In particular, Commander Reno has adapted to her present situation far more easily than almost every other member of your crew." He paused before adding, "Including you, and you fared rather well, all things considered."

"Additional consultation and assistance," said Burnham.

"Such a thing should not be unexpected, and neither is it automatically a cause for concern. Your crew is still adapting to the reality of their situation. Each individual is doing so at their own pace and while confronting their own feelings and issues relevant to them, of course. Feeling homesick for the life they left behind. Missing loved ones, and wondering what became of them." Looking at his hands as they rested on the table, Arbusala sighed. "Not everyone will be able to find answers, and so they imagine the possibilities, good and bad. They ponder what their own lives might have been like had they elected to remain behind."

Considering all of this, Burnham said, "It's been a difficult path to travel, but I have to believe they'll succeed. It's just going to take time."

Arbusala replied, "Time, and patience. Two things that are often in short supply when one commits themselves to a life of duty and responsibility, as the crew of *Discovery* has done."

Releasing a sigh of mild resignation, Burnham forced a smile. "Tell me about it." She recalled the reports and other administrative flotsam still waiting in her ready room. "But we'll figure it out, Doctor. That's what we do."

Nodding in apparent understanding, Arbusala replied, "Indeed."

Before the doctor could offer anything further, he was interrupted by the whistle of the ship's intercom, followed by the voice of her first officer, Lieutenant Commander Gen Rhys.

"Bridge to Captain Burnham."

Tapping her tri-com badge, Burnham replied, "Go ahead."

"We're picking up a distress call, Captain. It's weak, but enough to help us plot its location, and . . . well, I think you need to see this for yourself."

Rising from her seat, Burnham headed for the door. "On my way."

The paperwork in her ready room would have to wait.

07

"What have we got?"

Passing through the hatch leading onto *Discovery*'s bridge, Burnham acknowledged Rhys as the first officer vacated the command chair. She moved to position herself between the helm and operations consoles at the bridge's forward area. Around her, the alpha-shift bridge officers were taking over their stations, relieving their beta-shift counterparts.

"We detected the signal six minutes ago, Captain," said Rhys. The Asian man moved to stand beside her, gesturing to the transparasteel aperture that also was the bridge's main viewscreen. "It's coming from . . . in there."

Displayed on the screen was a formless violet mass contrasting against the utter darkness of the surrounding space. Burnham knew the image was the main computer's translation of telemetry delivered by the ship's array of sensors, rendered in a manner that made it easier to be studied by the naked eye. Scrolling down both sides of the screen were columns of text, a translation of supporting information captured by the scans.

"The Larasini system," she said, reading the legend depicted at the bottom of the image. "I've seen it on star charts, but I've never been there."

Rhys replied, "It's not along our present course. According to the data we have, the system consists of five planets orbiting an orange star, all contained within a nebula that looks to be all that's left of another star that went supernova."

"So, interstellar dust, fragments from the star, and however many planets, moons, and whatever else that system may have contained." Burnham shook her head. "One big mess. What about the remaining system?"

"One planet has a single natural satellite, and two others have three apiece." Rhys pointed to data scrolling down the viewscreen's right side. "According to our information, the system is uninhabited."

A voice from behind her said, "Because it's a shithole."

Burnham turned to see Booker walking onto the bridge. As was his habit, he remained behind the captain's chair and any of the workstations, doing his best not to distract the other bridge officers from their duties.

"You've been there?" she asked.

"The Larasini Nebula?" Booker nodded. "Once or twice, but not recently. For a long while it was a place to be avoided. The background radiation destabilizes warp fields, so you can only transit it at impulse speeds. Navigational sensors also get beaten up pretty good, making it one gigantic pain in the ass. The Chain and other independent pilots liked it because the sensor disruption is enough to make it a great place for avoiding unwanted attention. A nice place to visit, but you wouldn't want to live there."

"What about the signal?" asked Burnham.

Turning from the viewscreen, Rhys replied, "It's coming from the Larasini system, but the nebula's background radiation is interfering with it. The message is garbled and largely unintelligible, but Zora managed to pull out enough fragments to issue the alert, and I'm convinced the distress call is real. I've already ordered a complete sensor sweep, but aside from the basic information, we're running into trouble. Whatever's disrupting their communications is also affecting our scans."

"And we're sure none of the planets are inhabited?"

Rhys said, "According to our information, none of the planets are Class M, and so far our scans show no indication of indigenous higher-order life. However, I had Zora do a cross-check of communications logs and there are unconfirmed reports of different temporary settlements."

"Mining camps, mostly," offered Booker. "Along with a few

other activities that aren't appropriate topics for polite company. Most reputable pilots give this system a wide berth."

"Which begs the question of who's sending a distress call and why they're in there," Burnham said. "Any idea who it is?"

"Given the sensor disruption," said Rhys, "we can't even isolate the signal's point of origin from this distance. We need to get closer. I already ordered the course plotted."

From the helm console to her left, Burnham heard Commander Detmer report, "Course looks good and is already laid in, Captain. We can be there in just under five minutes at our present speed."

Burnham nodded. "Let's do it." Turning from the screen, she made her way back to the command chair. "Yellow alert. All hands to emergency stations. Until we get a better handle on what this is, let's be ready for anything. Lieutenant Tilly, pull power from wherever you need it to boost our sensors."

"On it, Captain," reported Sylvia Tilly from the science console to Burnham's right.

As she moved to sit in her chair, Burnham watched the Larasini Nebula growing larger on the screen as *Discovery* made its approach. It already filled the screen, and the sensor data now formed a more comprehensive image of the cloud. Violet with areas of dark red and black, accented by flashes of energy that she figured to be static discharges caused by the unchecked radiation permeating the region.

"Definitely a nasty place," said Tilly. "It's like a soup in there, Captain, but sensors are definitely penetrating as we approach. The cloud is a mix of ionized gases, interstellar dust, and what looks to be large bodies of spatial matter, likely remnants of whatever planets orbited the star that went nova. The background radiation and electromagnetic distortion is something else. Not so bad as the Verubin Nebula, but bad enough."

Burnham was already thinking along the same lines. The nebula where they had found the dilithium planet Theta Zeta, the point of origin for the Burn, had proven to be a formidable navigational challenge. Though Tilly's report was encouraging, Burnham also knew the lieutenant's information was still sketchy as *Discovery*'s sensors fought to make sense of the jumbled readings they were collecting.

"It also reminds me of the Briar Patch," offered Detmer. Looking over her shoulder at Burnham, the helm officer added, "Basically a big gas cloud near the border between Federation and Klingon space. Well, where the border was in the twenty-third century, anyway. That line shifted a few times after we left. When I was a cadet doing my semester aboard the *Endeavour*, we ran sensor sweeps of the Patch's outer boundary. The background radiation made it pretty much impossible to maneuver inside, but we got close enough for it to give us a pretty rough ride."

Tilly said, "The good news is the bulk of the debris doesn't seem to be near the distress signal's location, but there are electromagnetic storms all over the place. I'm looking for a way to avoid the worst of them, but I don't think we can miss them entirely."

Having retaken his customary position at the tactical station, Rhys added, "Captain, if we go into the nebula, its effects will have a definite impact on our shields. We going to lose as much as seventy percent of their effectiveness, which will definitely make for a bumpy ride once we're in there."

"Transferring the latest sensor data to the helm," reported Tilly. "I'm trying to get us as close as possible to the signal source before we have to enter the nebula."

Looking toward the tactical station, Burnham asked, "What about the signal source? Is it a ship or coming from one of the planets?"

"We're close enough now I'm pretty sure it's a ship, Captain. The closer we get, the more comprehensive our sensor readings are becoming. I'm picking up an energy signature consistent with a dilithium-powered warp drive." Rhys did not look up from his console, interacting with the programmable-matter interface that sent tendrils of the adaptable substance washing over the first officer's hands. Composed of nanomolecules and capable of altering itself into what so far seemed like an endless variety of shapes and functions, it was just one of the many thirty-second-century technological upgrades *Discovery* had received from Starfleet. Burnham had benefited from an additional year of learning how to use what had seemed like magic to her when she first saw it aboard Booker's ship. Despite an unavoidably shorter and intense learning curve, the rest of the crew had taken to integrating with the adaptive interface with little difficulty. Though Rhys had been among those skeptical of the wondrous enhancements made to the ship, he was now an enthusiastic supporter, operating the modern interface as if having done it all his life.

"Definitely a vessel of some kind," he said a moment later. "Sensor readings are still garbled, but clearing up enough that I can separate the ship from the surrounding distortions. It looks to be approximately six hundred million kilometers inside the nebula, in proximity to the Larasini system's fourth planet."

Having heard enough, Burnham leaned forward in her chair. "All right, then. Maintain yellow alert. Full power to the shields. Helm, take us in. Half impulse."

She watched as Detmer entered the commands to execute the intercept course. On the viewscreen, the image of the nebula's roiling gases seemed even more intense as *Discovery* pushed forward, and even with the shields Burnham knew when the ship had crossed the region's outer boundary. Slight reverberations played upward from the deck, channeled through her chair to her. A mild yet still audible shift in pitch from the ship's engines made Commander Owosekun cast glances first to Detmer and then to Burnham.

"Fluctuations in the shield generators," reported the operations officer. "I'm routing additional power to compensate."

A massive flash made Burnham blink as static disrupted the viewscreen just before she felt the entire ship shudder around her. According to her stomach, inertial dampers seemed slow to compensate, with the ship listing to port as something struck the deflector shields. She gripped the arms of her chair to steady herself, glancing to her left to see Booker holding on to the science console as everyone else struggled to ride the wave.

"Electromagnetic discharge," said Tilly. "We have to get through a pretty rough patch, but the area around the ship looks a little calmer."

"Captain," said Rhys. "We're close enough I can provide a visual of the ship. It's not a configuration I recognize, neither is it coming up in the recognition database."

Without waiting for instructions, he entered the necessary commands and the image on the main viewscreen shifted to display an elongated, narrow vessel. Rhys enhanced the picture and the ship appeared to jump closer to the screen, offering more detail. The ship was not a single piece but a chain of linked modules, headed by a flared, egg-like component pockmarked with illuminated viewing ports. Similar openings were spaced at regular intervals down the length of a massive support joist running from the ship's forward section and along the top of the other linked segments to the vessel's far end, which then connected to a larger component that broadened into a housing that contained engine ports. Two more struts flanked the modules along the port and starboard sides, and Burnham knew these were the ship's warp nacelles, capable of disengaging from the rest of the vessel much like the comparable units serving *Discovery*.

Burnham recognized the ship's configuration, her eyes widening in realization. "It can't be," she said, low enough she was sure no one else heard her. A quick glance around the room showed everyone else's attention on the viewscreen or their stations. She glanced a second time at Tilly and saw the young officer looking at the screen, her eyes narrowed as she studied the vessel. It was while Burnham was considering what she might say to her bridge officers when Booker beat her to the punch.

"That's a Xahean ship."

As Burnham expected, Tilly's reaction was immediate. "Wait. What?" Her features morphing into an expression of shock, she cast frantic looks at her fellow officers, pausing a beat longer on Booker before her gaze locked on Burnham. "Captain?"

Damn it.

Burnham forced herself to keep her composure even as she felt Tilly's questioning eyes boring into her. While on occasion she had considered the possibility of *Discovery* encountering a Xahean vessel, it was not something she expected so soon after the ship's arrival from the twenty-third century. From her people's point of view, barely two months had passed since that final battle against Section 31 agent Leland and the Control program, a fight *Discovery* likely would have lost if not for the help of Me Hani Ika Hali Ka Po, queen of the Xahean people, who had through an improbable sequence of events befriended Sylvia Tilly. Had Po even survived that battle? If so, what had become of her and her reign as queen? Burnham had made a few attempts to learn about the Xaheans and how they might have prospered in the centuries she had skipped, both before and after reuniting with *Discovery* and Starfleet. What she had found had been disheartening, to say the least.

Later, she reminded herself.

Pushing herself from her chair, Burnham offered a reassuring nod to Tilly before returning her attention to the matter at hand. "Lieutenant, what can you tell me about the ship?"

With obvious effort, Tilly refocused herself on her workstation. "Sensors aren't detecting any external damage, but several systems are offline. Propulsion and life-support are the big ones, and there are entire sections showing no power readings at all." Once more, she looked up from her console. "Captain, what—"

"Not now, Lieutenant." Burnham tried to soften her response with a sympathetic look, but she still saw the astonishment and uncertainty in Tilly's eyes. Before she could say anything else, Commander Bryce interrupted from the communications station on the bridge's starboard side.

"Captain, I've managed to clean up the distress signal. I think I can establish a connection." His hands were already manipulating the programmable matter of his own console, moving with practiced ease. "Opening a frequency."

Nodding to Bryce, Burnham set aside the apprehensive looks from Tilly and the others around her and moved to stand between Detmer and Owosekun. "Unidentified vessel in distress, this is Captain Michael Burnham commanding the Federation *Starship Discovery*. We are on an intercept course to your position. What is the nature of your emergency?"

In response to her greeting, the bridge's intercom system crackled and hissed at the same time the damaged ship disappeared from the viewscreen, replaced by a static-filled image of a bald Xahean male. He was humanoid in appearance, and his pale skin was highlighted by the intricate design of facial tattoos as well as piercings in his nose, cheeks, and the brows above his dark, wide eyes. The transmitted image was shaky, and it took Burnham a moment to realize he must be transmitting from a portable communicator. She also noticed he did not appear to be standing on anything that might resemble the bridge or command deck of his vessel. Indeed, it seemed to her as if he were crouching in a dark corner.

"Is he hiding?" asked Booker, and when Burnham looked over her shoulder toward him, she saw him exchanging worried looks with Tilly.

On the screen, the Xahean said, *"Captain Burnham, I am . . . civilian vess . . . under attack, and . . . ediate assistance to help us . . . ship."* It was only when he blinked several times in rapid succession that Burnham was reminded of how Xaheans possessed inner eyelids that moved in perpendicular fashion.

Stepping closer to the screen, Burnham asked, "Bryce, can you clean that up?"

"Working on it, Captain," replied the communications officer. "The nebula is playing havoc with their systems, and ours."

The unmistakable sounds of weapons fire pushed through the open connection, filling the bridge. Something flickered off screen, and Burnham saw the Xahean flinch before raising his hand to reveal a form of personal sidearm she did not recognize. The Xahean aimed the weapon, firing at a target Burnham could not see.

"Captain . . . engers are attempt . . . ijacking. We need assist—"

The transmission ended, restoring to the viewscreen the image of the beleaguered vessel.

"Did he say hijacking?" asked Tilly. "I don't understand. What . . . I mean, who? Why?"

The questions would have to wait, Burnham decided.

"Helm," she said. "Full impulse. Let's go to work."

08

Cloaked in shadow thanks to the corridor's subdued lighting, the figure stepped into the junction, making themselves visible to Ko In Lah Pili Leb an instant before the new arrival saw him. Without hesitating, Leb raised his pulse disruptor, but the other person was too fast.

"Down!" he shouted just as the new arrival fired their own weapon. A pair of bright green energy bolts spat from their "pulser," racing the passage's length. Leb ducked to avoid taking the hit, and he saw his companions, Luhi and Vran, taking similar protective action just as the two bolts slammed into the bulkhead above them. From where he crouched, Leb fired his pulser, not so much with the goal of hitting anything but rather forcing their adversary to move for cover. Instead of stepping back out of the corridor junction and out of sight, the figure was moving to advance, already sighting their weapon in Leb's direction. Then they disappeared, engaging their personal shroud that still left a rippling effect in the air through which they moved.

Luhi saw it as well. She rose from her crouch, holding her pulser with both hands. The *Pilikoa*'s pilot fired once and the single bolt found its target, striking their cloaked assailant in the upper torso. The figure's body became visible again, going rigid before sagging against the nearby bulkhead and collapsing to the deck. The weapon fell from their hands, clattering against the metal flooring.

"Nice shooting," said Leb, keeping his weapon raised and aimed down the corridor, just in case someone else lurked around a corner. His ears still ringing from the abrupt outburst of high-pitched weapons fire, he made his way toward the junction while searching for shadows or movement or some other indication of danger. He found none. Reaching the fallen Xahean, he glanced down to see it was Nalo, one of the *Pilikoa*'s cargo specialists.

"Nalo?" It was Vran. The engineer was standing next to Luhi and staring down at their unconscious shipmate. He regarded his two companions with disbelief. "Surely he is not taking part in this insanity."

"We cannot be certain," replied Luhi. "We have no way to know who else can be trusted." She eyed Leb and Vran. "If I thought for a moment either of you were involved, I would stun you both."

Leb nodded in understanding, unable to resist a small, humorless grin. "I appreciate your vigilance, but it is unwarranted." As for Nalo, Luhi was correct. For the moment, it was impossible to determine with confidence who among the *Pilikoa*'s crew were friends or foes. If Nalo was among the former group, Leb would make the proper apologies, but for now? An abundance of caution was more than justified.

Meanwhile, of greater concern to Leb was that he and his companions were running out of time.

The uprising had begun in innocuous fashion, while the *Pilikoa* was making its way to a trading outpost in the Priplanus system. It was a routine assignment, with him and his crew sent to barter an exchange of dilithium for whatever they might find in the way of equipment, tools, food, and other items of interest. Leb had made four previous voyages to the region since taking command of this vessel, and while back home there had been reports of similar confrontations on other ships as well, this was the first time he had experienced it. Some of those other incidents had even escalated to violence, though they were put down and control restored without any injuries.

Based on what he knew of those revolts, the one currently plaguing the *Pilikoa* seemed to be different. The situation was chaotic and evolving, but frantic communications from around the ship relayed the belief that fifteen people—nearly half of the ship's crew—were participating in the current unrest. Leb understood and even sympathized with the grievances believed to be motivating such actions, but staging open rebellion in deep space, far from the safety and security of home? To him that was a fool's errand. What could such a small group, so isolated, accomplish? Were they trying to send some new message to those in power?

None of that would matter if reckless acts carried out by the people now hunting him and his companions resulted in irreparable damage to the *Pilikoa* along with its crew and cargo. Primary propulsion was already offline, doubtless the result of sabotage, and that action—whether deliberate or accidental—now left the ship at the mercy of the Larasini system's harsh environment. Until main power was restored, there would be no navigating within or out of the nebula. Life-support was also offline, either due to damage or the dissidents seizing control of those vital systems in order to use them as bargaining tools.

And what if they decide to bargain with us?

The question burned in Leb's mind, despite his best efforts to suppress it. So far as he was aware, there had been no casualties reported. He also knew that without the authorization codes only he as ship's captain was empowered to use, anyone attempting to seize control of the *Pilikoa* could not do so without him. Did this put his life in danger? What of Luhi and Vran, or anyone else not involved in the revolt?

"We need to keep moving." Pausing to retrieve the still-unconscious Nalo's pulser, Leb led his friends farther down the narrow corridor. He paid no heed to the directional indicators and other signage littering the passageway, having long ago committed the *Pilikoa*'s entire interior layout to memory. It was, he realized, perhaps one of the few remaining defenses he possessed against the chaos now being visited upon his ship.

"What if they have more people coming from engineering?" asked Luhi. "If they have enough people and split up, they can maneuver around us from multiple directions. We would be trapped."

Leb replied, "Not if we move faster than they do."

Focusing his attention ahead, he searched for signs of danger. Only the angled, claustrophobic corridor stared back at him. Like the rest of the ship, the passageway was designed first as a workspace, with simple movement let alone comfort for the crew being a secondary consideration. Ducts and conduits of varying sizes ran along the bulkheads and ceiling, linking to various junction modules that all contributed to supplying power, light, and life-support to the ship's interior spaces.

Designed primarily as a passage between the control sections at the *Pilikoa*'s forward end and the vessel's engineering and propulsion components, the spine connecting those two areas had very few places in which to hide. Narrow corridors like this one along with crawl spaces allowed for movement back and forth along its length, and access hatches permitted entry to the cargo modules secured between the vessel's fore and aft spaces.

Also available were maintenance conduits linking the spine to the support braces running along the cargo sections' flanks. Containing their own passageways and control sections, the braces were also the primary means by which the cargo sections remained secured to the rest of the ship. For this reason, access to these areas was tightly controlled. Only a handful of the *Pilikoa*'s already modest crew had this authority, but what Leb did not know was how many of his fellow Xaheans were now his enemy.

You should have anticipated this, he scolded himself. *You should have been prepared.*

Just as he knew they would, Leb, along with Luhi and Vran, arrived at the access hatch for the conduit linking to the brace on the *Pilikoa*'s left side. Across the aisle from that door was a hatch leading to a small passage connecting this corridor to its counterpart, which ran forward and aft along the vessel's opposite flank. Stepping closer to that door, Vran placed his hand on the control pad set into the adjacent bulkhead, and the unit responded by emitting an orange glow.

"Still locked," he reported.

Leb nodded. "Override the lock and disable it."

Hatches like these along with similar gangways were spaced at regular intervals throughout the ship. Such compartmentalization was vital given the ship's design and inherent vulnerability. If a cargo module unexpectedly separated from the ship or damage was inflicted by other means upon the spine or support braces, affected interior areas could quickly be isolated from the rest of the ship in the event of a hull breach. As he had done so far, Leb planned to continue exploiting this capability in the hopes of forestalling capture long enough for help to arrive. The distress message he sent, although intended for any other Xahean vessel that might receive it, had also caught the attention of the Federation starship. That ship was much closer than any of the *Pilikoa*'s counterparts and was perhaps better equipped to assist his ship while it remained adrift within the Larasini Nebula. How that vessel's captain might view the situation into which she was leading her own crew remained to be seen.

That is not a concern just now, Leb chided himself.

Placing his hand on the hatch's reader pad, he waited the moment required by the computer to recognize him and unlock the hatch. It did so with a satisfying click and the hatch slid aside, revealing the null-gravity vertical shaft beyond. Handholds peppered the conduit's interior walls, and a track running along the far bulkhead served as an anchor and transfer system for large equipment, tools, and other items that were too bulky to carry while negotiating the shaft.

"Go," said Leb, gesturing for Vran to enter the conduit and be their guide for the descent to the cargo brace. Once inside the shaft, the engineer oriented himself to the zero-gravity space, using handholds to turn his body so that he could descend headfirst while keeping his pulser aimed downward.

"Look out!"

It was Luhi, pushing Leb toward the hatch and raising her own weapon down the corridor they had traversed. Catching himself on the door's threshold, Leb was in time to see the pilot fire her pulser twice, then quickly add two more shots. The quartet of energy bolts zipped through the passageway, two of them scoring sections of bulkhead while the others struck a dark figure doing their best to seek cover. The double shot caught the Xahean in the chest and thigh, twisting them around and sending them tumbling to the deck.

Leb heard running footsteps coming from both directions in the passageway. "Get inside!" he snapped, pulling Luhi into the shaft. He followed as she started to descend, and he saw Vran below her, having grabbed another handhold to arrest his own drop. Using the reader pad, he secured the hatch, ensuring it was locked before using his pulser to destroy the controls. That would stall pursuit, but only for a few moments.

"They know where we are," said Luhi, who was reaching for handholds to increase her speed as she pulled herself downward.

Leb mimicked her movements. "It was inevitable." There were, after all, only so many hiding places aboard the *Pilikoa*. He considered their current course. There were evacuation pods situated along the cargo brace, but the thought of attempting to move such a small and vulnerable craft through the chaos that was the Larasini Nebula held little appeal. So what were they doing? Hoping to find crewmembers who were not part of the uprising? He suspected they were outnumbered by those in favor of seizing control of the ship, but what would happen once they succeeded?

"It makes no sense," said Vran, his voice echoing in the shaft. "If they wanted the ship, why sabotage the engines?"

Luhi replied, "Perhaps the damage was unintended. Either way, repairing those systems are the priority if they wish to escape the nebula."

"Maybe the damage was deliberate, and they meant to leave us here after rendezvousing with another vessel," said Vran.

Having considered that possibility even before transmitting the call for assistance, Leb had seen no other alternative. If those among his crew in favor of this uprising outnumbered those against it, he and others like him would need help, from somewhere. While he had not anticipated the Federation starship responding to his message, at the moment he would take help no matter the source if for no other reason than it might prevent the current situation from spiraling out of control. Regardless of how this revolt ended, the *Pilikoa* and its entire crew were still in very grave danger.

Vran reached another reinforced hatch, which Leb knew corresponded to the maintenance corridor running the length of the ship's left-side cargo brace. With practiced ease, the engineer flipped his body around and arrested his descent by latching on to a nearby handhold, righting himself before the hatch.

"We are here," he said to his companions. As Leb and Luhi maneuvered down next to him, he used his right foot to chock and steady himself against another handhold. Raising the pulser in his left hand, he pressed his other palm against the hatch's reader pad. Leb gripped his own weapon in both hands, feeling his hands tense as the interface recognized Vran's and the hatch cycled open.

Nothing waited for them on the other side.

First through the hatch, Leb lowered himself to the narrow corridor's deck. He felt the familiar quiver in his stomach as he transitioned back to the positive-gravity environment. As with the gangway running along the *Pilikoa*'s primary support spine, space here was at a premium, with the bulkheads and overheads all but obscured by conduits, junction boxes, lighting panels, and equipment lockers. Checking in both directions, he saw no one lurking in the passageway. Down here, the brace was even further segmented into compartments, and the hatches at both ends of this section were closed. An additional hatch to his left offered access to this compartment's evacuation pod. Each hatch featured a circular port set into it with a thick pane of transparent polymer, through which one could see into the adjacent section. A quick inspection verified no one lurking beyond either hatch.

"Are we certain we do not wish to use the pod?" asked Vran as he maneuvered himself into the corridor.

Luhi replied, "It is too dangerous to launch into the nebula. The protective shielding would be insufficient against the region's background radiation."

"Even if that were not the case," said Leb, "there remains my responsibility to the ship and crew." He could not accept the idea of abandoning them. "Even those who now stand against us are in my charge."

"A noble sentiment," said Vran, "but unhelpful if the separatists choose to expel us through an airlock."

Grimacing at the thought, Leb shook his head. "I cannot believe they would do that. No revolt has ever escalated to such extreme measures."

Luhi said, "Let us hope these rebels choose to honor precedent."

A metallic click echoed in the corridor, making the three of them raise their weapons. Leb turned toward the sound, aiming his pulser at the hatch to his left. At the same time, he heard another click behind him, and knew without looking it had to be from the door at the compartment's opposite end.

"They are on both sides of us," said Vran. Standing next to Leb, he faced the other direction and aimed his own weapon at the other hatch.

Luhi said, "It was only a matter of time."

The hatch in front of Leb began to slide open, but stopped when only a sliver of light from the next compartment shone through the narrow opening on the door's left side. Without thinking, Leb stepped to his right, hoping to minimize his silhouette as a potential target. He glanced toward the still-open hatch leading back into the maintenance shaft, but knew he and his companions could not get through it and seal it behind them before their pursuers caught them. They were, as he had known when he began this all but hopeless course of action, out of options.

They were trapped.

"Leb," said a low voice, filtering through the hatch at the end of the compartment. "There is nowhere left for you to go. Please let us end this situation as peacefully as possible."

"Iku? Is that you?" Leb's eyes widened as he recognized the voice of the *Pilikoa*'s senior computer systems technician. "This is your doing?"

Standing away from the hatch opening, Ke Ho Maha Iku replied, "I would be the last person to call myself a leader, but circumstances have seen to it I now carry that burden because I believe in the cause we champion. I told the others you would listen to me if I asked you to cease resisting us. No one has been injured, and we wish no harm on anyone. All we seek is our freedom."

"Then why sabotage the engines?" asked Luhi. "All you have done is endanger us all."

Iku said, "An unfortunate accident, my friend. We are well aware of the jeopardy we now face thanks to that act, which is why we wish to bring a peaceful end to this. We need Vran's help if we are to return the ship to working order."

"So you can do what?" asked Vran. "Take the ship and throw us out like refuse?"

"Of course not." There was a pause as the hatch opened the rest of the way, and a lone figure made itself visible. Tall and lithe, with a thin stripe of black hair running from his forehead over the top of his skull and down to his neck, he held up empty hands to show he was unarmed. The corridor's low lighting glinted off the silver studs in his cheeks and nose.

He said, "Anyone not wishing to join us would be placed in the evacuation pods and set adrift, with a signal sent to other Xahean vessels to come retrieve you."

Behind Iku, other members of the *Pilikoa* crew stepped

into the compartment. Only some of them carried weapons, but their numbers were still sufficient that Leb knew there was no use attempting to fight. At the room's far end, the other hatch opened, and he glanced over his shoulder to see still more crew-members filtering in. It was plain to see he along with Luhi and Vran were outnumbered. Blowing out his breath in resignation, he lowered his weapon and gestured for his friends to do the same.

Apparently satisfied with this development, Iku smiled as he lowered his hands. "We could never harm our friends, but neither can we stand by and allow our lives to be controlled any longer. It is unfair—"

Whatever he might have said next was lost as the deck lurched beneath Leb's feet and everyone reached for something to balance themselves. Nervous looks were exchanged and Leb considered seizing the opportunity to escape, but he was stopped as other members of his crew aimed their weapons at him. He paused, holding up his hands before an alert tone sounded from the ship's internal communications system. It was followed by a frantic voice belonging to another of his crew, Kijon.

"The Federation ship is here! They have seized us with their tractor beam!"

Leb turned to once more face Iku, whose expression had softened, and he even released what appeared to be a sigh of relief.

"I am hopeful this will all be over soon, my friend." Iku offered a small, grim smile. "For all our sakes."

09

Her hands gripping the arm of her command chair, Burnham kept her gaze fixed on the Xahean ship at the center of the main viewscreen. The vessel's forward hull section was bathed in the pale glow of *Discovery*'s tractor beam, but the beam itself flickered and warbled as it fought to maintain its grip.

"The background radiation's playing hell with the tractor beam," reported Commander Owosekun. Hunched over her console, the operations officer tapped at controls with one hand while the fingers of her other hand, linked via programmable matter to the workstation, manipulated that interface. "I'm routing emergency power to the emitter."

"Helm, get us out of here." Burnham had no desire to remain in the chaotic nebula any longer than was absolutely necessary. To Commander Bryce, she said, "Send a message letting them know we'll be preparing repair teams to assist them once we're free of the nebula. See if they need any medical assistance."

The communications officer nodded. "Aye, Captain."

Looking to where Commander Rhys once again crewed the tactical station along the bridge's port bulkhead, Burnham said, "Number One, any sign of other vessels? Somebody who might've sent a boarding party to the Xahean ship?"

Her first officer shook his head. "According to sensor readings, we're all alone out here."

The brief, static-filled message from the Xahean ship's apparent captain still weighed on Burnham. Hijacking? By whom? During *Discovery*'s transit of the Larasini system to rendezvous with the damaged ship, scans had revealed no indications of other craft anywhere within sensor range. It was true the nebula continued to wreak havoc on those systems, but so far there had not been a hint of anyone else nearby.

"Stay on it," she said. "They may be lurking somewhere outside the nebula, waiting for us to do the heavy lifting for them."

Rhys replied, "Now that we're close enough for a decent scan, sensors show the ship is much better armed than I'd expect for a cargo hauler. Disruptor-style particle-beam weapons and heavy-duty shield generators that look to be operating at about twenty percent of their total capability. It's a wonder that ship hasn't taken a bigger beating in here. And speaking of cargo, I'm picking up concentrations of dilithium. High grade and refined, from the looks of it."

"That's what they do," said Booker. "They trade dilithium to various outlets."

"Are the weapons online?" asked Burnham.

"Negative." The first officer looked up from his station. "I'm keeping an eye on them."

Another electromagnetic discharge played across the viewscreen at the same time Burnham felt the deck quiver beneath her feet for the sixth time since *Discovery* entered the nebula.

"Steady as you can, Helm," said Burnham, keeping her voice level. She knew Commander Detmer had her hands full maneuvering the ship through the mess around them. This latest distortion wave was the roughest they had encountered since their arrival at the Xahean vessel and securing it with a tractor beam. As Lieutenant Tilly predicted, the area around the disabled ship had been somewhat calmer than the surrounding region, but now both ships were being buffeted as Detmer guided them through a much rougher patch on their way out of the Larasini system and toward open space.

"Owo," said Detmer. "Can you route more power to the impulse engines?"

Tapping several controls across her station, Owosekun replied, "Hang on. I'm pulling from the warp engines to compensate. I don't know if I can draw too much in here without destabilizing the warp core."

"Don't need much," replied Detmer, her attention focused on her own console. "Just a little juice for a minute or two."

Owosekun nodded. "Hang on. I think I've got it."

There was a noticeable shift in the omnipresent hum of the ship's warp drive as the operations officer completed her adjustments and drew power from the engines, which were still active. Useless as an actual mode of propulsion inside the nebula, they could still provide additional power to critical systems like the deflector shields, to the tractor beam grasping the Xahean vessel, and now to *Discovery*'s impulse drive. No sooner did Burnham sense the shift in energy to the engines than the reverberations coursing through the deck plating eased.

"Almost there," reported Detmer, not turning from her helm controls.

Burnham keyed the intercom from the arm of her chair. "Bridge to engineering. How are your preparations coming?"

Over the intraship communications system, Commander Paul Stamets replied, *"Commander Reno and her team will be ready at your signal, Captain."*

Although he did a decent enough job hiding it, the irritation in his voice was still noticeable, at least to Burnham. It was obvious the astromycologist still harbored lingering resentment toward her, even weeks after their struggle to bring down the Emerald Chain. Even if his feelings had been somewhat mollified by that brief passage of time, Burnham understood why Stamets had not yet fully processed his emotional responses, then or now.

There's no time for this right now, she reminded herself.

"Excellent, Commander," she said. "We're going to get a better feel for the situation over there before sending anyone. Continue your preparations and stand by."

"Acknowledged." Stamets's reply was crisp, though not quite curt. *"Engineering out."*

On the viewscreen, the violet mass with its undulating areas of red and black moved and stretched in response to the ceaseless electromagnetic distortion permeating the nebula, but Burnham could see some dissipation as *Discovery* moved along its exit course. Already, alert messages and other indicators were fading from the viewscreens and workstations around the bridge. Within seconds, the last of the background colors swept past the screen's borders as the ship reached the nebula's outer boundary, revealing nothing but the utter black curtain of interstellar space and the countless pinpoints of light indicating distant stars.

"We're out," said Detmer, and this time she leaned back in her seat. "Please don't ask me to do that again."

Next to her, Owosekun shifted in her chair. "Closing out power transfers and running diagnostics on key systems. We had a few near overloads along the way, Captain, but no actual damage. I'm sending a report to engineering."

Burnham rose to her feet. "Well done, everyone. Mister Bryce, reestablish communications."

"They're already trying to contact us, Captain," replied the comm officer. "Looks like some of their onboard systems have stabilized now that we're out of the nebula. Connecting the frequency now."

A moment later, a column of energy showered into existence at the front of the bridge, coalescing into the holographic projection of a Xahean male. He was not the one who had greeted her earlier.

"Greetings," she said. "I'm sorry, but I spoke to someone else earlier. My name is Captain Burnham, commanding the Federation *Starship Discovery*. Are you and your crew all right?"

The holographic Xahean nodded. *"We have suffered no injuries, Captain, though the damage to our vessel is substantial. My name is Iku, and I serve as a computer systems engineer."* His expression grew more serious. *"That is to say, it is what I have been until now. Today, I am a criminal, at least in the eyes of my people."*

Struggling to keep her own expression neutral, Burnham said, "I don't understand. Where is Captain Leb? Is he—" She stopped, realization dawning. "He said something about a hijacking. Are you the one responsible? What have you done with him?"

Iku raised his hands. *"I can appreciate why Leb described our actions the way he did, but I promise you we mean no harm to him or anyone else. Indeed, our only desire is to live our lives in peace. Unfortunately, achieving that goal meant undertaking acts we would ordinarily view as distasteful. Our seizure of this vessel was meant to be a temporary measure, designed to keep Leb and others who might resist us under control until we could be retrieved by allies. We would have departed the ship without harming anyone."*

Burnham scanned the faces of her bridge crew, each of whom was observing the conversation with varying levels of confusion and disbelief. For her part, Sylvia Tilly appeared all but beside herself, fidgeting from where she still stood next to Book behind her science console. It was obvious the young officer had much to say and was doing her best to remain silent, and all Burnham could do was offer a small nod of acknowledgment and sympathy before returning her attention to Iku.

"I hope you understand this changes the dynamics of our ability to assist you," she said. "First, I must ask: What is the status of Captain Leb and anyone else who may have . . . resisted your attempts to take control of the ship?"

As though relieved to hear the question, Iku's expression softened. *"I assure you everyone is unharmed, Captain. We have secured Leb and others in one of our ship's cargo modules, and I promise they are being treated with care and dignity. They are not hostages, and if you wish, we can arrange to have them transferred to your vessel."*

"Giving up a bargaining chip?" It was Book, making no effort to conceal his skepticism. "That doesn't make any sense."

"I cannot deny that others who share my desires might resort to such tactics, but I do not share their views." Iku held out his hands, seemingly to Burnham. *"We simply wish to live our lives*

according to our beliefs, Captain. Indeed, on behalf of those I lead, I formally request asylum with your Federation."

Silence hung over the bridge for a moment as Burnham and her officers digested this. Though she had anticipated such an appeal, to hear it spoken aloud was still unsettling. Into what sort of sordid internal cultural dispute had *Discovery* stumbled?

This, Burnham decided, was now a completely new thing.

10

The atmosphere in her ready room was a mixture of tension and bewilderment, itself a subset of the much larger mix of feelings permeating the bridge and—Burnham suspected—working its way in rapid fashion throughout the rest of the ship. She could understand and appreciate the reactions this new information was likely evoking from her crew, as represented by Lieutenant Tilly, who was, at the moment, pacing back and forth across the room.

"This is horrible," said Tilly, shaking her head as she continued her circuit, seemingly oblivious to the presence of Burnham, Commander Rhys, Ensign Adira Tal, and Book. "I mean, what happened to *them* is horrible, but I *feel* horrible for not knowing. How could I not know? How did I completely space on checking to see how they were doing? How did I do that? What—"

"Lieutenant," said Adira, their voice gentle but firm. "You're being too hard on yourself. You've been a little busy since your arrival in our century." They directed their gaze to Burnham. "You all have."

The colossal understatement would have made Burnham laugh if the situation were not so serious. "Ensign Tal is right," she said, as Tilly halted her pacing and turned to face her. "You've barely had a chance to get your feet under you, and we had more pressing concerns." For the second time in as many hours, she found herself reflecting on what she had learned about the Xahean people. More accurately, she ruminated on what they had presumably allowed to become public knowledge about their society and affairs. Even more so than they had in the twenty-third century, the Xaheans kept to themselves. Far from the world they once called home, they had chosen a new life for themselves for reasons described in only the most superficial details in Federation and Starfleet historical records. That by itself was enough to upset her, and Burnham could only imagine the effect it had on Tilly. Reaching out, Burnham placed a hand on the lieutenant's arm. "What's important is that we're here now, and we need to figure out how to proceed. So where are we?"

Leaning against the back of a chair in the ready room's sitting area, Commander Rhys said, "Iku has offered reassurances Captain Leb and anyone with him won't be harmed. He also agreed to your request that he and Leb come here to continue the discussion."

Book added, "He actually seemed eager for that, but I'm too much of a cynic to see that as a good sign."

"What did he say about our offer?" asked Burnham.

Crossing his arms, Rhys replied, "He appreciates your willingness to send our team over to have a look around. He insists it's not necessary and that he trusts you to give him a fair hearing, but he's happy for the help."

"Well, there's another reason I was hoping he'd go for that," said Burnham. "I figure it shows Iku we're not just laying some kind of booby trap for him over here."

Rather than venture over to the *Pilikoa*, she had decided the best way to proceed with any discussions about Iku's asylum request was to have him accompany Leb to *Discovery*. At least here, she could control the situation with a greater degree of effectiveness, and allowing her own people to assist with the Xahean vessel's repairs demonstrated a level of trust she hoped Iku would appreciate. A scan of the ship had already shown its defensive systems could not block any attempt to transport personnel to or from the *Pilikoa*, so Burnham was not overly concerned about sending an engineering team into a potential hostage situation. That said, a security detail would accompany Commander Reno and her people, all of whom were on standby, awaiting further instructions.

Knowing the conversation was about to take an unpleasant turn, Burnham looked to Tilly. "Lieutenant, what can you tell us about the Xaheans since we last saw them?"

Gesturing to Book, Tilly replied, "According to Mister Booker, they're basically nomads, these days."

Book replied, "So far as I know, that's all they've ever been. They keep to themselves, moving around either as individual ships or as part of convoys, staying well away from the usual shipping routes. They don't seem to call any one planet home. There've been rumors for years about some kind of commune, but if it exists, then the Xaheans know how to keep a secret. Every so often they make their way to some outlying world to trade dilithium for whatever they need."

"Dilithium," repeated Tilly. Her gaze was fixed on the deck before her. "I guess that explains their cargo, but wouldn't moving dilithium in such quantities attract attention?"

"The Emerald Chain knew about them," said Book, "but even they were smart enough to leave well enough alone, at least most of the time. A couple of Chain ships tried hijacking them, but the Xaheans can definitely defend themselves. Starfleet might have the only ships that can give them a run for their money."

Rhys said, "Sensor scans bear that out. For a cargo ship, it carries sophisticated weaponry and defensive shields. If they travel in convoys, that gives them numbers if they're attacked, but it sounds like only the Chain had the resources to even consider it."

Nodding, Book replied, "And for whatever reason, they decided it wasn't worth losing ships and people. Maybe it's because the Xaheans never seem to have enough dilithium to offset the risk?" He shrugged. "Nobody knows, just like nobody knows where they even get their dilithium."

"And that's the part I don't get," said Tilly. "Their homeworld was rich in dilithium. In our time, Xahea was on the brink of becoming one of the most important planets in the quadrant.

I would've thought the Federation would try getting them to join, but that never happened." She shrugged. "They likely had their reasons." She paused, her gaze shifting to stare at the deck. "And then I guess those reasons no longer mattered."

Book asked, "What happened?"

"In the early twenty-fourth century," replied Adira, "Xahea was occupied by the Cardassian Union—that's what their main governing body called itself during that period. Xahea was just one of numerous worlds colonized or simply conquered by the Cardassians."

"The Cardassians had depleted most of their homeworld's natural resources by the late twenty-third century," added Tilly. "By then, their government had evolved along more militaristic lines, and they began pushing outward from their own solar system. By the mid–twenty-fourth century, they'd taken over hundreds of worlds and enslaved who knows how many people. The Federation fought a war with them for several years, and as part of an eventual peace treaty, a demilitarized region was established." She grimaced. "Xahea was one of the worlds the Cardassians ended up keeping."

Burnham said, "And of course they continued to mine the planet's dilithium."

"Hell yeah, they did." Tilly frowned. "Sorry, Captain."

"It's okay." Smiling, she gestured to the lieutenant. "Go on."

Tilly nodded. "The Cardassians maintained control of Xahea and other worlds and continued their exploitation of those planets' natural resources."

"Their treaty with the Federation acted as a check against the worst abuses," said Adira, "but it was only marginally successful. Things took a turn for the worse less than a decade after that conflict, when the Federation became embroiled with the Dominion, a power from the Gamma Quadrant. The Cardassians formed an alliance with them, dissolving the formal government and allowing themselves to be annexed, which included any worlds they controlled."

"Including Xahea," said Rhys. The first officer pushed himself away from the chair. "Damn. Talk about bad break after bad break."

"The Klingon Empire joined forces with the Federation, and eventually the Romulans even joined them," continued Tilly. "Ultimately, the Cardassians broke away from the Dominion, which led to the Dominion's defeat."

Book asked, "What about Xahea?"

"It was just one of numerous worlds laid waste over the course of the war," replied Adira. "Between that and the Cardassians' earlier strip-mining efforts, their society was reportedly in shambles." The ensign shook their head. "Not much is known about what happened to them following the war. The Federation and other interstellar powers had their hands full rebuilding, and there would be . . . a number of crises in the ensuing decades that shifted the Federation's focus inward."

Having read high-level summaries of Starfleet and Federation history that had unfolded during those centuries *Discovery* skipped over, Burnham could only nod in sober agreement. While she understood and sympathized with the struggles endured by the Federation during those ensuing decades and centuries, the idea of abandoning a potential ally for political expediency and then seemingly forgetting about them altogether was difficult to comprehend.

"So, we think they've just kept to themselves for all these centuries?" asked Rhys. "Do we even know how the Burn impacted them?"

Book shook his head. "Nobody knows for certain. The dilithium they traffic is unrefined but of exceptional quality. It's possible the Burn destroyed only a fraction of their world's remaining deposits. I've never even encountered a Xahean myself, but the stories I've heard are pretty consistent. They're not the sort to trust anyone." He cast a sidelong glance toward Burnham. "Especially the Federation."

"And yet they sent a distress call and didn't balk when we

answered or when Captain Burnham offered help," said Adira. "No doubt there's more going on here than we know, but we're still going to help, aren't we?"

Walking to the ready room's outer bulkhead, Burnham stared through the viewing ports at the *Pilikoa*, still being held by *Discovery*'s tractor beam. "Whatever's gotten the crew of that ship into this situation, it's enough for some of them to resort to radical tactics to change their status quo." She turned from the ports. "We may have an opportunity here to reopen a dialogue with the Xaheans."

"Captain," said Rhys, "Admiral Vance may not appreciate us postponing our mission to Evora."

"I'll brief him once we're done here," replied Burnham. "I'm confident that after he hears what we've just talked about, he'll give us some room to run." It was true the admiral was a stickler for protocol and regulations. Following a rough early going with her that Burnham knew was largely her fault, she believed her relationship with him had improved to include a great deal of trust. If she was up front with him and explained the situation to his satisfaction, she was certain he would be on her side.

"If we can help with these Xaheans' current problem," she said, "they may consider further engagement with the Federation, and we go from there. Admiral Vance of all people will understand the benefit of reaching out to another former friend." She looked to Tilly. "Besides, I think we owe Po that much."

11

In the weeks following their rather abrupt and very much un-expected transition to host for Tal, Adira faced acclimating to existence with another sentient being living inside them. This also meant a reacquaintance with their own body and mind, and how they needed to adapt to better join with and accommodate the Trill symbiont. Tal had of course assisted in that effort, helping to ease its host through the joining process without the benefit of either Adira having trained for the demands placed upon them or the ministrations of the Guardians or the Symbiosis Commission on the Trill homeworld. With Tal's guidance, Adira learned how their body interacted with that of the symbiont, including determining which of the internal sensations they experienced came from Tal or themself.

It was because of this training, much of it improvised and only later augmented with more practiced instruction thanks to the Guardians and the Commission, that Adira could tell the odd feeling in their stomach was not Tal but instead unrestrained anxiety.

I'm nervous, they thought. *Why am I so nervous?*

"This is so ridiculous."

"What is so ridiculous, Ensign?" said a voice behind them, making Adira turn to see Doctor Arbusala walking at a brisk pace up the corridor toward them.

"Oh, damn," said Adira. "Was that out loud?" They placed a hand on their stomach in a futile attempt to quell the admittedly mild discomfort.

The Denobulan slowed his pace as he came abreast of them. "Not very loud, if that helps." He glanced in both directions along the corridor. "Worry not, though. I think your secret is safe with me." Adira watched as he seemed to study them for a moment before his eyes narrowed. "Are you all right, Ensign?"

"I think I'm going to throw up."

"Because you're nervous?"

Adira nodded. "Yeah. Dumb, right?"

Arbusala clasped his hands before him. "May I ask what's making you feel this way?" The way he spoke—gentle, indulgent, and with genuine concern lacing every word—already seemed to be having a calming effect on them. Adira forced a small smile.

"You're going to think I'm being silly, but Captain Burnham's called me to a meeting in her ready room. I'm not sure, but it's possible Admiral Vance might be there via comms too. That's not usually the sort of meeting an ensign gets invited to, unless you're senior staff, and even then you'd think the captain would want someone else from the sciences department. I mean, Lieutenant Tilly will probably be there, so why would they need me?"

Arbusala started to reply but stopped himself, and Adira realized he had noted another crewmember approaching them. He waited until they were out of earshot before replying, "I'm sure the captain has her reasons."

Blowing out her breath, Adira said, "What I don't understand is why I'm so nervous. So what if she invites Admiral Vance to the meeting? Why should meeting an admiral make me nervous? *I used to be an admiral.* I mean, *Tal* was an admiral. Or Senna was the admiral and used to be Tal's host." They rolled their eyes. "I swear I thought I'd gotten the hang of this, but every so often I get caught up in it all and it's like I've forgotten everything the Guardians tried to teach me."

"You haven't forgotten," said Arbusala. "You're simply racing to catch up to the level of training Trill hosts spend years undertaking. In a number of ways, you've been thrown into the deep end of a very large pool." He stopped himself, looking away as if to consider his words before adding, "Given what I know of how Trill symbionts are cared for, that was perhaps an unfortunate choice of words."

Despite themself, Adira could not suppress a small chuckle, recalling their time with the symbionts residing within the Caves of Mak'ala on Trill and the communing they had undertaken to release the memories of Tal's previous hosts. They now had access to the accumulated life experiences of six previous lifetimes spanning nearly three hundred years. This meant trying to sort through not just the memories of those other people but also the associated initial and lingering emotional reactions each of them felt. Adira was still coming to terms with all of that as well as what it truly meant so far as their own life and how they bonded with their predecessors. While they could recall the memories of an eighty-year-old male Trill, Adira at seventeen years of age had no comparable understanding of their own. Every day, each memory plumbed from the depths of their consciousness brought with it a new challenge.

Arbusala asked, "Why do you think the captain asked for you?"

"If I had to guess, I'd say it's because she thinks Tal's past knowledge and experience might provide some insight into what things were like a few hundred years ago. Historical perspective?" Adira shrugged. "That's the best I've got."

"That seems like a reasonable assumption," said the doctor. "Based on my observations of her to this point, Captain Burnham is very deliberate and precise when it comes to command decisions. If she's requested your presence, she believes you bring value to the meeting."

He's right, you know.

Feeling the new presence even before they heard the words, Adira turned to their left to see Gray standing next to them. As was often the case in these situations, he greeted her with an impish grin, but in this case Adira also noted a hint of understanding as they regarded Tal's former host and their late lover. He appeared as Adira had last seen him when he was alive, with his short black hair that he always loved accenting with cobalt-blue highlights. The added color emphasized the piercings in his ears as well as the dual rows of subtle spotting that traced from his forehead down the sides of his face and neck, disappearing below the collar of his dark tunic.

Don't sell yourself short, Gray continued. *Listen to him.*

"I'm not selling myself anywhere," replied Adira. Realizing they once more had spoken aloud, they returned their attention to Arbusala. For his part, the doctor appeared not at all put off by the proceedings.

"Is that Gray you're talking to?" He asked the question in a candid manner, and Adira sensed no skepticism or judgment, but rather a simple request for clarification.

"Yes, he's here." They gestured to where Gray was standing, and Arbusala turned and nodded in what Adira could see was a sincere gesture of greeting. "He says you're right and I should listen to you."

"Always good advice." His smile communicated Arbusala intended the response as a joke. "In all seriousness, it's my experience that good advice is where you find it." He raised a hand toward Gray as if able to see him. "It also seems to me you already have an excellent counsel to guide you through your nervousness along with so many other things."

I like the way he thinks, said Gray. *He gets us. He gets you.*

Frowning, Adira asked, "Are you familiar with the Trill and joining?"

"I studied the Trill along with various other species while undertaking my medical training," replied the doctor, "but I'm not an expert. When I was asked to observe *Discovery*'s crew and learned you were a member, I took it upon myself to refresh that knowledge. I've read a great deal about the joining, including how candidates are selected and prepared and ultimately guided through the process. It's rather a lot to take in, and of course my knowledge remains very limited compared to someone who's experienced it firsthand. Your status as the first known human to serve as a permanent symbiont host makes you

exceptional even by the standards to which all hosts are held."
Once again, he nodded toward Gray. "And that's even before
your unique relationship with Tal's previous hosts. You may
have much to learn from Trill, Ensign, but I also believe they
have a great deal more to learn from you."

This is what I've been trying to tell you, said Gray. *Tal knows it
too. You can always count on us. We're here to help you.*

"I know the Guardians back on Trill are still trying to figure
it out," said Adira before smiling toward Gray. "I like how it's
turned out so far, and I know I still have a long way to go, but
when it comes to Tal and the others, I'll get there."

"It's all quite fascinating," said Arbusala. "However, if I
may offer an outside observation, it seems to me you're consumed with how you, as an outsider of another sort, will learn
to harmonize your life not only with Tal but also Gray and the
memories of Tal's other previous hosts. That's an admirable
goal, of course, but don't forget that the joining is a communal
experience. You are supposed to benefit from the bonding just
as Tal reaps similar rewards. It is you, Ensign—the culmination
of seven lifetimes spanning hundreds of years—that Captain
Burnham now looks to for guidance. Let Gray and the others
help you be the best version of that very special and unique person that is Adira Tal."

Gray smiled. *It's official. I love him.*

"Thank you, Doctor," said Adira, opting not to pass on
Gray's sentiment. "I'll try to keep that in mind."

"Excellent." Nodding once more to Gray, Arbusala excused
himself and continued down the corridor, leaving Adira alone
with Gray. Once the doctor was gone, they sighed.

"I actually do feel better now. I hope I can carry this into
the meeting."

You'll be fine, said Gray. *But don't be afraid to lean on me if
you think you need to. I've got your back.*

12

Burnham had no idea what might happen when she suggested this meeting, but so far it was defying her expectations, mostly by how sedate the entire affair seemed to be.

"Would anyone like to get us started?" she asked. From her place at the head of the seating area in her ready room, Burnham considered Leb and Iku. The two Xaheans sat across from each other, each doing their best to outdo the other with their own impassive expression. Upon their arrival after being escorted by a security team from the transporter room and following the exchange of the usual greetings and pleasantries, neither seemed to have much to say. Aside from the odd glance, they did not even look at each other, preferring instead to take in the rest of the room, including the keepsakes Burnham displayed on the shelves and her desk. Their gazes did not overlook the quartet of security officers positioned a few meters outside the seating area, who maintained a discreet distance from Burnham and her guests.

"Would anyone like to say anything at all?" she prompted after another moment passed in silence. When neither Xahean rose to the occasion, she forced herself to keep her voice even. "We answered your ship's distress call, but I obviously don't understand your situation. Help me to do that, and perhaps there's something I can do to help you."

Iku replied, "I appreciate your caution, Captain, and your sensitivity to our plight. I repeat my request for asylum, for myself and the others who wish to join me." He gestured to Leb. "I regret that our pursuit of freedom came to fruition by the actions we took aboard the *Pilikoa*, but we harbor no ill will toward Leb or anyone else. We simply want to live our lives in peace."

Now it was Leb's turn. "Live your lives in peace, no matter what it does to our people. No matter the damage to our community inflicted by your actions along with those who surely will follow you. It is nothing less than an undermining of our very way of life."

"Life? We are not *living*, Leb. We are *surviving*. Stagnating while expending tremendous energy to maintain a feeble grasp on a way of life we've never really known, and which was taken from those who came before us generations ago. It is an existence into which you and I were born. We had no say in the matter, and we are expected to continue subsisting without question, for no reason other than because it is what we have always done." He waved his arms to indicate the room before pointing to one of the viewing ports and the open space beyond it. "There is so much more. Why do we deny ourselves the chance to experience it?"

It was the most emotional response Burnham had seen Iku offer since her first conversation with him. For his part, Leb seemed unfazed by the comments. She suspected he had heard them or variations of them numerous times in the past. Still, his silence was more than sufficient to communicate his stance. His sole reaction to Iku was to release a barely audible sigh.

"I need you both to understand my position," she said. "We responded to your distress call because we were obligated to do so. Even without that obligation, I would still have answered because it was the right thing to do. However, the same regulations that require me to offer assistance also prohibit me from inserting myself into a society's internal affairs. I can't help you unless you ask me to help you, and so far the only request I've received is one for asylum."

For the first time since sitting down, Leb spoke directly to her. "Captain, would granting such a request constitute inserting yourself into our affairs?"

Expecting that question, Burnham offered a sympathetic expression to the Xahean. "I'm afraid it's not that simple, which is why we have diplomats and mediators who provide oversight when the Federation becomes involved in delicate situations like yours. Our goal is to provide assistance when it's wanted, but not to impose our beliefs on your people. I admit it's a fine line to walk and we don't always get it right, but I hope you can believe me when I tell you our intentions are honorable."

Now Leb's features darkened. Burnham saw his jaw tensing and sensed him processing what he had just heard. Instinct told her that despite her best efforts, she had overstepped.

"We know all about 'Federation honor,' Captain. It is an indelible part of Xahean history. While I obviously cannot blame you or your crew for the actions of your forebears, neither does your presence here today erase what we know to be true. I cannot convince you to leave us to address this situation as we think best. May I at least implore you not to complicate matters any further with some misguided notion of selfless charity?"

And there it is.

The simple statement echoed in Burnham's mind, casting aside any hopes that history had softened the harsh reality of whatever the Xaheans had endured over the past nine centuries. There could be no refuting that, just as there seemed to be no contesting, let alone justifying, whatever role the Federation had played—or failed to play—in the tragic circumstances visited upon these people. Just as Leb chose not to indict her and *Discovery*'s crew for past sins, neither could she pretend they were not the Xaheans' reality, or an intrinsic part of their story.

All that remained was the here and now, and the circumstances in which Burnham and her people now found themselves.

Before she could address that point to her guests, the ship's intercom activated.

"Bridge to Captain Burnham," said Commander Rhys, who had the conn while Burnham participated in this meeting. *"Commander Reno has made contact and wishes to speak with you. She has a status update regarding the Xahean ship."*

"Put her through, Number One."

In response to her instructions, a human figure flashed into existence near Burnham's chair, coalescing into a holographic representation of Commander Jett Reno. She held a spanner tool of some kind in her right hand, and to Burnham it appeared the engineer was ready to swing it at anyone or anything that might draw her ire, which potentially was everyone and everything.

"Commander," said Burnham. "How's it going over there?"

"Right down the toilet, Captain." Reno waved the tool in her hand as though indicating something Burnham could not see. *"We've completed a survey of the damage and my preliminary report is that while I think we can do something with the propulsion system and main power, life-support's hosed."*

Burnham glanced to Leb and Iku to gauge their reactions, but neither Xahean offered a meaningful response. To Reno, she said, "Any idea what your complete report might say?"

"That life-support is completely hosed," replied the engineer without batting an eye. *"For all the talk of trying to minimize the damage, they did a spectacular job of . . . you know . . . not doing that. There are main power junctions down across the ship, so the whole thing's running on auxiliary batteries, which by my guess are good for another seventy-two hours or so. Their systems incorporate their own version of programmable matter, but it might take a bit for our tech to learn how to talk to their tech. They also don't seem to have any spares for the parts that can't be replaced by their own programmable matter. We might be able to pull some of the components and replicate them aboard* Discovery, *but we'll have to disassemble them and figure out just what they do. It'll take more time than they have oxygen over here."*

Leb asked, "What does that mean?"

"I'm thinking slumber party," replied Reno. *"Drop some sleeping bags on the hangar deck, have Zora throw up a good movie, and we roast some marshmallows. It'll be fun."* She shrugged. *"Well, maybe in that 'everybody shows up for Thanks-*

giving at the same time and I get stuck with the fold-out couch' kind of fun, but I figure it beats suffocating."

Ignoring Reno's commentary, Burnham turned her attention to her guests. "She's saying we need to evacuate your people to our ship. Given the nature of Iku's asylum request, I believe it best to keep your two groups segregated until the repairs are complete, but I promise we'll make you all as comfortable as possible. We'll have separate areas prepared to receive you." She was already considering the security implications of bringing the Xaheans aboard, but teams overseeing both groups would be sufficient to keep things under control. "Is this acceptable to you both?"

Instead of replying to her, Leb glared at Iku. "If not for her, you would have left us adrift in the nebula, sitting in evacuation pods after you made off with our ship."

"That was not our intention." Iku leaned forward in his seat. "Our aim was never to harm anyone, but we had no choice but to act. The queen and the council ignore our pleas, and you support their stagnant vision for our future. Just let us go in peace."

Leb shook his head. "Even if I wanted to, it is too late for that. Your actions endangered my ship and my crew. At least, those of my crew who did not join your cause. Justice for those crimes must be served. If allowed to go unpunished, they will motivate others to follow your lead, and eventually someone will be harmed."

"Wow," said Reno. *"This really is like family Thanksgiving."*

Shooting the engineer a disapproving look, Burnham dismissed her with orders to return with her team to *Discovery*. As the hologram faded, she rose from her seat. "Regardless of your feelings, we have no choice but to transfer your crew here. My security people will see to your relocation and get you settled. With luck, Commander Reno and my engineering staff will make short work of the repairs to your vessel, and you can be on your way." She turned to Iku. "While that work's underway,

I'll contact my superiors to report your desire for asylum. Under Federation law, we're not allowed to refuse such a request, but the power to grant it isn't mine. For that, I must seek direction from higher authority."

Iku nodded. "Very well, Captain. I appreciate your consideration."

For his part, Leb seemed defeated. "It appears we have no other options, Captain. I thank you for your hospitality."

It was a start, Burnham decided. A rough one, but a start nonetheless. She would take the win and hopefully find a way to build on it.

13

Making her way through the *Pilikoa*'s narrow corridors for a second time, Jett Reno decided the best and perhaps most diplomatic term to describe what she was seeing was *Spartan*.

"Watch your head, Commander," cautioned Vran, who led her along one of the Xahean ship's narrow passageways. He ducked under a section of oversized conduit—mounted along the ceiling between the opposing bulkheads—that felt cool to Reno's touch as she passed beneath it. Vran had bumped against it, dislodging dust that Reno brushed from her close-cropped dark hair and the shoulders of her uniform tunic.

"From what I know of Federation starships, our vessel might come as something of a shock," continued Vran as he guided them along this latest corridor on what had become an impromptu tour. "I assure you the *Pilikoa* only represents a practical class of spacecraft that we use. It's designed for the sole purpose of transporting bulk cargo. We have other ships that are much more luxurious."

"Well, it's certainly cozy," said Reno. From what she had seen so far, most of the *Pilikoa*'s interior spaces were devoted to onboard systems or the infrastructure required to support its cargo transport operation. Crew workspaces were small and utilitarian, crammed with computer stations and other equipment. Berthing areas were little more than bunks fastened to walls with just enough room between them to allow an occupant to perhaps prop themselves on their elbows without hitting their head on the bunk above them. These sections lacked any sense of home or belonging. As with this vessel's other areas, function took a much greater priority over aesthetic.

"This reminds me of one of my first deep-space assignments," she said. "A long-range scout ship. Covert reconnaissance, that sort of thing. Get in, take a look around, and get out without anyone ever knowing we were there. Our ship was so small you could fit a dozen of them inside one of your cargo modules. We had a crew of fourteen, and damned near every centimeter of the ship's insides was devoted to onboard systems or storage. Me and my shipmates? We were practically an afterthought."

Vran said, "That doesn't sound very pleasurable at all."

"We weren't supposed to be out that long." Reno shook her head. "But sometimes it was long enough that someone would start acting goofy. One of my shipmates was a Tellarite. Big, burly guy who insisted on walking naked from our bunks to the shower. Nobody really cared until he started showing up for his duty shift that way. Didn't even have the decency to bring a towel for his chair. I thought the captain was going to report him to headquarters."

Smiling as he listened to her recounting the story, Vran asked, "What did you do?"

"Wore a blindfold most of the time. And I drank a lot."

The *Pilikoa*'s cramped crew spaces along with her memories of her earlier assignment reinforced her guess that this ship, along with the others like it from which this craft had become separated, were intended for missions of short duration. If that was the case, then where was home? It was a question Reno had already asked Vran, but the supposed dissident had, with little subtlety, avoided offering any sort of answer.

"Everyone's accounted for, yes?" she asked. "I'd prefer to do this all at once, rather than wasting time looking for stragglers." She knew the reported ship's complement was thirty-three crewmembers, just enough to oversee the ship's systems and cargo.

Vran replied, "Leb and Iku are aboard your ship. The fourteen members we identified as co-conspirators have been gathered in one of the cargo service compartments near the front of the ship. The rest of the crew are in a similar area near engineering. My understanding is that both groups are under guard by your soldiers."

"Sweet. And then there's you, my escort," replied Reno. "And they're not really soldiers so much as general security personnel. I mean, I suppose some of them are or were soldiers. I haven't really had a chance to get to know everyone yet." When Vran regarded her with a questioning expression, she added, "Been kind of busy, ace."

She knew Captain Burnham had refused to lend any assistance to the Xaheans until her security conditions for the *Pilikoa*'s crew were met. Further, Commander Rhys had independently verified all Xahean life-forms detected by sensors aboard the *Pilikoa*, which did indeed number thirty-three. The security detail that had transported with her and her engineering team had rounded up all weapons. Captain Burnham had cautioned Reno against becoming embroiled in whatever disagreement might have fueled the revolt. Getting to the bottom of that and determining if there was a role for Starfleet or the Federation to play was the captain's responsibility, which she was addressing while in conference with Leb and Iku.

Even with that in mind, Reno still had her own job to do.

Following him through a reinforced hatch at the end of the corridor, Reno knew she had entered the *Pilikoa*'s primary crew-support spaces near the front of the ship. She recognized the layout based on a quick look at the Xahean vessel's schematics as rendered by *Discovery*'s sensors. Though still stuffed to overflowing with all manner of equipment, conduits, and workstations, along with what appeared to be storage lockers, the compartment at least was a bit more spacious. She was greeted by a pair of *Discovery* security officers, Ensigns Derek Attico and Kelli Fitzpatrick. Both were human. Attico was of African lineage while Reno guessed Fitzpatrick's ancestors likely were from Europe or North America. Reno had always been terrible about remembering personal information of that sort. Indeed, recalling the officers' names was a triumph for her. They stood before yet another reinforced hatch, into which was set a round porthole. A Xahean woman peered at her through the aperture.

"Are they behaving?" asked Reno.

Fitzpatrick nodded. "Yes, Commander. Not a peep."

There was a tone from Reno's tri-com badge on her uniform tunic and she pressed the device to enable its holo tricorder feature. An array of displays materialized before her, arranged like a curved computer station. She flicked one of the virtual controls and perused the resulting data display.

"There's an energy source online inside that compartment," she said. "It's too low power for a force field. Looks more like some kind of dampening field." She eyed Vran. "What are you dampening in there?"

Vran replied, "There are those among my people who are capable of generating a natural shroud to conceal us from the electromagnetic spectrum that is visible to most humanoids. We believe it is a trait that once protected us from predators in the earliest ages of our civilization. With each successive generation, the attribute has become much less common, but there are those among our crew who possess the ability, if only to a very limited degree."

"A personal cloaking device? Neat trick."

Ensign Attico said, "Saw it with my own eyes, Commander. Only one Xahean seemed to possess the ability, but she wasn't really invisible. I could see a vague shimmer in the air, and she still showed up on tricorder scans."

"Okay," replied Reno. "So we've got them locked up. A dampening field seems like overkill."

"Some Xaheans carry another gift," said Vran. "An ability to manipulate objects using only our minds. As with the shroud, it is limited in application, and even fewer of us seem to possess the trait. I have never seen the phenomenon for myself."

Reno made a point to scan the field being generated around the room, logging details with her holo-tricorder. There were

those civilizations who utilized technology to effect similar results as Vran described, and she had heard of other species that
possessed similar natural abilities. She had never before encountered any herself. It was an interesting development now, given
Captain Burnham's plans to bring the Xaheans aboard *Discovery*.

What could possibly go wrong?

Eyeing Vran, Reno said, "This doesn't sound like the sort of
thing you'd share freely with strangers."

"We believe these gifts were intended as a means of defend-
ing ourselves, but there are those who have used them for less
noble purposes." The Xahean shook his head. "I want you to
trust us, Commander."

With that opening, Reno considered trying to get the Xahean to offer more about whatever situation had caused the riot
in the first place, but the echo of Burnham's warning still rang
in her head. Instead, she tapped one of her holo-display's virtual
controls and sent the scan information about the dampening
field back to *Discovery*. That would give Stamets, Tilly, Adira
Tal, and the science and other engineering geeks something to
work on now that these Xaheans were about to become guests
aboard the starship. With the information sent, she pointed to
the door.

"Can I talk to them?"

Vran replied, "Of course." Moving to the hatch, he indicated a control panel set into the adjoining bulkhead and pressed
his hand to its flat surface. In response, there was a snap and a
low-level buzz followed by the sounds of multiple hushed voices.
Reno listened as the voices faded, and when she stepped closer
to the hatch to look through the porthole, she counted fourteen
Xahean faces looking in her direction.

"Hi," she said. "My name's Reno. I'm an engineer with
Discovery. Here's the deal: We need to evacuate you before we
can get on with the repairs to your ship. My people are setting
up separate areas aboard our ship for your two groups. Naughty
on one side, nice on the other." She paused, wondering if that

comment might have crossed a line before deciding she didn't really care.

"We'll have security teams watching over all of you once you're there. Turning yourself invisible or remotely operating an airlock door is the kind of thing that might make them decide to stun the whole bunch of you and let you sleep for a month, so don't screw with them or piss them off, all right?" Given these revelations about the Xaheans, Reno almost preferred that option from the outset, but there had to be at least one Starfleet regulation against incapacitating people one might be in the midst of rescuing. After their efforts to repair the *Pilikoa*'s damaged systems were complete, she would have to look that up at some point.

Nah, she thought. *Never happening.*

From inside the sealed room, the Xahean woman Reno had seen earlier stepped closer to the hatch. Through the intercom, she said, *"You have our word we will make no trouble, Commander. Can you tell us anything about our asylum request?"*

Though she had no discernible knowledge regarding Federation diplomatic practices, she was familiar enough with a few of the regulations pertaining to Starfleet involvement in such things. "My captain has relayed your request to her superiors. Last I heard, she was waiting on instructions, but it's not our policy to reject asylum seekers if we can help it. That's all I know, which is why they give me tools and tell me to fix things."

Before the Xahean could respond, the compartment's overhead lighting flickered and a distinct warbling reverberated through the metal bulkheads.

"That can't be good," said Reno.

Looking around the room, Vran said, "It could be a fluctuation in one of the ship's auxiliary power generators."

Already ahead of him, Reno once more called up her holotricorder. "That's exactly what it is." Swiping at the displays, she zeroed in on one that troubled her. "Power surges. I'm already seeing burned-out relays and junctions in some areas. That won't be good news for the secondary antimatter containment system."

Over her communicator came the voice of Lieutenant Mark Haynes, one of *Discovery*'s junior engineers.

"Haynes to Commander Reno. We've got a serious problem back here."

Reno replied, "Yeah, I see it. What can you tell me?" She knew Haynes was working with his fellow engineer Lieutenant Jason Kovalik to diagnose the full extent of the *Pilikoa*'s damage while compiling a list of impaired or destroyed components, including those items that might require manufacturing aboard *Discovery*.

"We're trying to run down the source of the problem," replied Haynes. *"But the power surges are causing instabilities in the antimatter containment system. If we don't get it settled down—"*

Reno cut him off. "Never mind. If my scans are right, we don't have that kind of time. Stand by to return to the ship." She tapped her badge to change the frequency. "Reno to *Discovery*. We need an emergency evacuation of all live bodies, right now."

"We're reading the power fluctuations," said Captain Burnham. *"According to our scans, you've got less than four minutes at this rate before the antimatter containment field becomes too unstable."*

"I had it at about three." Reno shook her head. "I hate being right all the time."

Burnham said, *"We're prepping to receive the Xaheans now, and we're sending recall signals to every member of the away team."*

"Copy that, Captain."

From behind her, Reno heard Ensign Fitzpatrick ask, "Commander, what can we do?"

Still studying her tricorder displays, Reno replied, "Beam back to the ship. They're going to need help once we get everyone transported over there."

"What about you?" asked Ensign Attico.

Before Reno could answer, the lights above her flickered again, this time in more erratic fashion. Several of them flared to what had to be their maximum illumination level before an audible crackling echoed in the room, and Reno flinched as three of the fixtures shattered, raining fragments of transparent composites onto the deck. At the same time, a pair of junction boxes on the bulkhead behind her, as well as the control panel next to the hatch, sparked and crackled. Reno smelled the residue of burned insulation and conduit lining, but she ignored that as she saw the control panel go dark.

"Does that thing still work?" she asked.

Reaching out with tentative fingers, Vran pressed his palm against the panel's faceplate but nothing happened, and he shook his head.

"The surge must have overloaded it." He looked around the room. "We may be able to initiate a bypass, if other power relays running through this section were not impacted."

Pulling up her tricorder's holo-display, Reno scowled as she studied its scan readouts. "Power disruptions are popping up all over the ship. There's a circuit fused down the line from here, and the surge overloaded the panel. Any kind of workaround will take more time than we have." She was already turning over scenarios in her mind, pondering different ways of jury-rigging the damaged systems to coax just enough life out of them to get everyone off the ship. For a moment she was reminded of her time on the wrecked *Hiawatha*, where ingenuity and improvisation had become primary survival tools not just for herself but the injured crewmates in her care. Without warning, her current circumstances had grown even more desperate than that previous crisis.

"*Commander Reno,*" said Burnham over the open comm frequency. "*We're under two minutes, and we've got everyone off the ship but you, Attico and Fitzpatrick, and the fifteen Xaheans you're with. Rhys reports there's an active dampening field preventing transporters from locking on to fourteen Xahean life signs.*"

Reno gestured to the disabled control panel. "Let me guess. That thing controls the field?"

Offering a grim nod, Vran replied, "Yes."

"Well, this just went all the way to total shit show in a hurry, didn't it?" Reno looked to Attico and Fitzpatrick. "You two, back to *Discovery*, now."

Attico asked, "What about—"

"Working on it." Reno raised her right hand and made a gesture as if she were holding a weapon. In response to her targeted movements, a phaser materialized in her hand, generated by programmable matter courtesy of the small control chip on her uniform sleeve. With practiced ease, she thumbed the phaser's power setting to increase its output before aiming it at the hatch. When she fired, the weapon emitted a thin stream of orange energy that she began tracing along the reinforced door's seams. Without being asked, Attico and Fitzpatrick mimicked her movements and added their own phasers to the effort.

"Sixty seconds," said Burnham. *"We're only locked on to four of you, but we have to beam you back."*

Reno snapped, "We're almost there, Captain. Hang on."

She eyed their progress. Even with the three phaser beams working on the task, it was going to be close.

"Reno." It was Burnham, in full captain mode. *"Scans show the antimatter containment system is starting to buckle. You're out of time!"*

Attico finished cutting across the bottom of the hatch at the same time Reno's phaser beam met Fitzpatrick's. Without preamble, Attico planted the bottom of his boot against the hatch and it buckled inward, clattering to the deck inside the adjoining compartment.

"Everybody out!" Reno waved toward the Xahean rebels, trying to get an accurate count at the same time she felt the deck rumbling beneath her feet and another surge of power coursed through the *Pilikoa*'s bulkheads.

Then everything was lost in a flash of light and in the next instant she found herself standing along with Attico and Fitz-patrick at the forward part of *Discovery*'s main bridge, staring into the tense faces of Captain Burnham and the rest of her senior officers. The one person she did not see was Vran, and she looked around the bridge for the Xahean engineer but did not see him.

"Hangar bay to the bridge," said a voice Reno did not recognize over the intercom. *"That's it. We've got everyone. All away-team members and Xaheans accounted for."*

From the tactical station, Gen Rhys called out, "Captain, it's starting to go!"

"Full power to forward shields," ordered Burnham, already rising from her command chair and moving toward the front of the bridge. "Helm, back us out of here."

Reno turned to face the main viewscreen in time to see a brilliant flare erupt from the *Pilikoa*'s aft section, signifying the last gasp of the vessel's antimatter containment system. The sphere of energy stretched to consume the Xahean ship, obliterating it from existence. A fleeting ripple across the screen was the only indication of *Discovery*'s forward shields reacting to the impact of the explosion's resulting energy wave. When the flash faded, the ship was gone.

Blowing out her breath, Reno turned to face Burnham. "I'm getting a little old for that sort of nonsense."

The captain smiled. "Nice to see you, too, Commander."

14

Leaning against the corridor bulkhead, Hugh Culber studied his holo-padd, scrolling through various status reports in rapid fashion. Only when a door to his left hissed open did he look up from the streams of text and figures, and he saw Ensign Rebecca Relph step into the passageway. Like him, she was dressed in the dark pants and white uniform tunic denoting a member of the ship's medical staff. Shoulder-length brown hair framed her fair complexion. Noticing him, she began walking in his direction, and Culber swiped away the entire holo display.

"That's it," he said as the reports vanished. "I've completed my preliminary checks of both groups and there's nothing to worry about from a medical standpoint."

Relph said, "Everyone has a place to sleep and clean clothes. They've been fed and they know how to use the replicators in their rooms."

With only a minor bit of extra effort, Culber and teams from the ship's medical and security staffs had succeeded in finding berthing space for the thirty-three Xahean evacuees. A surplus of unassigned crew quarters along with an artful shuffling of beds and other furniture had seen the *Pilikoa*'s crew relocated to a set of eight rooms, four on the starboard side of the ship's primary hull and four to port. This simplified the task of separating Iku and his group of would-be mutineers from Leb and the rest of the ship's crew.

Looking past Relph, Culber saw the security detail already moving into position to stand watch on the guest quarters here on the port side, and he knew similar precautions were already in place on the other side of the ship. He also confirmed the installation and activation of the security fields for both sets of quarters, which would prevent any of the Xaheans from displaying their odd cloaking and telekinetic abilities, limited as they might be. Commander Reno's scans of similar systems aboard the *Pilikoa* had simplified replicating the functionality. That, Culber decided, should go a long way toward minimizing any potential disruptions.

"I don't know who thought to upload all that Xahean cultural information to the computer database," continued Relph, "but it sure came in handy. Zora's already integrated dietary data with the replicator menus."

"Thank Lieutenant Tilly." Culber smiled. "She took something of an obsessive interest in the Xaheans after our last encounter with them."

"You mean when Queen Po helped us with the time crystal?" asked Relph. "I can't imagine where she found the time for research like that." She shook her head. "We've been on the go pretty much since then, not counting those bits of shore leave."

Culber replied, "That's right. You came aboard after the war, but before Captain Pike took command." He paused, considering the true weight of that statement. "It just occurred to me that you were with us for such a short time, and yet you still made the choice to come with us. I don't know why I didn't think to ask you about that before."

It was the sort of thing that should have come up during one of those moments when he sought out each individual crewmember in an attempt to see how they were adjusting to their new reality. The sudden and very much irreversible change of circumstances they all had accepted by staying with *Discovery* and leaving behind families, loved ones, and indeed their entire lives was not to be taken lightly. He had worked to ensure he did no such thing, and yet here was Rebecca Relph, perhaps a year at most out of Starfleet Academy—subjectively speaking, of course—and facing an existence she could not possibly have foreseen. Making matters worse was the fact that she was a member of Culber's own staff. How had he overlooked such an important opportunity for conversation?

For her part, Relph shrugged. "I'm an orphan. My parents died when I was very young, and I was raised by my grandmother, who died while I was attending the Academy. I don't have any siblings, and the closest friends I have are here on the ship. Three of us from my graduating class were among the crew replacements after the war ended." Her expression fell. "About half of my classmates were shipped out early during those final months, and only a third of them survived. I guess I was one of the lucky ones."

"That had to have been rough." Unlike her, his position aboard *Discovery* had ultimately seen to it he was shielded from the worst aspects of the Federation's war with the Klingon Empire. From the outset, the ship's activities took place beneath an unyielding cloak of secrecy. That was before Gabriel Lorca—rather, the captain's doppelganger from the other, "mirror" universe—had surreptitiously maneuvered Paul Stamets into a spore-drive jump that moved the ship from this universe into that parallel dimension. Upon its return from that other realm, nine months had passed in this reality, a brutal stretch of time during which the Federation had nearly been defeated by Klingon forces.

Then there were Culber's own experiences, in which he— or the original version of himself—was killed by Ash Tyler, a Klingon surgically altered to appear human. It was that Culber who uncovered the elaborate deception, though too late to warn anyone before Tyler broke his neck. That was the end of Hugh Culber's participation in the war effort and indeed everything else, until *Discovery* found him—the version that now existed—trapped within the mycelial realm in which the experimental spore drive allowed the vessel to travel.

"I lost a lot of friends during the war," said Relph. "My classmates who came with me to *Discovery* were pretty much all who were left. We decided it had to be fate, or something like that." Culber saw that her eyes were reddening, and she reached up to a single tear that had begun falling along her left cheek.

"Then everything with the Red Angel happened. After we heard Captain Burnham was bringing the suit here into the future, and so many of the crew were going to follow her so she wouldn't be alone here, I decided to join you. My friends weren't going to come, at first, but when they realized I was serious, they took the plunge with me." She forced a smile. "It seemed like the right thing to do."

As he recalled from her service record, Relph had opted for a career in medicine that included time spent first as a nurse, with an ultimate goal of pursuing her medical degree. Relph had not yet mentioned anything about a preferred field of study or specialization, instead throwing herself into whatever task or range of duties she was assigned or sought on her own initiative. She had played an important role tending to injuries during the battle with Control and the crash landing following *Discovery*'s transit from the twenty-third century. Then there were more wounded following the encounter with Minister Osyraa and her Emerald Chain agents. Like nearly every member of the crew, Relph had committed herself to her shipmates, even more so than to Starfleet or any order given to her by Captain Burnham, Admiral Vance, or anyone else. Though she might have only joined *Discovery* just before the hunt for the Red Angel began, she and others like her were as much a part of the ship's family as Culber or any of his colleagues.

Reaching out, he placed a hand on Relph's arm. "I don't know if it was the right decision for you or your friends. What I do know is that we're better off with you here."

"Thank you, Doctor." She caught another tear before drawing herself up. "I appreciate it. I appreciate *you*."

Sensing movement in the corridor behind him, Culber turned to see Paul Stamets walking toward him. Though his husband's expression was neutral, the doctor still recognized the tension Stamets was doing his best to hide. Sensing an incoming conversation where privacy might prove beneficial, Culber instructed Relph to return to sickbay and see if the ship's other medical officer, Doctor Tracy Pollard, might need assistance. The ensign nodded in greeting to Stamets before departing.

"What's going on?" asked Culber, once Relph was out of earshot.

Stamets shook his head. "It's been pretty busy in engineering. I needed to get out of there for a few minutes. You know, clear my head." He smiled, but Culber could tell it was forced. "How are things going with our guests?"

"As well as might be expected, I suppose." Remembering he wanted to return to sickbay to finalize the status updates for Captain Burnham, Culber started walking and Stamets fell into step beside him. "Everyone's healthy and behaving themselves. Now we're just waiting to see what's next."

"Yeah," said Stamets. "That should be something."

"What's that supposed to mean?"

Before answering, Stamets glanced up the passageway and then over his shoulder as though verifying he would not be overheard. "It looks like the captain's getting us involved in someone else's internal squabble again."

"This isn't just some 'squabble,' Paul." Culber stared at him with confusion. "We're talking about their right to self-determination, to live the life they choose to live. There are legitimate questions being raised by some of these people that deserve answers. *Straight* answers."

Frowning, Stamets replied, "But are they *our* questions to answer?"

Culber could not help his shocked expression. "They asked for our help. Are we supposed to turn our backs on them?"

"Of course not. It's just . . ." Stamets stopped himself. Pressing his lips together, he held up a hand. "It just seems like whenever we go looking to help someone, we bring a lot of trouble down on ourselves. You have to admit the captain is pretty good at that."

"That's the second time you've referred to her as 'the captain,' and you did it with a pretty dismissive tone." Culber knew his husband could get into occasional moods, in particular while focused on his work, where he lost track of "nonessential" things like social graces and simple good manners. Swings of this sort tended to manifest themselves when he was deep into trying to solve some complex problem, but they could also appear if something or someone else rubbed him the wrong way at the wrong moment.

As they approached an intersection in the corridor, Culber held out a hand and stopped walking. "Seriously, Paul. This isn't new. I've heard the same thing before over the past few weeks. At the time I didn't think anything of it, but there's something about Captain Burnham that's bugging you. What is it?"

"I'm just worried she'll pull us into something that's more than we're expecting, or can even handle, and then once we're all in the thick of it, she'll fly off to save the universe in her own way and leave the rest of us to clean up the mess."

Where is this coming from?

Even as the question echoed in his mind, Culber realized he already knew, at least on some level, what had to be bothering his husband. "This is about what she did to you while we were fighting to take the ship back from Osyraa." He shook his head and silently cursed himself for missing yet another obvious clue. "I honestly thought you'd put that behind you."

"I thought I had too." Stamets grimaced, obviously embarrassed that this subject was coming up. "I mean, on an intellectual level, I know she was looking out for me and taking responsibility for my safety, but with her it always seems so much more . . . personal? Like she's driven to be a martyr. No one else is allowed to take a risk, even if it's for some greater good." Using both hands, he gestured as if to indicate the ship around them. "I mean, we all risked everything to be here, *with her*. We gave up *everything* and everyone we left behind so that she wouldn't have to be here alone."

"And you don't think she understands that?" asked Culber. "You don't believe she absolutely knows what we all gave up? She had a family, too, Paul. A mother and father. A brother. A crew. *Us.* And when the time came to make a hard decision—to give up all of that in order to save them, and us, and *literally everyone else in the entire galaxy*—she didn't flinch. She knows what we did, and I think it's our choosing to follow her that gave her the strength to see the mission through to the end. To do what was necessary for that greater good."

Closing his eyes for a moment, Stamets nodded. "I know. I hear what you're saying, and I know you're right, but I could've helped her against Osyraa. She didn't have to go up against her by herself. I still . . . I can't . . . I can't help thinking there's some part of her that insists on being the only one meant to suffer on our behalf. I think it sometimes clouds her judgment."

"We're all susceptible to that." Culber stepped closer, putting a hand on Stamets's shoulder. "Even Captain Burnham, but it's worth remembering there was a logic to her ejecting you from the ship. Osyraa needed you to make the spore drive work. She didn't know about Book. Denying her a chance to get her hands on you kept you safe, but it also saved the rest of us and probably everyone at Federation Headquarters."

Stamets blew out his breath. "I know that too. I *do* know it, Hugh. I've been trying to convince myself of that for weeks now, but I still keep coming back to it. I don't know how to articulate other than it should've been my choice to stand and fight with her."

"Why didn't you say anything to me about this before?" Culber frowned, realizing just how much he had failed to pick up on the feelings of the one person he cared about the most.

"I didn't want to worry you," said Stamets. "Your plate's been pretty full since we got here, and even before that." Reaching up to where Culber's hand still rested on his shoulder, he covered it with his own. "You've been looking out for the entire crew, and I didn't want to burden you with one more set of problems."

Culber pulled him closer. "Your problems are my problems. That's what we've always told each other, right?"

"I thought I was helping you by letting you focus on the crew." Stamets squeezed his hand. "I'm sorry." He drew a deep breath. "We'll get through this, just like we've gotten through everything else. I promise." When he smiled this time, Culber could tell it was genuine. "Just talking about it has made me feel a little better. Maybe I am being silly."

"Don't dismiss yourself, Paul. You're entitled to your feelings, but keeping them to yourself won't do you any good."

A new voice said, "He's right, Commander."

Culber and Stamets turned to see Arbusala. The doctor had come around a corner in the intersection, stopping a few paces from them. His hands were in his pockets, which Culber decided was an odd look for a Denobulan to affect.

"Doctor," said Stamets, his voice neutral.

Arbusala smiled. "I apologize for interrupting, and I most certainly didn't intend to eavesdrop." Pulling his right hand from his pocket, he reached up to touch his ear. "Unfortunately, my people possess hearing that's a bit more acute than most humans. As you might imagine, it can sometimes present something of an occupational hazard."

How does he do that? Culber wondered to himself. Since arriving aboard *Discovery*, Arbusala had demonstrated an uncanny knack for appearing as if from the ether, unencumbered by distance or obstacles and without the aid of modern transporter technology. Was he skulking about the ship in search of hapless crewmembers, eager to engage with them about whatever troubles and feelings they might be carrying?

"We were just talking," said Culber, hoping to keep the irritation from his voice as he removed his hand from Stamets's shoulder.

Arbusala replied, "Indeed you were, and I certainly did not mean to interrupt. Please excuse me." He moved as if to continue walking past them before stopping again, and when he regarded them both, it was with an expression of concern and understanding. "Commander, if I may, the good doctor is quite correct." He nodded to Culber. "Keeping your feelings bottled up is ultimately harmful to your mental and emotional well-being. I'm certainly available if you wish to—"

"Commander Stamets," said Zora over the ship's intercom. *"Please report to engineering."*

With a fleeting look to the overhead as if trying to find the artificial intelligence residing within the ship's computer, Stamets said, "I have to go." He reached out to touch Culber's arm. "I'll see you in a while. Thanks for listening." To Arbusala, he said, "You too, Doctor."

Culber watched him go before noting the Denobulan was still looking at him.

"Anything you'd like to talk about, Doctor?" asked Arbusala.

"Maybe later."

Perhaps he should consider his own feelings and speak with the doctor, Culber decided, including those he harbored for Arbusala, but he suspected that was a much longer conversation for which he presently did not have time.

Later.

15

People were not supposed to get headaches, or if they did, then such minor afflictions were supposed to be treatable with only negligible effort. Among the many technological, scientific, and medical advances that had come about over the past nine hundred years was a greater understanding of the humanoid brain, managing the discomfort visited by such ailments, and even their root causes. No one in the here and now was expected to suffer from such discomfort for any appreciable length of time.

Burnham had always prided herself on her ability to confound expectations. The dull ache behind her eyes had begun at some point during those last moments overseeing the evacuation of the Xahean ship. Waiting while Commander Reno dared antimatter to come for her while she worked to free the group of trapped Xahean dissidents only exacerbated the stress as Burnham struggled to navigate the odd situation in which she and her crew now found themselves.

Explaining all of this to Admiral Vance certainly did not help.

"Nothing's ever routine with you. Is it, Captain?"

Vance, or rather a holographic projection of the admiral, faced Burnham in her ready room from the opposite side of her standing desk. Despite his remark, Vance delivered it with a small, knowing grin that indicated his understanding of the circumstances Burnham faced.

Resisting the urge to rub her temples, she said, "I figure you have enough captains covering your quota for 'routine,' Admiral."

"Fair enough." Vance's hologram turned to where Leb and Iku stood behind him watching the two Starfleet officers. *"My*

name is Admiral Charles Vance, commander-in-chief of Starfleet. On behalf of the United Federation of Planets, I apologize that we meet under such circumstances, especially given our past history with your people. I cannot speak to whatever events, action, or lack of action brought us to a point where a friend became a stranger, but I certainly hope we can rectify what I consider to be a grievous oversight."

Leb replied, "Thank you, Admiral." He gestured to Burnham. "I also wish to express my sincere appreciation to Captain Burnham and her crew for rescuing my crew. *All* of my crew."

Burnham caught the fleeting glance he directed to Iku, and for a moment she wondered if she should reconsider not having a security team in the ready room as she had during the previous meeting. She had wanted to put the Xaheans at ease, and the security detail was seconds away thanks to the personal transporters each crewmember wore. Both Leb and Iku seemed to respond favorably to the change, so she was reluctant to backtrack on her decision. Her doubt was fleeting, and she dismissed it as Vance kept talking.

"Captain Burnham has explained to me what she understands of your situation, and the Federation would like to assist, if that's possible and desired." Vance held out his hands. *"Perhaps if you explained your dispute in greater detail and the reasons for the request for asylum, we can work together to find a mutually beneficial solution."*

As though uncertain how whatever he said next might be perceived, Leb remained silent for a moment, but Burnham caught another wayward glance in Iku's direction before his gaze shifted between Vance and Burnham. The Xahean ship captain's jaw was tensing, and he drew a long breath. Finally, he directed his attention once more to Vance.

"I have endeavored to maintain a degree of discretion with respect to what I believe is strictly an internal matter among my people, Admiral, but given all that has happened and with the risk inflicted upon my crew, I no longer have that luxury. We stand before you today due to the actions of extremists—selfish fanatics who give no thought to anything or anyone but their own desires. They are content to disrupt not only our government but our society and indeed our very way of life. That you now consider providing them safe harbor is an affront to everything we hold dear. They must be held accountable, not just for their actions against my ship and crew but for their crimes against the Xahean people."

Iku glared at him with obvious astonishment. "That is a ridiculous accusation. Extremists? For wanting to live our own lives in peace? To choose our own path rather than living by some edict created generations before we were born?"

"We have survived as a civilization because each of us understands our commitment to the whole." Turning from Iku, Leb glared at Burnham and Vance. "Thanks to uncounted severe lessons, we have come to understand we can rely on no one but ourselves. In the end, we are the only ones who have never disappointed us—or betrayed us." He redirected his unflinching gaze to his Xahean counterpart. "At least, that used to be true."

It was as much emotion as Burnham had seen from the *Pilikoa*'s captain since his arriving aboard, matching Iku's earlier outburst as he implored his counterpart to understand the desires of those requesting asylum. From Leb's reaction, she suspected he was the sort of person who was content to let others live in peace so long as he and those about whom he cared were afforded the same courtesy. His initial responses to Iku during their earlier meeting suggested as much. Only now, with time to consider all of the disruption and damage caused by the rebels' actions up to and including the destruction of his ship, the Xahean was allowing his emotions free rein. Burnham was certain this outburst was fueled more than anything by the realization it could have gone so much worse for his crew, including those responsible for the disruption.

"*Simply existing* is not a life, Leb," said Iku. "When you

were a child, you did not dream of commanding a cargo freighter, traveling back and forth from our home to exchange a few precious rocks for food and other things we want or need in order to continue *simply existing*. There had to be a time when you wanted more. Perhaps not even a great deal more, but something you wanted, *for yourself*, rather than carrying on the profession you were assigned or trained to do. Tell me I am wrong."

"You are not wrong." Leb paused, and Burnham saw his jaw clenching as the Xahean wrestled with his feelings. "Unlike you, I came to understand my role in our society, and the value of doing what we can to preserve what remains of our heritage. If each of us decided our individual destinies took precedence over our responsibility to the community, what remains of our civilization would vanish. Is what we have perfect? Of course not, but we have struggled too much and for too long to maintain some grip on what it means to be Xahean, and you would see it all risked for your own personal gain."

"Gentlemen," said Vance, attempting to keep the meeting from spiraling out of control. *"I can only guess this is a debate that's raged for quite some time. Do either of you know how long this . . . resistance . . . has been occurring? Is it a relatively recent phenomenon?"*

Leb replied, "There have always been those who railed against the status quo, Admiral. It is an admittedly small movement, representing only a small yet very vocal minority of our population. I cannot say when it started, but its momentum does seem to be increasing." With another glance to Iku, he added, "And to be honest and fair, the vast majority of demonstrations, protests, and other acts of civil disobedience have been nonviolent and even peaceful. I truly believe no harm to individuals has ever been intended, except perhaps by a still smaller segment of those who have chosen to follow this path. In the beginning, they seemed content to voice their concerns by holding rallies where our leaders could see and hear them."

"And that got us nothing," replied Iku. "We have attempted to voice our concerns. We have invited discussion, to no avail. We have asked to leave, and been denied. Some of us have even put forth the notion of simply being allowed to explore on our own what might await us out here and bring newly acquired knowledge back to our people, and even that is viewed as a step too far. How can one seek reasonable accommodation when every entreaty is ignored and all we seek is a place we can call a home of our own?"

Burnham eyed the would-be dissenter. "I understand your homeworld suffered a great deal of environmental and other damage due to a series of tragic events, and I have no idea what its present condition is, but I'm certain the Federation would allow us to return you there. It would give us an opportunity to open a dialogue, something I think we all can agree is long overdue."

"Open a dialogue with Xahea?" Leb regarded her with an expression of astonishment that surpassed even the look of confusion on Iku's face. "Do you really not know what happened to our world?"

Realizing she had stepped into a figurative minefield, Burnham fought to choose her words with greater care. "I confess that I don't. I can guess the Burn affected Xahea as it did other dilithium-rich planets, but I don't know to what extent. Perhaps you—"

"There is no Xahea," said Iku. "Not anymore. At least, not the way we are told it once existed. So far as we know, all that remains of the world that was the cradle of our civilization is a hollow, burned-out shell of what it once was."

Vance asked, *"Xahea was destroyed?"*

"In every way that mattered, Admiral," replied Leb. Then, for the first time, he seemed almost embarrassed, even sharing a look of uncertainty with Iku. "From the time we were children, we have heard about the trials our world suffered. War, oppression, exploitation, but the details about what happened are lost to us. The stories our parents told us or the history we learned in school is . . . incomplete."

Iku said, "Have you ever considered there might be a reason for that? That the people we are supposed to trust the most have kept from us the truth about our heritage?"

"Of course I considered it." Leb's response was sharp, and the Xahean paused a moment as if to compose himself before continuing. "I have also considered that our elders simply do not know because, like you and I, their elders did not tell them, for whatever reason. Do I believe there is a conspiracy to withhold from us the full reality of our history? I do not. Perhaps, in the beginning, the struggle simply to survive and preserve our civilization took precedence, and, over time, concerning ourselves with a past we could never alter or repair became less and less important."

Burnham asked, "So, your people left Xahea behind? Where did you go? Did your ancestors find a suitable world?"

Iku shook his head, and his expression fell. "No. There can be no replacing something so unique and treasured."

Even as she had asked the question, Burnham wondered if it might be insensitive, given Xahean culture as she remembered it. She recalled what Tilly had told her about how the Xaheans were intrinsically linked with their homeworld, believing both their race and the planet itself were "born" at the same time. No one seemed to know what that actually meant, and even the one Xahean Burnham had met, Me Hani Ika Hali Ka Po, could or would not articulate the belief beyond a simple statement of unflinching conviction.

"What we have done," said Leb, "is create a home for ourselves, in a way we hope honors the world our ancestors left behind. We call it 'Sanctuary.' It can never replace the planet our people once called 'sister,' but there we strive to preserve all that we believe it means to be Xahean."

Vance asked, *"And where is this Sanctuary?"*

"The exact location is kept secret," replied Leb. "For our

own security, you understand. Generally speaking, the only Xaheans who leave it are, like me, crewmembers on one of our cargo vessels. Only ship captains possess the coordinates, and even then there is an extensive security procedure through which every vessel must pass before it is allowed entry. Though it has not happened in my lifetime, I am told there have been incidents where unsavory parties attempted to gain entry to Sanctuary by hijacking one of our freighters and posing as its crew." His expression grew taut. "We have also had a few encounters with pirates and even with the Emerald Chain. While the latter opted to give us a wide berth, and we did engage in the occasional commerce with their representatives, the independent pirates were another matter."

Burnham said, "That explains the weapons on your ship. We thought you were rather well-armed for a cargo vessel."

"An unfortunate necessity, Captain," said Leb. "I would be content to go through the entirety of my life without ever once having to ponder using any sort of weapon."

Stepping forward, Vance held out his hands. *"Leb, would you consent to allowing Captain Burnham and* Discovery *to escort you back to your Sanctuary?"*

"Wait," said Iku, and Burnham sensed his sudden heightening agitation. "You want to take us back? What about our asylum request?" He looked to Burnham. "You said—"

"The Federation is still considering your request," said Vance. To Leb, he added, *"While they deliberate the question, I'm inclined to allow Iku and his companions to remain aboard* Discovery. *But I see no reason why we cannot assist the rest of your crew in returning home. It would also give us a chance to . . . renew our relationship with your people. If nothing else, I believe that is an oversight in dire need of addressing."*

Leb replied, "After all that you have done for us, that seems like a reasonable request. If you will allow me access to your communications system, I can dispatch a message to Sanctuary and seek instructions." He offered an apologetic look to Burnham. "Given our people's lack of interaction with the Federation for generations, I cannot promise you will receive a warm welcome."

"You just have to arrange the meeting," said Burnham. "After that, I guess we'll see what we see."

16

For all intents and purposes, travel via *Discovery*'s spore drive had become routine, but Burnham never felt that way. Despite a technological advancement with the potential to render warp drive obsolete, that had never happened. In the nine centuries she and her crew skipped over, it appeared as though no one had been successful in replicating the work pioneered by Paul Stamets and his professional colleague Justin Straal. A secret at the time of its development and experimental deployment, no information about it appeared in any Federation or Starfleet database. At least, none Burnham could access. Upon *Discovery*'s reuniting with Starfleet, she and the crew had learned of the purging of the ship and its mission from all official accounts. It was just one more layer of security protecting them from possible exploitation by some would-be successor to the Control artificial intelligence.

Despite such precautions, Burnham was certain some record of Stamets and Straal's work was archived somewhere, perhaps long forgotten, in whatever deep, dark hole in which such secrets were kept. So far as she was concerned in a post-Burn reality, it was only a matter of "when"—not "if"—Starfleet would approach Stamets about working to improve and reproduce the technology, whether that meant retrofitting existing starships or designing new classes of vessels.

Until that happened, *Discovery* remained unique, and that was all right with Burnham.

She felt the familiar twinge in her stomach as the ship emerged from its latest jump, those stars visible on the bridge's forward viewing screen shifting as *Discovery* all but instantaneously transited to its destination. Using the mycelial network to sidestep normal space while laughing in the face of many known laws of physics, the ship now found itself in the middle of . . . nothing.

"Secured from black alert," called out Commander Eva Nilsson from her station behind Burnham. Around the bridge, status indicators shifted to green or else deactivated, signifying the ship's return to normal operations.

Acknowledging the report, Burnham continued to study the viewscreen and the image of open space visible through the transparent port. Status updates scrolled down the screen's edges as the ship's sensors forwarded their telemetry.

"Detmer," she said. "What's the story?"

From where she sat at her helm console, Commander Detmer replied, "Navigation shows we're right where we're supposed to be, Captain."

Shifting in her chair, Burnham looked to where Leb and Iku stood near the rear of the bridge, flanked by a team of security officers. She noted how both Xaheans appeared somewhat dazed by the ship's jump from the Larasini Nebula, a typical reaction from anyone experiencing the *Discovery*'s spore drive for the first time.

"Are you all right?" she asked.

While Iku nodded, Leb replied, "You did warn us it would be something of an odd transit."

Burnham offered a sympathetic smile. "I promise that feeling will pass. Are you sure you gave us the correct coordinates?"

Nodding toward the viewscreen, Leb replied, "Please be patient, Captain. As I told you during our meeting, there is a process for entering Sanctuary."

"A process." Burnham pursed her lips. "All right, then."

Following that meeting, Leb had requested permission to transmit a message over a specific subspace frequency on an omnidirectional signal. This offered no opportunity to monitor who might be the intended recipient, but the Xahean had delivered his message on the bridge in full view of Burnham and her people. It was a short missive, indicating the *Pilikoa*'s status and its crew, along with the attempted takeover as well as Burnham's request to return the evacuees to Sanctuary. The reply his transmission evoked had been short and direct, extending permission for *Discovery* to proceed. There had been no comments about the uprising or the asylum request, and no further messages.

And now here we are, thought Burnham.

"Book," she said, looking to where Cleveland Booker stood next to Tilly at the science station. "Have you ever been to this region before?"

He shook his head. "No. It's well off the normal courier routes, and too far from any of the major trade hubs. The only reason to be out this far is if you're lost, or you don't want to be found."

"We're being scanned," reported Gen Rhys from the tactical console. "It's a pretty comprehensive scan too. Right through our deflector shields. I'm trying to pinpoint the source, but something's blocking our sensors."

At the science station, Lieutenant Tilly added, "Hang on, I'm making some adjustments to try and compensate."

Burnham asked, "Is it dangerous?"

"No signs of anything harmful, Captain." Rhys moved his hands across his station's holographic displays. "But it is very thorough. I'm picking up residual energy traces throughout the ship, even in the protected areas."

Trying not to let that thought fester, Burnham returned her attention to Leb and Iku. "All right. You said it was a process. What part do *we* play in that?"

Before either of the Xaheans could reply, Tilly said, "Captain, I've completed adjustments to the sensors. We're now picking up a massive energy field. It's on a frequency outside our normal scanning range, but it's . . . it's ginormous."

"What do you mean?" asked Burnham.

Tilly replied, "The affected area is roughly spherical, covering an area just over sixty kilometers in diameter." She looked up from her science console. "There's no way this is a natural phenomenon. The energy readings are too balanced."

"It is not a natural occurrence," said Leb.

"Some kind of distortion field." Burnham fixed the Xahean with a knowing look. "Protecting your Sanctuary, in a manner similar to how we shield Federation Headquarters." She looked once more to the screen. "But yours is quite a bit more powerful."

"That's, like, a heinous understatement," said Tilly. "Now that I can read it, I'm telling you this thing is amazing. Our scans aren't even being reflected back. They're just . . . stopping. It's like running into a wall, but there is no wall." Burnham heard the lieutenant blowing out her breath. "Crazy."

From the communications station, Commander Bryce called out, "Captain, we're being hailed. The signal appears to originate from within the distortion field."

"Open a channel." Burnham rose from her chair and strode toward the viewscreen, stopping when she stood between Detmer and Owosekun at the forward stations. When Bryce indicated a communications link had been established, she said, "Hello. I'm Captain Michael Burnham, commanding the *Starship Discovery*. We bring you greetings from the United Federation of Planets."

In response to her salutation, a column of energy appeared before the viewscreen as a hologram took shape. It configured itself into a projection of a Xahean female. She was dressed in a dark gown decorated with patterns of silver swirls. The gown featured a high collar that framed her pale, thin neck, and her long, dark hair was arranged atop her head in an elegant updo style. Like Queen Me Hani Ika Hali Ka Po, the only other Xahean Burnham had met prior to this mission, this woman sported an elaborate pattern of understated yet distinct facial tattoos that served to highlight her eyes, cheekbones, nose, and mouth. Her eyes, dark and wide, seemed to brighten as she beheld Burnham.

"Captain, I am Queen Lini Kah Si Shafis Ki. On behalf of all Xahean people, I bid you welcome and extend our heartfelt thanks for coming to the aid of the Pilikoa *and its crew."*

Burnham said, "We're happy to help, Your Highness." She gestured to where Leb and Iku still stood near the back of the bridge. "However, as I'm sure you're aware, there is a situation that we've become aware of, and I'd like to discuss it with you."

"Yes, Captain, I've been made aware of the attempted rebellion. It is, of course, an internal matter, and one we prefer to address ourselves." Ki's features remained composed, but Burnham still heard a subtle shift in the queen's voice.

"I understand, Your Highness, and it's certainly not our intention to insert ourselves into your affairs, but members of the *Pilikoa*'s crew have made a formal asylum request that I'm simply not authorized to refuse. I've already referred this to my superiors, and they've dispatched me here in the hopes we may have a dialogue." Burnham stepped closer to the hologram. "I know the Federation and your people have not had a relationship for quite some time, and I confess my knowledge about the reasons for that is sorely lacking. I asked to come here because I believe there's an opportunity to address these failings, and perhaps renew the connection our peoples once shared."

Silent for several moments, Ki said, *"We know who you are, Captain Burnham, and a select few of us know about your past interactions with our people. Tell me, is there still a Sylvia Tilly among your crew?"*

Not expecting such a direct question, Burnham blinked a few times before turning to gesture to where Tilly stood behind her science console, her expression one of barely contained shock. "This is Lieutenant Tilly."

At this, the queen's demeanor changed again, and for the first time she smiled. *"We are aware of the lieutenant's unique re-*

lationship with one of my distant predecessors, who came to your aid so very long ago. To be honest, I only just learned about this, after an aide retrieved Queen Po's personal journals from our protected royal archive. It is not public knowledge, but Po's writings of these encounters make for rather fascinating reading."

While the truth behind *Discovery*'s arrival in the thirty-second century was a closely guarded secret among the highest echelons of Starfleet and Federation leadership, this was the first time Burnham had considered another party might well possess the same knowledge.

Admiral Vance will love that, she thought.

"In light of this new revelation, I find myself eager to speak with you," said Ki. *"Please accept my invitation to join us here in Sanctuary. Coordinates will be provided, and I hope you'll bring Lieutenant Tilly with you when we finally meet in person."*

Burnham smiled. "It would be our honor, Your Highness."

After bidding farewell, Ki closed the communication and her hologram vanished. At the same time, an alert tone sounded from Tilly's science station.

"Change in energy readings from the distortion field, Captain. It's directly in front of us. Distance, one hundred five thousand kilometers."

Still standing near the back of the bridge, Leb said, "Do not be alarmed, Captain. This is standard procedure when a vessel is granted permission to enter Sanctuary."

All eyes on the bridge turned to the viewscreen in time to see space itself appear to bend and stretch, bulging toward them before an opening appeared at the center of the image. Expanding outward, it assumed an ovular shape, its boundary defined by a ribbon of vivid blue-white energy. Space was visible beyond the new aperture, but so was something else. At first Burnham thought she might be gazing upon an asteroid or perhaps a small moon, but within seconds it became obvious the spherical shape now visible to them was clearly of artificial design.

"It's a space station of some kind," said Commander Rhys

from the tactical station. "But it's the biggest damned thing I've ever seen."

From the helm console, Detmer said, "It's beautiful, is what it is."

Dwarfing even Federation Headquarters, a transparent shell surrounded a byzantine, weblike construct with massive conduits extending from the sphere's inner surface down to its central core. Burnham could make out areas of land and water scattered throughout the intricate latticework, and cityscapes of varying size and density situated across those areas as well as the conduits supporting the entire structure.

"The sphere measures over thirty kilometers in diameter," reported Tilly. "Sensors show a massive power plant at its center, as well as energy signatures from hundreds of ships of varying size. I'm also picking up programmable matter in quantities like you wouldn't believe. It's in active use throughout the entire facility, almost like it's moving at will."

Leb said, "We use it for a wide variety of autonomous functions that are necessary to sustain the habitat, far more so than—for example—our cargo vessels."

"There's also enough dilithium to supply every ship in Starfleet for at least a century," added Rhys. "Sensors show a sophisticated refining facility beneath what I guess you'd call the surface of the sphere's core."

Burnham asked, "What about life signs?"

"Over one million inhabitants." Tilly grinned. "It's like San Francisco, but in space."

To Burnham, it was an orb of sheer beauty, hanging before them. "Sanctuary."

Discovery passed through the opening in the distortion field, its effects forgotten as the mammoth sphere filled the viewscreen. The closer they approached, the more impressive the construct looked to Burnham. Even from this distance, she could see small dots sailing through the air inside the self-contained ecosystem, likely a form of personal conveyance. She also spotted what had to be monorails or a form of magnetic-levitation trains arcing up, around, over, and under the orb's extravagant support lattice. More than a simple construct, Sanctuary was indeed a work of art.

"How long did it take to build this?" asked Tilly.

Iku replied, "My grandfather once told me that from his earliest memories until he married my grandmother, his father was one of thousands of people working on its construction, and it had been underway before he joined the effort."

"I remember seeing early designs for a starbase like this," said Owosekun. "More like concept drawings. It was while I was at the Academy. We were talking about how long-term deep-space exploration could be supported even in those regions where there are no habitable planets. Something like this was supposed to be a better alternative to typical starbase stations, mimicking the features you'd find on a planet-based facility."

"Starfleet did get around to building a few," said Burnham, remembering what she had read in historical texts as part of her remedial education following *Discovery*'s arrival in the present. "They were lost during the Burn too."

Rhys said, "Captain, we're receiving a signal from the sphere." Looking up from his console, he gestured toward the viewscreen. "Instructions for maneuvering inside. It looks like an area of null gravity with docking ports for their cargo ships."

"It is an approach vector, Captain," said Leb. "Once inside the sphere, you will be directed to a docking umbilical where you will be provided assistance and instructions for disembarking your ship."

Iku asked, "What about us?" There was no mistaking his troubled expression or the note of worry in his voice.

"Of course, Leb and your crew are free to leave once we've docked," said Burnham. "As for the rest of you, I'm allowing you to remain here as we agreed. Federation Headquarters is still considering your asylum request." She nodded toward the viewscreen. "Given your queen's invitation to meet with her,

I'm hoping we can find a mutually satisfactory option on how to proceed."

Burnham could only hope Ki was as amenable to discussion as she appeared to be a few moments earlier. How would the queen's unexpected familiarity with *Discovery* and its past history with Xahea play into whatever came next?

An advantage or a detriment? Her unspoken question taunted Burnham. *I guess there's only one way to find out.*

17

Materializing on the transporter pad in his office, Hona Ko Mah Sen's first sight was the computer terminal on his desk. Even from here he could see the litany of alert indicators telling him he had messages and reports of numerous types to review and answer, but all of that would have to wait. Instead, he focused his attention on his executive officer, Ona La Nako Tol, who had apparently been waiting for him.

"Sen," she said, acknowledging her counterpart and friend. He had known her since they met while undertaking the security ministry's introductory training course. In an environment where trust and loyalty could be rare commodities—and even weapons—his confidence in Tol was total. She had been his first and only consideration to serve as his second-in-command upon being assigned to lead this unit.

A holographic tablet floated in the air before her, generated by the bracelet she wore on her wrist. Like him, she wore nondescript civilian attire rather than her Ministry of Security uniform. This was standard procedure for the Internal Security Section, the ministry's clandestine subordinate agency that he currently commanded. Along with Tol and the section's other members, he neither wore nor carried anything that might connect him to the secretive organization.

Stepping off the transporter pad, Sen asked, "Do we have a report on the protest in the Kalyadi Province?"

Tol consulted her control pad, scrolling through several columns of text. "There was an altercation, started by someone who took issue with the separatists, of course."

"Was it one of our people?"

Tol shook her head. "Not this time. This was just a regular citizen taking issue with people causing a disturbance near her home. Others joined in, but it was mostly verbal exchanges. There was only the one physical confrontation, but security officers quickly addressed it."

"Continue monitoring the situation," said Sen. "Inform me the next time the information channels release a new opinion poll. I have observed a small increase in those voicing support for the separatists."

Using agitators to promote unrest during these separatist demonstrations was a calculated risk, and one Sen chose to use with care. A significant percentage of the public actively opposed the cause these rebels championed. Forsaking Xahean heritage and the society they had built over the course of generations as a means of overcoming the stark tragedies visited upon their civilization tended to inflame opinions. However, there was still a vocal segment of the population who supported the idea even if they had no such aspirations of their own, or else held no overriding opinion on the matter. It was those people about whom Sen worried, as it might be their views that could sway the council toward favoring separatist agendas. He knew such behavior could be anticipated and even manipulated, but it was something to be undertaken with great care.

He stepped onto the security section's main floor. Ambient sounds greeted him from the larger chamber filled with people and equipment. Workstations and other offices filled the room, all active and overseen by security officers. It was there that the ministry monitored all of the communications and information transferred throughout Sanctuary. The mandate for Sen and his people was simple: observe, study, analyze anything and everything, and prepare for any and all contingencies. Such a mammoth effort was aided by a powerful computer apparatus buried deep beneath the habitat's peaceful veneer, separate from the system used by civilians to inform and entertain themselves as they went about their lives. Only a select few persons even knew of the Internal Security Section's existence. That very short list did not even include the queen or the Xahean council. The section had its own procedures, its own rules, and Sen was accountable only to Security Minister Vomin. Given the nature of the duties required of him, he had long ago come to terms with the belief this was a good thing, not just for the throne and the leadership caste but all the Xahean people. The challenge, he knew all too well thanks to the inappropriate actions of some of his predecessors, was in not overstepping the limits of the authority granted to him. For better or worse, the section had its own rules for addressing those sorts of unfortunate occasions as well.

"I can only remain for a short time," he said to Tol as she followed him onto the main floor. "The queen is due to meet with the Starfleet captain."

Tol swiped away her control pad. "I thought you would want to see this as soon as we had a preliminary report. We have completed our initial scans of the Federation vessel. It is as we suspected after the *Pilikoa* shipmaster made contact."

"The ship from our historical records." It was almost impossible for Sen to believe. "After all this time?"

"It appears so," replied Tol. "I find it difficult to accept myself, but the proof is now in our midst. It did in fact just appear on our long-range scans as if from nonexistence itself. I am at a loss to explain this, but we do know there are a host of technologies that allow for concealing a vessel from sensor detection."

Sen allowed himself a small chuckle. "Indeed there are, but that is not the case here, my friend."

Upon hearing the initial report from Leb just prior to the ship's arrival at Sanctuary, Sen knew there would be precious little opportunity to confirm this news. It was therefore fortunate the Starfleet captain, in her haste to make a goodwill gesture to Queen Ki, had wasted no time releasing the cargo ship's crew. Sen had personally seen to Leb's debriefing, and the shipmaster's description of the alien vessel had matched those on record in the security ministry's data files in vague terms. That much was understandable, considering many Starfleet ships were essentially variations on a standard design in use since well before Xahea's first encounter with the Federation. As for this vessel, *Discovery*? Its configuration was, so far as Sen was able to determine after conducting his own research of the ministry's historical databases, rather unique. A search of Starfleet ships known to Xaheans in the time following that initial contact revealed no apparent instances of this craft.

But it was Leb's descriptions of the vessel's abilities that had given Sen his first true hope.

Tol said, "According to Leb, they traversed the distance from the nebula to Sanctuary in near-instantaneous fashion. Even if this is some other type of propulsion system—something the Federation has developed without our knowledge—it still presents an opportunity for us."

"You have no idea," replied Sen. "This represents the goal that has eluded us for generations: a permanent means of keeping us all safe, and never again having to rely on any outsider for anything. Perhaps once that is achieved, those who seek to leave Sanctuary will finally realize the uselessness of such desires and keep their rightful place here with us."

Like Tol, he had never known life before Sanctuary. The immense habitat's construction was completed even before his parents' forebears were born. However, the separatist cause was well known even when his own mother and father were children. When he first heard about it, Sen admitted it was a fanciful, even romantic notion. Seeking a new life on some heretofore unknown world carried a certain appeal. Building an existence of one's own rather than simply inheriting the society created by those who had come before him seemed like it could be an adventure.

However, with ancestors tracing all the way back to before the great exodus from Xahea, Sen's family had in the generations that followed put forth much effort into maintaining their status. Their civilization's "elite class" had suffered greatly during times of strife such as occupation under the Cardassian Union and further subjugation by the Dominion during its war with the Federation. Such distinctions were of little interest or use to their oppressors, so Xaheans of any societal stripe were re-purposed as laborers. If they did not contribute to strip-mining the planet of its valuable dilithium reserves, they were taken to other worlds to contribute to whatever effort their overseers deemed appropriate.

In the aftermath of those trials and the eventual abandon-ing of Xahea, families such as Sen's struggled to regain their status. It was a process eased by an innate desire by much of the population to restore as much normalcy as possible to the civilization they were attempting to salvage. What little wealth survived the hardships of occupation and conflict was collected before setting out in convoys for deep space, while the effort to return themselves to their former places in Xahea's social hierarchy slowly continued. As time passed, with each genera-tion giving way to the next, and with no small amount of help from the leadership council and the throne itself, the elite class returned to something of its former glory. Understandable concessions to the greater good, first as the convoys made their way among the stars and later with the construction of initial habitat colonies and culminating with Sanctuary itself, made those in the upper echelons of Xahean society appear mag-nanimous to the rest of the populace. Sen's family took things even further, forgoing many of the benefits of its previous sta-tus in order to serve within the government. He was the first member of his clan to join the Ministry of Security, and now had spent the balance of his adult life in service to the throne. Never comfortable with the shield of privilege, Sen preferred instead to do something of value not just for his family but for all Xaheans.

Now that meant safeguarding their heritage as well as their

future. The means to do that very thing appeared to have delivered itself into their midst as if provided through divine intervention.

Conjuring a holographic display of the Federation ship, Tol allowed the representation to hang in the air before them. Slight gestures allowed her to turn and rotate the computer-generated representation as rendered thanks to the array of sensors aimed at the ship from the moment of its arrival.

"The ship does contain a modern dilithium-based warp-drive system," said Tol. "The metallurgy suggests a type of construction from many generations in the past, but the vessel's relative age belies that. If this is indeed the same ship you say Queen Po described in her journals, where has it been all this time?"

Sen nodded, offering her a knowing smile. "The ship carries with it an amazing story, my old friend." His own research into this mysterious ship had taken him back generations within the ministry's vast storehouse of information, to the time of Me Hani Ika Hali Ka Po, the young, spirited woman whose reign as queen intersected with Xahea's first contacts with *Discovery*. Her voluminous private journals were available in the royal archives, of course, but those versions along with those of her predecessors and successors lacked various segments and other documents deemed too sensitive for public release. All of that material was available to the throne, of course, but also to the Ministry of Security.

"According to Queen Po, the ship was still rather new when she encountered it for the first time, having been recently constructed as a platform for various emerging technologies the Federation thought might aid them in their war with the Klingon Empire. The vessel later entered a temporal rift, disappearing from its own time on a course for a point in the distant future." Sen held out his hands. "Our present, as it happens. Her Highness chose not to include the reasons for this journey in any of her journals, perhaps as a means of protecting some secret the ship harbored."

"The truth almost certainly lies within the vessel's own computer system," said Tol. She manipulated the hologram and the *Discovery* model continued rotating, offering a range of angles and views as both security officers studied it. "And what of this propulsion system the *Pilikoa* captain described?"

Sen replied, "At least there, Queen Po's recollections were quite vividly described. She called it a 'displacement-activated spore hub drive.' It apparently employs spores harvested from the mycelia of a particular type of fungus that exists on this dimensional plane as well as another realm that lies in proximity to the subspace our ships enter when they travel faster than light. Interfacing with these spores—with the proper equipment, of course—allows a vessel to traverse this other realm, at which point it can exit at a predetermined point anywhere within that domain. In effect, this process permits interstellar travel of a sort that renders our current technologies obsolete."

"This sounds like fantasy," said Tol, making no attempt to hide her skepticism. "It has to be a deception, an illusion or trick performed to amuse children. Even if such technology existed generations ago, how or why was it never duplicated? My understanding is that Queen Po was something of a prodigy when it came to complex engineering concepts. Did she not ever attempt to reproduce this astounding feat?"

Once more, Sen laughed. "Queen Po was a gifted engineer. That much is historical fact. She is lauded for a number of technological advancements that were of great benefit to our people. Many of these developments were never shared with the masses, as she feared they would be used to further damage our world or—worse—enable our people to exploit and harm other worlds. I suspect she harbored similar feelings with respect to something like *Discovery*'s drive system, but that did not stop her from scanning the ship when the process was employed, and documenting everything she understood about it."

It was almost amusing for him to watch Tol's expression turn to one of astonishment. "Are you saying she found a way to re-create this technology?"

"In a manner of speaking," replied Sen.

18

It was not until Doctor Arbusala took the chair across from her that Sylvia Tilly realized he had been speaking to her. How long had he been doing that?

"Lieutenant?" asked the Denobulan, settling into his seat and resting his hands in his lap. "Are you all right?"

Startled from her reverie, Tilly blinked several times before looking around the crew lounge. A few of the tables were occupied, mostly by lone crewmembers or the odd pair, and no one seemed to be paying any attention to her.

"Doctor," she said by way of greeting. "I'm sorry. I didn't hear . . . I mean, I wasn't . . . I'm sorry." She frowned. "I guess you can say it's been one of those days."

"I would imagine so." Arbusala took a moment to peruse the room for himself. Tilly had selected a table near the lounge's far corner, near the bulkhead where she could look out the viewing ports. When he redirected his attention to Tilly, he gestured toward the cup on the table before her. "Espresso?"

Tilly nodded, reaching up to wipe a rogue lock of her bright red hair away from her left eye. "Only a double, this time. Just enough to give me a little pick-me-up but not so much I end up bouncing off the walls. I don't think Captain Burnham would appreciate that when we meet with Queen Ki." It was early for the evening meal following alpha shift, but she had only stopped for the espresso as a way to relax for a few moments before continuing with her preparations to transport with the captain to Sanctuary. In a lower voice, she added, "Also, Zora gets snippy if I order a triple, and I think there's an override in the system that won't let me order anything more than that. I really need to dig around in the code and see if she's just screwing with me."

Before Zora, the ship's computer would simply advise against the extra allotments of caffeine—often, Tilly decided, in a rather judgmental manner. While Zora's approach was more maternal, she could be just as condemnatory whenever Tilly came looking for a supreme energy boost that could only be found in the warm embrace of her very best friend, a quadruple espresso. With milk alternative, of course. If early developments with their current mission were any indication, she might well have to burrow into the replicator system's software and install an override to ensure her supply of espressos remained unimpeded.

Looking up from her coffee, Tilly said, "I'm sorry, Doctor. My head must be in subspace. Is there something you needed from me?"

The counselor shook his head. "That was going to be my question for you, Lieutenant. Given recent developments and what I know of your personal history with the Xaheans, I thought you might like to talk about what you're feeling. I suspect gaining some insight into how they've fared in your absence came as something of a shock."

"Remind me to nominate you for the Galactic Understatement Awards." Without meaning to, Tilly released a single, humorless chuckle in response to her own feeble joke. "I'm sorry, Doctor. That wasn't fair." Attempting to mask her shame, she took a sip of her espresso and blanched upon realizing it had gone cold. "I'm just feeling out of it. Pulling up all that information about the Xaheans was more than I bargained for." She blew out her breath. "Everything they went through after we left. It's insane. I tried looking up information about my friend Po, but there wasn't much in any of the historical databases."

Arbusala said, "Me Hani Ika Hali Ka Po, who took her place as queen of the Xahean people in 2257 at just seventeen years old, at least as humans measure such things. Quite the remarkable achievement."

"I wish I'd gotten to see her in action," replied Tilly, then waved her hand. "As a queen, I mean. She had all these grand ideas about how to lead her people. They'd only just discovered faster-than-light travel, and I've wondered what they might've done once they had the ability to leave their homeworld." She grimaced. "Not much, as it turns out. I don't even know how long she ruled, or lived, or how she died. Did she have kids? None of that is in any of the files."

Leaning forward in his chair, Arbusala offered her a sympathetic expression. "You feel as though history has forgotten them."

"Exactly!" Her reply came out louder than she intended, and Tilly offered sheepish grins to those few people who were close enough to hear her. To Arbusala, she said in a quieter voice, "Exactly. It's like Xahea just fell off the galactic map and nobody gave a damn. And then we find what's left of their civilization out in the middle of nowhere and living inside a giant ball." Feeling a rush of anger welling up within her, she placed her hands flat on the table. "I'm sorry."

Arbusala smiled. "It is certainly understandable for you to feel as you do. Is it possible you're identifying with the Xaheans—and Queen Po in particular—even more so than you did before, because you feel history has treated you and your crewmates in a similar fashion?"

The question caught Tilly by surprise. She stopped herself from replying, pondering for an extra moment what the doctor had posed. Was it really that simple?

"I honestly hadn't thought about it that way," she said, continuing to turn the question over in her mind. "I suppose I never considered our situation from that perspective, but after hearing the words out loud, I . . . guess there's something to the idea."

How had her parents reacted to the news of *Discovery*'s apparent destruction and her own death—the cover story created by Starfleet to conceal the true purpose of the ship's journey to the future? While she had dwelled on such questions, it had been through the lens of her personal situation and its impacts on her family. She had given less thought to the larger ramifications of the ship's removal from official records and, indeed, the annals of history. On an intellectual level, she knew the ship's documented fate was merely an extension of its mission, shrouded in secrecy given *Discovery*'s original status as a testbed for experimental and highly classified technology. Every member of the crew was aware of their assignment's clandestine nature and the risks inherent in such an undertaking. She also understood the subterfuge was necessary to keep anyone else from ever getting their hands on *Discovery* and the Sphere data it harbored. All of that would likely have been of little comfort to those left behind, even if they could have known about it.

"I sometimes wonder if any of our families or friends ever learned the truth about what we did," she said. "I doubt it, and I suppose in some way that makes our choice all the more meaningful. I know what we did was right, and I'd do it again if faced with the same choices. Even if my family never really knew what happened to me, I'm at peace with knowing I did something to save them. You know, along with everyone else. I mean, there are worse things to do with your life, right?"

Her words sounded like a jumble to her, but they evoked a small laugh from Arbusala. "That is a wonderful perspective, Lieutenant. I know you've perhaps had second thoughts, and it is of course natural to miss your home and those you left, but it's good that you take comfort from knowing your actions had meaning, even if those for whom you made such an incredible sacrifice could never fully appreciate what you and your colleagues did."

Validation from an outside observer brought Tilly an additional measure of peace. "Thank you, Doctor." She cast her gaze toward the viewing ports. "What it makes me wonder is why the Xaheans have apparently made this choice of their own accord. According to what Po told me, her people believe their species was born at the same time as their planet. They were bonded and balanced with the planet itself. So what does it say that whatever happened to them was so bad they felt they had to leave?"

Arbusala replied, "It seems fate has provided an opportunity for you to answer that very question. I can only hope it might also offer a means for you to ask your other questions, Lieutenant."

"Which brings us to me going with Captain Burnham," said Tilly. "All of a sudden I'm the Starfleet expert on the Xaheans, and all because I once gave their queen some ice cream. Who could've seen that coming?"

"A most fortunate meeting, as it turned out." Arbusala shrugged. "At least, based on what I've read. It was your relationship with Po that allowed Captain Pike to seek her assistance and gain her trust as you all worked to safeguard the Sphere data and bring *Discovery* here. None of that could have happened without Queen Po's support, and that might not have been possible but for your chance meeting with her."

Always self-conscious when receiving praise, Tilly placed her hands in her lap. At the same time, the doctor's words made her realize something she had not previously considered. "Well, when you put it like that, it sounds like all of this was my fault."

"It's no one's fault, Lieutenant. What happened was meant to be and indeed what had to happen, not just to protect the Sphere data but all life in the galaxy. Your relationship with Queen Po factored into Captain Burnham's decision to set one of the Red Angel's signals near Xahea. Thanks to you, she knew Po was the one person who could help charge the time crystal Captain Pike retrieved from the Klingons at Boreth. She and Captain Pike made the ultimate decisions, of course, but they were guided by your relationship with Po." Arbusala's expression turned thoughtful. "Of course it's not your fault. Just the opposite, I think. If not for you, none of us would be here."

"Savior of the galaxy." Tilly pondered that. "Talk about peaking early, huh?"

Arbusala rose from his chair. "I suspect we haven't yet seen the best Sylvia Tilly has to offer. All in good time, I imagine."

"Let's see what happens after I go with the captain." Reaching for her cup, Tilly frowned as she examined its contents.

Maybe just one more espresso. A single this time.

19

The transporter sequence faded, replacing Minister Sen's office with an expansive underground cavern. Here, Sanctuary's underlying structure was prevalent, with massive columns supporting whatever lay above their heads on the surface as well as conduits for power and environmental and other systems Xaheans relied upon for daily life. Walls towered above them toward a high arched ceiling. Workstations, many of them older or discontinued models and requiring constant attention from the technicians charged with their care, provided most of the room's illumination. Light from other subdued sources ran along the ceiling or were mounted to the sides of support columns scattered throughout the subterranean cavern.

At the center of the chamber sat a large, intricate mechanism. Mounted within a reinforced framework, the device had its own system of ducts and tubes branching outward to connect to the existing conduits. While it was inert at the moment, Sen knew it was capable of producing tremendous power.

"Is this what I think it is?" asked Tol.

Sen nodded. "It is indeed what you think it is. At least, most of what you think it is."

"Queen Po," said Tol. "All of this, from her journals?"

Sen smiled. "No, not all of it. Po never had the chance to examine the ship's systems in sufficient detail. The notes she left behind were comprehensive, to be sure, and scientists did attempt to develop computer models based on what little information she included as well as sensor scans obtained during *Discovery*'s visit to Xahea. Research into the spores and the mycelial realm progressed with more success than development of any actual system to exploit it. Of course, those efforts were abandoned once our world suffered under the Cardassians and the Dominion, and were largely forgotten once the relocation began. We still had the information, but as you might imagine, there were other priorities for quite a long time. Given the prosperity our forebears made for themselves, particularly with the creation of Sanctuary, that early research might never have been revisited." His expression fell. "Then the galaxy changed."

Tol nodded in understanding. "The dilithium cataclysm."

"Precisely," said Sen. "Even though our high-grade, unrefined dilithium survived that disaster, there was renewed value in seeking possible alternatives to warp drive. With that as a driving factor, a group of our scientists discovered the long-forgotten research and set out to re-create it." He gestured toward the gargantuan mechanism.

"And it works?" asked Tol.

"No." Sen led her across the cavern toward the machine, around which a group of Xaheans moved and worked. "What you see here is the product of an effort that began in the aftermath of the Burn, extrapolating from the information in Po's journals and those limited sensor scans to create this device. Smaller versions have been constructed as test subjects, installed aboard unmanned probes and other small craft. Computer simulations show it is possible, but numerous attempts to establish even a fleeting connection to the mycelial realm have failed. When a successful link is made, there is no control. Our test objects end up disappearing with no trace, or else come back with significant damage. Until we understand why that happens and what *Discovery* does to mitigate or eliminate this danger, the risk to a living test subject is far too great, at least at this stage."

Standing a respectful distance from the machine so as not to interfere with the scientists and engineers hovering around it, Sen watched as his friend studied it with unguarded astonishment.

"Such a massive undertaking," she said. "Carried out across

generations." She turned to stare at him. "How have I worked with you for so long and never heard of such a thing?"

"Because it remains a closely guarded secret," replied Sen. "Knowledge of this work has been limited to a select few, even within the security ministry's already compartmentalized structure. I only became aware of it when I joined the Internal Security Section and was given oversight of the project." He paused, recalling the day he learned of the effort's existence and the staggering amount of time and resources devoted to it. Personnel, equipment, financial and logistical support, all in service to the Ministry of Security's ongoing mission to shield it from the rest of the population. "I am the fifth such officer to carry this responsibility, and until today I assumed I one day would transfer it to a successor. Now we find ourselves at a point where the dreams of so many Xaheans over such a significant span of time might finally be realized. I brought you into this section because I trusted you to safeguard such information."

As if attempting to comprehend all she had learned in the past moments, Tol said, "It seems unlikely that we would exert this much time and effort into something where we had no reasonable belief it would succeed." She turned to stare at him. "Queen Po. She knew the Federation ship would arrive at this point in time. Our ancestors knew this?"

"It appears so," said Sen. "Though the exact point of arrival was not known, it was still a milestone to which they might work. I do not believe they counted on waiting such a span of time, and while efforts on the project did wane for significant periods, they never fully stopped. The ship's arrival has infused us all with renewed vigor. There is obviously an aspect to this process our version lacks; perhaps some additional component that assists with successful passage through the mycelial realm. Whatever that might be, we need to find it, determine how to integrate it with what we have built, and successfully test it before we can ever share it with the public."

"Agreed," said Tol. "A revelation of this magnitude might

escalate the strife we already see between traditionalists and separatists. Such a technological progression would certainly renew the former's desire to relocate Sanctuary while keeping us all united. The latter would see it as yet another means of seeking a new permanent home, either for everyone or simply for those who share their views."

"That is a very valid concern, but of even greater concern is the fear of this technology being discovered and exploited by outsiders." Sen paused, casting another long look at the dormant machine and considering the hopeful as well as the adverse potential it represented. "We cannot allow our people to face such a threat ever again."

They would have to proceed with caution, he knew. At the moment, there was mutual respect between Queen Ki and the Federation captain. Each would be doing their level best to foster trust with the other. The queen's aims were obvious, as she acted to protect the Xahean people, but the Federation was an entity that could not be ignored. Circumstances had seen fit to bring its representatives here, ostensibly on a mission of mercy and aid. It was possible, even likely, the Federation captain's motives were pure. Would that be enough to convince those who remained fixed in their long-held beliefs about how Xahean society should proceed and endure?

Sen knew it was a question with no easy answers.

20

"Are you sure this is such a good idea?"

Checking herself in her lavatory's mirror to ensure her fresh uniform was not just presentable but indeed as perfect as possible for a mere mortal like herself, she looked up to see Booker reflected from where he stood behind her, awaiting an answer to his question.

"You know first contact is always tricky," she said. "I know this isn't technically a true first-contact situation since we have a history with the Xaheans, but in reality it's much more like that than a meeting between old friends. I'm going to treat it as such."

Booker said, "Yeah, but does that make it a *good idea*?"

"We're going to find out. Want to come along?"

"Now, I know that's not *at all* a good idea."

Turning from the mirror, Burnham smiled. "Can I take Grudge?"

"Go ahead." Booker gestured to where the cat had taken up a position of unchallenged authority atop the pillows on Burnham's bed. "Queen to queen? My money's on her."

Taking no apparent notice of the conversation or her role in it, Grudge instead opted to focus on preening herself.

"Yeah," said Burnham. "I think I'm on my own."

Booker shrugged. "You're scrappy. You'll be fine."

Satisfied with her appearance, Burnham nevertheless brushed her hand across her shoulder, sweeping away a stray hair that appeared to exist only in her own mind. She realized she was acting like a newly commissioned ensign preparing for a uniform inspection, the way she had after entering her Starfleet tutelage. Her former captain's ability to find the smallest flaw was unmatched, so even Burnham's own heightened attention to detail had found itself thwarted on several occasions.

Having moved to sit on the foot of her bed, Booker studied her as she stepped out of the lavatory. "You seem nervous."

"I'm not in the habit of meeting with a queen." Before Booker could respond, Burnham bowed to Grudge. "Present company excepted."

Booker offered a noncommittal grunt. "She seemed pretty welcoming when we arrived. They didn't have to let us into their Sanctuary if they didn't want us, and based on what I saw of the sensor scans, their weapons were more than enough to fend us off, if not worse. There's nothing to gain by letting us in that they didn't already have by keeping us outside."

"They have us," replied Burnham.

"Not as hostages or anything like that." Booker glanced down to his left side as Grudge, having moved from her perch on the pillows, had now moved to rub up against his arm. "From the way their queen sounded, they don't want anything to do with the Federation. I figure the only reason they invited us in is because there's history between you and their ancestors."

Burnham smiled. "Exactly. We represent perhaps one of the only links to their world as it was nine hundred years ago, before everything that happened to it and their people." She shrugged. "We're an anomaly. A crazy, impossible quirk of fate, and they're curious."

Now stroking Grudge's flank, for which he was rewarded a satisfied purr from the cat, Booker said, "And you think you can establish a dialogue with them after all this time? After everything they've had to deal with for centuries, and knowing the Federation failed them when they needed it the most." He shook his head. "Fixing that's a pretty tall order."

"I'm used to tall orders." Stepping forward, Burnham extended her hand toward Grudge. The cat appeared unperturbed by her proximity, continuing to purr as Burnham scratched behind her ears. "And this is what Starfleet's supposed to be about. New civilizations." She shrugged. "Okay, so they're not exactly a new civilization, except they are in all the ways that really matter. The Federation drifting away from them is so far in the past, most of the people in this bubble probably know next to nothing about what life was like in my time. How different everything was, and how much promise the future held."

She started to pace in front of the bed, back and forth across the room with her hands clasped before her. "The Xaheans had just discovered warp drive back then. They were at the point of making their first major leaps into the galaxy. Who knows how differently things might've gone if the Federation hadn't gotten caught up in all the things that made it so a planet like Xahea somehow managed to fall through the cracks."

"You sound like you're practicing a speech," said Booker, smiling when she threw a mock glare in his direction. "No one's ever going to doubt your passion or sincerity, Michael. I saw enough of that first interaction with Queen Ki to believe she's willing to hear you out, but what about other Xaheans? She's the main ruler, but from what Tilly told us about Xahean society, she has a council of advisors who represent different constituencies. Who knows how many Xaheans favor trying to leave Sanctuary versus those who want to stay, and how many of the latter want to force the rebels to stay as well? Likewise, how many Xaheans do you think want our help, as opposed to those who'd rather we leave them alone?"

Burnham stopped her pacing and realized she was once again checking her uniform for wrinkles or other flaws. Forcing herself to leave well enough alone, she turned to Booker. "One thing at a time, Book. First, we accept the invitation. We've earned a little grace thanks to saving their people, but I know it won't be enough. I can't expect to sway Ki or her advisors on my own. I'll probably need Admiral Vance before this is over, but if I can at least start a discussion and give them a chance to air their grievances, then that's more than the Xaheans have gotten from the Federation in . . . what? Eight hundred years?" She drew a deep, calming breath. "This is an opportunity. We have to take it and see where it leads."

"I know." The blunt reply caught her off guard, especially when Booker smiled again. "I just like hearing you get all high on Starfleet and Federation ethos and ideals."

Burnham could only hope those would be enough to impress Queen Ki.

21

The flash of transporter energy faded, leaving Burnham standing with Lieutenant Tilly at one end of a grand hall. A high glass ceiling curved downward to form the chamber's outer walls, offering an unfettered view of the habitat's interior space. Only the floor itself, composed of a smooth jade finish that reflected the room's subtle interior lighting as well as the brighter exterior illumination, blocked her view outside.

"Rhys to Captain Burnham," said her first officer over her tri-com badge. *"Scans show you transported to the precise location indicated by the coordinates we received. We're only detecting the two of you in that immediate area, however."*

Burnham replied, "That's correct. We're alone here."

"Couldn't help noticing the total lack of doors either," said Tilly.

Within seconds of materializing, Burnham had observed the same thing after taking a quick look around the room to get her bearings. Like Tilly, she saw no means of entry or exit. If such ingresses were present, they were well hidden even from sensors. What she did see was a quartet of simple straight-backed chairs in each of the corners nearest to her, while a grouping of nine larger and more opulent chairs sat positioned behind a long table at the room's far end. Burnham noted the chair at the center of the group was a bit more ornate than its companions.

"We've still got good transporter locks on both of you," said Rhys. *"We can pull you back in a heartbeat if it comes to that."*

"Let's just take it easy for the moment," replied Burnham. "If they didn't want us here, we'd still be sitting outside wondering if we'd jumped to the wrong coordinates. We're going to play this out."

"Aye, Captain."

Turning in place, Burnham took her first real look at her immediate surroundings. A number of buildings of varying sizes rose up around the hall in which she and her companion found themselves, while others extended from all sides of the enormous struts forming the sphere's elaborate support lattice. A maglev train sped past on their right side, with none of the sounds of its passing audible through whatever material comprised the hall's transparent walls and ceiling, and Burnham also saw a handful of smaller vehicles flying on their own, in and around the lattice and the nearby buildings. Forming a backdrop to all of that was what appeared to be a clear blue sky with just a few wisps of clouds that did nothing to dim the brilliant sun high overhead. She knew that aspect was an illusion, a visual effect cast upon the inner surface of Sanctuary's protective sphere, but it was most effective, and she was not alone in thinking so.

"Wow." Tilly stood next to Burnham, her mouth agape as she looked up and beheld the wonder that was Sanctuary's vast interior.

"Is that your official scientific observation, Lieutenant?" Burnham smiled, which was enough to elicit a giggle from the young science officer.

Tilly shrugged. "I'll add some bigger words to my official report. *Impressive* works, right? It's all pretty impressive."

"It certainly is." If Burnham did not know better, the view alone was sufficient to convince her she was standing on a planet rather than an elaborate artificial habitat.

A flash of light in her peripheral vision caught her attention and she turned toward the table at the hall's far end in time to see nine bursts of energy appearing before the chairs behind the raised table. Each of the flashes faded to reveal a Xahean, five women and four men. All of them were dressed in ornate robes of varying colors, while they wore matching dark maroon sashes across their left shoulders. Standing at the center of the formation was Queen Ki, dressed in darker robes accented with streaks of silver. Neither she nor any of her companions said anything.

"Talk about an entrance," said Tilly, keeping her voice low so only Burnham could hear.

Moving to face the table, Burnham assumed a position of attention that Tilly mimicked as she stepped up to stand beside her. "Your Highness, thank you for granting us an audience. It is a privilege to stand before you today."

Ki offered a cordial smile. "Welcome, Captain Burnham and Lieutenant Tilly." She gestured to the hall around them. "This receiving hall has not seen visitors in quite some time, and certainly none of your stature." She indicated for Burnham and Tilly to move closer to the table, and she gestured for her companions to take their seats.

"Captain," said the Xahean male sitting to Ki's left. "I wish to add my thanks to those already offered by Her Highness, for coming to the aid of our cargo vessel's crew. It's reasonable to say they wouldn't be alive if not for your actions. I'm told Leb and his people have disembarked your vessel and are being processed by our Ministry of Security."

Debriefings, most likely. Burnham decided to keep that observation to herself, and instead said, "I'm just glad we were in a position to help."

"And what other sort of help do you feel you can provide?" asked another of the Xaheans, this one an older woman. Though her expression was passive, there was no mistaking even the subtle tone of accusation lacing her words.

Ki seemed to notice it, as well. "Hilo, please." With both hands, she gestured to indicate her companions. "Captain, this is my leadership council. It's with their assistance and wisdom that I'm able to lead our people. While we all may not always see things the same way, I trust each of them to give me their honest, even frank opinions and perspectives no matter the situation. I doubt it would surprise you to learn not everyone in Sanctuary is enthused by your arrival. Even after all this time, there remains some resentment toward the Federation. However, thanks to what I've recently learned about you and your crew, I feel such feelings toward you are somewhat unfair."

Somewhat unfair. Burnham repeated those last words in her mind. The queen, she decided, was someone faced with walking a tightrope when it came to ministering to the needs of her people. That likely meant catering to a broad spectrum of beliefs and sentiments while trying to build consensus. It took an extraordinary individual to succeed in such an environment, and Burnham suspected Ki walked such a tightrope on a daily basis.

"As I mentioned earlier," said the queen, "Po kept a journal. Several of them, actually, throughout her reign." She paused, smiling. "Her behavior was always somewhat unorthodox, and that extended to expressing herself through the written word."

Tilly asked, "How long was she queen?" Glancing to Burnham before returning her gaze to Ki, she cleared her throat. "I'm sorry, Your Highness. I was just wondering—"

"Queen Po's rule was a long and prosperous one, Lieutenant," said the Xahean woman seated to Ki's right. "Her methods and mannerisms may have been unconventional, but a review of the historical record tells us she faithfully and enthusiastically carried out the duties of her crown to the best of her ability, remaining one of our people's most popular rulers until her death. She passed quietly, in her sleep, surrounded by her family, and her legacy was continued by her successor."

Ki added, "Councilor Pani is correct. During Po's rule, we were at peace. She oversaw our first real interactions with your Federation, which according to our records were quite positive. Your leaders at that time respected our people's wishes to remain an independent society. We traded dilithium with a number of Federation worlds, and your Starfleet even assisted during our initial efforts to colonize the other worlds in our home system."

"We only wish our relationship with the Federation had continued in such a positive fashion after Queen Po's passing," said Councilor Hilo, and Burnham thought she detected quiet acceptance in her eyes.

Burnham knew she was stepping into a minefield, but there was no avoiding it at this point. All she could do was proceed with caution, sensitivity, and, above all, the truth as she knew it, and hope Ki and her council would recognize she had no desire to diminish the history of the Xahean people and the Federation's role in it.

"I've come to know about what happened to your people at the hands of the Cardassians and the Dominion all those centuries ago." Burnham gestured to Tilly. "Sylvia and Po had a much closer relationship than I did, and she's told me of your people's unique relationship to your planet. That you were forced to leave it tells me everything I need to know about the damage and pain inflicted upon you and your homeworld."

Ki said, "The annexation of Xahea by the Cardassians following its conflict with the Federation was the beginning of the end for life as my people knew it. Over the generations, our historians have attempted to put those events into a proper context, even going so far as to remove some of the blame from the Federation. With such a delicate peace between the two powers hanging in the balance, sacrificing our world along with so many others to avoid resuming hostilities makes some sense." Her expression grew flat. "Except for those who called those worlds their home."

"Then the Federation acquired a new enemy," said Hilo, leaning forward from her chair. "One that threatened not just them. The Dominion were on the verge of conquering the entire Alpha Quadrant. When the Cardassians aligned themselves with the Dominion, all of the worlds under their control were ceded to the war effort. The ravaging of Xahea continued unabated. Our people were considered expendable. Even now, centuries after all of the misery inflicted upon our world, we still have no idea how many Xaheans died under Cardassian and Dominion oppression."

Pausing, the council member waved his hands and Burnham's eyes went wide as the receiving hall seemed to disappear around them. She heard Tilly's sharp intake of breath as their surroundings morphed—thanks to holographic immersion—so they now appeared to be standing on a barren, mountainous ridge overlooking a valley. The scene before Burnham was one of devastation, with enormous gouges and craters scarring the scene around her. Smoke and dust hung in the air, all but blotting out the sun, and her nostrils were assailed by the stench of pollution and destruction. Oversized machines moved across the ravaged terrain, and even from this distance Burnham could make out small figures moving around the equipment or in and out of craters and tunnels tarnishing what she knew had once been a lush, thriving landscape.

"Even with the war over," said Hilo, though Burnham could not see her or Ki or any of the other council members, "the Dominion forced back from whence they came, and Cardassia granting Xahea and other worlds their freedom, the damage was done. Decades of strip-mining our dilithium with little regard for environmental impact left us at the precipice of an ecological disaster."

Struggling to keep her voice level as she beheld the generated images of destruction, Burnham said, "I read that the Federation tried to offer assistance."

Ki replied, "By the time the war ended, so deeply did the feelings of betrayal run among our people that our ruler at that time, King Buhi, refused all such offers. He was determined we would resolve our own issues without the need for outside aid. It became something of a rallying cry that only Xaheans could heal Xahea." There was a distinct pause before she added, "It was a noble sentiment, if not an accurate one."

As the queen spoke, Burnham watched the scene before them shift away from the somber images of wanton environmental destruction. Instead of efforts at reclaiming what had been damaged or destroyed in the face of oppression and enslavement in service to war, she saw depictions of renewed mining efforts. These accompanied representations of spaceships under construction both on the surface as well as in orbit above what could only be Xahea. The world before her bore little resemblance to the one Burnham recalled from her single visit. Thick cloud cover masked what she knew had once been brilliant blue oceans and green landmasses.

"Eventually, it became all too apparent that Xahea would be incapable of supporting life within just a few generations," said Ki. "So King Buhi put into motion a bold plan: Evacuation. Fleets of colony vessels were constructed over the course of more than a century, orbiting Xahea as what remained of our population relocated to these ships. Not everyone agreed with this idea, naturally. Those people were granted their freedom to travel to other worlds and seek out a new beginning for themselves. In the earliest days of this initiative, a significant number of Xaheans even migrated to the Federation."

"I don't understand," said Tilly. "You could've asked for help. Terraforming, climate and ecological restoration. We . . . I mean . . . *they* could've helped you." Burnham heard a slight wavering in the lieutenant's voice and placed a hand on her arm.

To Burnham's surprise, Ki appeared, standing before the depictions of spaceships in orbit above Xahea. "I can see your emotions are sincere, Lieutenant. You must understand that King Buhi came to the throne in the aftermath of so much suffering, and resentment toward the Federation was very high. He was dedicated to leading our people out of that dark time, but he was rather headstrong. Perhaps if you or someone like you had been present during that time, he might have been persuaded to act differently."

Tilly shook her head. "I can't . . . it just doesn't make sense."

"To be fair," said Ki, "the Federation did make numerous overtures, at least in the beginning. They were dealing with their own problems in the aftermath of their war with the Dominion, but they continued their outreach attempts despite repeated rebuffs from King Buhi. Even so, the Federation accepted any Xaheans wishing to emigrate. Then your people became involved in the effort to relocate the Romulans from their homeworld and other planets they believed would be affected by the supernova that eventually destroyed the Romulan star system. You know what happened during this period, of course."

"The Mars attack." The words were almost a whisper as Burnham spoke them. Learning of the devastation wrought upon the Utopia Planitia facility and indeed the whole planet had made her heart heavy, but not so much as what happened after that tragedy. Wounded in so many ways both literally and figuratively, the Federation retreated. In the immediate aftermath of the attack and with the loss of so many vessels being constructed for the evacuation effort, Starfleet suspended its attempts to assist the Romulans. Two years later, the supernova consumed the Romulan system, shattering the once powerful empire and annihilating billions of people.

Perhaps motivated by shame, Earth and other core worlds disengaged from the interstellar stage. Turning their focus inward, they began reassessing the advantages and detriments of adhering to principles that had guided them since the Federation's founding. By the end of the twenty-fourth century, borders were redrawn, severing lifelines to planets and civilizations that relied upon trade and mutual cooperation with the Federation despite not being members themselves. Regions once patrolled and secured by Starfleet vessels found themselves on their own and forced to improvise their own methods of enforcing law and order, with varying degrees of success. While never seeming to gain traction in mainstream circles, "Federation First" and comparable slogans and troubling sentiments were prevalent for a number of years.

"After nearly a century of preparation, which included a concerted effort to mine as much of our planet's remaining dilithium as our ships could carry," said Ki, "our remaining population took to the stars, leaving behind our beloved Xahea in search of a new home."

The simulation vanished, revealing the receiving hall along with the queen's council leaders. "However, during the time between our preparations and those first few years transiting the void, something began to happen among our people. We began realizing we no longer wished to become tethered to another world that might one day see itself a victim of the same oppression and abuse suffered by Xahea. Instead, we chose to remain in space. 'Children of the Stars,' if you will."

"Talk about your paradigm shifts," said Tilly.

Smiling, Ki nodded. "Precisely. We ventured to unexplored regions of space. Though we searched for a suitable home, it was not our primary goal. Eventually, Buhi's successor, Queen Mino, put forth an initiative that we should simply build our own home. A tribute to Xahea. It was she who first envisioned what we now call Sanctuary."

"What began as a simple process—fusing together several of our ships to make a larger habitat—spiraled far beyond the queen's original idea," added another councilor. "We sent other vessels in search of the raw materials we needed for manufacturing the necessary components. The effort took even longer than assembling the original fleet, but eventually that habitat grew and expanded to what we have today." He gestured toward the viewing ports. "A fully sustainable ecosystem that is itself a memorial to the planet that nurtured our ancestors."

Burnham said, "You obviously survived the Burn."

"Not without cost." Ki's expression grew somber. "Sanctuary suffered only minor damage, as our stores of refined dilithium at that time were relatively low. We learned long ago to refine only what we needed, lest we became a more inviting target for pirates and others who might discover our location. We did lose thousands of our people aboard ships traveling at warp when the cataclysm occurred. In the wake of that tragedy, we knew dilithium would become an even greater commodity, and so we turned our efforts to improving our technology and our defenses."

"But you're still a stationary target," said Tilly. "Even with your protective shield, you're vulnerable. We could help with that."

Ki smiled. "That was once a very real concern, but no longer. Sanctuary is quite capable of moving under its own power, albeit at great energy cost. For this reason, we prefer to keep such an option as one of last resort. Therefore, we go to great lengths to keep our location secret, and remain vigilant for the day we may have to defend our home against another enemy."

She held out her hands to Burnham. "As leader of my people, I am obligated to consider whether you represent such an enemy, Captain. While I believe you and Lieutenant Tilly to be trustworthy—perhaps along with your entire crew—what of the Federation? It abandoned us during times of great need. How can we be sure that won't happen again?"

Before Burnham could answer, a tone echoed through the receiving hall, drawing the queen's attention to the raised table and her assembled council. Without saying anything, Hilo offered a formal nod.

"I apologize, Captain, but duty once again calls us to service. As you might imagine, the business of leadership is unending." Though Ki offered the statement with little in the way of emotion, Burnham had little doubt the interruption was expected, whether for actual demands on the queen's time or simply as a means of ending their meeting on her terms. Burnham knew it was just another aspect of diplomacy, and perhaps even a test of her own mettle and patience and to gauge her reaction.

Smiling, Burnham said, "Of course, Your Highness. I'm grateful for the time you've shared with us today, and I'm eager to continue at your convenience. We still have so much to discuss."

"Indeed we do." Ki regarded her for a moment. "Trust, Captain. We both have much to ruminate on regarding that topic. This is especially true in my case." She paused, and Burnham noted the glance she directed toward Hilo. "You arrive here with the intention of inserting yourselves into what, in reality, is an internal matter best addressed by those to whom our people look for leadership. Please reflect on that until we meet again."

The queen and her council disappeared as they arrived, leaving Burnham and Tilly alone in the receiving hall.

"That last comment," said Tilly. "It wasn't meant for us but for her own people, right? She's really walking a line with all of this."

Burnham frowned. "No kidding."

Where was that line drawn, she wondered, and on which side would the queen ultimately land if forced to choose? Her people's welfare would always be Ki's top priority. What if her decisions put her at odds with her advisors? Burnham had noted the obvious dissension among some of the council members, so what were these leaders telling their queen?

She knew her own role here was to mollify the situation however possible, but Burnham could not help thinking *Discovery*'s arrival might well have done nothing more than stoke a long-smoldering fire. What could she do to keep everything from spinning out of control?

22

Though she understood its necessity, Ki had little affection for the Ministry of Security's operations nucleus. To her, the chamber was little more than a shrine to paranoia, fear, and negativity. Cloaked in secrecy, the Ministry of Security carried out its unenviable yet essential mission. This facility and the personnel and resources it employed through this office monitored Sanctuary and all its denizens. Ever vigilant, they watched for anything that might constitute a threat, whether from outside the habitat or within its confines. It was here, she knew, that difficult decisions had to be considered and executed in service to a higher calling.

"Your Highness," said a voice from behind her as she materialized at the center of the operations nucleus, completing the transport from her private chambers. She turned to see Walo Ji Vomin, her minister of security, moving from behind his desk to greet her. Much older than many if not most of the other Xaheans working around him, he was dressed in the distinctive gray uniform worn by all ministry agents and officials. His long gray hair was braided, with the tail resting across his left shoulder, and deep lines accented the familial markings on his face. Despite his age, he moved with energy and grace as he rushed across the floor to offer a formal bow of greeting. "Thank you for coming so quickly."

"You asked to see me," said Ki, taking the opportunity to survey her surroundings. Unlike her chambers or even her office, which were both appointed in a manner that helped to quell her mind and offer her places of refuge from the demands of the throne, the nucleus pulsed with activity. Octagonal in design, the room's high walls were dominated by an array of oversized display screens. The lighting here was subdued, with most of the illumination provided by the screens and various other status readouts. At present, all but one of the screens offered different views of Sanctuary's interior areas, with that last one reserved for a scene of the open space outside the habitat. Beneath the screens and positioned around the walls were a host of workstations, each augmented with holographic displays that could either hover in the air above their respective consoles or else stay with their operator as that individual moved around the room while carrying out their duties.

In response to her statement, Vomin directed her attention to the display screen on the wall opposite his desk. An upward swipe of his hand called forth a holographic interface that he used to direct the screen to shift its image to an open-air marketplace. Ki thought she recognized the location from the arrangement of covered dining tables situated on a patio near a walking path. The most obvious difference between her memory of the area and the reality depicted onscreen was the concentration of people in what was normally the quiet, inviting atmosphere of a market square.

"The Lantrix Province?" she asked.

Vomin nodded. "Correct, Your Highness. Another separatist demonstration. It started modestly enough, with just a few people standing in the square and making statements that could be heard by patrons visiting the market. Then others started to join in. Some of them carried signs or flags with an assortment of slogans they typically employ."

"But it's been peaceful to this point?"

"Yes, Your Highness, but it is the fourth one in as many days. Like those incidents, the people involved with this protest do not appear to be causing any overt disruption, but the ministry has logged a number of complaints."

Taking advantage of Vomin's holographic interface, Ki swiped at the controls to enlarge the screen's image. The quality of the visual feeds was such that she could see individual expressions on the faces of many taking part in the protest.

"They all look so young."

Vomin replied, "Young, and misguided."

"Were you not young at any point, perhaps in the distant past?" Ki smiled, conveying her gentle teasing of the security minister, who responded in kind with his own knowing grin.

"Perhaps at a point well before all recorded history, Your Highness."

Ki knew Vomin had served in his capacity as security minister since early in her predecessor's reign. He had a well-earned reputation for taking his duties quite seriously, and he brought experience, wisdom, and measured calm to the leadership council. Though he could be abrasive toward those with whom he disagreed, Ki appreciated his direct yet considerate approach. It was a welcome respite from those who sought to earn her favor by presenting themselves in annoyingly sycophantic or otherwise ersatz fashion.

"You said it's a peaceful demonstration," she said, gesturing to the screen. "And that does appear to be the case, so why summon me?"

"As I said, Your Highness, it is the fourth such protest in the past few days. These rallies are increasing in both frequency and the number of people participating in them. Complaints from merchants in the areas where the activities take place express their fear their customers will seek accommodation with other establishments that are less publicly accessible."

Ki frowned. "None of this is new. We've been dealing with protests of this type for quite a while now, both from separatists and traditionalists. When someone from either side oversteps the boundaries of good order, your security ministry sanctions them."

Tapping his controls, Vomin changed the screen's image away from the market demonstration to another scene. The feed now depicted an area Ki did not recognize, but the presence of grass, trees, and other foliage suggested one of the parks or meadows scattered throughout Sanctuary. In the middle of the screen was a team of ministry agents, at least ten, though they moved in and out of view as they dealt with a number of unruly citizens. She also noted smoke clouding the images.

"This is from Aellud Gardens," said Vomin. "A protest that overstepped the boundaries of good order."

She watched the scene of what likely began as a peaceful demonstration deteriorate to shouting and hand gestures as another group—traditionalists, Ki knew—lodged their counter-protest against the would-be separatists. Then the gestures and verbal sparring devolved to physical violence, demanding action on the part of the ministry agents.

Swiping at his holographic controls, Vomin paused the screen's visual feed. "Note the signage, Your Highness."

Studying the halted imagery, the queen felt a pang of discomfort welling up within her. "Asylum for everyone. We should all be free. Let us live. Free us, Federation."

Gesturing to a member of his staff, Vomin said, "Your Highness, this is Deputy Minister Sen. I've tasked him with monitoring these new developments and coordinating our range of response scenarios."

Ki took in the other Xahean, who appeared a bit younger than Vomin and wore a similar uniform but with fewer decorations signifying awards and a lengthy term of duty. Perhaps it was a function of the responsibilities he held, but the queen wondered if the Ministry of Security did not prematurely age those who pledged service to the agency.

"Your Highness," said Sen after bowing to her. "News about the revolt on the *Pilikoa* has been made public, despite our best efforts to prevent that." He directed her attention to another screen along the nucleus's right wall. "What has not yet been reported to the population at large is that it was not an isolated incident. We've received reports of similar uprisings from three other ship captains. Word about the Federation's rescue of the *Pilikoa* is spreading. Minister Vomin has already ordered com-munications to the rest of the ships currently in transit restricted to official matters only, but I'm afraid no one can ever stop the flow of information indefinitely."

Again, Vomin tapped his controls and the screen changed to a view of the Federation starship. "Your Highness, perhaps we should consider retrieving our citizens and directing the ship to depart. Their presence is already causing disruptions, and I fear this may just bring an expansion of the protests we've seen to this point. The longer the ship remains here, the more it will serve as a symbol for those who wish to continue causing disorder within our community."

"I allowed the *Pilikoa* separatists to remain with Captain Burnham as a sign of good faith. You know from your scans of her vessel that she's not taken any measures to prevent us from retrieving them ourselves. That is her offer of sincerity and an invitation to trust her. It appears she wishes to establish a dialogue with us on behalf of the Federation, and given her actions with the *Pilikoa*, I believe she's earned that opportunity."

"You have also invited her and her crew to visit Sanctuary," said Vomin.

Ki nodded. "Yes, with escorts from your security forces."

"Several of them have accepted the offer," said Sen. "They are currently touring various areas. Their security escorts are in constant communication with their superiors and have been advised to keep them isolated from any protests, particularly of the sort seen at Aellud Gardens."

"You think if they see such a display, they may feel the need to intervene?" Ki frowned. "That doesn't sound consistent with Captain Burnham's demonstrated behavior to this point."

Vomin replied, "Nevertheless, Your Highness, we feel it's best to avoid even a possibility of incident." He gestured to the display of the Federation vessel. "So long as they remain in our midst, they carry with them the potential to incite further unrest. After all, there are those who have not allowed past failures to be forgotten."

Her gaze lingering on the ship, Ki pondered what it represented. A symbol for a people who might once have been trusted allies and friends. Like every living Xahean, she could not know all the details that contributed to those unfortunate and even tragic events so long ago. There might well have been legitimate reasons for the Federation not seeking out and assisting Xahea. Perhaps the aftermath of the conflicts and crises it faced during those years had impaired its ability to offer meaningful aid to a far greater degree than was known to her people during that time. Regardless of what occurred centuries ago, no one alive today had been a party to any of it, and neither could Ki in good conscience hold Captain Burnham or her superiors to account for it.

Deactivating his holographic interface and dismissing Sen, Vomin fell into step alongside Ki as she began a slow circuit of the nucleus. "We've lived for generations without the need to depend on the Federation, or anyone else for that matter. The life we have made for ourselves is a good one, Your Highness, as much through your efforts as those of any of your predecessors. You should not lose sight of that."

"I know our life is good. It can also be better. What kind of ruler would I be if I dismissed such possibilities without first investigating them? Perhaps there is a place for us in the galaxy where we can once again live among friends."

Despite the serious demeanor that was a function of his duties, Vomin allowed a small smile. "You are an insufferable optimist, Your Highness."

Ki nodded, accepting the compliment. "It comes with the crown, my friend."

23

The grass was real, as were the trees and other foliage. At least, that was what Hugh Culber's holo-tricorder told him about the grounds on which he stood. An open expanse of green space nearly one hundred meters in diameter, the park was a welcome contrast to the clusters of buildings towering above the trees that formed the glade's perimeter. There were other smaller plots of trees scattered around the area, including a larger patch at the park's center. All around him, Xaheans of all ages enjoyed the open space. Children ran or played games, adults reclined in chairs or on blankets or just lounged on the grass itself.

Lifting his face toward the sky, Culber felt a warmth he could believe was generated by the representation of a sun displayed in the artificial sky above the tallest structures. High overhead, Sanctuary's extensive support lattice extended up from the central core, weaving in and around the habitat's sprawling interior. Each massive strut hosted its own collection of buildings and green spaces. Some of these appeared upside down from Culber's vantage point, owing to the variable gravity regions inside the sphere. This, along with the gridwork of the facility's enormous outer shell, rebelled against the illusion that he was standing on the surface of a planet.

"This is incredible," said Joann Owosekun, standing a few paces from Culber. Her infectious smile beamed as she took in her surroundings. "It reminds me of the terrestrial enclosures on Watchtower-class stations."

Next to her, Keyla Detmer replied, "I think those were bigger, but even then you still knew you were on a space station."

"Yeah, but this place has a couple dozen of them." Owosekun pointed to the large tree at the park's center, which to

Culber resembled an aged oak. "On Earth, something that big would be centuries old. Do you think they let it grow naturally, or terraformed it?"

On Culber's opposite side, Adira Tal said, "I suppose they would've had time to do it either way." They shrugged. "We had small arboretums on our generation ship, so we grew our own flora. We also experimented with genetic modification to accelerate development." Turning to the pair of officers from the Xahean Ministry of Security assigned as the away team's chaperones, Adira asked, "Were the trees and other vegetation planted and allowed to grow naturally?"

The Xaheans, one female and one male, and dressed in matching gray uniforms, glanced to each other before the man replied, "I believe they were genetic alterations, planted generations ago when Sanctuary's construction was complete, then allowed to grow naturally." He gestured to indicate the green space around them. "Areas like these have always been a part of our environment."

"It's really very beautiful," said Detmer.

With no particular emotion or warmth, the female officer replied, "It's our home."

"And we're grateful to you for sharing it with us," said Culber.

His reply seemed to land with her. For the first time since being introduced as their security escort while visiting Sanctuary, her expression softened and Culber thought she might be relaxing just a bit.

"You're not what I expected," she said as the group began crossing the park, retracing their steps toward one of the nearby mercantile districts.

Owosekun asked, "What were you expecting?"

Instead of answering, the Xahean looked again at her male counterpart before he replied, "There's been much discussion about you. Rather, the Federation. All we know is what we've read in our history texts, many of which don't present you in a positive light." After a moment, he added, "I admit it's difficult to look at you, here and now, and compare you to those accounts."

"What are your names?" asked Adira.

"I am Hala Mi Von Yovi," said the woman. "You may call me Yovi."

Her companion added, "And I am Numa, a shortened form of Bonu Jen Kal Numa."

"Have either of you ever left Sanctuary?" asked Detmer.

"No," replied Yovi, both she and Numa shaking their heads. "But it's not uncommon. Aside from the merchant vessels and their crews, there have been scouting expeditions sent to worlds that show promise of containing resources we might be able to use to sustain us, but those are always uninhabited planets. There are also exploratory missions to find a suitable location if the queen and council decide it's time to move Sanctuary."

"Do you move often?" asked Culber.

Numa replied, "A stationary target tends to be a vulnerable target. However, doing so requires a great deal of power, so it's not something undertaken lightly. The development of the shield that surrounds Sanctuary has proven to be a more efficient means of protection."

"We've not moved from our present location during our lifetimes," added Yovi. "The ships traveling to and from Sanctuary do so in a manner that preserves the secrecy of our location, and while there have been encounters with pirates and other unsavory parties, no one has challenged us directly." She almost succeeded in hiding her skeptical expression before adding, "Not yet, at least."

"I promise you we're not a threat," said Owosekun. "The only reason we know about you at all is because of the *Pilikoa*'s distress signal. Our intention has always been to render whatever assistance we could."

"And if our queen asks you to leave?" asked Yovi.

Culber replied, "Then we'll leave, without argument. It's

our highest law that we're not allowed to interfere with another society's internal affairs." Sensing a rebuttal, he held up a hand. "I know we can never properly apologize for what the Federation did or didn't do all those centuries ago. We can only acknowledge that horrible mistake and try to make amends." He placed a hand on his own chest. "*We* have to try, and we hope your people will have that discussion with us, but if respecting your desires means leaving you in peace forever, then that's what we'll do."

Nearing the park's perimeter, they moved onto a paved walking path, and Culber saw they were already nearing the exit leading from the park toward a cluster of high-rise buildings. At first glance the scene appeared almost the same as when they had entered the meadow. Even from here he could see a number of Xaheans on the streets and sidewalks, on foot or else standing upon small hoverboards, maintaining balance with subtle body movements to effect changes in direction and speed. Other people occupied tables outside restaurants and other shops, and it was easy for Culber to think he was walking through a borough of San Francisco on Earth or ShiKahr on Vulcan.

"Are you hungry?" asked Numa. "We were instructed to provide guidance should you wish to sample any of our offerings. The Jovahna Province is known for its diverse selection of delicacies representing different regions from our homeworld. Several of the establishments are centuries old, operated by descendants of families who departed Xahea aboard those first colony ships. Many of the meals they create are based on recipes handed down through the generations."

Adira said, "I wasn't even hungry until I heard all of that, but let's eat."

"I'm in," added Detmer.

More activity caught Culber's attention as they neared the park exit, and he noted a gathering of Xaheans near an open area that was bracketed by buildings on three sides. It was a courtyard of some kind, he decided, and he counted more than three dozen people standing in proximity to one another. Standing some distance away, others observed whatever was happening. Some of those in the larger group carried signs of varying sizes and shapes, each inscribed with colorful text in at least one of the Xaheans' native languages.

Owosekun asked, "What's going on over there?"

"A demonstration." Yovi gestured for the group to stop. "Separatists, clamoring to be heard by our leaders." She frowned. "Your arrival has emboldened them to intensify their rallies. They've remained mostly peaceful to this point, but we've had a few isolated incidents that were more than that."

Pointing toward the crowd, Adira said, "There's another group moving toward them."

"Counterprotesters." Culber eyed the new arrivals making their way to the square. Some of those Xaheans carried their own signs, which he also could not read.

Numa said, "As you've likely been told, the separatists are a small movement, but they're gaining attention and sympathy for their cause. Some people are not pleased with how the situation seems to be evolving."

"We should avoid this area." Yovi's expression had grown serious, and Culber noted her right hand now rested atop the holstered weapon on her hip. She signaled for them to follow her back into the park. "We can cross the meadow and make our way to the security ministry's station in the Kalyadi Province."

"There will be security officers at the rally," said Numa. "Should we not join them?"

Shaking her head, Yovi replied, "No. Our instructions are to keep our guests away from such gatherings."

"There! In the park! Federation people!"

Detmer said, "Um, I think the gathering might be coming to us."

Touching a control on a wide, silver bracelet she wore on her wrist under the sleeve of her uniform, Yovi spoke into the device. "This is Officer Yovi, requesting assistance near the demonstration at the Jovahna Province." Static was the only reply to her call, which she repeated with the same results. "Something's interfering with our communications."

"Let me try." Culber tapped his tri-com badge. "Culber to *Discovery*. We may have a situation brewing down here."

Nothing but silence greeted him.

"Something's definitely wrong," said Owosekun.

Numa suggested, "You should return to your ship."

Less than fifty meters away, the gathering of perhaps a dozen Xaheans seemed to be picking up their pace, and now Culber could hear other shouts.

"We don't want you here!"

"Go! You have nothing we want!"

Reluctant to leave the officers, Culber realized they would be far better able to handle the approaching crowd without him and the away team as distractions. "Everyone, use your personal transporters." He tapped his tri-com badge to activate the built-in transporter recall feature, but nothing happened.

"The signals are being jammed," said Adira. "Nothing else makes sense."

Yovi gestured toward the approaching crowd. "If we stay here, I cannot guarantee your safety."

"Then let's not stay here," said Culber as they searched for an exit, his attention divided between the park ahead and the mob coming toward them.

24

Even though Burnham knew Ki was only present thanks to a holographic projection, she sensed the queen harbored no grand expectations so far as being the point of focus in any room she entered. Unlike other heads of state, diplomats, and even a few Starfleet officers Burnham had known, no arrogance or other air of superiority emanated from the Xahean leader. Despite the demands of her office, she seemed eager to project attentiveness even in situations like the one she now faced.

"Your Highness," said Ke Ho Maha Iku. The Xahean stood at the entrance to the room in which he and a handful of separatists had been confined aboard *Discovery*. A force field covered the opening, which Burnham knew was intended to neutralize any possibility of the Xaheans utilizing their peculiar abilities, and a pair of security officers flanked the doorway. Iku offered a respectful bow toward Ki. "Thank you for agreeing to meet with us. You honor us with your presence."

The queen replied, *"As with all Xaheans, you are my constituents. If you have grievances against the government or the throne, you have the right to bring them forward."*

Burnham could not help but be impressed by the queen's demeanor. Here was someone who approached her role with the gravity and poise it required, while remaining conscious of those over whom she ruled. It was an unusual attitude for someone descended from aristocracy, and one Burnham found refreshing.

"I appreciate and can even sympathize with your desires," said Ki, *"but you must understand my position. I simply cannot allow attacks against other citizens to go unchecked. Your actions aboard the* Pilikoa *placed the ship's entire crew in danger. That vessel is now lost."* She gestured toward Burnham and her colleagues.

"Further, your attempt at rebellion necessitated another ship—an outsider *ship—coming to your aid, placing their crew at risk. It is only with the assistance of Captain Burnham and her crew that no lives were lost. Otherwise, we would be having a very different conversation."*

Iku nodded, his expression solemn. "Your Highness, I promise our intentions were to harm no one, but I accept full responsibility for what happened. On behalf of those who followed me, I willingly accept any punishment you order." He glanced over his shoulder at the Xaheans behind him. "All I ask is you at least consider allowing them to proceed with our request to seek asylum with the Federation."

"I'm not in the habit of negotiating with criminals." The reply was harsh, one of the first times Burnham had heard the queen toughen her voice in such a manner. Then, as if realizing the severity of her words, Ki cleared her throat. *"I apologize. There is a great deal for me to consider, just now, but I shouldn't let that distract me from the fact many people are asking the same questions you pose."*

Turning to Burnham, the queen said, *"As you've likely guessed, the ideas put forth by separatists are not new. It's existed in many forms for several generations, and there have always been those who harbor a desire to find some new planet all Xaheans might call home."*

"Her Majesty is quite correct," said Iku. "At first, it was what one might consider a benign movement, particularly among younger people studying history in school. Astronomers also assisted with this endeavor, studying stellar maps and searching for planets that might meet our needs. Efforts of this sort date back well before Sanctuary's creation, you understand."

"So, when you were just a fleet of ships?" asked Burnham, looking to Ki. "What did you call yourselves? Children of the Stars?"

The queen smiled. *"A rather romantic notion, I agree. It was an outlook born out of necessity, as at the beginning of our journey our goal was simply to survive. What Iku describes is actually something we as a people originally sought. Our initial hope was to find just such a world, far away from the Federation, its allies and enemies, and anyone else who might attempt to assert their will over us."*

Burnham asked, "Your Highness, is it accurate to say not all Xaheans agreed to the idea of creating Sanctuary as a substitute for colonizing another planet?"

"Of course. A significant number opposed the idea. Even after the advantages were weighed against potential risk. In particular, our ability to create a habitat large enough to sustain us while offering a facsimile of life on an actual planet caused much consternation. However, a world—even a small one—that you can move away from danger held a powerful appeal. In the end, the matter was put to a vote and all Xaheans were afforded the opportunity to make their choice. A majority of those voters chose what ultimately became Sanctuary."

"But those who voted against it," said Burnham. "Didn't they want to continue the colonization effort?"

Ki nodded. *"They did, but at the time there was a prevailing view that keeping as much of our population together was better from a security standpoint. To be fair, the nomadic existence we'd adopted after leaving Xahea still appealed to a great many of us, including a number of those who later generations would identify as supporting the separatist cause. It was a time of great uncertainty for our people as they moved into the void, searching for a new home. This was followed by gradually coming to believe anchoring themselves to any one world carried with it the risk of enduring a fate like the one visited upon our forebears. We essentially turned inward, never again leaving ourselves vulnerable to those who might subjugate us."* Her expression fell. *"Unfortunately, that lack of trust extended to nearly anyone not born of Xahea."*

"I don't understand," said Burnham. When Ki turned to face her, she swallowed a sudden nervous lump before continuing, "I'm sorry, Your Highness. There's no denying you obviously care for your people. Surely there has to be a way to reach some kind of understanding. Some compromise."

"I truly wish it were that simple. Perhaps in the beginning, we should have listened more to those raising these concerns. I can't deny many of those in positions of leadership could have been more receptive to such matters."

Iku added, "It's not as though we're completely radical with our ideas. A few members of the council have even attempted to put forth new laws allowing for greater debate and a vote to approve requests to leave Sanctuary permanently. However, such measures face resistance from the more hard-line traditionalists who continue to see the value in maintaining our current course."

"Unfortunately, too much has happened for me to simply accommodate such desires," replied the queen. *"Discussion along with other attempts to reach any sort of compromise grow increasingly more difficult due to the escalation of disruptive actions carried out by extremists on both sides of the issue. They've only served to lock far too many others even further into their respective mindsets."* To Burnham, she said, *"Your arrival has only exacerbated a situation I fear will become untenable if left unchecked, and it seems any course we choose in this moment would only serve to further inflame hard-line sentiments."*

"Ideological entrenchment." Burnham sighed. "On both sides." She could understand it, of course. To an outside observer without knowledge of the circumstances that had brought the Xaheans to this point in their civilization, the entire affair might seem difficult if not impossible to appreciate. As was often the case whenever deeply held beliefs clashed, after a point the emotional investment had become so great that neither side seemed capable of hearing anything short of total capitulation. Somewhere in the midst of all that chaos, compromise wandered adrift. Empathy screamed mute into the face of cacophony. Burnham refused to believe this situation was beyond rescue, and she suspected Ki and a large number of other Xaheans felt the same way regardless of their position on the issue at hand. She also knew the queen found herself navigating a treacherous path as she sought to lead her people toward concession.

Burnham stepped forward. "Your Highness, perhaps we can assist with some form of mediation? Providing a forum where representatives from both sides can be heard on equal footing might go a long way toward cooling at least some of those hot tempers."

"I can't imagine anyone on our side of this issue objecting to that," said Iku. "We'd welcome the chance to tell our story to anyone willing to listen."

The queen could not hide her skepticism. *"But you're not a neutral party, Captain. While I don't doubt your intentions were honorable when you assisted the* Pilikoa *crew, I can see you're sympathetic to the separatists' cause."*

"My personal feelings are irrelevant, Your Highness," replied Burnham. "My duty requires me to remain a neutral observer during any such proceedings. I'd offer no thoughts of my own unless specifically asked, and even then I wouldn't be permitted to advocate for any one position. Indeed, an outside perspective might be just what both sides need to help articulate their stance."

"Your passion and desire to help is heartening, Captain. You are a credit to your people." She paused, and Burnham noted from her body language that she likely had been interrupted by something. Perhaps an assistant or another call. When she returned her attention to Burnham, the queen looked concerned.

"Captain, I've just been apprised of some potentially troubling news. Some of your people have been reported near a separatist demonstration that appears to be escalating beyond a simple peaceful protest."

Burnham frowned. "Escalating?"

"A group of traditionalists have apparently launched a counterprotest, and the event is drawing greater attention from the

surrounding citizenry." Ki held up a hand. *"Captain, my security ministry has strict instructions to safeguard your people from anything of this sort."*

Iku said, "No one who feels as I do would knowingly seek to harm your people, Captain. Please believe me."

Ignoring the Xahean's plea, Burnham said, "Burnham to the bridge. Number One, do you have a fix on our away teams?"

A moment later, Commander Gen Rhys replied over the ship's intercom, *"We had contact with everyone until a moment ago, Captain. But a check shows we've lost the lock on seven combadge signals. We can't make contact or recall them via transporter. It's like we're being blocked."*

25

Closing her eyes, Tilly savored the delightful blend of cherries, nuts, and the closest approximation to vanilla she had tasted beyond the replicators aboard *Discovery* or even Federation Headquarters. The mouthful of gelato melted in her mouth and she swallowed, not realizing she had released an audible sigh until she heard Cleveland Booker chuckle.

"What?" she asked, opening her eyes to see Booker and Doctor Arbusala regarding her with broad smiles. Like her, they each held a bowl of the concoction they had obtained from a street vendor, one of dozens to be found on the streets of the Jovahna Province.

"You seem to be enjoying yourself well enough," said Booker.

Tilly adopted a mock official air. "I'll have you know I'm conducting research, sir, and it is my considered official opinion that this is delicious."

One of the two Xahean security escorts accompanying them, a younger male named Duko, said, "One of my elders used to make it from her own recipe, which she said was given to her by her own elder. Apparently, it's an old invention from before our people left Xahea."

"You bet your ass it's old." Tilly held up her bowl. "Nine hundred and thirty years ago, I introduced your people to spumoni." Holding up her free hand, she waved away that statement. "Okay, I introduced Queen Po to spumoni. This is almost the exact same recipe I figured out when I was nine years old. She loved it."

Arbusala lifted his own bowl closer to his face, sniffing at its contents. "I'm familiar with a few Earth-based confections, but not this one. It has a rather pleasing aroma."

Looking back to the vendor cart where they had obtained their snack, Tilly blew out her breath as she gave the matter deeper thought. "That it ever became popular on Xahea, much less survived this long, is . . . wow. That's pretty heavy stuff to take in."

Having consumed his portion without fanfare, Booker followed directions from their other escort, Jahn, and dropped the empty bowl into a nearby reclaimer. "The way I heard Michael tell it, your befriending Queen Po played a major role in how and why you all ended up in my time. And to think it all started with ice cream."

Smiling, Tilly shared a look with Arbusala, recalling their earlier conversation before she turned to study the bustling Jovahna Province. Just one of several such areas scattered throughout Sanctuary, the borough was abuzz with the comings and goings of numerous Xaheans. Retail and dining establishments abounded, and a gently arching footbridge crossed a small stream to an expansive park filled with trees, open meadows, and still more people moving about. It was a tranquil scene, she decided.

"I'm still wrapping my head around everything these people have been through," she said after taking another bite of her spumoni. "They fell so far, and yet look how far they've brought themselves." She looked up, taking in the buildings and other structures buoyed by the sphere's immense support lattice. Clusters of this sort thrived in all directions around the habitat's core.

Booker said, "They could've given up, but they endured. No, they did more than that. They laughed in the face of defeat and pressed on. They created a new life for themselves. Certainly a better life than if they'd stayed on their homeworld."

"But they gave up so much," said Tilly, remembering again what Po had told her about the Xahean people's connection to their planet. "It must've taken them generations to come to grips with losing all of that, and yet I see things here that remind me of things Po showed me." She gestured toward some of the nearby buildings. "Architecture. Some of this looks like the images she sent me of her home on Xahea, and the city where she grew up. I recognize bits of fashion, too. Mixed in here and there with the newer styles, but I still see it. 'The more things change,' and all that." Po had sent only a handful of images from her homeworld, but Tilly had saved them all in her personal computer files and had called them up soon after the encounter with the *Pilikoa*. She had smiled upon seeing the one image of Po herself, dressed not in full royal regalia but instead a dark bodysuit and big furry slippers with only her ceremonial crown denoting her title. Tilly often wondered how much of the requirements and customs of her office the young queen had ignored during her reign, and almost laughed at the thought of Po dispensing with all of it just to irk the older, more traditional members of Xahea's leadership cadre.

"If you think about it," said Booker, "they're still adapting. Take the people who want to leave. They're not trying to hurt anyone. They just want to live life on their own terms. A chance to find their own way rather than living out an existence defined for them centuries before they were born."

"There may be some of that at work for you, too, Lieutenant," said Arbusala, who also had finished his ice cream and discarded his bowl. "That is to say, you and other members of your crew. You've experienced feelings of displacement and detachment, and you are all dealing with your own ongoing efforts to adjust and adapt to your current circumstances."

He gestured to the district streets and shops around them. "The Xaheans have, through learned behavior, come to accept their existence, at least on some level. Others have either read what life was once like on their former homeworld, or enough of them have seen the galaxy that resides beyond Sanctuary, and they want to experience that for themselves. Their expression of these feelings only seems abrupt to those who have either ignored such sentiments and voices for too long, or else they are simply set in their ways and fear what change to their status quo might bring." The doctor turned back to Tilly. "Asking you and your friends to face such a stark new reality and not giving you the time you need to adapt—in whatever form that takes—is demanding more than a bit much, in my opinion."

A sound caught their attention, and Tilly looked up to see a small flying craft zipping by overhead, banking as it turned to fly over the nearby park. She saw a handful of similar vehicles flying over the city. A few others rested on the grass of the park, but she noted none were visible on the streets or indeed anywhere in close proximity to the nearby buildings.

"I've seen those things flying around," she said. "What are they?"

Security Officer Duko replied, "They are personal conveyances. We call them skimmers. Though most forms of transportation here are automated or even obsolete thanks to transporter technology, many Xaheans still prefer moving around on their own terms for recreational purposes."

"Moving around on their own terms," said Booker, his expression communicating the irony of his statement. "There's a thought."

Tilly's gaze followed the skimmer until it arced downward to disappear behind a stand of trees perhaps fifty meters away. Then she took note of a concentration of people in the middle of the park. While Xaheans naturally composed the bulk of the group, it was easy for Tilly to discern Starfleet uniforms worn by four of the people.

"That's Doctor Culber," she said, pointing toward the gathering. "And Detmer and Owosekun." She also noted they seemed to be heading in her general direction.

Booker said, "The real question is why are they being followed?" He looked to their Xahean security escorts. "What's going on?"

"It appears to be a group of demonstrators," replied Jahn. "From the signs being carried by various individuals, there are both separatists and those opposed to them in the group." She raised her left hand so she could activate the communications device on her wrist, and Tilly heard her speaking with someone she guessed was a superior.

"You mean counterprotesters?" Arbusala looked to Tilly and Booker. "We should probably think about returning to *Discovery*."

"Over there! More of them over there!"

Tilly jerked her head toward the source of the yelling to see another, much smaller, group of Xaheans making their way down the street. Other people were watching, emerging from storefronts, looking up from tables, or simply standing on the nearby walking paths. A few signs were visible, featuring Xahean script Tilly could not read. She watched as other Xahean security officers moved to intercept the group, slowing its advance.

"Traditionalists," said Duko. "Judging by the signs." He pointed to another group. "Separatists." Along with Jahn, he moved closer to Tilly and the others. "We should get you away from here."

"And go where?" asked Booker.

Jahn replied, "There's a security ministry precinct two blocks from here." She nodded toward the park. "Your friends are likely heading there as well."

As the rest of the group began following Duko, Arbusala asked, "Why does everyone seem mad at *us*?"

"For the traditionalists, you represent a radical shift to our existence." Duko's hand rested on his holstered weapon, but he did not draw it. "Whereas the separatists view you as a form of validation of their beliefs, and perhaps their salvation."

"So, which one are you?" asked Tilly.

The security officer frowned. "I wish everyone the opportunity to live life as they choose, so long as it brings no harm to others."

"Well, that's certainly a radical viewpoint," said Booker.

Jahn said, "Our communications are being interfered with. I was speaking to the local security ministry office when I was cut off."

"Is that something your security would do during a protest?" asked Arbusala.

The Xahean nodded. "Yes, but our communications would be insulated from such measures."

Tilly pressed her tri-com badge. "Tilly to *Discovery*." When no response came after a second attempt, she frowned. "Whatever it is, it's affecting us too." She felt a knot of worry forming in her gut.

"And it started when the protesters began heading our way." Booker looked around, and Tilly followed his gaze to the protesters still being challenged by the security officers. "It must be localized. Probably someone in that gang."

Then Tilly flinched at the sound of a loud, intense report, followed seconds later by a rush of displaced air, the mild yet still obvious shock wave from an explosion somewhere behind them.

26

"An explosion?"

Having just returned to the bridge, Burnham did not even bother with her command chair but instead moved to where Gen Rhys stood at his tactical console. "Near our people?" she prompted.

"A few of them, yes." The commander's right hand swiped across one of the station's holographic displays. "It was very small, but located near a gathering of Xaheans. Scans show some people are on the ground as though they've sustained injuries."

Turning to the science station on the bridge's opposite side, Burnham asked, "What's the latest on transporters?"

Crewing the console in Sylvia Tilly's absence, Lieutenant Linus replied, "Transporter signals along with communications are still being blocked, Captain." His bulging black eyes blinking several times, the tall, lanky Saurian pointed toward the main viewscreen.

"But only at that location," said Burnham.

Linus nodded. "Correct. With the exception of those seven individuals, all away teams have returned to the ship. I am still attempting to pinpoint a source for the interference."

"Keep after it." Burnham pushed back against the anxiety growing within her. Six of her people—seven, counting Doctor Arbusala—in potential danger and cut off from the ship. Her first impulse was to go after them herself, but she forced herself to maintain her command presence. Looking back to Rhys, she said, "Number One, have two security details grab a pair of shuttles and prep for immediate launch. We'll do this the old-fashioned way."

As she expected him to do, Rhys stared at her with an expression meant to convey concern while not outright questioning her. "Captain, Queen Ki might not like that."

"I'll worry about the queen after our people are safe."

"Captain," said Linus. "Scans are showing similar disruptions at multiple locations around Sanctuary. Large gatherings, a few with small explosives being detonated. I'm picking up numerous unconfirmed reports of injuries, though the situation is evolving."

More explosions? Burnham could make no sense of the sudden deviation from what had to this point been peaceful protests. From everything Queen Ki had told her, previous demonstrations where separatists and traditionalists clashed had for the most part remained peaceful. In very rare and isolated exceptions, when encounters had become heated, those disagreements were limited to verbal exchanges. While Burnham would categorize the events aboard the *Pilikoa* as an obvious escalation in tactics, it paled when compared to the situation now unfolding within Sanctuary. That was before she considered what had to be a deliberate effort to interfere with communications. Was it aimed at the demonstrations themselves as a means of disrupting Xahean security, or was *Discovery* being purposely hampered as well?

Those questions could wait.

Looking to Commander Bryce at the communications station, Burnham asked, "Can you monitor any official comm traffic?"

After a moment working the controls at his station, Bryce nodded. "I think so, Captain. Some frequencies are encrypted, but I've already tapped into other channels that sound like those used by security and other first responders."

"How are they doing?" asked Rhys.

"According to sensors," replied Linus, "demonstrators currently outnumber security personnel, but my scans show reinforcements are moving on that location."

"Dispatch a message to Queen Ki and the Xahean leadership," said Burnham. "Let them know we're offering whatever assistance we can."

Bryce looked up from his station. "What about the shuttles?"

"You can leave out that part."

"Captain," said Rhys. "Security reports shuttles are prepped and ready to go."

Burnham nodded. "We may lose comms with them when they get down there, so tell them nothing fancy. Get in, get them out, and get back. Go."

Around her, the bridge crew tended to duties at their various stations, and she knew they were readying to support the retrieval operation. That left her to watch the main viewscreen as a pair of shuttlecraft appeared, banking away from the ship and heading deeper into Sanctuary's interior. Her people were well trained, which meant all Burnham could do for the next few minutes was wait.

She hated waiting.

———

Culber heard the detonation just before a body slammed into him and drove him to the grass. He grunted from the abrupt impact, realizing only as he turned on his side that it was Detmer who had hit him. Her eyes were wide, taking in everything around them before she pulled herself to her feet. She extended one hand to him.

"Doctor, are you all right?"

Nodding as he let her pull him up, Culber looked to see Owosekun protecting Adira in a similar manner. Then his gaze turned to Yovi and Numa as they moved to place themselves between Culber and his companions and those demonstrators who had not yet dispersed. Both Xahean security officers had drawn their weapons, which to the doctor looked like slimmer, lower-profile versions of the phasers now carried by Starfleet personnel.

"What's happening?" asked Adira.

Her attention on the people in front of her, Yovi replied, "Some kind of explosive device, but from what I can tell, it was very small."

Around them, Xaheans had moved away from the apparent point of the explosion, and Culber could see a handful of people lying or sitting on the ground. Though he needed to get closer to be sure, what he did not see was obvious evidence of wounds sustained from any sort of explosive shrapnel or concussion.

"I can help the injured," he said, starting forward. That was enough for Detmer to grab him by the arm.

"Hang on a second, Doctor." Her grip was firm, and Culber noted the helm officer had conjured a phaser from the programmable-matter pendant affixed to her uniform sleeve. The weapon was held out and away from her body, as though daring anyone to approach. "We don't know what's going on just yet."

Culber replied, "What's going on is there are people hurt, and I can help them."

Her lips pressing together as she weighed his response, Detmer said, "You know I'm coming with you."

"Well, yeah." Culber forced a smile. "I'm not a *complete* idiot." The comment was enough to make Detmer relax enough to let go of his arm and her expression softened.

With the immediate area cleared of anyone who could move under their own power, Culber now could see what remained of the device. Pieces of it littered the ground, and there was a circle of burned grass perhaps a half meter in diameter. Approaching the nearest victim, a young Xahean male, the doctor was relieved to see no sign of shrapnel wounds. Instead, the man was holding his left ankle and there was a cut above his right eye. Culber held up his hands as he stepped closer.

"I'm a doctor," he said, keeping his voice calm. "Is it just your leg?"

His expression pained, the Xahean nodded. "I tripped when people started running, and someone stepped on it." He pressed his lips together, in obvious discomfort. Culber knelt beside him and Detmer took up a protective position within arm's reach.

"Emergency response teams are approaching," said Numa as he moved toward them. "There was another explosion just outside the park. Another demonstration."

"You! This is all your fault!"

Culber snapped his head up to see a group of four Xaheans walking toward them. Leading them was an older male carrying a sign in one hand while pointing an accusatory finger in his direction.

"You should never have come here!" said the man, raising his sign in defiance. "Go back to wherever you came from and leave us in peace!"

"I'm guessing he's a traditionalist," said Owosekun, who along with Adira was moving toward Culber and Detmer. She had produced her own phaser but held the weapon along her right leg. Mimicking her movements, Adira took up a defensive position on Detmer's opposite side, establishing a partial perimeter around Culber.

"They don't seem to like us very much," said Adira.

Detmer asked, "Is understatement a Trill thing, or is that all you?"

"It's definitely Tal," replied the ensign.

Culber heard the nervousness in their voices but knew Owosekun and Detmer would watch out for them if the situation continued to deteriorate. Ahead of them, he noticed Yovi and Numa moving to disperse the small group. Looking past the security officers, he saw more Xaheans returning to the area, perhaps realizing the explosive had inflicted no real damage. Most of the would-be demonstrators seemed to heed the security officers, either their spoken commands or the weapons they waved in the air. Forcing himself not to focus on what was happening around him, Culber returned his gaze to his unlikely patient.

"I don't have any of my equipment with me," he said. "But I'm going to try to make you a little more comfortable until more help arrives. Okay?"

The Xahean nodded. "Thank you. You are not what I expected from the Federation."

With gentle movements, Culber moved the cuff of the Xahean's trouser leg to expose the injured ankle. "What were you expecting?"

Shrugging, the Xahean replied, "I'm honestly . . . not sure anymore."

His patient's sharp intake of breath told Culber that even his gingerly touch was painful as he noted the discoloring around where the tibia would be in a human. There was already some swelling. Any attempt to walk or place weight on the ankle would cause the Xahean greater pain.

"Incoming!"

Culber flinched at the warning before instinct took over and he threw himself across the Xahean's chest. He felt Detmer's hand on his back just before another loud snap popped off somewhere to his left. The muffled explosion was similar to the others. His near certainty the device served more as distraction than weapon did little to ease his growing anxiety.

"This isn't the worst port call I've ever had," he said as he pushed himself off his patient. "But it's up there." He took in their immediate surroundings, noting how those demonstrators—he could tell who represented what cause—who had scattered after the last detonation seemed to be regaining their courage.

"Why do I get the feeling they're blaming us for all this?" asked Adira.

Culber replied, "I don't want to wait around to chat about it. Where's the nearest medical or security facility?"

Turning from where she maintained watch for trouble, Yovi pointed along their original path across the park. "There's a security ministry office in Jovahna Square."

"Then that's where we're going."

Assisting his patient to his feet while favoring his injured ankle, Culber then situated the Xahean across his shoulders in a carry position. With Yovi and Numa covering him from the rear, he set off after Detmer, Owosekun, and Adira. Behind him, he heard more shouted voices.

"Are you all right, Doctor?" asked Adira.

"It's just been a while since my field fitness and survival training at the Academy." Despite the weight on his back, Culber quickened his pace to keep up with Detmer and Owosekun. He did his best to ignore the commotion around him and cringed when he heard Numa's weapon fire. It was a discharge into the ground, which seemed to convince a small group of Xaheans to maintain their distance.

"I'm still not able to raise *Discovery* or activate my transporter," said Owosekun.

Adira replied, "Same here."

"Forget it," said Detmer. "Even if they can't pinpoint us on sensors, they know something's going on down here by now. If they can't reach us, they'll send someone to get us."

The group reached the edge of the park, and in the street beyond, Culber could see still more Xaheans but also several security officers, their drab uniforms standing out from the more colorful and informal fashions sported by the civilians. More protesters, he decided, from their movements and the security detail's attempts to corral them away from what must have been the center of their demonstration. One security officer produced a form of baton and began swinging it, forcing back a pair of Xaheans.

"All citizens in this area are required to disperse immediately," said a voice over some kind of outdoor broadcast system. *"Those failing to heed this directive face detainment and prosecution. All citizens in this area, disperse immediately."*

"Watch out!"

It was Adira, their warning coming a second too late before Culber felt something hit him in the back just as he stepped from the grass to the street's unyielding surface. The impact of the collision sent Culber's assailant tumbling to the ground, and only then did the doctor see it was a Xahean. His body shimmered as he dropped the personal shroud that had rendered him nearly invisible and allowed him to get past Adira and their security escorts.

You sneaky son of a bitch.

Still off-balance from the hit, Culber did his best to protect his patient before tripping on the edge where park and street met. He pitched forward, dropping hard onto his right knee. Pain shooting through his leg, he gasped for breath while fighting to stabilize the injured Xahean. He tried pushing himself to his feet, but it was impossible with the man still across his shoulders. Hearing movement nearby, he turned his head to see his assailant lunging toward him.

The attempt was thwarted as another, larger figure rushed into view and with a commanding growl slammed into the Xahean, sending the would-be attacker tumbling back to the ground.

"Book!"

His back to Culber, Cleveland Booker took up a defensive position between the doctor and the Xahean who was in the midst of regaining his feet. Pausing as if to take quick appraisal of his new opponent, the protester turned and ran back across the park. Only when it was obvious he would not be returning did Booker turn back to Culber and his patient.

"Hang on, Doc!"

It was Sylvia Tilly, running across the small square where demonstrators were scattering. Within seconds she was helping Booker lift the wounded Xahean off him.

"The security office isn't far," said Booker. "We were heading there when we saw you."

"Doctor, let me help you."

Culber looked up to see Arbusala holding out his hands, and gratefully accepted the offer of assistance. With the therapist's help he was able to stand, though the pain in his knee was severe. Despite his own injury, he looked around to account for Detmer, Owosekun, and Adira. They along with Yovi and Numa were there, and all seemingly unharmed. The security guards turned their attention to the injured citizen Booker was still supporting.

"Can you walk, Doc?" asked Booker.

Nodding, he glanced to Arbusala. "I've got help. I'll make it." His knee was killing him, but he knew it would be a quick fix once he was back in *Discovery*'s sickbay. "Are there any serious injuries?"

Yovi replied, "Nothing life-threatening. The explosives appear to have been simple concussive devices, intended to disorient and distract rather than inflict any actual damage. Indeed, grenades used in our training are more powerful, but to the uninitiated in a crowded setting, they can have a most disruptive effect."

"Doctor Culber." It was Owosekun, who now was pointing toward the sky. "Check it out. The cavalry's here."

With Arbusala helping him to shift around, Culber gritted his teeth against his pain and looked up to see a pair of Starfleet shuttles navigating through Sanctuary's upper support structure and arcing downward toward the ground. This was more than enough to agitate several of the Xaheans still lingering in the area despite ongoing warnings to leave.

"Go back to your ship and leave us!" shouted an older Xahean woman. Culber heard variations on the sentiment yelled by other Xaheans, interspersed with the commands of different security officers to leave or face arrest.

"I must admit it certainly doesn't sound like the worst idea just now," said Arbusala.

Culber replied, "I'm with you." He hissed as he attempted to shift his stance. The movement only caused more pain to lance through his knee. "I'm just glad no one looks seriously hurt."

Having been relieved of the injured Xahean by the security officers, Booker moved to stand next to Culber and their companions, watching the shuttles make their descent. Xaheans in close proximity ran, while others stood some distance away and observed the pair of utility craft settling to the park grass. Xahean security officers seemed to be quelling what little remained of the disruptions, and Culber allowed himself a small, relieved sigh as he confirmed all of his shipmates safe.

Detmer said, "Am I the only one who thinks things got way out of hand way too fast?"

"I'll do you one better," replied Owosekun. "I think we were the target."

Adira asked, "Us? You mean on purpose?"

"Somebody riled up that crowd," said Detmer. "And it had nothing to do with the normal demonstrations they told us about."

Owosekun added, "Start a riot and point the finger at us." She shrugged. "Stand back and watch the chaos."

"Why would they do that?" asked Tilly. "Can't they see we just want to help?"

Booker said, "I'm guessing there's a whole bunch of people who'd be really happy if we just minded our own damned business."

27

Exiting his office, Minister Sen struggled to keep his emotions in check. As a proponent of detail and precision, he had little patience for carelessness, and in particular when it came in the form of someone misunderstanding or outright disobeying his instructions. While he knew the former could in some instances be attributed to him given his position of leadership, he gave no quarter to the latter.

"What happened?" he asked, stalking onto the Internal Security Section's main control center. Around him, Xahean ministry officers and assistants seemed to take heightened interest in their workstations or whatever task lay before them. The only person with any apparent willingness to turn toward him was, as he expected, Tol.

"Several demonstrations today, throughout Sanctuary," she said, her holographic display pad hovering in the air before her. "A few we knew about in advance, but the bulk of them appear to be more impulsive. They were almost certainly provoked by the presence of the Federation ship."

Sen glanced at the information scrolling past Tol's control pad. "Separatist rallies, or counterprotests?"

"Both, actually. Given the volume, we opted to refrain from any direct action and allow these to proceed without interference. There was an increased security presence in the various provinces, of course, following the incident at the Aellud Gardens. Subsequent events proceeded without issue for a time, but one of the first rallies to spawn additional trouble was the traditionalist rally in the Stederra Province. It was organized by a group of university students and was peaceful until a group of counterprotesters challenged them. Although the situation threatened to deteriorate, security officers were able to restore order."

Growing irritated with the hologram's reduced-size display, Sen directed her to call up the latest information on the various protests, rallies, and other demonstrations and put it on the control center's main screen. What appeared was a wall of text similar to what Tol showed him, but now he could make out the reports submitted by different security ministry precincts as well as officers in the field. There also were correlations with logs of previous incidents the ministry was tracking for these activities. Citations, arrests, injuries—though thankfully only a few of the latter—and other related data. A series of faces and identity data belonging to prominent individuals such as known activists and other persons of interest also was presented. Sen recognized a few of the faces, either protesters who had run afoul of the security ministry or others who had proven themselves worthy of enhanced scrutiny for assorted offenses.

"How many protests were staged today?" he asked.

Still working with her own control pad, Tol replied, "Nine actual assemblies, but there also were a number of informal gatherings with just a few people. Most of those were staged outside official offices or establishments belonging to citizens who have given public statements about various issues. We conducted pattern analysis and found no correlation we could ascribe to all of them, but we have indications at least three were coordinated events. We have evidence linking separatists at each of those locations. Known associates, surveilled together during previous demonstrations, and so on."

"But none of these protests were planned by our people, correct?" Sen knew the answer to his question before voicing it. No covert actions designed to influence demonstrations of this sort were conducted without his express review and approval. "No one was cleared to insert themselves into any of these rallies or events, and certainly not with an eye toward escalation."

Tol's jaw clenched for a moment before she shook her head.

"It appears some of the independent assets we employ for these types of actions took their own initiative." She transferred that information to the main screen.

Recognizing the faces of two male Xaheans, Sen gestured to the screen. "These two were at the Jovahna Province protests today?"

"That is correct." Checking the data streams on her pad, Tol added, "According to initial reports from the local security precinct, they were observed by several witnesses tossing concussive devices near gatherings of rally attendants. Neither party has offered any statements to explain or defend their actions, but investigation of unused devices found on their persons shows they were not capable of causing serious injury. Their intention appears to have been disruptive rather than destructive. Security officers processed them, and they are currently being held in custody pending an appearance before a province magistrate. Their cover identities were not penetrated, so there is no link to us."

"That does not alter the fact they acted on their own and without authorization. They should not have been there at all." Sen felt anger swelling within him, and with practiced effort held it at bay. "I gave explicit instructions for the Federation people to be left alone while visiting Sanctuary. I directed security officers to keep them away from any rally or other demonstration."

Consulting her pad, Tol replied, "The Jovahna Province protest was unplanned. From the reports I have received, it began with three citizens standing outside a dining establishment whose proprietor has expressed pro-separatist sympathies. The security officers accompanying Federation people touring the province had no advance knowledge, and to their credit they acted to avoid the area once they were informed. The situation escalated before they were able to take further corrective action."

Struggling to keep his growing ire in check, Sen began pacing. "Concussion devices to agitate the crowds? It will only draw greater scrutiny. The local precincts conducting their own investigations will want to know where they obtained such ordnance." He drew a deep breath, releasing it slowly as he contemplated his next steps. "It appears I will be having a conversation with the magistrate, in hopes of dispensing with this matter in quiet fashion." It would help if the officer of the court assigned to adjudicate their charges could be persuaded to believe the two agents were acting on behalf of the ministry in an official albeit furtive capacity. The prospect did not enthuse Sen, but there would be just enough truth in that explanation to cover up the larger falsehood.

"Would you like me to see to this?" asked Tol.

"I will see to this myself, if for no other reason than to ensure such idiocy is not repeated." Feeling discomfort swelling behind his eyes, Sen reached up to rub the bridge of his nose. "It will be fascinating to learn what they hoped to accomplish."

Sen began pacing along the length of the center's main floor, Tol keeping pace with him as he examined the various workstations, display screens, and tables featuring holographic maps of different Sanctuary provinces. There was an undeniable surge of activity in the wake of the latest protests, which he knew would spawn other types of disruptive behavior. It would be easy for him to dismiss much of these actions as those of separatists or others committing assorted illegal activity, but that would be naïve. He knew there were plenty of Xaheans who subscribed to traditional beliefs and cultural norms and yet were not above illicit acts to further their own agenda.

Some of them work in this room, he reminded himself. *Some of them even look back at you when you see your reflection.*

He could not deny the ever-growing divide between those espousing separatist notions as opposed to the more mainstream concept of observing traditional Xahean values and the ideals of the community that had thrived for generations within Sanctuary. Although he wanted to be sympathetic to those seeking life outside the habitat, the very real impact to those left behind could not be ignored. Bypassing the minister of security, members of the leadership council had come to him to explain their concerns in no uncertain terms. All reasonable measures to quell the growing separatist movement had to be considered. This included surreptitious manipulation of public opinion.

Though reluctant to engage in tactics of this sort, Sen understood if he did not acquiesce to the council members' wishes they would find someone else to do their bidding. At least if he oversaw the effort, it could be controlled and restrained. This sometimes placed him at odds with the councilors, but so far, he had managed to convince them discretion and patience were the keys to success while avoiding detection. This was of paramount importance to him, for if the truth of the security ministry's involvement in these actions ever came to light, repercussions for the Xahean Council, to say nothing of Queen Ki, would be devastating, though those members who had ordered the action would likely suffer no consequences. Instead, the ministry would shoulder the blame, and he in particular would never escape unscathed.

And now there were other factors to consider.

"Involving the Federation crew was a mistake," said Sen, continuing to study the different stations and monitors they passed. "Perhaps their original intentions were to avoid miring themselves in our affairs, but it was obvious from their captain's first meeting with the queen that they are sympathetic to the separatist cause. Granting even temporary asylum to the *Pilikoa* crew is certainly proof of that."

Tol replied, "We should be thankful none of them suffered serious injuries."

"Yes, but now their captain and the rest of her crew will be on guard." Sen shook his head. "What happened in the Jovahna Province may only have deepened their commitment to finding a solution that benefits those seeking separation. Indeed, our assets' stupidity might even alter opinions among those who oppose the idea."

"And you believe the Federation captain will be more vocal

in her support." It was a statement on Tol's part, rather than a question. "Based on my limited observations, she seems quite passionate, and that can be channeled into persuasiveness."

"Indeed it can."

"According to recent news broadcasts," said Tol, "a growing number of citizens are concerned the Federation may disrupt our way of life, even if their intentions are honorable. They think we should tell the ship to leave and never return."

Sighing, Sen shook his head. "It's not that simple. Not anymore."

He had read enough reports from freighter captains in recent weeks to know the Federation was attempting to reconnect with worlds where contact had been lost in the wake of the Burn. With the origins of that calamity now known—along with assurances the circumstances behind its manifestation would not be repeated—the once powerful interstellar cooperative was endeavoring to reestablish itself as one of the quadrant's dominant voices.

"I honestly do not believe there is reason to fear the Federation," he said. "However, who else is out there? Uncounted civilizations fell victim to the Burn. While many among them will emerge from their enforced isolation and present themselves as allies, others will doubtless reassert themselves as adversaries. Now that the Federation knows about us, how will all of this maneuvering aid or threaten us?" Even after all these generations managing to live largely at a remove from the rest of the galaxy, Sen did not discount the possibility of his people once again finding themselves caught in yet another dispute that did not directly involve them.

That could not be allowed to happen ever again.

"It now seems even more urgent that we find a way to extricate ourselves from affairs of this sort, Minister," said a new voice.

Sen turned to see Nan Joma Hilo, dressed in casual, even nondescript, clothing, rather than the more formal attire she preferred while sitting on the Xahean Council, crossing the control center floor toward them. Even her hair was styled in a manner different from when she undertook her official duties, flowing freely about her shoulders rather than pulled back from her face or styled atop her head. She was almost unrecognizable, which Sen decided might well be the point.

"Councilor Hilo." Tol threw a nervous glance to him before returning her gaze to the new arrival. "This is quite unexpected."

Holding up a hand, Hilo replied, "Do not be concerned, Officer. I have been an overseer of this effort even longer than Sen. Indeed, it was I who advocated for giving him the responsibility he now holds."

"That is correct," replied Sen.

He should have expected the councilor to make an appearance in the wake of the protests, and given the revelations about the Federation ship. Hilo was one of the more ardent detractors of the separatist movement and had long championed not simply maintaining Sanctuary's restrictions against outsiders but indeed a much more extreme isolationist policy. Along with other council members who shared her views, she had promoted the idea of moving Sanctuary as far away from known space as was feasible. As she had discussed over the course of many open debates in the council's chambers, somewhere in the known galaxy there had to be at least one place untainted by the machinations of others. There, she envisioned, Xaheans could retreat and live in peace far away from the squabbles of others, to say nothing of enemies seeking to exploit everything the Xahean people had managed to salvage, restore, and cultivate.

"It seems we have an opportunity here," said Hilo. "If your preliminary reports about the Federation ship are accurate, it likely holds the answer to our most pressing question: How do we protect our people for all time? If we are to seek a new safe harbor, that vessel will be our guide."

Tol tried and nearly succeeded in hiding her skepticism.

"Councilor, long ago the Federation was in a position to assist us, and they failed. The vessel's captain seems eager to rectify that mistake."

"I would like to believe that," replied Hilo, "but for the good of the people we are sworn to protect, we cannot afford to be wrong. We must act in their best interests." She looked to Sen. "Is that not correct, Minister?"

Despite his misgivings, Sen could only answer, "That is correct, Councilor."

Hilo nodded. "And this time, the Federation will not stand in our way. Indeed, they will be the instrument of our salvation."

28

Alone in her ready room, Burnham felt her temptation to unload on the holographic presence of Queen Ki threatening to overwhelm her. The only thing preventing her from speaking her mind was the knowledge that the Xahean leader was not alone in whatever location from which the hologram was generated. For the sake of her staff, advisors, or whoever else might be in the room, Burnham forced herself to keep her emotions in check and focus on the more important issue.

"Your Highness, I understand that none of the injuries reported so far are serious. That's very good news."

"We are all grateful for that, Captain," replied the queen. *"Just as we are thankful none of your crew was injured."*

"A few bumps and bruises, and one leg injury I'm told has been treated and the patient is already back to full duty."

Ki studied her for a moment before saying, *"There is the matter of your landing craft being launched without our permission."*

Burnham maintained her bearing, hands clasped behind her. "I take full responsibility for that, Your Highness. We had no way to contact our people or retrieve them with transporters, and from our vantage point, the situation on the ground necessitated quick action to ensure their safety."

"I understand you feeling the need to protect those you lead, Captain. I certainly hope such action isn't necessary again, but if it is, then I request you seek my approval first."

"You have my word it won't be repeated, and that no one will leave this ship until we've secured that authorization."

What Burnham did not say, as it would likely serve only to increase tensions during what was a civil conversation, was that she had no intention of allowing any more visits to Sanctuary's surface. She did not yet know the reasons for the attacks, but statements from the away team that they felt targeted—or that the entire incident felt somehow like a pretext for such targeting—made her uneasy.

Instead, she opted for the moment to pivot away from focusing on her own people. "If there's anything we can provide to assist with treating injuries or contributing to any investigations currently underway, we're happy to do so."

The queen nodded. *"My minister of security informs me that order has been restored and investigations are underway. As you know, there were demonstrations similar to the one your crew witnessed in several provinces. A few of those involved explosives, but I'm told none of these appeared intended to cause harm."* She paused, and Burnham got the impression she was uncomfortable with what she might say next. *"Captain, though the investigation is still in its earliest stages, we have also responded to incidents of assaults against portions of Sanctuary's infrastructure. We believe the demonstrations may have been intended as cover for these other activities, which were aimed at power systems as well as computer and environmental facilities. So far as we have been able to determine, no damage was caused. The Ministry of Security is still determining whether the computer facility intrusions yielded any compromised information or access to other, more vital systems."*

Aware of no such activities, Burnham asked, "Is there anything we can do to assist with that effort?"

The queen shook her head. *"There has been much discussion about how to proceed on that front, but I'm afraid at the moment we don't have any information to go on. The obvious deduction is that these acts were perpetrated by separatists, and if that's the case, then it's a troubling development. Today's demonstrations were atypical compared to those we've seen on other occasions. The level of violence, despite the lack of severe injuries, is a noticeable escalation from past incidents. Several of my council members are calling for swift, decisive, and punitive action."*

"They think we're responsible," said Burnham.

"I don't believe you caused any of this, of course, but your presence has proven to be a disruptive influence. I'm not discounting the obvious possibility that members of our community are engaging in such acts in the hopes they'll persuade you to leave. I must stress that, at this time, I do not want that to happen. I've made that clear to the council, but I'm aware of dissent among the members. Even if we were unanimous, the prospect of you being a target means I think it's best for your crew to remain aboard your ship unless we specifically invite you to visit with us."

Feeling no need to press the point, Burnham replied, "Agreed, Your Highness."

When the queen paused again before speaking, it was obvious she was listening to someone Burnham could not see or hear, and the nod she gave to that unseen person was curt, and there was an ever so slight hardening of her features.

"Also, and after listening to advice offered by members of our council, I formally request you return to us those members of the Pilikoa *crew who've requested asylum."*

Having expected something like this, Burnham nevertheless struggled to keep her composure. "That would not be how we normally address asylum requests, Your Highness. I understand our two governments have no formal process for such matters, but I hoped you and I could come to an understanding, based on the considerable trust you've already shown us."

"You presuppose there's a path forward for any long-term relationship between the Federation and my people, Captain."

Burnham wanted to pace as was her habit while contemplating a problem or issue in private. She never cared for desks, not even the standing variety like the one that had been a feature of the ready room when it belonged to previous *Discovery* commanding officers. For her, desks were not conducive to personal reflection, concentration, or decision-making. In Ki's presence, she called upon her Vulcan upbringing and Starfleet training to remain still as she contemplated the queen's words.

"Presuppose? No, Your Highness. I'm merely optimistic we can reach agreement on this issue, and then use that as a foundation for moving forward along such a path."

Ki smiled, though to Burnham it felt forced. *"If I had not already met you in person, I'd be tempted to think you were presenting a façade. Thankfully, I have that perspective to help me see you, and I do not doubt your intentions. However, given the turn events have taken, I feel it's best that there be no misperceptions about what the* Pilikoa *separatists attempted, and the crimes they committed in service to that cause."* As if sensing Burnham's hesitation, the queen added, *"If it's their safety that concerns you, I offer you my personal assurance they will be treated well while in custody and receive the due process afforded to anyone accused of a crime in our society. Further, I'll see to it you can visit them any time you wish, without restrictions."*

Despite herself, Burnham could not help a small sigh of resignation. "Your personal assurances mean a great deal to me, Your Highness. I'll arrange for their transfer."

To refuse the queen's demands at this point would be detrimental, Burnham decided. That action would spell disaster for any future attempts at diplomacy. The consequences for the Xaheans currently seeking asylum aboard *Discovery* would be immediate, as they would face whatever prosecutorial action awaited them. At least now there was still a form of grace being extended if the queen was to be believed, and Burnham had no reason to do otherwise. For the uncounted people in Sanctuary waiting to see how this entire situation proceeded, this was a chance for her and Ki to show that reasonable people could work together to seek solutions. Burnham sensed the queen comprehended this. The issue was no longer just about the *Pilikoa* separatists, but anyone who dreamed of such a future for themselves, as well as the impacts to larger Xahean society if Ki and the Federation could reach some form of agreement. This compromise action bought both sides time. Somewhere in the midst of such concessions and in the face of so many questions, Burnham knew answers waited.

The needs of the many, she reminded herself of the Vulcan axiom taught to her long ago by her foster father, Ambassador Sarek, *outweigh the needs of the few.* She could only hope Iku and his companions would see things her way.

29

"I can't believe the captain would do that."

Pacing her quarters, Tilly stopped herself before she ran into her sleeping area's far bulkhead. She turned around, caught up in her own thoughts, those already given voice as well as so many others as yet unspoken. For that reason, she started upon seeing the figure standing in the middle of the room.

"Oh, right. You're still here."

"I am still here, Lieutenant." Long fingers laced together as Captain Saru clasped his hands before him. He was not dressed in a Starfleet uniform but instead a long gray coat with gold highlights over dark gray trousers and matching boots that rose to his knees. The coat's front panel was a field of royal blue, its only ornamentation the brilliant silver-and-gold pendant symbolizing the Kaminar High Council. The decoration was worn only by members of the council and those selected to serve as envoys to the planet's highest leadership body. Envoys were treated with the utmost respect, and it warmed Tilly's heart to see her former commanding officer and dear friend honored in this way.

"Kaminar looks good on you," she said, appraising his attire.

Pressing his hands to the sides of his coat, Saru affected a meek smile. *"I admit it took some getting used to. It had been so long since I had worn anything other than a Starfleet uniform, at first I felt uncomfortable with anything else. Change comes in many forms, as does our reaction to it."* He cocked his head, and Tilly thought she saw a twinkle in his brilliant blue eyes as he considered her with that patient, almost paternal expression Tilly had come to know so well and truly missed seeing in the flesh. Holograms were good, especially the kind generated in this century, but they could never replace a real person. If the actual Saru stood with her now, Tilly was sure she would be trying to hug the stuffing out of him.

"You did not contact me to ask about my wardrobe," he said, once more affecting the air of the patient listener and mentor. *"This is about you and your feelings about the Xaheans. I can only imagine what seeing these people, descendants of those we left behind not all that long ago, must be like for you."*

Tilly had given Saru a full accounting of the encounter, up to and including the protests and attacks. "I'm still coming to grips with just how much their civilization went through after we left. After everything they were forced to endure and the decisions they had to make, that they've managed to come this far after this many centuries and still hold themselves together." She held up her hands. "No, more than that. They've *thrived*, Saru. This Sanctuary they've built? It's *amazing*."

"And yet there are those Xaheans who feel it is not their true home," replied Saru. *"They seek something more. That is natural for many species, even mine and most especially yours."*

Tilly said, "Their true home is gone. At least it's not the planet we remember. They can't live there anymore."

She knew that without actually venturing to the planet; there was no way to know the exact condition of Xahea, but she had no reason to doubt the sincerity of people such as Queen Ki. Like everyone else who called Sanctuary home, the queen relied on the history as passed down through the generations succeeding those who centuries earlier had left the planet in search of a new home. After hundreds of years, was their former homeworld in even more dire straits? Could anything be salvaged? Tilly had even researched current terraforming techniques, in the hopes of devising possible alternatives for the Xaheans. Efforts such as those begun by humans in the early twenty-second century were now far more advanced, as were the capabilities of other civilizations, including several Federation-member worlds.

"There are ways to help them," she said. "The stumbling block is the Xaheans themselves."

Saru replied, *"You refer to their evolved cultural sensitivities and their desire to remain unchained from any single world."*

"I mean, I get it." Tilly blew out her breath. "They don't want what happened to their ancestors to happen to them, but it doesn't have to be like that. They don't have to exist alone, out in the middle of empty space, hiding from the rest of the galaxy. We can help them. They can have friends, if they want them." She could sense her emotions threatening to get the best of her. It required effort, but she forced herself to relax.

"While we might see it as an isolationist and even extremist point of view, they have a right to regard the galaxy through that lens." Saru seemed to contemplate her for a moment before asking, *"Have you considered that your feelings for the Xaheans are rooted in something deeper and perhaps more personal?"*

The question caught Tilly off guard. "What do you mean?"

"It is fair to say we have all faced a period of adjustment since our arrival in this century. Trying to build a new life nine hundred years removed from everything we have ever known is no easy task." Saru held out his hands, and Tilly almost reached out to take them. *"We have been forced to seek closure for our past lives, to put everything in a proper context that allows us to move forward. While I believe most of us are adapting to our circumstances, it is easy to feel as though we are relics from a history that long ago forgot us. We no longer belong in the twenty-third century, but we ask ourselves if we truly belong here."*

"You have no idea how many times I've asked myself that question." Her reply evoked an involuntary laugh, and Tilly reached up to wipe her nose. She could feel her eyes reddening as she fought to keep her emotions at bay.

"I asked that same question, several times," replied Saru. *"Most recently, upon my return to Kaminar. Much has changed here over the centuries, but there are still reminders of what my life*

*was like before I joined Starfleet. I am still finding my way here,
but working with Su'Kal has helped me to adapt."*

Saru had taken into his charge the much younger Kelpien,
an orphan found by *Discovery* on a dilithium-rich planet in the
Verubin Nebula. His parents' vessel crashed on the planet while
he was still *in utero*, and the nebula's odd radiological proper-
ties resulted in him developing a deep bond with the planet's
vast dilithium resources. Witnessing his mother's death, Su'Kal
inadvertently released a psychic shockwave that triggered an
explosive reaction not just in the planet's dilithium, but in a
shockwave cascading outward, causing similar effects in starships
throughout the galaxy: the Burn. After his rescue by *Discovery*,
Su'Kal accompanied Saru back to Kaminar with the goal of creating a new life for himself among his own people.

"Perhaps you see parallels between yourself and the Xaheans,"
said Saru. *"Many if not most of them have adapted to their circumstances, but there are those who question their existence. They
are not certain where they belong. I suspect even those who wish to
maintain their status quo still ask themselves that question from
time to time. Maybe they truly have found their home in Sanctuary, but just asking the question is enough to engage in discussion
and seek common ground."* He gestured to Tilly. *"I suspect Captain Burnham knows this. She possesses great empathy, and she will
find that foundation of mutual understanding. However, I also
believe your counsel to her at this time would be most valuable."*

"I mean, she's asked me about the Xaheans, sure." Tilly
frowned, not certain what Saru might mean. "I've done the research, helped get her up to speed, but—"

"No," said Saru. *"It's more than that. You are also a person of
deep feelings, Lieutenant. Your ability to see the needs of others and
respond to them with profound compassion is a wonderful asset to
Michael, particularly now."*

"Michael has more than enough compassion for all three of
us, Saru."

It was Saru's turn to laugh at the unexpected joke. *"Lieu-*

tenant, no one else alive possesses your relationship with the Xa-
heans. You alone hold the greatest perspective about the world they
left behind, about how their civilization existed before the tragedies
visited upon them. Use that to your advantage, Sylvia. I know
Michael will appreciate your efforts, and perhaps the Xaheans will
as well."

Tilly cleared her throat. "Wow. No pressure. How will I
know I'm doing the right thing, and not just making things
worse?"

"I find that highly unlikely, Lieutenant. I know you will do the
right thing, because I believe you are incapable of anything else."

That got to her, and now she did feel tears welling up.
"Damn it, Saru." A nervous giggle escaped her lips as she wiped
her eyes. "Why do you have to make me cry?"

Saru's face stretched as he smiled, and his eyes seemed to
shine even brighter as he regarded her. *"It tells me you are pure of*
heart, Sylvia Tilly. No matter what course you choose, I have every
confidence you will find your way, and help others to do the same."

30

Even as a junior officer, Burnham had perfected the art of stealing whatever precious few opportunities for rest might present themselves during those lull periods in any situation. Sometimes that meant the luxury of lying down for a brief interval of actual sleep. Even just the ability to close one's eyes and ignore other external stimuli for a handful of minutes could be restorative.

Sleep fast, as her former captain, mentor, and friend Philippa Georgiou used to say.

Having learned the value of meditation thanks to her Vulcan upbringing, Burnham discovered the two mental exercises complemented one another in a way she found satisfying. They allowed her to process information while still taking advantage of those transient intervals where rest was needed in order to best see to her overall mental health.

It also made it easier to return to full wakefulness when her nap was interrupted.

Walking onto *Discovery*'s bridge, Burnham sensed the tension hanging in the air. She neither saw nor heard any alert indicators from any of the stations, but a quick glance around the room revealed her people crewing their stations with the sort of heightened awareness that told her something was wrong. This was expected, of course, given the apologetic call from Commander Rhys that had broken into her all-too-brief respite in her ready room.

"Captain," said Rhys, drawing her attention to where he stood at the tactical station. "I'm sorry to disturb you, but I thought you'd want to see this."

Moving to stand next to her first officer, Burnham eyed the displays and status indicators arrayed on the tactical console as well as the holographic interface suspended above it. She noted the reports coming from the ship's internal and exterior sensors, starting to piece together what Rhys had found.

"They're scanning us again," he said. "It started about five minutes ago and has continued since then."

Burnham replied, "Given the Xaheans' views on security, this is something I'd expect. They want to know if we're a threat." As things stood now, she suspected *Discovery* would be tested by Sanctuary's internal defenses if it came to that. Could the starship fight its way out if necessary? She believed that was likely, and once out in open space, it would be a different story.

"This is different," said Tilly, who had moved from her science station to stand next to Rhys and was also perusing the tactical readouts. "They'd already taken a good look at our weapons and defenses when we first arrived. That made sense at the time, but most of these new scans are concentrated on the engineering section."

"They seem really interested in the spore drive," said a new voice, and Burnham turned to see Paul Stamets stepping onto the bridge, followed by Adira Tal. "Zora says they've focused most of their scans at engineering on the spore chamber including the reaction cube."

Burnham pondered that. "They would've scanned our arrival when we jumped to the coordinates Leb provided, and you can't blame them for wanting to know how we got here without being detected by any long-range sensors." It was never far from her thoughts that *Discovery*'s drive system was a unique advantage not just for the ship itself but also the Federation. Before its dissolution, the Emerald Chain tried and failed to exploit such knowledge for its own ends. It would be foolish to think no one else, whether they represented whatever remained of the Chain or some other party, would want *Discovery* for their own ends.

"They're also trying to scan our computer banks," said Ensign Tal, "but Zora's encryption schemes are doing a good job of keeping them out."

"We keep saying 'they,' but who are we talking about?" Burnham looked to the main viewscreen and the null-gravity docking umbilical to which *Discovery* had been directed upon its entry into Sanctuary. "Where are the scans originating?"

"That's the weird part," said Rhys. "For the scans we detected when we arrived, we could trace back to the habitat's central hub. Based on the energy readings we picked up, that's probably where they've concentrated the bulk of their command-and-control facilities as well as Sanctuary's primary power source." He gestured to his console's holographic displays. "These? They're not coming from the same place, and the readings are piggybacking off other data and energy transmissions being sent across the entire sphere. If our scans aren't being bounced back, then they're pretty much just getting lost in the shuffle. Whoever's doing this? They know how to cover their tracks."

"If they were so interested, they could've just asked." If this action was being conducted under the direction of Ki, Burnham conceded it as being consistent with at least some of the queen's guarded statements during their initial meeting, including her emphasis on the need for trust. Feathers had been ruffled following the demonstrations down on the surface, but she hoped the queen and her council could move past that. Were they searching for evidence in order to calm or rationalize their wariness about Federation intentions?

"I activated a scattering field around the spore chamber and the drive itself," said Stamets. "That should prevent any more nosing around. I don't suppose just asking the queen about any of this is a good idea?"

"Probably not." Burnham sighed. "Things are pretty delicate at the moment, but it seemed to me like we were making some progress, at least before the protests."

Tilly added, "Do you think returning Iku and the others helped?"

"I'd like to think so." Despite her own reservations, Burnham had to hope the queen understood the gesture of trust

Burnham offered. "I can see she wants to approach this fairly, but others aren't too happy about that idea."

"A couple of those council members were giving off some bad vibes," said Tilly. "I'm pretty sure they don't want us here. I mean, *at all*."

Stamets said, "What else could we expect? The Federation failed them. Imagine how the last nine hundred years would've gone for them if we'd been there at those critical moments in their history. We may not be completely to blame for everything that happened to the Xaheans, but we certainly weren't much help."

"When you consider all of that," said Adira, "it's hard to believe they agreed to meet us in the first place."

"It could just be a matter of them wanting us where they could control the situation better," offered Rhys. "In here, we're on their turf."

Tilly asked, "If they thought we were a threat, wouldn't they have taken some sort of precautions by now?"

"There's nothing we can detect," said Rhys. "Our own scans show no indications of weapons or other energy sources targeting the ship."

Burnham considered her initial meeting with Ki and the leadership council. "I have to believe there are Xaheans who don't hate us. They understand the Federation as it exists today isn't responsible for what happened. What we can do is show them a sincere desire to make amends. I think at least some Xaheans want that too." That much was evident from Ki and one or two of her council leaders, even as Burnham picked up on the resentment carried by others. She also knew the queen was obligated to listen to and address the concerns of her people, and that meant any interactions with outsiders would be carried out with an abundance of reasonable precautions in place. That alone, as Burnham saw it, would be enough to justify the scrutiny to which *Discovery* had been subjected.

"Plus there's the matter of Iku and the other asylum seekers," said Tilly. "Even though we returned them, how many more Xaheans know it's a possibility? We've already seen them starting to act out about it. The queen and the council can't be happy about that."

Rhys added, "On that front, Queen Ki seems to be acting on good faith and wants a reasonable solution that benefits all sides of the issue."

"But we know there are people within her inner circle who don't agree with her," said Tilly. "What if they're able to convince her we really are the bad guys and we should leave?"

Burnham crossed her arms. "Then we'll leave. It'll be up to Federation diplomats to decide if and how we engage with the Xaheans again. I don't think we're there yet, so until then? We keep doing this by the book. I'll be meeting with the queen soon enough, and hopefully we can continue the discussion we started and make some real progress." Her instincts told her Ki was being truthful with her, at least about those things they had discussed. "I don't doubt she and everyone else knows more than they're letting on. That goes with the job, but my instincts tell me she's honestly looking for a mutually agreeable solution to all of this. For now, I think we're just going to let this play out."

Play it out, she thought, *and wait to see who shows their cards first.*

Looking to Stamets, Burnham asked, "Can we jump out of here if we need to?"

"Absolutely. We ran diagnostics after the last jump, and all systems show green. Since we learned about the scans, I set up an alert if anything changes. So far, so good." His reply was clipped and formal, and Burnham thought she detected the barest hint of irritation in his voice. She could understand him being irritated at the thought of someone poking around the spore drive, but was there something else lurking beneath the surface?

"How's Doctor Culber?" she asked, and was relieved when Stamets's face softened at the mention of his husband.

"As good as new," he said. "He won't admit it, but I think he did the surgery himself."

Burnham smiled. "Doctors make the worst patients."

"Almost as bad as captains."

And the moment's gone, Burnham thought. Whatever was bothering Stamets, it ran deeper than his normal and often unpredictable mood swings. Could it be explained by simple worry about Culber and the events on the surface? That would be natural, she knew, but she sensed there had to be something more in play here. Whatever the source of his irritation, it would have to wait for a more appropriate time, but she made a note to follow up with him when the opportunity presented itself.

An alert tone from the tactical console drew Rhys back to his instruments at the same time other stations around the bridge began flickering. Display screens and holographic interfaces wavered, their images becoming distorted or engulfed in static.

"What's going on?" asked Burnham.

Intent on his station, Rhys shook his head. "I'm not sure, Captain. Some kind of localized distortion. It came out of nowhere. At first I thought it might be a power spike, but it's not coming from us."

Tilly, having crossed back to her science console, called out, "Scanning. It's definitely an external reading."

"Shields up," ordered Burnham, then stopped herself. "Belay that order. We can't raise shields while we're connected to the docking umbilical. Go to yellow alert."

"Incoming!" Tilly's warning was frantic enough to make everyone on the bridge turn toward her. "Brace for impa—"

Something punched the ship. It was the only thing Burnham could think as she felt the deck heave beneath her and she flailed for anything to keep from being thrown across the bridge.

31

Materializing in *Discovery*'s engineering section after transporting from the bridge, Paul Stamets took in the sights and sounds of what had to be every single alert indicator on the ship screaming for attention.

"Engineering, what's the story? We're blind up here."

It was Burnham, now in full captain mode as the ship weathered whatever sort of attack was being thrown at it. Stamets heard the determination in her voice, could almost see the set of her jaw as she processed the rapidly unfolding situation and formulated responses in that deliberate, hyperfocused manner that made her good at her job and even a bit awe inspiring while at the same time being a tremendous pain in the ass.

"Working on it, Captain," replied Commander Jett Reno from where she stood at one of the main engineering master systems consoles. Stamets saw her enter a series of commands and the audible alarms stopped their wailing. Lighting returned to normal, but the alert indicators continued to flash. "Whatever that was, it kicked us right in the onions."

Stamets crossed the floor to a console next to Reno's, swiping across its surface to activate its holographic interface. "I'm pretty sure something collided with us." He called up a damage report, and a schematic of *Discovery* appeared before him. Rotating the model, he took note of the crimson icon on the underside of the ship's secondary hull.

"Point of impact," said Reno. "Near engineering and the main computer core."

"I'm not seeing evidence of a hull breach." Stamets frowned. "And I'm also not seeing any foreign object."

Reaching across to his console, Reno swiped at the diagram.

"Yeah, but look at this, Sparky." She enhanced the highlighted area of the secondary hull, then tapped it, changing the image from a technical schematic to a view of the ship's underside as if rendered by sensors for a viewscreen. The perspective was close enough for Stamets to note the seams between the dull silver plates comprising *Discovery*'s hull. He also saw that the center of the image wavered and blinked as if the visual feed was out of focus.

"A distortion field," he said. "Something's there, but blocking our sensors."

"Give that man a cigar," replied Reno as she shifted back to her own station. "Just not one of mine."

Stamets frowned. "You smoke cigars?"

"Only when I'm called in to work at the last minute." Switching between engaging her console's tactile controls and the holographic display, she said, "The field is similar to the one surrounding the station but using way less power. If we can isolate the frequency, we might be able to cut through it."

"I see where you're going." While he considered himself no slouch when it came to his technical acumen, he could appreciate Reno's approach. Years of training, combined with hard-won experience forged in peacetime and war along with a knack for improvisation and a wealth of sheer talent and determination, made her a formidable engineer. While it was true they had rubbed each other the wrong way at the beginning of their relationship—and in truth he still found himself irritated with her on occasion—there was almost no one he would rather have caring for *Discovery* and its crew when the heat was on.

After a moment, Reno said, "I think I've got it." Another series of commands to her console and the sensor image cleared to reveal a squat cylinder lying on its side and affixed to the ship's belly. Using the surrounding hull plates to provide perspective, Stamets guessed it to be at least a meter in length. It was composed of a gray metal that almost made it invisible against the ship itself. Then the image started breaking up.

"Bridge to engineering," said Burnham over the intercom. *"Did I hear you right? There's something on the hull?"*

"It must be magnetized." Reno tapped another control. "It's putting out a massive amount of energy that's starting to screw with our sensors. We might be able to depolarize that section of the hull, but—" She stopped herself when another indicator began flashing. "Okay, kids. Bad idea. Scans are showing that thing's carrying some kind of explosive."

Stamets called out, "Adira! Evacuate that section and seal it off."

Working at a nearby console, the young ensign nodded as they got to work. "Aye, Commander." As they dispatched those instructions, Stamets saw them pull their hands from the console as everything in front of them blinked and the station's holo display broke apart. Then every console in the room began following suit.

"Warning," said Zora. *"Outer hull breach detected. Deck seventeen, section nine."* As always, the artificial intelligence's voice remained almost serene even in the face of chaos.

"Holy shit. That thing just detonated," said Reno, and Stamets looked over to see her struggling with her own console. A moment's wrestling restored the image of the ship's underside, and the device was still there, affixed to the hull.

"I don't get it," said Adira, moving to stand next to Stamets. "It's still there."

Reno grunted in obvious irritation. "Some kind of shaped charge, aimed downward into the ship. The hole's only about thirty centimeters in diameter, but it punched right through the outer and inner hull. What the hell is that about? And it didn't even use all of the explosive material I'm seeing inside its shell, so the whole thing is still a bomb."

"Warning," said Zora. *"Computer system intrusion. Primary operating systems breach. Emergency firewalls and encryption protocols activaaaaaaaaaaaa—"*

Stamets, struggling to get his station back under control,

stopped cold as he took in what was happening. "I'm picking up multiple strings of unfamiliar code attempting to infiltrate the main computer. It's already breached one firewall. Zora, are you there?"

"I am attempting . . . block . . . trusion." The computer's voice was halting, almost a stutter.

Working with Stamets to wrestle his station back to working order, Adira said, "Whatever this thing is, it's picking up speed as it moves through the network's security perimeter."

Through the intercom, Burnham said, *"Engineering, we're detecting multiple attacks throughout the computer network. Whatever that thing pushed in here is targeting as many system entry points as it can at the same time."*

"It's a brute-force attack, Captain," said Stamets. "Trying to overwhelm our safeguards and exploit any weakness it finds or just creates for itself. Zora's staying ahead of it, but the attack program is spawning clones of itself and launching a multi-pronged assault on the system firewalls."

"Primary power is fluctuating," reported Burnham. *"We're switching to emergency power. We're without main propulsion and still linked to the docking port umbilical."*

Adira reported, "Secondary and tertiary security protocols are online. That'll buy us some time, but not much."

"How do we stop it?" asked Burnham.

Reno said, "Getting that thing off the hull would be a great start." She scowled as she reviewed the data scrolling across her displays. "Hang on a second. It's literally anchored itself to the ship." She used her fingers to zoom in on a section of the sensor feed, and Stamets saw a trio of what could only be metallic umbilical cables running from the device to *Discovery*'s outer hull. The image was clear enough for him to make out the puncture marks where the cabling, likely fitted with some kind of compressed-force projectile, had penetrated the duranium plating.

Another alarm echoed across the room, drawing Stamets's

attention to the new indicator flashing across his display. "Fire-walls and encryption protocols are still in place, but the way this thing is hammering at us, it's only a matter of time."

"What about a tractor beam?" asked Adira. "To grab it off the hull."

Stamets replied, "The emitters can't reach it at that angle. Same with phasers." He stopped, catching himself. "Ship's phasers, that is."

"Right," said Reno. "The angle for those is all wrong too." Then her expression shifted. "Hang on, cowboy—"

"I can go out there and cut it loose by hand." Crossing to a nearby equipment locker, Stamets extracted a tactical vest and began strapping it around his chest and back.

"Paul," said Burnham over the open channel. *"Wait. We don't know what that thing might do if you get too close to it."*

"Then I won't get too close to it, but if we need to defuse or deactivate that thing, it should be one of us. We've all gotten a look at it thanks to Reno's sensor scans." The vest secure and in place, he returned to his console and began entering commands. "She and Adira can feed me more information once I'm out there, but we don't have time to argue about this."

"You're right," said Burnham, much to his surprise. *"But you might need backup. I'm coming with you."*

Though he started to protest, Stamets saw the logic in her decision. "Yes. That's . . . that's a good idea, Captain." With a final check of his console, he transferred the device's location to his tri-com badge. To Reno and Adira, he said, "Keep monitoring that thing. No surprises, okay?"

"No surprises," said Adira.

Reno smirked. "No promises. Try not to get blown up out there."

Feeling a sudden urge to laugh, Stamets pressed the control on his vest and its built-in programmable-matter environmental suit began forming around him. It took only seconds for him to be encased from head to toe in the protective garment, a helmet with clear face shield coalescing around his head. That transition completed, he tapped his tri-com badge and the engineering room disappeared, replaced with *Discovery*'s hull.

He felt his suit's gravity boots attaching themselves to the duranium plating, and there was a moment of vertigo as he realized he was upside down in relation to many of the Sanctuary islands and clusters of buildings. The sphere's immense support lattice was even more prominent here, high above the main population centers, with the inner shell curving away from him to disappear beyond the habitat's inwardly curved horizon. While he thought he might expect a strong wind to buffet him the instant he was outside the ship, Stamets instead found the air here to be calm, and almost deathly quiet. If not for his present location, he could just be out for an afternoon stroll.

Just so long as I don't throw up, he thought.

"You okay?"

It was Burnham, walking across the hull toward him. She wore a suit like his, and she moved with practiced ease along the ship's outer skin.

"This is a little outside my normal wheelhouse," he said. Despite any lingering resentment he might feel toward her, Stamets was glad to have the captain watching his back.

Turning toward the rear of the ship, they began making their way along the hull. Out here in simulated daylight, the rogue device contrasted more noticeably against the ship's silver finish. Beyond it, Stamets could see the underside of the warp nacelles, which at present were connected to the ship via programmable matter. Their Bussard collectors still glowed blue even though he could tell they were operating at less than full power. It was an obvious indication the assault on the ship's computer systems was manifesting in numerous ways, only a few of them observable to the naked eye at this point.

As he and Burnham closed to within twenty meters of the device, he called up his holo-tricorder and set it to align with the information being collected by *Discovery*'s sensors. "It's broken through a second firewall. Zora's managed to throw up a new one on top of our existing perimeter, but it took this thing less time to get through that than the first one."

Tapping her tri-com badge, Burnham said, *"Engineering. What's your status?"*

Over the open comm link, Reno said, *"We've got a penetration into the backup memory banks, and we're seeing new scans coming from the device, sweeping the interior of the ship. Almost like it's searching for something. The code it deployed is directing search algorithms throughout the system. Firewalls and encryption are holding for the moment, but if you've got some awesome plan to get rid of it, now's the time."*

"Something's controlling it," said Burnham. *"What if we can overload its transceiver or whatever it's using for communication? If we can avoid damaging it, we might even be able to track back to a point of origin."*

As if in response to her suggestion, Stamets heard a groan of protest from ahead of them, and he saw the collectors on the warp nacelles go dark. He also noted illumination fading from the various portholes along the hull as well as the ship's exterior lighting.

"That's it for primary power," said Reno over the link. *"And it just busted through a third firewall. It's launching attacks against the main operating system. We're not going to keep it out much longer."*

His tricorder's visual display flashed red and Stamets threw out an arm, indicating for Burnham to stop her advance. "Hold it," he said. "It just scanned us and activated some kind of proximity sensor." He cast a glance in her direction. "Looks like you were right about getting too close. It definitely knows we're here."

"Heads up, kids," said Reno. *"That thing's getting feisty. We're tracking a new energy reading connected to its remaining ordnance payload. I think it's on a buildup to detonation."*

Burnham said, *"We can't let that thing blow while it's still attached to the ship."*

Almost in sync with her, Stamets flexed his wrist to activate the programmable-matter pendant on his suit sleeve. Phasers materialized in their hands, and he checked his weapon's power setting. "Any ideas on how hard we hit it?"

"*As hard as we can.*" Taking several steps backward, Burnham adjusted her weapon's power to maximum. Stamets mimicked her action before they both took aim at the device.

Burnham's eyes shifted toward him. "*Ready?*" When he nodded, they both returned to sighting in on the device. "*Fire.*"

Both phasers unleashed their own torrents of energy with sufficient power to penetrate the drone's outer casing. Sparks erupted from its interior and Stamets even saw it tremble before it tore free of the hull. He and Burnham fired again, sending the device away from the ship.

"*We need to get out of here,*" said Burnham. "*Back inside.*"

Stamets felt what he thought was the tingle of a transporter beam forming around him even before he tapped his tri-com badge. This was different from the familiar sensation he associated with Starfleet transporters. The process was slower, enough for him to see the cascade of energy coalescing to envelop him.

"*Paul!*" shouted Burnham, and he saw her reaching toward him before everything faded to black.

32

Burnham stood near an expansive window forming the outer wall of Queen Ki's sitting room. The chamber itself was appointed in elegant detail, beginning with heavy, colorful tapestries featuring abstract art that decorated the walls. The carpet was thick and plush, giving beneath her feet even though Burnham noted how it seemed immune to footprints or other signs of traffic. Sculptures and other mementos and personal effects occupied space on shelves or the small desk in the room's far corner. The large window offered Burnham a breathtaking, unfettered view of one of Sanctuary's larger population centers. Suspended between cross sections of the habitat's colossal support lattice, it was an artificial island in the sky with structures stretching upward toward the curved shell and plunging down to anchor points along the sphere's central core. Standing at the window, Burnham could almost believe she was flying. If only she could enjoy the obvious beauty Sanctuary offered.

Not today, she reminded herself. *Maybe tomorrow, but that depends on what happens right here, right now.*

"I cannot even begin to express my horror over what has happened," said Ki as she paced the length of the sitting room. "This attack on your ship is appalling, and the abduction of your officer is inexcusable. I have ordered our minister of security to direct all available resources toward securing his safe return." She stopped her pacing and shook her head. "I know your arrival has raised concerns among the population, but it has been obvious from the beginning that you presented no threat. If I believed otherwise, I would never have permitted you to enter Sanctuary. One might reasonably think a queen's decisions had a bearing on matters of this sort, but I am apparently mistaken."

Her arms were clasped behind her back as she attempted to affect a composed demeanor. There were no guards with them in the sitting room. No advisors, and no aides or assistants. That alone had to have sent the queen's security detail into an apoplectic fit, but still she sent them away, seemingly confident that her well-being was not at risk. To Burnham, it was the ultimate gesture of trust and respect, one perhaps rarely if ever afforded to anyone, let alone an outsider. She suspected it was a privilege extended to no non-Xahean in centuries, and certainly not to anyone representing the Federation. The magnitude of this moment was not lost on Burnham, and if circumstances were different, she would be nothing but honored and humbled to stand here.

At the moment, however, circumstances were what they were.

"I understand there's been a new wave of protests," said Burnham. She already knew about the unrest, thanks to *Discovery* continuing to monitor local broadcasts even as the crew completed repairs from the drone incident and assessed the full impact of its attack. "Opinions seem rather divided on what happened."

Ki sighed. "Indeed." She tapped a control on the bracelet adorning her left wrist, and in response to that simple command an array of six holographic displays appeared at the center of the room. Each window depicted a different scene, but it was easy for Burnham to recognize the theme connecting them.

"These six demonstrations are just the most recent," said the queen. "They are but the latest in a series that began after the first reports of the attack against your ship became public. Opinions cover a broad spectrum, with many either applauding or denouncing the incident. As you can expect, outspoken voices championing many different positions are using this to fuel their rhetoric." She activated another half dozen displays. Each featured columns of scrolling text interspersed with images, most of it moving too fast for Burnham to decipher.

"Our social interaction platforms are peaking at levels I have not seen in quite some time. Regardless of what some might believe, your arrival continues to have a great influence on my people, Captain." Ki turned away from the displays and they vanished. "Unfortunately, there are those who would be quite happy for you to leave and never return, and we cannot discount the possibility of motivated individuals doing whatever they could to facilitate or even hasten your departure. Likewise, we cannot rule out the possibility this attack might be punishment for your releasing the separatists back to us. There are those who would see that as you aligning yourselves against their cause."

"We haven't ruled out simple sabotage or retaliatory action," said Burnham. A full assessment was still being compiled, but aside from the point of impact where the device landed and then blasted through the hull, physical damage to *Discovery* itself was minimal. Of greater concern was the penetration of the computer system and the attention paid to key areas of the ship's vast storehouse of information.

"If that is the case, then anyone could be the responsible party. Separatists, traditionalists, or simply people acting out for your having disrupted our community." Ki sighed. "It only makes the task of apprehending them that much more difficult."

Burnham said, "Your Highness, you should know I don't believe this was an act of simple civil disobedience or even retaliation against us. This was someone with an agenda. They scanned our ship and attacked our computer. They seemed to be looking for information. Specifically, information about our spore drive. I don't know if that means they see it—and by extension, my ship and crew—as a tool or a threat, but they could've taken any member of my crew and they chose Stamets. I don't believe that's coincidence."

What she chose not to say—even though she suspected the queen already knew it—was that *Discovery*'s entire sensor array was being employed in a search effort for Stamets. Finding a single human among millions of Xaheans presented a challenge, the effort hampered by an inability to track his communicator. Whoever had taken him understood the lifeline that represented and had taken appropriate steps to neutralize it. Simply scanning for his human life signs would take far longer, and Burnham had already received reports that areas of Sanctuary were proving resistant to scans. She was certain he was alive, as there was no logic in abducting him for the sole purpose of killing him. The apparent interest in the ship's spore drive only strengthened her suspicions.

Moving to stand before the window, Ki placed a hand against the portal's surface and closed her eyes as if taking in whatever warmth might be making its way through the material. While Sanctuary did not have a sun, of course, the sphere's internal environment suggested a formidable climate system designed to simulate for its inhabitants the sensations one could only experience on a living, breathing world.

"I have never set foot upon any planet, except in my dreams," she said, keeping her eyes closed. "When I do this, I can almost imagine what that must be like."

Even though she had spent the bulk of her own life living aboard starships or within other enclosed, artificial ecosystems, Burnham still relished the feel of an actual sun's rays on her skin, the sound of waves breaking against a beach, or wind rustling through the leaves in a dense forest. All of that could be re-created on a holodeck, of course, just as a facsimile could be constructed, as was the case with Sanctuary, but none of that was a substitute for the real thing.

"You understand what at least some of your people want," said Burnham. "Perhaps it's something they all want but are afraid to admit it. They don't want to put themselves at risk and suffer the fate their ancestors endured. I understand that, but there's no reason your people have to face that fear alone. Not anymore."

Opening her eyes, the queen said, "Even after what has happened, you still feel this way? You believe there is a path forward for us, working together?"

"I do. We can start by working together to find my officer. Then we find common ground where all Xaheans can stand and have their concerns heard, and we go from there."

"Your optimism is admirable, Captain." Turning from the window, Ki said, "I am expecting an update from the security minister at any time. I will inform you of any new information I receive, including any developments in our investigations. I know you are scanning Sanctuary in the hopes of finding your officer. If your efforts uncover anything, I trust you will share it with me?"

Burnham nodded. "Absolutely, Your Highness."

Taking her leave of the queen, she activated her transporter and the sitting room vanished, replaced by *Discovery*'s bridge. Along with the bridge crew, Cleveland Booker was on hand as she materialized.

"Welcome back," said Booker. "How'd it go?"

"As well as I could expect, or hope." Burnham looked around the bridge. "What's our current status?"

Rising from the command chair to make way for her, Commander Rhys replied, "Repairs to the hull and related areas are completed, Captain, but we're still determining the extent of the computer intrusion. It appears the attack was designed to interrogate our systems and design software for insertion into our core processes. We've detected a number of compiled object modules and even more source code introduced into the active operating system and a number of application and data libraries." He gestured to where Tilly stood at the science station. "Lieutenant Tilly is working with engineering and Zora to root out everything, but they're running into problems."

Taking her cue from the first officer, Tilly said, "Malicious software is adaptive by design, but this is like that times ten." She waved her arms as she spoke, as if the gesture would emphasize the magnitude of the situation. "It's aggressive, apparently designed to infiltrate a computer system, translate whatever source code it finds, and immediately begin writing new code to either disrupt, bypass, or just outright replace what's already there with its own embedded routines. I'm seeing indications it can corrupt or redefine anything from a simple request to turn on the lights or replicate your lunch to the navigational systems or even the calculations we need for the spore drive. And it has its own detection countermeasures. It can literally sense when it's being hunted and reconfigure itself to avoid being caught by a code scan. I've never seen anything like it."

"So what do we do about it?" asked Burnham.

Tilly replied, "Zora is in there, fighting it her own way. She's basically trying to play their own game against them, laying logic traps and seeing if these infiltration routines take the bait. Meanwhile, the bad code is still loose in our system. Our biggest success so far is keeping it out of our data banks. It tried at least three times to access files about the spore drive but couldn't break through the firewalls. We've tried restoring from backups, and that's worked to keep us in control of vital systems, but it's not enough. Until we figure out what makes it work, we're just trying to predict its next moves based on what it's already done."

"Let me guess," said Booker. "It's good at anticipating that as well."

"You got it." Tilly blew out her breath. "Devious little shit, is what it is."

"But we're still in control?" asked Burnham.

Reaching up to wipe her forehead, Tilly nodded. "For now. Between the restores from protected backups and Zora figuring out how to outflank it, we might be able to stay ahead of it long enough to flush it out once and for all."

Her response was punctuated by the bridge's overhead lighting and several consoles blinking, turning off, then resetting.

"Work in progress," said Tilly.

"Pull whoever and whatever you think you need to solve this." Burnham looked to Booker. "Feel like lending a hand?"

The courier nodded. "No problem." To Tilly, he said, "Where do you want me?"

"Engineering," replied the science officer. "Adira and Commander Reno are down there, but without Commander Stamets they could use the extra hand."

With a mock salute toward Burnham, Booker said, "I'm on it," before tapping his personal transporter and vanishing.

Burnham watched him leave before returning her attention to the bridge crew. "Are we having any luck trying to find Stamets?"

"Nothing so far," replied Tilly. "Whoever took him masked their transporter signature. It's how they were able to drop that drone on us at near-point-blank range. So far, we have no way to track either of those transports to a point of origin."

"Whoever took him did it for a reason," said Keyla Detmer at the helm console. "Either they grabbed the first person they could, or they want him specifically."

"If they'd just wanted a hostage," replied Joann Owosekun, shifting in her seat at the forward operations station next to Detmer, "they could've grabbed one of us down on the surface." The operations officer shook her head. "Between Commander Stamets and scanning our computer for information about the spore drive? This was targeted."

Already convinced of this on her own, Burnham still liked hearing others arrive on their own at the same conclusion. It told her the suspicions she had harbored since watching Stamets disappear before her eyes were on the right track.

Fine, she told herself. *Now what?*

"Whoever took him knows we'll be scanning for his life signs, so count on those being blocked, too, but there has to be some other way to run them down." She pondered the question for a moment. "How many transporter nodes are active inside Sanctuary?"

"Hundreds, probably," said Rhys. "We'd need to run a more comprehensive scan of the interior."

Owosekun said, "Maybe we can filter out units that weren't operational, or at least in the midst of an active transport cycle at the time that drone arrived or Commander Stamets vanished. That might narrow the number of possibilities."

Detmer asked, "Captain, what did the queen say about all of this?"

Burnham replied, "According to her, their security ministry is mobilizing all available resources to search for him."

"That tracks," said Rhys, who had returned to his tactical station. He swiped at one of his console's holographic control surfaces and gestured to the main viewscreen, where Burnham now saw a comprehensive map. It took her a moment to recognize it as a representation of Sanctuary's interior surfaces. Dozens of flashing blue icons were scattered across the map.

"What are we looking at?" she asked, taking in the schematic.

Rhys replied, "More protests. There's been a definite uptick in them since the one involving our away teams. And they seem to be escalating. The reports we're monitoring indicate infrastructure and property damage along with physical altercations and associated injuries."

"Don't tell me," said Burnham. "It's because of us."

"We've been listening to official communications," said Owosekun. "Some of it is encrypted, and we're working on decoding, but a lot of broadcasts are on open channels anyone can monitor. There's chatter about following up leads not just for the commander but also suspects believed to have instigated protests or other actions that turned violent. It's a definite escalation from what we saw before the attack on us. According to media reports, there are as many incidents triggered by separatists as there are by those who stand against them."

"But we were the trigger," said Burnham. "Not directly, of course, but our presence here is influencing the situation."

Rhys said, "That seems to be the prevailing opinion. Separatists want us to do more to help them, while other parties want us to leave. As for the civil unrest, there are demands for heightened action from the security ministry. Two Xahean council members have called for curfews and a greater law enforcement presence in public." He frowned. "From what I can tell, that's not normal for these people."

"There's a lot of that going around." Burnham sighed. That all of this had spawned from a simple rescue operation was not a development she had envisioned after leaving Federation Headquarters. Now she and her people were neck deep in the internal squabble of a sovereign state. Their very presence was being viewed as antagonistic, and even if they left right now, the effects of their influence would likely be felt for the foreseeable future. *Discovery* and its crew had unwittingly added fuel to a smoldering fire, threatening to unleash an inferno.

Admiral Vance is going to kill me, she thought.

"It's probably going to get worse the longer this goes on," she said, looking to each member of her bridge crew. "We need to find Stamets, and fast."

33

The two Xaheans flanking him were dressed in nondescript clothing, but Stamets's gut told him they were law enforcement officers or military members or something similar. The way they carried themselves and the weapons they wielded suggested considerable training and familiarity based on experience. Speech patterns, body language, and other subtle cues only served to reinforce his suspicions. Were they mercenaries? Given his surroundings and how he had come to be here, he decided that was as plausible a theory as any other he might contemplate.

The path from the oversized cargo container that served as a makeshift brig took Stamets and his escorts on something of a guided tour through portions of what had to be a vast subterranean cavern. Unlike natural cave formations and tunnels carved by millions of years of rushing water, the passages here were of obvious artificial design. He decided they had to be somewhere beneath one of Sanctuary's population centers. An artificial construct like this habitat was at its most basic an immense machine, built to sustain the fragile organisms who called it home.

"I'm guessing this isn't on the regular tour," he said, earning him annoyed expressions from each of his escorts. Neither said anything. Whether that was due to orders given by a superior or a simple lack of interest was anyone's guess.

It was his first look at what Stamets supposed he should call his prison, having materialized inside the container after being snatched from *Discovery*'s hull. Two other Xaheans, a male and a female, were waiting for him and upon his arrival quickly relieved him of his phaser, tri-com badge, and tactical vest. He suspected those articles were destroyed by now, if for no other reason than to make it more difficult to track him. The badge was the biggest loss, for without it he had no way to contact the ship. While he might be able to repurpose some piece of communications equipment he found here, Stamets doubted he would have such an opportunity. This was the first time he had seen anything beyond the confines of his cell.

How long had he been here? Not more than a few hours, Stamets suspected, given hunger or fatigue was not a factor. Even if that was the case, his cell featured enough light to see by along with a rudimentary food replicator and lavatory that addressed the most pressing reasons for him to require leaving confinement. The duration of his captivity was also important so far as the efforts he knew were underway to find him. Captain Burnham would not rest until that happened, just as he knew her patience with the Xahean leadership and anyone else standing in her way would have a limit. Unless things progressed to her satisfaction, there would come a time when she took matters into her own hands, regulation or diplomacy or good manners be damned.

Nice when it works in your favor, isn't it?

It was a variation on the same wayward thought he had pondered since his capture. While he might have his issues with Michael Burnham and her methods, right now he was counting on them. He knew that presented a conflict of sorts, with himself rather than anyone else, including Burnham. Assuming he managed to get out of his current situation, he knew it was an issue that could no longer go unaddressed.

Ahead of them, Stamets could hear the sounds of people and equipment at work. Maneuvering around a series of oversized storage containers and worktables arranged in haphazard fashion revealed an area of the cavern where the walls extended even higher toward a curved ceiling. Even here, the distinction between a natural cave and a space created for a deliberate purpose was obvious. At the center of the spacious chamber was an immense construct, which to Stamets resembled a form of power generator. Dozens of meters in height, it still did not reach the ceiling. Scaffolding, ladders, and smaller equipment along with numerous Xaheans moved in, on, and around the machine, if indeed that's what it was. A web of conduits and support struts ran from the construct to the cavern walls. Several of the conduits glowed, channeling energy from some unseen source. What if it *was* the source? Stamets could feel the raw power emanating from the machine, but there was nothing to suggest its purpose. Recalling Captain Burnham's report that Sanctuary was capable of space travel on its own, he wondered if this might be part of what had to be a massive propulsion system. Despite his chosen field of study, he possessed little in the way of actual knowledge of warp drive or other aspects of pushing a starship through the cosmos. He understood the basic theories and principles of warp travel, learning what he needed to pursue his own goal of rendering such technology obsolete. What little knowledge he possessed was enough to tell him this was not a warp core or a component to such a system.

"Commander Stamets."

The voice came from behind him, and he turned to see two Xaheans. Both male, one was older with long, unkempt gray and black hair, dressed in a dark-green utilitarian coverall garment that, like its bedraggled wearer, looked in desperate need of laundering. His somewhat younger companion, on the other hand, sported a crisp gray jacket and slacks that had a military air about them. His black hair was pulled back from his face and secured behind his neck. Each Xahean's face was anointed with its own facial tattoos, with the older, scruffier male's markings somewhat faded while being much more elaborate.

"How do you know my name?" asked Stamets, uncomfortable with what this simple revelation suggested. "Who are you?"

The Xahean in uniform replied, "We know a great deal about you, Commander. Learning about people is just one of my duties. My name is Deputy Minister Sen. I am an officer serving the minister of security and Her Royal Highness, Queen

Ki." He held out his hand as if to indicate their surroundings. "My responsibilities include safeguarding the Xahean people and our home from threats both within our community and beyond its boundaries."

"Does safeguarding the Xahean people mean kidnapping people who've come in peace, mean you no harm, and in fact have offered to help you?" His voice growing louder as he talked, Stamets noted how his two escorts stepped closer as though offering silent warnings about his conduct.

"You can go," said Sen, waving away the guards. Another gesture was enough for them to move a respectful distance away, leaving Stamets alone with the security minister and his companion. Stamets watched as they made their way to an archway leading to a connecting tunnel or perhaps another chamber, taking up positions near that entrance while keeping their attentions focused on him.

With the escorts out of the immediate area, Sen gestured to his fellow Xahean. "This is Professor Fostra. He is the current leader of a scientific project that has been underway here since not long after the dilithium cataclysm, or 'the Burn,' as it is more commonly known."

Though he did not wish to be obvious, Stamets could not help taking in his surroundings. With the guards well out of arm's reach, it occurred to him there were any number of hiding places within the cavern. The sounds of work continuing elsewhere in the chamber told him there had to be tools or something else he might use as a weapon. While he had never seen much point to the armed and unarmed personal combat classes given to cadets at Starfleet Academy, now he was thankful even for that rudimentary training. All he needed was an opening and a bit of luck, he decided, and then he would see where that took him.

"If you are wondering about possible escape," the minister said, as if reading Stamets's mind, "I will save you the effort. The only way in or out of this facility is via transporter. All physical exits, like the transporter, are coded to authorized personnel only. You will not be leaving without my express permission."

Stamets asked, "Will I be leaving?"

"That is certainly my intention, Commander, for I have no desire to harm you. As I said before, we know much about you, but there remain things as yet unrevealed to us. Everything we do know tells us you are potentially of great value to all the Xahean people. Harming you would be a waste of a precious resource, and indeed a detriment to those I am sworn to protect."

Unable to keep his irritation in check, Stamets said, "That's an awful lot of words to say you need something from me." To his surprise, Sen laughed.

"I am trying to convey what you represent to us. You are not a simple hostage. We brought you here because you are a singular individual, someone we believe holds the key to everything to which Professor Fostra and his colleagues have devoted the better part of their lives, continuing the work begun and furthered by uncounted Xaheans who came before them."

Scowling as he processed the unexpected yet effusive praise, Stamets shook his head. "You talk about me being able to help all of your people. I'm not a medical doctor, and I'm not an engineer. I'm an astromycologist. A *scientist*. I've spent most of my life in a lab. The only reason I was ever assigned to *Discovery* in the first place was because—"

Realization dawned, and Stamets froze in midsentence. It took him an extra second to realize his mouth was still open in the midst of trying to form the next word of his reply. Pulling himself together, he turned to look once more at the massive construct dominating the cavern behind him. The basic shape was unfamiliar, its size reinforced by the ladders, ramps, panels, and hatches he suspected enabled engineers and other technicians to access internal components. The power conduits, he now decided, could be input as well as output paths. It had to be a generator of sorts, but that was the most basic definition that could be applied. He imagined it receiving enormous sums of energy in order to channel it outward, but what happened between those two processes?

Someone who holds the key, he reminded himself. *To everything.*

"You built . . . a *spore drive?*"

For the first time, Fostra spoke. "It is more accurate to say we have endeavored to build such a device. The initial efforts began generations ago, not long after your vessel came to our world. Queen Me Hani Ika Hali Ka Po extrapolated various aspects of your ship's propulsion system based on scans collected at that time. Among her various talents, the queen was a gifted engineer, but despite her best efforts, success eluded her, and much of what you were able to accomplish remained a mystery. She eventually abandoned her efforts, but all of her research was preserved in the royal archives, labeled as little more than a scientific and engineering curiosity."

Stamets was already racing ahead, piecing it together. "Then the Burn happened. People tried developing all sorts of alternatives. Nothing worked, or at best worked but not nearly as well as dilithium-based warp drive."

"That is correct," said Sen. "We know of one race, the Laguzai, who attempted to replicate Romulan warp technology from a time after your ship disappeared. They developed an artificial quantum-singularity energy-generation matrix, but it ended in failure. The moon on which they built their prototype was destroyed, resulting in catastrophic damage to their homeworld's atmosphere and killing most of its population. A fraction of their race remains, living as refugees on various other planets." The security minister shook his head. "We obviously wish to avoid a similar fate."

Stamets had heard of the tragic event, which in turn led to him reading up on the twenty-fourth-century technology that inspired it. The forced quantum-singularity method devised by the Federation's former adversaries had proven quite effective, but not without its share of problems and dangers. No form of faster-than-light travel was completely safe, he knew, but redundant protective measures had served to mitigate such risks for centuries. The Romulans had taken such systems even further, owing to their need to mask the energy emissions of a vessel's warp drive while employing a cloaking device. In his estimation, the risks posed by the Romulan method were greater than those inherent in conventional dilithium-based methods, which were of course hardly foolproof, as the Burn had demonstrated in rather dramatic fashion.

Studying the immense mechanism with fresh eyes, he realized now what it represented. "This is your version of the spore reaction cube?"

"That is its intended purpose," said Sen. "Acquiring and cultivating the proper species of mycelium spores proved quite challenging. That alone took several generations of searching before we found a world where the fungus grew indigenously."

Fostra added, "However, we believe there may still be obstacles to navigate in that regard. To date, all of our testing has been conducted via computer simulation models, or with much smaller vehicles we can control outside of Sanctuary. While computer modeling reveals the potential, our actual testing efforts have yielded no success. Our theory is the spores we cultivated are not the correct species, allowing at best a fleeting contact with the mycelial realm. Beyond that, all of our attempts to control passage to and from that realm have failed. We obviously cannot risk exposing Sanctuary to that sort of danger."

The professor looked past Stamets to the machine. "This version is connected to the habitat's primary energy plants and its conventional warp drive in a manner similar to your drive's installation aboard your ship, so that it might draw the power necessary to achieve a proper transition."

For the second time since the conversation began, Stamets felt his jaw slacken in disbelief as he turned back to Sen and Fostra.

"You want to push *Sanctuary* through the mycelial network?" he asked.

Now the machine's size made sense. The amount of energy required to produce a controlled entry to the mycelial plane for something the size of the Xahean habitat would be staggering, but Sanctuary was already equipped to move itself at warp speed. In some ways, it was not that big a leap. The calculations necessary to make a safe transition and back again would be orders of magnitude more complex. Or would they? Stamets realized he was already pulling the problem apart, breaking it down into smaller pieces so he could solve each component before reassembling everything once he had a solution. Was it feasible? Perhaps, with the appropriate preparation and everything computed and tested to within a centimeter of its life, but Stamets was beginning to think it was not so impossible as he at first envisioned.

It doesn't make it any less insane, he thought.

Sen nodded. "That is our intention, yes. Even with the Burn's lingering effects, the galaxy once again grows too small for our comfort. We are reminded how our discovery of faster-than-light propulsion introduced us to so many spacefaring races, many of which saw nothing in us but something to be exploited." He paused, leveling an accusatory glare at Stamets. "While others stood idle, observing such atrocities from afar. We have spent generations ensuring no Xahean will ever again endure such oppression. To that end, we have worked toward a singular goal: finding a home for our people where we will forever be free from the threat of subjugation."

He gestured to the machine. "We thought this device would be our salvation, but we have come to understand it is but one part of a much grander solution, Commander Stamets. We now know the critical component we lack . . . *is you.* Even more remarkable was that as generations passed and our work stalled, we knew—thanks to Queen Po—that you eventually would arrive, traveling from the distant past to your future and our present reality. Fate has seen fit to bring you to us, Commander, like a spiritual savior."

It was not the first time Stamets had been called a "solution," or even a "savior." During the Federation-Klingon War, Gabriel Lorca—in actuality, his doppelganger from the dark, alternate universe—had referred to him that way. Lorca had pushed the idea of service to the war effort while in reality manipulating Stamets for his own selfish agenda. Still, Starfleet had given Stamets a platform for his work, hoping the spore drive would give them a tactical advantage over the Klingons. It had galled him to be used in such a manner, but it allowed him to prove his concepts and make instantaneous interstellar travel a reality. He had hoped such a technological leap might be used for good, but of course it ended up not being used at all. *Discovery* remained the only real expression of his life's work. Stamets knew he was at best a minor footnote in a version of history known to but a precious few.

He seemed now to have an opportunity to change that.

But at what cost?

34

Culber could not stop pacing.

It was not until he nearly ran face-first into one of the oversized display monitors set into sickbay's angled bulkheads that he realized he was doing it again. Then the screen flickered before its display reset, jolting him out of his near trance. He stopped before colliding with the monitor, blinking several times as he turned to reorient himself. He was alone, of course. None of the treatment beds were occupied, and he knew if he looked into the recovery unit, he would find no one there either. With no one else to talk to, he was left to himself to figure out how he had managed to leave and cross the length of the room.

"Damn it," he said, shaking his head.

More than once, he had tried to do something, anything, to keep his mind occupied. He had forced himself to focus on work, but with no injuries or illness among the crew requiring treatment or otherwise demanding his attention, there was precious little to occupy his attention. The idea of devoting time to the never-ending stream of medical-record updates, consultation updates, or reports for the captain and Starfleet Medical was laughable, at least right now. Although he took all of that seriously, along with the myriad other responsibilities that came with being the medical officer on a Federation starship, for the moment none of it seemed important. It would all be there, waiting for him, at the conclusion of the current situation.

No matter how it turns out.

"Stop it," he snapped. With no one else in the room, Culber felt free to chastise himself.

Except he was not alone.

"Doctor?"

Startled by the unexpected voice, Culber whipped around to see Adira Tal standing at the sickbay entrance, accompanied by Doctor Arbusala. Each sported matching expressions of obvious concern, aimed at him. His own features must have been anything but welcoming, as Adira held up both hands.

"I'm . . . sorry," they said. "We didn't mean to surprise you. I just wanted to—"

Culber waved away the apology. "No, it's all right. I'm the one who's sorry. I didn't see you standing there."

"In the ensign's defense, we only just arrived," said Arbusala as he and Adira stepped farther into the room.

Clearing their throat, Adira added, "I was just . . . I wanted to check up on you."

"And after encountering them in the hallway, I decided to pay my own visit." Arbusala eyed him in that way all therapists seemed to exude. "I also wanted to see how you're doing."

Do they teach that level of annoying at therapist school? Culber gritted his teeth to prevent voicing the question aloud. Instead, he asked, "How I'm doing?" He knew as soon as the words left his lips they were too harsh, laced as they were with an unfair indictment. On an intellectual level, he knew Arbusala meant well.

"I'm sorry," he said, composing himself and taking care to speak with a gentler tone. "That was very rude of me."

"No apologies necessary, Doctor," replied the Denobulan, his voice, as always, even-keeled. "We all empathize with what you must be feeling just now."

Empathize, Culber thought. *Not understand.* Yes, the words were synonyms to each other, but he felt there was a subtle yet very important distinction in how they were to be used, in particular when employed in a health-care setting or when attempting to offer comfort or consideration to someone in the grips of crisis. It made sense for Arbusala to comprehend the need for such sensitivity, but Culber suspected that awareness was less about the professional training he received than the doctor's own character. It brought Culber another measure of reassurance that he decided he needed just now.

Looking to Adira, he said, "I thought you were in engineering."

"I am. I mean, I was. Zora's managed to contain most of the invasive software, and now she's running a deep diagnostic. She's pretty much taken over all computer functions as a protective measure. There's nothing we can do until she lets us back in, and I wanted to check on you." Adira tapped their chest. "Gray did too."

That made Culber smile. "I appreciate that." He released a heavy sigh. "I just wish I could help," he said. "Just do *something*. I know the captain's doing everything she can, and I've tried to concentrate on my work, but it's all a blur in my head." He gestured to the empty sickbay. "Doctors are supposed to be thankful when they have no patients, but here I am, hoping for the chance to help anyone, with anything."

For the first time, it occurred to him that he had no appointments for the informal counseling sessions he offered to the crew. Those had trickled off while *Discovery* and its crew were enjoying the brief shore leave granted to them by Admiral Vance. He had expected them to resume, even in limited fashion, when the ship departed Federation Headquarters. The mission to deliver dilithium to the planet Evora and hopefully reestablish formal contact and interstellar relations with the people of that world was supposed to provide Doctor Arbusala an opportunity to observe the crew while carrying out its duties, but Culber had hoped at least a few people might take advantage of the four-day voyage to see him as well. With very few exceptions, that had not been the case. Rather than feel disappointed, he chose to interpret this as the crew just needing a break from what had been a very hectic routine. It was reasonable to assume such a respite included not being harangued by the ship's would-be therapist.

Especially now that we have an actual therapist aboard, Culber mused. *One who knows what he's doing.*

"It's natural to want to feel useful," said Adira. "I hate just standing around, waiting for something to happen or someone to tell me what to do. It's worse when there's someone we think needs our help, and we can't do anything about it."

Arbusala added, "This is especially true for humans, and particularly so during emergency situations. It is just one of the things that makes your species so remarkable."

Culber sighed. "I don't know about that. You've probably been around humans long enough to know we can be pretty self-involved when we want to be."

"Perhaps." To his credit, the Denobulan capped his reply with a knowing look, and Culber wondered if he saw a gleam of humor in the doctor's eyes. "To answer your question, I have observed your people over a great many years, Doctor, and I am impressed with your seemingly inherent ability to set aside such perspectives and behavior and come to the aid of someone in need. It is a trait Starfleet cultivates, but it also is a quality that must be present in the first place. The raw material, if you will. Starfleet simply polishes the rough stone."

"I guess you're right," said Culber. "Maybe that's why I'm upset with myself. I'm alone in here, moping and pretending I'm attempting to work, when I could be doing something to help someone else. So the ship doesn't need a doctor right now. I could go help Tilly, or engineering."

Gesturing toward him, Arbusala said, "There may be occasions when a bout of self-involvement is inappropriate, but this is not one of those times. You are *entitled* to your feelings, Doctor. Your feelings for your husband, and your feelings about yourself."

Adira stepped closer. "You have to take care of yourself, Doctor, because some of us are counting on you to take care of us." They extended their arms. "And sometimes that means we have to look out for the one who's looking after us." When

Culber hesitated, they added, "This is Gray asking to do this, too, by the way."

His own laugh caught him by surprise, at the same time as he felt tears. "Well, how can I refuse that." He let Adira embrace him, wrapping his arms around their back. "Thank you. You too, Gray."

Once Adira released him, he asked, "I promised myself I wouldn't bother Captain Burnham asking about Paul every five minutes. Have you heard anything?"

"Not yet, I'm afraid," replied Arbusala. "I have tried to avoid the bridge and other areas that are devoted to the search effort so as not to be a distraction. Rest assured there is a comprehensive effort to find and retrieve Commander Stamets."

Despite the reassurance, Culber knew it was not that simple, and he once again felt despair welling up within him. "I can't help thinking about what he might be going through."

"You can't do that," replied Adira. "You have to remain positive about this."

Arbusala said, "The ensign is correct, Doctor. Captain Burnham is all but certain the commander was taken for a purpose, which means they cannot harm him if they hope to achieve whatever goal they have."

"And what if they achieve this goal before we find him?" asked Culber. He knew it was unwise and even unhealthy to fixate on such negative thoughts, but they came unbidden. Nothing he did could combat them.

"Captain Burnham won't let that happen," said Arbusala. "She will do everything in her power to ensure that does not happen." Before Culber could protest, Adira held up a hand.

"He's right, Doctor." When Culber eyed them, they straightened their posture. "I haven't known her as long or as well as any of you, but I've known more than a few Starfleet captains." They shrugged. "Well, Tal has, but you get my meaning. Not all of them were great leaders, but the ones who were? They all had the same drive to succeed, to face adversity and beat it.

They'd get very obstinate and protective when their crews were concerned. Nothing would stop them from keeping their people safe. Not rules, not laws, not being outnumbered or outgunned. Nothing. They're the ones we read about in history books. Captain Burnham is one of those leaders. If it can be done, she'll do it."

When they paused, Culber got the sense they were realizing how uncharacteristically vocal they were being. These were not the words of a young, untried ensign on their first assignment. This was the experience of multiple lifetimes coming to the fore. Triumphs and failures, accumulated knowledge and unanswered questions, wondrous achievements and roads not taken. In this moment, all of that came pouring out of this sixteen-year-old with hundreds of years of memories, wisdom, and attitude at their disposal.

For his part, he was amazed by the conviction in their voice. It was as much confidence as he had heard them put forth since their arrival aboard *Discovery*. At any other time, he might take a cynic's view and dismiss their words as so much naïveté. Instead, he chose to take strength from them.

"I have to tell you," he said after a moment, "I like this side of you."

Adira nodded. "Yeah, that actually felt pretty good."

The sickbay lighting blinked at the same time every bulkhead and display monitor went dark. All of this was followed by an alert tone and the voice of Zora.

"Attention, all personnel. Noncritical systems are being deactivated until further notice. Ensign Tal, please report to engineering."

"That doesn't sound good," said Arbusala. "You should go. I'll remain here."

"I don't need a babysitter." Culber tried to make it sound supportive, but to his ears it came off as petulant. "What I mean is, if you have somewhere else you need to be, I understand."

When the Denobulan smiled this time, the entire lower

half of his face stretched in order to commit to the effort. "I'm where I think I can best serve *Discovery*'s crew, Doctor."

Wasn't it just a couple of days ago that I hated him? Culber almost laughed at his unspoken question. "I'd like that."

As if satisfied their work here was done, Adira turned to head for the exit. They had reached the door, which opened at their approach, when Culber called out to them.

"Adira. Thank you." He placed a hand to his chest. "Both of you."

The ensign straightened as they drew themself up, their expression one of gratitude. "We both figure we owe you at least one."

35

This was not Burnham's operation. If she were in charge, they would already have dropped the hammer.

Clenching her jaw as she pressed herself against the wall, with both hands she gripped her phaser in a low ready carry position. To her left, Officer Maja Hin Bo Yina of the Ministry of Security adopted a similar pose, one hand holding the Xahean equivalent of a phaser while the other grasped a small cylindrical object. Beyond him, a member of his security reaction team, Kar Tibi Ovo Dran, crouched next to a door and the open access panel set into the wall next to it. The security officer held a small device in her left hand that projected a holographic image of a technical schematic onto the wall before her. Her other hand was inside the wall cavity, working on internal components Burnham could not see.

To her right, four more members of Yina's security reaction team waited. Burnham wore a standard Starfleet tactical uniform and vest that was not so different from the protective clothing and equipment harnesses used by the reaction team. Like the Xaheans and the rest of her team, Burnham wore the hearing protection and tinted eye shields provided by Yina. The ear coverings blocked out most outside noise while also featuring a communication system the reaction team used when conducting a covert infiltration, such as the one in which Burnham and her people were now participating.

"Will you be able to open it?" asked Yina, looking at his subordinate. His voice was low and just audible in Burnham's ear coverings.

Dran nodded. *"The internal alert system is active, and it appears to have been modified from most standard residential models. I can bypass it, but it takes more time."*

The message from Queen Ki had come just as Burnham arrived on the bridge, having stolen away for an hour to catch a catnap. Brief respites of this sort had been all she allowed herself since Stamets's abduction, as she wanted to be close if anything changed regarding the search effort. She was therefore on hand when the queen invited her to participate in raiding the residence of two Xaheans suspected of contributing to the protests involving *Discovery*'s away teams and with a startling connection to the attack on the ship itself. Rather than bring a security detail of her own, Burnham had opted to come alone and follow the security ministry's lead.

To her right, a younger male Xahean agent had activated his own tricorder-like scanner. A small holographic representation of the residence's interior hung in the air. *"Yina, I can confirm two life signs. One male, one female. I am also detecting trace amounts of the explosive compound. I do not believe there are any actual devices on the premises."*

Yina nodded. *"Excellent. One less variable in this equation."*

During the pre-mission briefing, the security officer had used the term "variable" to describe any of the dynamic elements the team might face when making this entry. One of these elements was the presence of a transporter inhibitor located on the premises. Beaming the suspects out of the residence to a location where they could be safely questioned was not an option, so Yina and his people were forced to rely on more traditional apprehension methods. Complicating the issue was the visual record of the residence's owner, which appeared to have been a falsified document using another Xahean's photograph. At least one of the people now inside the residence was using a forged identity to camouflage their movements.

"Stand by," said Dran. Turning to look past Yina, Burnham saw an orange indicator on her holoprojector change to blue. The hologram disappeared and she nodded to Yina, pocketing the device before brandishing her own weapon.

Yina raised the hand with the cylinder. *"Open it."*

The subordinate reached into the wall cavity once more and the door slid aside. With what Burnham suspected was practiced ease, Yina flung the cylinder into the room, and Burnham heard it strike something. A loud flash erupted through the doorway and into the corridor, followed by a deep booming sound Burnham heard, despite her ear protection, and felt against her body. The stun grenade's detonation was still echoing into the corridor when she detected the first cries of surprise and fear.

"Go!"

First in line, Yina charged through the open doorway and was stopped by something striking him in the chest. The force of the impact was enough to drive him back into the hallway and slam him into the opposite wall, where he collapsed in a heap. Burnham started to move toward him, but two more projectiles burst into the corridor, driving into the wall above Yina's head.

Crouching low, Burnham leaned just far enough into the entryway to fire her phaser. She angled the shot up from her near-kneeling position as she saw a figure run down a hallway at the back of the residence's front room. Advancing through the entry, she sidestepped to her left away from the door. Dran followed her, mirroring Burnham's movements and dodging to her right. Burnham glanced back, confirming the rest of the team entering behind her.

As indicated on the schematic she had studied before the raid, the small residence began with a large room near the front entrance. Furniture of varying and mismatched styles and condition was arranged in rather haphazard fashion around the room, as if the owner had no sense of design aesthetic. One of the Xaheans was there, on his knees, pitching forward to the floor while holding his hands to his ears. Two of Yina's agents were already moving to secure him, leaving Burnham to track the other threat down the hallway.

Something moved at the corridor's far end, and Burnham saw a shimmering, almost imperceptible form crouching near a doorway. Instinct told her the figure was raising an arm in her direction, and Burnham fired her phaser. The weapon's bolt of energy struck the figure in the chest and sent it falling backward to the floor, and Burnham watched it solidify into the form of a now unconscious Xahean female. She also saw the weapon that had fallen from the woman's hand and landed on the floor to lie next to the Xahean's right hip.

"Excellent shooting, Captain," said Dran as she and another agent moved past her, advancing on the fallen Xahean and ensuring she was no longer a threat.

"All parties in custody," said one of the agents.

Turning back toward the door, Burnham headed for the corridor to check on Yina when she saw him standing in the entry, grimacing in pain as he rubbed his chest. He had holstered his weapon and removed his ear coverings and eye shield.

"You're okay?" she asked.

The security officer nodded, though he was in obvious pain. "A riot-suppression round. Nonlethal, but also very unpleasant." He tapped the protective vest over his chest. "I will have a very colorful bruise in short order."

Burnham allowed the programmable-matter pendant on her uniform sleeve to reclaim the phaser from her hand. It dissolved and disappeared, and she reached up to remove her ear coverings and eye shield. For the first time since entering the residence, she caught a whiff of something unpleasant, perhaps coming from the small, disheveled galley to the left side of the domicile's main room.

"You overcooked your *ansa,*" said Yina, to no one in particular, as he continued to rub his chest. "You are supposed to wait until your meal's final preparation, then with great care add the *ansa* root, cooking it over a low heat to ensure it reaches the optimum temperature while retaining its texture and flavor. Now the entire meal is ruined." He shook his head in mock disgust. "We fail our younger generations when we do not teach them such things."

Was this Xahean humor? Burnham managed to suppress a chuckle. "It's possible our entry may have upset his cooking timetable."

"Details." Yina motioned as though to dismiss her suggestion, but then offered a wry smile before returning to the business at hand. Moving back into the main room, he gestured for his two agents to pull their detainee to his feet. "Let us see if we might learn something useful today."

Guided by the agents flanking him, the male Xahean was helped to his feet. His hair had fallen across his face, obscuring his features, and when he reached up to brush it aside, Burnham could not help the involuntary sharp intake of breath.

"Vran?" She did not even know how to react and made no effort to hide the shock on her face.

"You know this person?" Now it was Yina's turn to be confused. "According to the file we were given, his name is Nadeb."

Still processing this revelation, Burnham replied, "He was a crewmember on the *Pilikoa*, the cargo freighter we assisted."

Yina nodded. "With the separatist uprising. I read the report of that incident." The security officer eyed their detainee. "So, your real name is Vran? Confirming this should be a simple matter of contacting the Ministry of Trade, unless that is also an alias."

For the first time, Vran spoke. "It is my real name."

Turning to where two other agents held the second suspect, Burnham was not as shocked to see she recognized the female Xahean. "Luhi." The woman at least had the grace to appear embarrassed.

"Her name is listed as Dizon," said Yina. "Very interesting."

"Yina." It was Dran, her holographic scanner once more out and active. She had emerged from the corridor leading out of the main room, and now carried a black octagonal container, which she held out for her leader. "I found this in a storage compartment in the sleeping area. It is the source of the explosive residue we detected."

Taking the container, Yina examined it for a moment before returning his attention to Vran. "Captain Burnham and her crew risked their own safety to come to your aid, and you repay them by attacking her people during the protests. Then you launch an assault against her ship. You were among those members of the *Pilikoa*'s crew released, were you not? Is it possible you were part of that failed uprising and did not get caught, then crept away to hide while your friends face the consequences of their actions? And now we find you with contraband materials we know to have been used in the commission of crimes against the Xahean people. Is this the statement you separatists are trying so hard to make? Is this how you attempt to garner support for your cause?"

"We are not separatists."

Burnham turned to Luhi, her eyes wide with surprise. For her part, the Xahean woman seemed at ease with herself. Her expression and body language suggested she had not a care in the world, perhaps having expected she and Vran would be apprehended.

"You were involved with the civil unrest in the Jovahna District," said Yina, holding up the container. "Your faces were captured by surveillance drones. Why your actual identities were not immediately flagged due to your affiliation with the Ministry of Trade is a question I shall be asking the proper authorities in due course, but the simple answer is that someone there is sympathetic to your efforts. As for the protests, devices with explosive materials such as those stored in this vessel were used to escalate the incidents there. You placed your fellow Xaheans at risk."

Vran replied, "We never intended to hurt anyone."

"And yet people were injured due to your actions." Yina handed the container back to Dran. "There will be a tribunal for those crimes, but cooperating with us now may grant you leniency from the magistrate. We seek the captured Federation officer. Where is he?"

His expression of confusion was almost genuine, but Burnham doubted it as he said, "How would I—" He stopped when Yina raised a silencing hand.

"I have little tolerance for this sort of fruitless interaction. The explosive compound you used during the Jovahna District protests is the same employed against the Federation ship. It is a specific compound, limited in its use and accessibility to our security and defense forces. Even I must make formal, documented requests to obtain modest amounts for training purposes. That it would be involved in two separate and seemingly disconnected incidents in as many days stretches the limits of believability."

Burnham said, "So you were acting out against separatists during those protests. You knew you could turn it into a riot and aim counterprotesters at my officers. Counterprotesters, not separatists, so you essentially egged on your own people." Stepping closer, she pointed a finger toward his face. "People who want us to leave and never return. Is that why you attacked my ship?"

"We were not involved with that," said Luhi. When Yina turned his unflinching stare on her, she added, "It is the truth. We participate in escalation tactics during gatherings such as the Jovahna District demonstrations. Instructions are sent on where to go and what to do. Our aim is to cause disruption and provoke animosity and distrust for the separatist cause. Anything beyond that is the action of someone else."

"Even if that is true," replied Yina, "there is still the matter of the explosive material, which you obtained or were given." When neither suspect said anything, the security officer shook his head, and his expression grew thoughtful. "Very well. You have already shot me, and now you wish to test my patience. You will regret that choice." He gestured to his team. "Take them into custody. We will continue this discussion in a more appropriate venue."

"Yina." Another of the agents had emerged from the room,

carrying a palm-sized device Burnham did not recognize. He handed it to his leader.

"What is that?" she asked.

Examining the device, Yina replied, "An encrypted communications device, of a type not typically available to the general public." He sighed. "Without the proper decryption key, these are all but impossible to access." Looking to Vran and Luhi, he said, "And even if we succeed in getting the key from them, the communications it receives and transmits are further encrypted from origin to termination point. They are designed to evade all attempts at tracking." ｜

Burnham's eyes fixed on the device. "My people can break it."

Appearing to consider this for a beat, Yina frowned. "To surrender this to you without proper authorization would earn me a reprimand at the very least." He held it out to Burnham. "Please return it to me when you are finished."

"Thank you." Burnham took the device, feeling her pulse already beginning to increase with anticipation. In truth, she was not even sure her crew could break through the thing's protective measures, at least not while *Discovery*'s computer was compromised, but it was the first solid lead to finding Stamets. So far as she was concerned, there was only one play here.

Hang on, Paul, she thought. *We're coming for you.*

36

"It won't work."

Stamets knew his blunt statement would not be received well by his captors, but it had the virtue of being true. The challenge now, he knew, was convincing them of this fact in a manner which avoided him ending up dead.

"You mean to say it does not work at present," said Minister Sen, standing with Stamets and Professor Fostra inside the oversized chamber of the Xahean spore-drive hub. In many ways, the sealed room with its transparent walls bore more than a passing resemblance to the reaction cube in *Discovery*'s engineering test bay. Outside the chamber, a half dozen scientists and technicians tended to various tasks.

"That's true too," replied Stamets. Hanging in the air before them was a large holographic schematic Stamets had created to act as a visual aid. It represented the interior of the Xahean spore drive or "XPD," as he had taken to calling it. After conducting a thorough scan of the enormous mechanism and incorporating the project team's own design notes and specifications, he had used their equipment to generate the new diagram. He was thankful Xahean technology was almost as easy and intuitive as its Federation and Starfleet counterparts. It not only aided in his learning curve but also boosted his confidence in the conclusions he was reaching.

Realizing his response sounded more flippant than helpful, Stamets added, "In its current configuration, I don't believe it can work on its own. The power needed for the spore reaction cube won't be sufficient to keep the connection to the mycelial plane stable." For emphasis, he held up the thumb and forefinger of his right hand, a centimeter apart. "If Sanctuary deviates from its entry into the network even this much, that's enough to cause an instability that could severely damage or even destroy the entire sphere."

Professor Fostra grunted in obvious annoyance. "How is that possible? Our computer models—"

"Are all projections," said Stamets. "Each of your actual tests have provided data to support this conclusion. The failures for those tests stemmed from several reasons, from using the wrong kind of spores to insufficient power to faulty navigational calculations." He had pored over the notes from each of those unsuccessful attempts, comparing them to the analysis of computer-based simulations dating back more than a century. "The good news is many of the lessons learned during those earlier tests and later simulations show you're definitely on the right track. What you're lacking is actual data from anything resembling a successful attempt." He indicated himself. "That's me, and based on literally hundreds of jumps I've made, I'm telling you this is a disaster waiting to happen."

"Or, perhaps you are attempting to deceive us."

At this point, Stamets was not surprised to see Hilo entering the open doorway into the reaction chamber. The councilor, already a fierce advocate for the Xahean spore-drive project, had taken a keen interest in his involvement. Stamets saw her more than the guards assigned to watch over him. She demanded constant status updates, almost to the point that Stamets felt he was spending more time explaining what he was trying to do than performing actual work. Even Sen, Fostra, and other members of the project team were content to leave him to work, albeit under close supervision. He suspected it was little more than a ploy designed to assert dominance and remind him of his station here, and to reinforce the implied threat of harsh penalties for his failure to assist them.

After two days with little rest, Stamets had grown tired of the game.

"And why would I do that?" he asked, squaring up in front

of Hilo. He gestured to the holographic schematic. "Better yet, show me where I'm lying."

Her eyes narrowing as she regarded him, perhaps deciding whether his insolence warranted punishment, the councilor replied, "I am not a fool, Commander. You know I am not technically inclined and therefore unable to read that gibberish in which you and your kind are so fluent. I do not understand machines, but I do comprehend people and their various behaviors. Is it not reasonable to assume you would find any means of delaying whatever progress you might make, in the hopes your captain will find you?"

"Captain Burnham *will* find me," replied Stamets. "You need to start getting comfortable with that idea. It's inevitable, and you've brought it on yourselves. She won't stop until she's found me and knows I'm safe, and if I'm not?" He shook his head. "There won't be anywhere for you to hide." It was a bit of embellishment on his part, but offering the veiled threat gave him a small bit of comfort. While he intended the warning as bluster, Stamets knew it also was true. Burnham would never stop looking for him, doing everything in her power and letting nothing and no one stand in her path. In her own way, Michael Burnham was a force of nature, and right now Stamets pitied anyone who chose to oppose her.

If Hilo was impressed with the display of bravado, she did not show it. "You should focus on convincing me why we remain at an impasse."

Drawing a deep breath, Stamets held up his hands. "All right, let's try again. I'm not saying this will *never* work. I'm saying it's not workable at the moment. At least, not in its current configuration." He gestured to the diagram still hovering in the air before them. "Your people have done a remarkable job reverse engineering our system. Queen Po gave you an excellent starting point, and even though she never made it far enough for it to work, she was making real progress." Indicating Fostra with a nod, he added, "I'm told the work done in the years since the Burn required going back to the beginning and starting over just so your scientists and engineers could gain an understanding of what Po started. I get that. It's a very complicated process, even more so when you don't have all of the information."

"What have we done incorrectly?" asked Sen.

Stamets shook his head. "It's not what you've done incorrectly. What you have here is very impressive, but we're still talking about retrofitting a spore drive into a vessel that was not constructed to support it. *Discovery* was built specifically as a platform for our spore-drive technology. Everything about it was designed to survive traversing the mycelial network. Shields, inertial damping, structural integrity, delicate computer systems, even life-support. It all plays a part, and if any of those fail at a critical moment, then that's it. You lose."

He gestured to indicate the reaction cube and the rest of the immense mechanism around them. "This doesn't mean other ships can't do it, but the power required to stabilize a spore reaction chamber of that size so it can function throughout any transit of the mycelial network would be enormous. For *Discovery*, the ship itself is deliberately designed to assist with that stabilization process. For something as large as Sanctuary, we're talking about power on a scale big enough it makes my head hurt."

Hilo said, "Are you suggesting your ship is the only one that can utilize this technology?"

"No, I'm saying *Discovery* is currently the only ship where the spore drive wasn't an afterthought." He clasped his hands together. "Everything about *Discovery*, from its shape to the components of its hull, feeds into the process. You're familiar with quantum slipstream drive systems, yes? It was an experimental propulsion technology tested in the late twenty-fourth century. The vessels they built to utilize that system were constructed differently than regular Starfleet ships. Even then, it could be used only for short periods."

"I am familiar with that technology," said Fostra. "We

considered it as an alternative but discarded it, as we believed it unworkable for a structure as large and unwieldy as Sanctuary."

Stamets replied, "Exactly. The same issue is present here, only within an even smaller margin for error."

"You keep saying that," said Hilo.

"Because it's true." Stamets glared at the councilor. "It'll continue to be true every single time I say it." He paused, drawing a calming breath and reminding himself these people were attempting to reconstruct a technology they had never actually seen, based on notes from scans taken over nine hundred years ago from someone who saw only at most two times the thing they were trying to build. The progress they had made despite the proverbial shackles around their ankles was nothing to dismiss out of hand.

"Navigating the mycelial plane isn't like piloting a ship through a nebula or an asteroid field," he said. "The network is very fragile and exists in an environment where outside matter is interpreted as an invasion. Simply attempting to cross the mycelial barrier is hazardous, and could result in system overloads, warp core breaches, or any of a hundred other things that end up with a destroyed spaceship. Your own tests with drones and other small craft should have told you that."

Fostra replied, "That is correct."

"Okay, then." Stamets once more waved his arms at their surroundings. "What you can't know, because you haven't yet made it that far, is that if a ship from this universe becomes trapped on the other side of that barrier, the mycelia comprising the network start to attack it, breaking it down." He glanced around. "It almost happened to *Discovery*. It'd take some time for it to eat Sanctuary, or at least break it down enough that your warp cores explode, or you just vent your atmosphere and kill everyone inside, but it'd happen."

"So what have we been doing wrong?" asked Sen. "What has eluded all of our tests and simulations?"

"A fundamental understanding of our relationship with

the mycelial plane." Using the holographic pad's interface, he called up a crude map he had drawn of the network. "Everything about interacting with that realm hinges on precision and timing. It's not like traveling a system of trails or roadways, and even comparing it to warp through subspace is at best a crude comparison. The entire idea of using it for travel is that a ship enters it with a specific destination plotted, and once you cross the barrier, the network punts you where you need to go." He snapped his fingers. "It happens just that fast, mostly because the network wants to get rid of the foreign body it thinks is invading it. Ending up where you want to go is a side effect, not the intention, and that only happens with precise calculations and navigation."

Hilo said, "We understand all of this, just as we know you are the one who perfected the system. That is why you were brought here." She pointed to the oversized spore drive. "You insist there is insufficient power to operate it safely, and now you tell us our calculations for transiting this other dimensional plane are inaccurate."

"We can supply more power," said Fostra. When his colleagues looked at him askance, he added, "Obtaining power is not the issue. Sanctuary already is capable of producing more energy than we require for this to work. However, the simple act of calling upon it would trigger a number of alert systems to our presence."

Stamets replied, "So you're saying we only have one shot at this, and it has to be perfect, because either way everyone in Sanctuary is going to know. If we all survive the jump, of course."

"That is exactly what he is saying." Sen stepped forward. "So, assuming the power requirements are met, that leaves you to carry out the necessary calculations."

"In a manner of speaking." Stamets rubbed his temples. Fatigue was starting to become a factor. "*Discovery*'s systems are still the best suited to pull this off. I've been thinking about it, and I see a way we might be able to move forward. If we could link *Discovery*'s spore-drive system to your reaction cube, I may be able to synchronize a jump with the ship and Sanctuary. The calculations are liable to be far more complex than if it was just *Discovery*, but I think I can bridge the gap."

"The technical specifications for your drive system were among the files we accessed," said Fostra. "Why can those calculations not be performed here?"

Shaking his head, Stamets held up his hands. "Because it's not that simple. The calculations can't be derived and executed through a computer the way we understand such machines. It requires a translator of sorts; an organic connection to the mycelial plane in order for such computations to be understood."

"Organic," said Fostra. "You mean a living being."

Sen stared at him. "You are referring to yourself."

"I guess that wasn't in the computer files you hacked." Stamets eyed his three captors. "I am the key you've been missing. My DNA has been altered, giving me an ability to communicate directly with the spores we use to power our drive, and also interpret the mycelial network and guide our ship through it." He looked around, taking in the reaction cube and the rest of the spore hub around them. "Here's the short version: this won't work without me, and I can't do it without *Discovery*."

37

Hearing the summons from sickbay, Culber emerged from his office to the unexpected sight of Doctor Arbusala being escorted into the treatment ward by a member of *Discovery*'s engineering staff. The therapist was favoring his right arm and shoulder, and his expression conveyed obvious pain.

"Doctor?" Culber crossed the room, extending his hands toward his new patient. "What happened?"

Standing next to Arbusala, Ensign Wendolyn Johnson replied, "He fell."

"I fell," repeated the Denobulan. Despite his obvious pain, he offered a smile to the young African woman. "It was really rather clumsy of me. No one's fault but my own."

While he certainly did not enjoy having anyone visit sickbay to have an injury treated, Culber was grateful for the distraction. He could be useful, if only for a few minutes, rather than wallowing in his own rampant thoughts. Now, at least, he could compartmentalize his emotions and focus his attention on a patient in need.

Pulling up his tri-com badge's holo-tricorder and activating its medical diagnostic functions, Culber directed a scan at Arbusala's arm. It took only seconds to visualize the issue. "You separated your shoulder. There's some tearing of the coraco-acromial and transverse humeral ligaments. There's also a hairline fracture along your ulna."

"It certainly feels like I did all of that." Arbusala glanced to Johnson. "Given there is little demand for my particular skill set with everything else going on, I thought I might somehow contribute to the repair efforts. To Commander Reno's credit, she made certain not to assign me to any tasks that might be hazardous or required technical expertise I obviously lack." He grimaced and his eyes narrowed, and Culber suspected he was enduring a fresh bout of pain. "It was a good idea, in theory."

Johnson added, "It was in a Jefferies tube between decks eight and nine. Doctor Arbusala was assisting us with replacing a damaged power junction. It can get pretty tight in some of those spaces, and there are also the vertical access points."

"And I found one of those," said Arbusala, punctuating his reply with a grunt as Culber gingerly probed his arm. "Unfortunately, grace and balance are not among my celebrated abilities."

After verifying Arbusala had no other injuries, Culber directed his patient to sit on a nearby treatment bed. "I take it you fell through the opening."

"Quite suddenly, as it turns out." Adjusting himself on the bed, Arbusala presented his arm to the doctor. "I tried to arrest my fall, and my arm impacted the deck plate adjacent to the access point." Once again, he directed an apologetic smile to Johnson. "I fear I may have lost or broken Ensign Johnson's diagnostic scanner."

"That's okay," replied the ensign. "We can make more of those. I'm just glad you're all right." She stepped closer, placing a hand on his uninjured shoulder. "Thanks for lending a hand, but I also wanted to thank you for our conversation. I appreciated your perspective, and I'm feeling much better about things now. Thank you for that."

Arbusala, his attention now on Culber and his ministrations, said, "I am happy you found our discussion constructive. Please feel free to call on me again if you feel it necessary."

"I will." Stepping back from the treatment bed, Johnson looked to Culber. "I need to get back, but please let me know if you need anything else from me, Doctor."

"Thanks for bringing him in," said Culber. "I may reach out to you for comments on my official report, but otherwise this looks pretty much like just a simple accident. You're dismissed, Ensign."

As Johnson departed, Culber returned to his holo-displays. From the treatment cart next to the bed, he retrieved a bone regenerator. Activating the device, he held it over Arbusala's injured forearm and the area was bathed in a warm yellow light.

"This should only take a minute," he said, glancing to Arbusala. "Then we'll take care of the ligaments in your shoulder." Medical advancements over the course of nine hundred years had rendered obsolete most of the equipment on which Culber had trained. Skin, bone, and muscle and tissue repair were much faster than in the twenty-third century and required less recuperative time on the part of the patient. New organs could be grown in a controlled laboratory setting, mitigating in significant fashion deaths resulting from catastrophic injury. While Culber had at first been hesitant about adopting such new technologies, common sense and a desire to remain an effective physician won out.

"How's that?" he asked after a moment of applying the treatment.

Arbusala flexed his fingers. "Much better, Doctor. Thank you." Then the Denobulan released an unexpected chuckle. "I cannot believe I was so careless. I suppose my injuries could have been much more severe."

"There are variable gravity areas inside the Jefferies tubes and other maintenance conduits," said Culber. "But they're designed to prevent the really dangerous falls. I guess they can't account for the occasional stumble." He set aside the bone regenerator and reactivated his tricorder to examine the results of his efforts. "That's healed rather nicely. You might have some soreness for a day or so, but I can prescribe something for that."

Arbusala replied by gritting his teeth as Culber touched his shoulder in what he thought was a gentle manner. "Perhaps after you address the more serious injury."

"I know it hurts," said Culber, "but it's actually not too bad." From the treatment cart, he retrieved a tissue stimulator and checked its power setting before activating it. "This still might sting a little more as I apply the treatment, but I promise it'll pass quickly."

To his credit, Arbusala almost succeeded in hiding the slight expression of discomfort as Culber directed the stimulator to his shoulder. As he moved the tool over the affected area, he monitored the status from his tricorder, noting with satisfaction that the torn ligaments were responding to the treatment.

"I can already feel a difference," said the Denobulan. "Very warm and soothing."

Culber smiled. "That's exactly what's supposed to happen."

"I take it you've experienced this treatment yourself?"

With a slight chuckle, Culber nodded. "A few times, like overdoing it with sports or a workout. Then there were one or two where I was just a clumsy idiot."

"It is refreshing to know we represent our respective species in similarly graceful fashion."

His attention divided between the stimulator and his tricorder readouts, Culber said, "I have to say, Doctor, you manage to keep surprising me. I've never met a therapist with such an unconventional approach to engaging with his patients."

Arbusala eyed him with appreciation. "You are quite perceptive, Doctor. While I did have a genuine desire to lend a hand wherever I could, I cannot deny I also saw an opportunity. However, rather than initiating any discussion on my own, I instead waited for someone to take advantage of our working together. Ensign Johnson was the first to do that when she broached the subject of her feelings."

Continuing to monitor the progress of his treatment, Culber asked, "Her feelings? Is she all right?" In other circumstances, he would have refrained from asking about interactions with a patient, but Arbusala had informed each *Discovery* crewmember with whom he interacted that he planned to withhold nothing from Culber, and no one had objected.

"Ensign Johnson is fine," replied Arbusala. "Like many

of her colleagues, she endured the initial shock of *Discovery*'s transit through time and your subsequent actions. Only after the Emerald Chain matter was resolved did she, along with the rest of the crew, begin to examine her new reality. As one might expect, she longed for home: her family and friends from your century. Coming to accept all of that as forever out of reach is a daunting task."

Culber said, "You can say that again." Deactivating the tissue stimulator, he ran a new scan of the treated area and nodded, satisfied Arbusala's injured ligaments were healing as expected.

"Can you raise your right arm for me?" he asked, and Arbusala responded by extending his arm and then raising it above his head. Culber noted his patient's slight grimace. "You can expect some lingering tenderness for the next day or so." He guided the therapist through a full yet gentle range-of-motion test, and while Arbusala frowned once or twice, that was the extent of his reactions.

"A slight, dull ache," he said, "but otherwise there's no real pain." Arbusala nodded. "Excellent. Thank you, Doctor."

Returning the tissue stimulator to its place on the treatment cart, Culber replied, "I should be thanking you, Doctor. The manner in which you interact with those in your care is remarkable." He paused a beat before adding, "It's easy to see why the crew feels comfortable speaking with you."

He should have known Arbusala would pick up on his hesitation. "They are quite comfortable speaking with you, as well, Doctor Culber. Yes, they have opened up to me, but I remain an outsider, albeit one with honorable intentions. You, on the other hand, are not simply their physician, but their protector. You offer them a space in which they can open up about what they are feeling, knowing they will not be judged but supported. To a person, every member of the ship's crew with whom I have spoken looks to you with the utmost respect. Several of them have gone so far as to tell me you alone are responsible for their ability to cope with their new circumstances." Leaning closer, the Denobulan said, "You must know that they trust you, Doctor. Implicitly."

The statement's direct nature caught Culber off guard. Of course he liked to think he had the crew's confidence, but one could never be sure; certainly not about every single person aboard *Discovery*. It was possible, even likely, that some did not hold him in the same high regard as Arbusala described, and they simply had not yet been afforded the opportunity to voice their concerns. Still, it was gratifying to hear such feelings conveyed from a third party.

"Thank you," he said after a moment. "I appreciate that."

Easing himself off the treatment bed, Arbusala once more tested his restored shoulder. "There is the 'lingering tenderness' you mentioned, but I do not believe I will require any pain medication." He bent his right arm at the elbow and tested his fingers by flexing them again. "Most impressive work, Doctor. Thank you."

"I'm glad you're feeling better," said Culber.

Arbusala studied him with a practiced, appraising gaze. "And how are *you* feeling, Doctor?"

"Me?" Culber waved a hand as if to push away the question. "I'm fine."

"With all due respect, I do not believe that is entirely true. Given the situation with your husband, it is perfectly understandable for you to be upset." Arbusala gestured around the sickbay. "You spend your time here, caring for your patients when you have them but also finding other ways to immerse yourself in your work. That likely does not leave you sufficient time to care for yourself."

Frowning, Culber replied, "There aren't that many people on board for me to talk to. I mean, I usually confess all my problems to Paul."

"What about Captain Burnham?" asked Arbusala.

"She has enough to worry about right now." Culber leaned against the treatment bed, crossing his arms. "The last thing she needs is me storming into her ready room and getting up in her face about Paul." ˙

Arbusala said, "Considering the current circumstances, I think she would understand you would want to ask questions, receive any updates about the search, and so on."

"When she has something to tell me," said Culber, "she'll tell me."

"You seem very confident." The Denobulan eyed him for a moment. "Is it because you trust the captain that much?"

"Of course." The response was out of his mouth before Culber even realized he was speaking. "I know she's doing everything she can to find Paul and get him back safely. I don't need to ask."

In a manner Culber did not think was normal for Denobulans, Arbusala placed his hands in his trouser pockets. "Interesting. And you believe the rest of the crew feels this same way about the captain?"

"I'd like to think so." Culber shrugged. "I mean, I can't deny there isn't tension with a few people." He recalled his earlier conversation with Stamets and his unresolved resentment of Burnham.

Nodding, Arbusala asked, "Doctor, if it is so easy for you to believe with such conviction that *Discovery*'s crew trusts their captain, why do you struggle with the notion of them feeling the same way about you?"

Well, I walked right into that one, thought Culber. "Nicely played, Doctor." It was a testament to his roiling emotions that he did not see the very easy exercise through which Arbusala had guided him.

"No games, Doctor," said Arbusala, turning as if to head for the exit. "A little positive reinforcement is rarely harmful, and you of all people certainly deserve it just now."

Culber found himself wondering how he could have resented the therapist. Nothing about Arbusala's demeanor justified the doubt and suspicion Culber had harbored. His initial feelings seemed so inane in hindsight.

As Arbusala made his way to the door, Culber stopped him. "Thank you, Doctor. I appreciate it."

Pausing as the doors parted for him, the Denobulan looked back, holding up his now healed arm. "I believe that makes us even."

When he was gone and Culber once more stood alone in sickbay, he allowed himself a small, relieved smile. Despite the knot of worry still churning in his stomach, it no longer threatened to consume him. He sensed his tension abating, and he could only shake his head at the ease with which Arbusala had helped elevate his mood.

"Well played, Doctor," Culber repeated to himself. "Well played."

But the therapist's efforts and even his full faith in Captain Burnham could not silence one question lingering in his mind.

Where are you, Paul?

38

Alerts. Warnings. Diagnostic messages. Status updates. More alerts. More warnings. Repeat. Information coming almost too fast to process. Their eyes burning with fatigue, Adira Tal blinked before stepping away from their console.

"You all right, kid?" asked Jett Reno from where she stood at an adjacent console. Like Adira, the engineer seemed to be stockpiling holographic displays above her station. Each virtual screen was packed to overflowing with information scrolling by at incredible speed. Some of the text was highlighted in one of several colors, while other parts vanished to be replaced by new script. If Reno was having any problems keeping up with the maelstrom, she did not show it. In fact, the engineer seemed to take no notice of it, her attention instead focused on a smaller holoprojection displaying the inner workings of the communications device given to her by Captain Burnham.

"I think I'm just tired, Commander." They rubbed their eyes and stifled the sudden urge to yawn. "I take that back. I know I'm tired."

Reno smirked. "Welcome to the club, Ensign. We have special hats and everything."

The strain had been mounting for several hours, taking its toll on them as they worked together in the test bay. With the bulk of Zora's attention focused on containing the intrusive software running loose within *Discovery*'s computer system, the artificial intelligence was fighting a war on multiple fronts. Reacting to changes in the software equivalent of a rampant viral infection, Zora was activating or creating all manner of new defenses. The work proceeded at a pace far greater than any living being could attain, coupled with Zora's ability to anticipate changes to the renegade code almost as they happened. On the other side of that conflict, the rogue software was introducing its own changes in response to Zora's efforts. There was, Adira knew, a legitimate battle royale unfolding within the virtual space of *Discovery*'s computer, the only evidence of which was the litany of advisories and alarms both entities left in their wake.

The overhead lighting chose that moment to flicker in manic fashion for several seconds before returning to normal, followed by Zora's voice over the intercom.

"Attention, all personnel. All replicator stations are unable to produce Chicken à la King at this time. Please seek alternative sources of nourishment."

Reno chuckled. "Thanks, Zora. You did me a solid. That's one fix I'm happy to see made permanent. Remind me to do that when we get done with today's crisis."

"You don't like Chicken à la King?" asked Adira.

Her hands stopping in midair over her console, Reno raised her head and looked up at the ensign. "When the *Hiawatha* crashed, it knocked the crap out of everything. There wasn't a day that went by where I wasn't fixing eight or nine things, all while trying to keep my crewmates alive. One day the replicator loses its mind and won't give up anything but Chicken à la King. That's what I ate for nearly three weeks until I figured out how to fix it. I haven't eaten it since and I don't plan on eating it ever again. If you offer it to me and it's the only thing between me and starving, I'm checking out. I *hate* Chicken à la King."

Still uncertain about what to do with this latest revelation, Adira chose to file it away for future reference. "Good to know." They waved to the storm of data raining down over their own console. "How can you concentrate on just one thing with all of that going on? How do you keep up with it all?"

"You ignore a lot of it." When Adira frowned at that response, Reno added, "What I mean is, right now Zora's running point for us, charging ahead and looking for the really big problems. The computer's regular diagnostic routines don't know that, so they're sending us everything that pops up and isn't normal for them. Trouble is, nothing's normal for them because Zora is shaking every tree and rattling every cage trying to run down this crappy code. The side effect is the diagnostic programs are losing their minds because while they're great tools, they're still dumb as dirt."

"That doesn't make any sense," said Adira. "It's software and, other than Zora, isn't even artificially intelligent. It does what it's programmed to do, which is identify and prioritize issues it finds." Once more, they indicated their console and the streams of diagnostic data. "Everything can't be an issue."

Reno shrugged. "They do what they're coded to do, which is raise hell when something's wrong. Right now? Everything's going wrong." She pointed to Adira. "You and me? We're the ones who have to tell the computer to take a pill and calm the hell down, because Zora's busy."

"How much do you actually know about computers?" asked Adira.

"Enough to know I'd like to throat-punch this one."

Reaching beneath her console, Reno pulled back her hand to reveal a long, thin piece of black licorice. She stuck one end of the candy into her mouth and let it dangle there as she resumed her work.

Adira asked, "You're hungry? Now?"

Eyeing her with her usual expression of aplomb, Reno replied, "This isn't food, kid. It's life-support."

"Warning," said Zora. *"Life-support is offline in hangar bay. Personnel should avoid that area until functions are restored."*

Stopping in midbite, Reno raised an eyebrow. "Okay, I'm done tempting fate for a minute."

The hatch leading to the port engineering spaces parted to admit Cleveland Booker. Adira could not help noticing the courier looked almost as tired as they felt.

"I've run every diagnostic in the database," he said. "Zora was able to keep the virus out of the warp-drive systems long enough for me to take them offline." He looked to Reno. "I've disconnected it from the main operating system and your team has powered down the warp core. The antimatter containment system's also been isolated, so there's no chance it can be deactivated."

Reno offered a thumbs-up gesture. "I think we all can agree that'd be a crappy way to close out the day."

Once more, Zora piped in over the intercom. *"Attention, all personnel. All turbolift operations are in standby mode until further notice. Please utilize secondary access points when moving about the ship."*

"See," said Reno, "now I think she's doing some of this just to be annoying."

It made a sort of sense to Adira. "If the intrusion software is probing for ways to gain deeper access to our system, it makes sense for it to probe every process for vulnerability."

Pointing to the Xahean comm device on Reno's console, Booker asked, "Any luck with that thing?"

Reno grimaced. "Not yet. It's protected by a randomly generated fractal encryption code that changes at irregular intervals. The only way to cut through it is with the right decryption key, which, based on the interface on its faceplate, could be billions of combinations if we're talking about the Xahean equivalent to our alphanumeric characters." She held up the device and pointed to a slot set into one side. "The decryption key goes here. Without it? This thing's a rock."

"They didn't find anything like that when they arrested those two fools," said Adira, recalling Captain Burnham's update when delivering the comm unit to engineering. "They must have destroyed it."

Reno said, "Yeah, so that means it's a pain in the ass to figure out, and that's before we add in I don't even have full resources because Zora's still on her snipe hunt through the computer."

"Intruder alert," said Zora. *"Intruder alert."*

The warning was only just starting to register when a dull hum began echoing in the engineering space, and Adira turned to see six flashes of transporter energy appear at the room's far end. They coalesced into the forms of five Xaheans, each dressed in dark clothing and brandishing weapons as they stood in a circle around the sixth figure, Paul Stamets.

"Commander!" Adira yelled at the same time the five Xaheans raised their weapons and took aim at the handful of *Discovery* crewmembers in the test bay.

"Reno to security! Intruder alert in main engineer—"

The rest of her call for help was cut off as one of the Xaheans fired their weapon at her and a bolt of green energy washed over the engineer's body. She fell unconscious to the deck at the same time Adira ducked behind their console in search of cover.

More shots rang out as the Xaheans dispatched the other crewmembers. Booker rushed one of the intruders, slamming them into a nearby bulkhead. They wrestled for the Xahean's weapon, with Booker clocking his opponent with a forearm to the intruder's chin. He followed that with another strike to the side of the Xahean's head before a bolt of green energy found him. He went limp while still grappling with the intruder, falling toward the bulkhead and sliding in a heap to the deck.

Within seconds everyone in the bay had been neutralized except for Adira. This realization was landing as two of the Xaheans trained their weapons on them.

"Not them!" It was Stamets, shouting to be heard above the weapons fire. He pointed at them. "They're coming with us."

Coming with you? Adira's mind screamed the question. What was going on? What had they done to Stamets?

Two of the Xaheans approached them and Adira raised their hands.

Still trying to believe what they were seeing, they looked to Stamets for an explanation. It was obvious from his face that the commander was fatigued. His chin and cheeks were fuzzy with beard growth, his hair was mussed, and there were dark circles under his eyes. He looked as if he had not slept in days. Adira noted one of the Xaheans pointing their weapon at him, and that at least made a sliver of sense.

He's here against his will, Adira thought. *He's being forced to do this.*

"Ensign," said Stamets, staring at Adira with tired eyes. "Just do what they say and you won't be hurt. I promise."

While they remained under guard, Adira watched Stamets enter the spore drive's reaction cube and begin disengaging the twin pylons of the interface he used to access the spore hub. Adira could not help but feel a sting of betrayal at seeing the device they had created for him apparently being poached while they watched.

"What are you doing?" they asked.

Emerging from the reaction cube, he pointed to the disconnected pylons. "Those come with us," he said to the Xaheans, and two of the intruders moved to retrieve them. Next, another of the intruders, perhaps the group leader, handed Stamets a device Adira did not recognize, which he affixed to the console dedicated to monitoring the spore-drive system. They watched as he crossed to the heavy storage unit set into the bulkhead behind the console and retrieved one of the cylinders Adira knew contained cultivated specimens of *Prototaxites stellaviatori,* the mycelia on which *Discovery*'s spore drive depended. Taking the cylinder, he loaded it into the receiving port used to deliver the spores into the reaction cube. Finally, Stamets placed small octagonal devices on three more of the cylinders.

"Commander," said Adira, their voice firmer this time. "Why are you doing this?"

When Stamets returned his attention to Adira, his expression was one of resignation as he stepped closer to them. Adira stood in muted shock as he removed their tri-com badge and the pendant on their sleeve before dropping them to the deck.

"I'll explain it all soon, but I promise you this is for everyone's sake. Just please trust me on this."

One of the Xaheans grabbed their arm and Adira felt the first tingle of a transporter beam forming around them. Adira had just enough time to glance around the engineering compartment and see the unmoving forms of Reno, Booker, and the others before they and *Discovery* vanished.

39

"Multiple intrusion alarms," reported Gen Rhys from the tactical station. "We're getting slammed all over the system."

From her chair at the center of the bridge, Burnham listened to her first officer's report, which was just the latest in a chorus of such updates. "This is still the software?"

"Looks that way, Captain," said Rhys. "I don't know what set it off. Zora didn't give us any heads-up, and judging by activity in the main computer core, this caught her off guard too."

At the communications station, Ronald Bryce called out, "All external comms are down, and primary internals are out too. We've lost connectivity with the various Sanctuary broadcast feeds. I'm switching to emergency systems for internal comms."

"Internal sensors are spotty," added Sylvia Tilly, "but transporters, shields, and turbolifts are all offline."

"What's the status in engineering?" asked Burnham. Jett Reno's truncated report about intruders in that part of the ship had left everyone wondering what happened. There had been no time to follow up before the latest round of cyberattacks delivered this new gut punch.

Tilly replied, "All hatches are sealed, and there's a force field around the entire section." She swiped at her station's holo-displays. "I can't make out any life signs, but environmental control is still active."

"Zora," Burnham prompted. "Report. What is your status?"

"I am currently engaged with multiple assaults against the central computer core. Operating system as well as primary and secondary data-storage hubs are impacted. I am routing functions to emergency fail-safe servers."

It might not be total chaos, Burnham decided, but it had to be close. From the moment the frantic call to security came to engineering, the situation continued to deteriorate. The main computer, already compromised from the earlier attack, had proven vulnerable to this new action. Burnham had to wonder if this was part of the plot against them all along, launched by an enemy that still eluded them.

"Captain," said Bryce. "I've got comm restored to engineering. No holos, though."

"I'll take it." Burnham pushed herself from her chair. "On-screen." She walked past the helm and operations consoles as the view of the Sanctuary docking port playing host to *Discovery* vanished, replaced by a visual feed of the engineering test bay where the spore hub was located. On the screen were a somewhat disheveled Jett Reno and Cleveland Booker.

"Commander," said Burnham. "Are you all right?"

Reno replied, *"That's a pretty open-ended question, Captain."* She reached up to rub her neck, closing her eyes and grimacing. *"For the record, getting hit by a Xahean stun gun sucks."*

Clasping her hands in front of her, Burnham tried to see the entire room behind the engineer. "Is everyone all right?"

"Nothing serious," said Booker, rubbing his left shoulder. *"But they took Adira. Xaheans. Some kind of assault team. They popped in and put us all down. Also, Commander Stamets was with them."*

"What?" Burnham heard several gasps from various members of the bridge crew, but ignored them. "He was with them?"

"Not by choice," replied Booker. *"They had him at gunpoint. I think he was helping them take what they wanted without anyone getting hurt."*

Burnham scowled, processing the startling new information. "What did they take?"

"The spore-drive interface," said Reno. *"Stamets disconnected it from the reaction cube and trucked it right out of here, along with three cylinders of mycelium spores."*

"*Captain,*" said Booker. "*It looks like he loaded spores into the port for the reaction cube. They're primed to be inserted into the cube itself. We also found a device attached to the spore-drive control console. It scans as Xahean in origin, and we can't get it off.*"

"Is it dangerous?"

Reno shook her head. "*It's not a bomb, if that's what you're asking. Near as we can figure, it's some kind of interface module. I scanned it, and there's an encrypted transceiver component, sort of like that comm unit you gave us to hack, but more powerful. We can't access the console itself, so we think it's locking us out.*"

"But why?" Burnham tried to connect the dots. "They've already wormed their way into our computer. Why do they need another interface? And why a direct link to the spore drive?"

They took Stamets for a reason, she reminded herself. *They took spores and the interface.*

"Could the Xaheans have built their own version of a spore drive?" Burnham looked around the bridge. "Is that even possible?"

Tilly said, "It's been over nine hundred years since Commander Stamets came up with the idea, and we're in the weird, wild future now. We missed out on people inventing a lot of neat new things. Seems reasonable they might figure out some older stuff too."

Another round of alarms sounded on the bridge, and Tilly, along with everyone else, turned back to their stations. Burnham looked around, noting the number of crimson alert indicators not just on the tactical and science consoles but also the helm and ops stations.

"We're moving," reported Detmer. "The port's docking clamps have released us and maneuvering thrusters are engaging." She swiped and pushed at various controls as well as the holo-display above her console. "The instructions are coming from the computer, Captain."

"Zora," said Burnham. "What's happening? Why are we moving?"

The computer replied, *"There is an override in the navigational subprocessor, Captain. I am attempting to diagnose and determine corrective action, but I am currently experiencing difficulties. An unauthorized subroutine has launched within the central memory core. It is beginning to impact a number of primary and secondary functions."*

"Captain," said Owosekun from the ops console. "The computer has just activated emergency isolation protocols. Turbolifts were already offline, but now emergency bulkheads have been closed and every interior hatch on the ship has been sealed."

Burnham asked, "What about transporters?"

The operations officer shook her head. "Still offline. At least we have life-support."

"But someone's still pulling the strings." Burnham looked to Detmer. "Any idea where we're being taken?"

"There were no coordinates entered to the helm, Captain. Whatever's happening, someone's guiding us remotely."

Pondering that, Burnham turned to Bryce. "Remotely. That means some kind of signal."

"On it, Captain." The communications officer brought up a new set of holo-displays and status screens.

Letting him work, Burnham started to pace the bridge. "We need to flush that virus out of the computer." She looked to Tilly. "Any ideas?"

Her expression one of uncertainty, Tilly said, "Short of a full power down and restart? I don't see how."

Sensing her mounting frustration, Burnham turned back to the viewscreen where she saw Reno had already returned to her console while Booker had taken up an adjacent station. "Reno, is there anything you can do from down there?"

"Taking a look now, Captain." Burnham watched the engineer fight with her controls, which included irritable swiping at the station's holo-displays and even smacking the console

with the flat of her hand. Then, as if realizing she was still being watched, she said, *"Sometimes they like it rough."*

"Captain." It was Bryce, who now seemed engrossed in several displays hovering above his console. "I think I've found it. After the intruders beamed in and out, and just before this new wave of cyberattacks started, we received an encoded transmission. It was on an encrypted subfrequency, and it sent a signal directly to the main computer from outside the ship." He swiped away one of his holo-displays and pulled up a new one. "It was very low power. They were trying to hide it, and it almost worked, but the initial contact still posted to the comm logs."

Detmer said, "They've taken control of the helm. They obviously want to move us somewhere, which means someone has to be driving."

"Even if that signal is encrypted," added Owosekun, "we can still track it, right?"

Bryce replied, "That's what I thought, but when I try running a back trace, it disappears into the rest of the broadcast noise filtering through the entire habitat. Whoever's doing this knows their stuff."

"So do we," said Burnham. "I want my ship back, and I want whoever's sending that signal. We find them, we find the people responsible for all of this, and hopefully we find Stamets and Adira. It's time to end this."

40

I'm scared.

Standing at a console positioned just outside the oversized reaction cube that was the heart of the Xahean spore drive, Adira looked over their shoulder to see Gray standing there. There was no charming grin this time. In their beloved's face, Adira saw nothing but fear.

"I am too."

They spoke softly, barely moving their lips and hoping their voice did not carry over the hum of power resonating through the compartment. There were Xaheans standing nearby or in their line of sight. A pair of guards stood mere steps away, flanking Adira. Two others, an older female and an older male, watched with intense curiosity as Paul Stamets worked inside the transparent cube. Neither Hilo, a member of the Xahean council, nor her companion, Hona Ko Mah Sen, a senior officer within the Xahean Ministry of Security, had seemed thrilled with Adira's arrival and had said nothing to them. Another Xahean, a scientist named Fostra, had at least been civil with them if not cordial, directing them to a console positioned outside the reaction cube and quickly tutoring them on its functions before moving to an adjacent workstation.

On the cube's far side, Adira saw through the chamber's transparent walls three Xaheans, two females and a male, working at a bank of consoles. With help from Stamets, Adira had learned enough about the technology around them to intuit the meaning of various indicators, a few of which glowed orange while the vast majority flashed a brilliant blue. The latter color meant that the system check was good and whatever the console monitored was functioning in an expected manner, whereas the former color suggested something different. Given what was being attempted, there were far too many orange lights for Adira's taste.

Inside the reaction chamber, Stamets stood between the pair of interface pylons taken from *Discovery*'s spore hub. He was in the process of installing the devices using programmable matter to bridge Federation and Xahean technology, and now was employing a portable scanner to check his work. In response to the controls he pressed on the palm-sized device, Adira noted updates to several of the holographic status screens floating above the console. Another display hovered nearby, offering them a translation key so Adira could understand the Xahean controls and indicators.

"Adira," said Stamets, his voice sounding distant and hollow from inside the reaction cube. "Are you confirming my readings?"

Studying the holo-displays, Adira nodded. "Yes, Commander." Despite their best efforts, they were unable to keep the anxiety out of their voice. "Everything appears nominal."

"Good." Stamets conjured a holographic schematic of the pylon, and Adira recognized the diagram of the interface's internal components. The commander was running a configuration diagnostic in a manner similar to what he would do in *Discovery*'s reaction cube. "The programmable-matter bridge worked even better than I expected. This might actually end up working, after all."

"It *might* work," said Sen. "You remain uncertain?"

Stamets glared at the security minister with an expression Adira recognized as one not just of disbelief but also impatience. "Unless there's been a successful spore jump with this thing when I wasn't looking?" He nodded. "Yeah, I'm totally uncertain. One shot to do this, remember? I'm just playing by your rules, Mister Security Minister."

With a scornful look toward Adira, Councilor Hilo said, "I still do not understand why you had to bring this child here. Surely one of our own engineers or scientists can observe status monitors just as well."

I don't like her, said Gray. *Not even a little.*

Adira nodded. "Neither do I."

Without looking up from the adjustments he was making, Stamets replied, "For this to work, we're basically going to remotely activate *Discovery*'s spore drive at the same time I'm engaging this one, and using the energy from Sanctuary's power generators to trigger the spore reaction and get this entire monstrosity through the mycelial barrier. You need me to make the jump, and while I'm in here I need someone to monitor the link between here and *Discovery* to make sure everything stays in sync."

Now he looked at the councilor. "I also need someone I trust to monitor me and my responses to the spore reaction from out there. I prefer people who don't abduct me or endanger my ship for that sort of thing, so that's why I brought them."

"I grow tired of this nonsense," said the councilor. "Remember, Commander, that your value lies solely with your ability to help us. If you are unable to meet that need, then there is really no need to continue this exercise any longer."

Continuing to make adjustments to the interface pylons, Stamets shrugged. "Does that mean we can go home?"

Her irritation obvious, Hilo looked to Adira. "Does everyone in your Federation comport themselves in similar fashion?"

Adira frowned. "Only when we're kidnapped."

Okay, said Gray. *That was salty. And funny. I think Stamets is having a bad influence on you.*

That might be true, Adira decided. There was something about the way Stamets seemed to have no fear for his captors or any possible repercussions if he succeeded in annoying them to some as yet undefined breaking point.

Adira had received a crash course in the bold plan Stamets had put forth to link *Discovery* to this much larger and more powerful version of a spore drive. It was the culmination of more than a century's worth of work in the wake of the Burn thanks to the efforts of uncounted engineers, scientists, and other technicians. Despite the decades spent re-creating the mechanism from a design imagined over nine hundred years ago, the time period *Discovery* had left behind to travel to their future, the effort had remained unrealized. Sen and Hilo had even said when all plausible options had failed or were dismissed as unworkable, they knew *Discovery* would eventually be arriving in this century.

What they did not know was where the starship might appear. Was it fate or simple good luck that the twenty-third-century vessel found its way to a beleaguered region representing but a fraction of the space once under the Federation's purview? No matter the reason, the ship with its extraordinary propulsion system along with the man who created it were here, within easy reach. Without the emergency situation aboard the *Pilikoa*, an opportunity to make contact with *Discovery* might not have come for years.

And yet, with the obstacles in their way, there was no denying the technical achievement of building a form of spore drive while working from such limited information. It was a bold endeavor, Adira decided, and an achievement to be celebrated in its own right. Still, it remained untested in the only form that mattered: its ability to transport Sanctuary in its entirety across the mycelial network to an as-yet-unidentified location.

His configurations and fine-tuning completed, at least for the moment, Stamets exited the reaction cube and moved toward Adira. With the console between them, he placed a hand atop the workstation's angled surface and regarded them. "Are you okay?"

"Compared to what?" asked Adira.

That was enough to evoke a small, humorless grin from Stamets. "Fair enough." Moving around the console, he began swiping at the holographic controls and inputting commands to the station's tactile controls. "I think we're almost there." He looked to where Fostra still stood at the other console on this side of the cube. "Professor, what's *Discovery*'s status?"

"On course toward the rendezvous point," replied the Xahean. "Due to the vessel's size, it was necessary to maneuver it around a few of the larger districts."

"And its computer systems remain under our control?" asked Sen.

The professor nodded. "Yes. Their computer features a very robust operating system and an impressive array of defensive features. It is still resisting our efforts at a complete takeover, but we have secured most of its critical processes."

The cyberattack, at first intended to force access to *Discovery*'s computer and extract information pertaining to the spore drive and allow for the commander's kidnapping, had continued to offer benefits. This, to Adira, explained the seemingly haphazard nature of the ongoing assault on the ship's systems. The software introduced into *Discovery*'s computer core was, in essence, figuring out things as it evolved and while in the midst of an unexpected battle with Zora. Facing off against a sentient artificial intelligence that now defined itself by its commitment to safeguarding the ship and its crew was something the Xaheans could not have anticipated. While the virus could evolve, even in aggressive action, to the obstacles Zora pitted against it, the renegade program still had limits to the responses it devised. Zora had far fewer restrictions as well as a greater capacity to learn and adapt. She might have been caught off guard at the beginning of this crisis, but Adira knew it would not take much to give her an edge and perhaps, ultimately, the upper hand.

Was there something they could do here to help with that? Other than the console at which they presently stood, Adira had been permitted to touch nothing. Their instructions were to monitor readings from the reaction cube and Stamets, and to follow his lead once he began the process of initiating the jump. The Xahean professor, Fostra, seemed to have some oversight of what was happening on *Discovery*, but there was no way Adira could take any action against him before their guards overpowered them.

Looking up from his console, Stamets said to Hilo and Sen, "We're just about ready. Where are we going?"

Sen exchanged glances with Hilo before the councilor reached into a pocket of her blouse and extracted a violet-tinged data module. "The coordinates are on this."

"What is it?" asked Stamets.

"An uninhabited star system approximately sixty light-years from our present location. It was charted long ago by automated reconnaissance probes, not long after my species discovered faster-than-light travel. Probes of that sort were dispatched using our new technology, and they catalogued numerous systems. This one has conditions similar to Xahea, where we might build our new home."

Adira asked, "Is it to be a home for separatists as well?"

"That is certainly the intention," said Sen. "It is hoped that once we reach the new system, those who harbor such rebellious notions might reevaluate their stance and see there is common ground for all of us. A new world, perhaps even a new Xahea."

"It sounds nice," said Stamets. "I honestly hope your people can be happy."

They heard Gray in their mind. *Even with Commander Stamets, this is completely crazy.* Gray still stood nearby, visible to no one but Adira, and they found his presence soothing.

"If anyone can do this, he can," they said.

"Your faith in your colleague is endearing," said Sen.

Hilo seemed less impressed. "Let us hope it is not misplaced."

If it did not work, Adira knew none of them likely would be around even long enough to lament the failure.

41

Over the course of her life, Michael Burnham had faced numerous situations in which she felt powerless to take any action on her own behalf. When she was a child, such incapacity—be it literal or figurative—had been an intimidating teaching tactic employed by her foster father. She remembered those many lessons, which often took the form of being forbidden to act, in favor of directing her energies inward while contemplating possibilities and consequences of action as well as inaction.

Then, as a child, it was an uncomfortable and even galling experience to endure.

Now, as an adult granted tremendous authority as well as latitude toward identifying all manner of issues and problems? It felt the same.

Burnham hovered at the bridge's main viewscreen, watching the artificial landscape of Sanctuary's interior slide past. Population centers, suspended islands, buildings rising up from its central core or extending downward from the web of its upper support lattice, all of it had seemed so wondrous and inviting upon their arrival. It was little more than an elaborate prison now, and escape was foremost on her mind. The notable absence of the omnipresent hum of *Discovery*'s warp engines, which had been powered down to protect them from the ongoing cyberattack, only heightened the sensation of helplessness.

"We're slowing down," said Detmer, still seated at her helm console. "Maneuvering thrusters are shifting to bring us to a hover."

"Can we see anything?" asked Burnham, and Detmer called up sensor imagery that afforded her and the rest of the bridge crew a view of the habitat beneath the ship. Mindful of the variable-gravity environment inside the sphere, Burnham had hoped *Discovery* might at least be guided away from areas that might pose a threat to anything or anyone beneath it. She was troubled to see the ship coming to an apparent stop above a densely populated area along the habitat's central core. Buildings, thoroughfares, support stanchions bore still more structures. Even from their present altitude, the signs of activity around buildings and in green spaces was obvious.

"It's not quite the exact center of the sphere," reported Tilly from the science station. "Scans show we're approximately thirty meters above that point. According to the sensor readings we collected when we first arrived, this is a null-gravity area. Sort of a buffer or transition point between different artificial gravity fields. As long as we stay put, we shouldn't pose a danger to anyone around us."

Trying to connect the dots, Burnham began pacing toward her command chair. "They already took Stamets and components of our spore drive. If the Xaheans had built their own, then why do they need *Discovery*? We were already secure back at the docking port, but they put that transceiver on the spore-drive console in engineering." Her semidistracted movements having brought her close to the science station, she looked at Tilly. "The transceiver they planted in engineering. What if it's to somehow link our spore drive to whatever the Xaheans built?"

"It might explain why Commander Stamets took the interface and a bunch of spores," replied Tilly. As if trying to order her thoughts, she held her hands before her and made a fist with her right hand. "This is us." She waved her left hand. "And this is whatever they have down there somewhere. They have to generate the energy necessary to push Sanctuary toward the mycelial barrier, but *Discovery* is the key to controlling a spore jump and—you know—not killing all of us."

Burnham said, "And Paul is the key to controlling *Discovery*. We're set up to travel the mycelial network. Sanctuary isn't.

The Xaheans need us to ensure safe passage. That's why he loaded spores to our hub, put that transceiver on the console, and had the ship maneuvered to this position. He's setting up some kind of synchronized jump." Now it made sense. At least, it made a kind of sense.

"We can't just destroy that transceiver with a phaser?" asked Tilly.

"Too dangerous," said Commander Rhys, crossing over from his tactical station. "If it's interfacing with our systems, it could have countermeasures to protect against tampering or sabotage. That might be more than Zora can handle right now."

At the communications station, Commander Bryce replied, "More importantly, if it's meant to connect our spore drive to whatever Commander Stamets is doing down on the surface, we might have a better chance of pinpointing his location." Before he could say anything else, an alert tone sounded from his console. "Captain, we're being hailed on a low-power frequency."

"Can you trace it?"

The communications officer frowned. "I'm not sure. Working on it."

"Open the channel."

On the main screen, the view of Sanctuary was replaced by an image of a visibly exhausted Paul Stamets. With dark circles under his eyes, beard stubble, and his hair out of place, he had removed his blue uniform tunic and rolled up the sleeves of his undershirt, which looked dusty and stained. There could be no mistaking the expression of shame on the commander's face.

"Captain, it's good to see you."

"It's good to see you, too, Commander. Are you all right? How's Ensign Tal?"

Stamets held up a hand. *"We're both fine. I regret the action taken against the ship, but it was necessary to protect everyone, both there and down here. At least, it's what I thought was necessary."*

"The Xaheans have a spore drive, don't they?"

Nodding, Stamets said, *"They do. I knew you'd see it. The Xaheans have actually managed something extraordinary here, but they were never able to solve certain problems."*

"Like safely navigating the mycelial network."

"Exactly." Stamets held out his hands. *"I'm the answer, but only to a point. Sanctuary wasn't designed for this kind of travel, but I believe with* Discovery*'s help it can work."*

Burnham stepped closer to the screen. "But why not just ask us for help? We could have come to some kind of agreement. We still can." She considered what Stamets had said. "How can you be sure this will even work? You couldn't possibly have had time to test it."

"You're right." Stamets looked around. *"All we have are computer simulations and projections. I've examined everything, and I think I've found a way to safely bridge the gap."*

"But what if you're wrong?" Burnham shook her head. "This could destroy Sanctuary and *Discovery*. It doesn't have to be this way."

"The people championing this effort feel differently." Stamets paused, looking at something off-screen. His body language told Burnham he was under close supervision, his words obviously being monitored. When he scowled and his body went rigid, she knew he was at odds with his handlers.

"They believe they've come too far to stop now," he said, *"and they want me to try, but I've at least gotten them to agree to abort the process if I think there's a real danger."*

"How do you know they'll keep their word?"

Stamets drew a long breath and released it before replying, *"Because they can't do this without me. I won't willfully endanger anyone. I'll die before I let that happen, Captain. You* have *my word."*

The transmission ended without warning. Stamets disappeared, replaced by the view of Sanctuary's interior.

"This is crazy," said Tilly. "These Xaheans, what are they hoping to accomplish?"

Rhys said, "It can't be the separatists. They've been trying to find a life outside Sanctuary. Why try to move it?"

"Why would those opposed to the separatists want to move?" Tilly pointed toward the viewscreen. "They just want to keep things the way they've always been."

Burnham said, "Maybe they think if they move Sanctuary far enough away from outside influences—like us, for example—they can get a better handle on maintaining the status quo."

"They don't think they'd go to jail once all this is over?" asked Tilly. "Assuming this even works?"

"Radical agendas aren't always logical."

Tilly snorted. "Guess that's why they're radical."

All around the bridge, workstations winked out and the overhead lighting blinked before fading altogether, replaced within seconds by emergency illumination. Holographic heads-up displays at the different consoles reset, and Burnham noticed more status indicators at various stations shifting from green to red.

"Captain," said Bryce. "We've got another incoming signal. It's encrypted like the last one, but much more powerful." He tapped and swiped at his controls. "It's a data link to the spore drive."

"Stamets," said Burnham.

"Engineering to bridge," called Jett Reno over the intercom. *"Things just got lively down here. The spore drive's online. Spores have been released into the reaction cube."*

Burnham said, "Is there any way for you to abort the process?"

"We're still locked out," replied Booker. *"The transceiver they planted on the console just launched a subroutine to do the pre-jump countdown. If we're reading this right, we'll be ready to jump in less than two minutes."*

Her feelings of helplessness continuing to mount, Burnham said, "Zora, what's your status? Can you abort the jump?"

"Negative," said the computer. *"There is a malicious subrou-*

tine isolating the spore-drive subprocessor. I am endeavoring to cir-
cumvent that process, but I have no estimated time for completion.”

Whatever Zora might do, Burnham knew it would not
happen in time. There was only one thing left for her and her
people to do.

“Bridge to all hands,” she said, triggering the intercom.
“Black alert.”

42

Standing behind the control console outside the oversized reaction cube, Adira watched as Paul Stamets placed his hands in the shallow basins atop each of the interface pylons. In response to his touch, pale-green synthetic nanogel flowed into the basin and over his fingers. The effect on Stamets was obvious as the gel touched his skin, initiating the quantum transduction process.

"Everything appears nominal, Commander," they called out.

Looking across the cube toward them, Stamets nodded. *"Excellent,"* he said, his voice filtering through an intercom now that the reaction cube was sealed. Despite the appearance of him falling into an almost trancelike state, Adira knew he remained aware of his surroundings. *"Keep an eye on the* Discovery's *position and readings. Everything has to be exactly in sync or we abort."*

"Understood."

"This is incredible," said Professor Fostra, who had moved from his own station to monitor the proceedings at Adira's console. "The idea of one of us being able to communicate directly with the spores. From the beginning of our efforts to re-create this process, it never occurred to anyone."

"I wouldn't feel too badly about that," said Adira. "It's a pretty crazy way to travel." For emphasis, they looked over their shoulder to where Councilor Hilo and Minister Sen stood, watching the proceedings with undisguised wonder and perhaps a hint of apprehension.

Good, they thought.

According to Stamets, linking the gel to the alien DNA fused with his own was not painful. He had previously described it as a warming and even soothing sensation washing over his entire body. This sounded far more pleasant than the cruder and likely more painful method he had concocted in order to forge his first successful connection with the mycelial plane. Adira still shuddered at the sight of the shunts in his forearms during their first meeting, surgically implanted ports allowing for a direct connection to *Discovery*'s spore-drive navigation system. Rejecting the need for Stamets to be in constant discomfort while providing his ability to guide the ship through the mycelial realm, Adira had taken it upon themself to create the new, modern interface using programmable matter and the nanogel.

"How did he ever come to this conclusion on his own?" asked Fostra.

"An accident of some sort." Adira knew it was a lie, but they decided the truth in this instance was something perhaps better left unspoken. To hear him tell it, the circumstances by which Stamets came to be a "living navigator" for *Discovery*'s spore drive resulted from a desire to protect an innocent, spacefaring life-form discovered to possess an ability to communicate with the mycelial realm, though at the cost of great pain to itself. Unwilling to allow such a creature to suffer while being exploited for such a purpose, Stamets injected himself with DNA taken from the life-form. This resulted in augmentation of his own genetic structure, allowing him to interface with the spores that guided him and *Discovery* through the mycelial barrier. While Adira did not know whether the Xaheans were as ethical as Stamets in this regard, it was a risk they were unwilling to take.

A status indicator on their console flashed blue. "Commander, *Discovery*'s spore-drive system is online. The spores you staged have been deployed to the ship's reaction cube."

His eyes closed while he stood with hands linked to the interface pylons, Stamets nodded. *"Send the initiation sequence on my mark."*

Directing their gaze once more to Hilo and Sen, Adira said, "You might want to sit down for this. It can be a little unnerving the first time you go through it."

Exchanging looks of uncertainty, the councilor and the minister moved to nearby seats.

———

"Come on, space cowboy. I'm out of ideas. Give me something."

Jett Reno cast an annoyed glance at Cleveland Booker as the two stood over the spore-drive console, studying the array of status updates. The workstation had come alive the moment the Xahean transceiver activated, generating a dozen different holo-displays above the console. Reno recognized most of the information as being related to the reaction cube, which now hummed with energy from the spore hub's own internal power source.

"I don't have a damned clue," said Booker. "I don't even know how he's managing to do this at all, let alone remotely."

Reno had to admit it was odd to see the entire operation progressing without Paul Stamets or even Booker himself involved. Another indicator on the console's status display went from red to green, and she tapped her tri-com badge. "Reno to bridge. It looks like he's sending the initiation sequence. We're under a minute until we jump."

Over the open channel, Burnham asked, *"And you're sure there's nothing we can do to stop it from our end?"*

"Not so long as the subprocessor is cut off from the rest of the system." As she spoke the words, Reno frowned. "Hang on a minute." She pulled up her holo-tricorder and reviewed the current status of Zora's ongoing fight with the virus attacking the main computer. "Zora reported the subprocessor had been isolated by a separate subroutine. So how is it they can get a signal into our computer from the ground while Zora is stuck on the outside looking in?"

Booker studied the diagram, his eyes narrowing. "That's a damn good question. Somewhere there's a back door into the code."

"Any chance Stamets was sneaky enough to prop that door

open when he set up the link between him and us?" In a louder voice, Reno called out, "Hey, Zora. You out there?" As she summoned the computer, she entered commands of her own to the system. "Come on, you beautiful hunk of sexy software. Show me what you've got." She sensed Booker eyeing her. "What?"

"You've got an interesting approach to engineering," he said.

Reno shrugged. "I'm adaptable. It's one of my quirky charms." Another alert tone made her look up to see millions of blue-white mycelial spores alight inside the reaction cube. "Bridge, we're just about there."

Then everything in the room shut down. Consoles, lighting, and the reaction cube all cut out, plunging the compartment into near darkness, with the exception of the illumination from the spores inside their chamber. Every ambient sound also faded, leaving Reno and Booker standing in silence. Instinct made Reno reach for the console to steady herself in anticipation of losing artificial gravity, but she sighed in relief when that did not happen.

"Spore-drive subprocessor is offline," said Zora. *"Intrusive software deactivated or contained. Restoration of primary computer core anticipated within sixty seconds."*

"Holy hell," said Booker. "It worked?" He looked around. "I guess the lights will be back on in a minute?"

"I for one am going to enjoy this unprecedented time-out from our latest pressing emergency and soak in the serenity." Crossing her arms, Reno smiled as she watched the spores dancing inside the reaction cube, their bright hue bathing the room in a comforting glow.

"Paul Stamets," she said. "You magnificent bastard."

43

Every indicator on Adira's console went from blue to orange. Eyes wide with confusion, they reached for the controls Stamets had shown them were designated for triggering the abort procedure.

"Wait!" shouted Minister Sen, rushing from his chair to the console. "What is happening?"

"The link to *Discovery*," replied Adira. "It's been severed. We're no longer in sync with the ship's spore drive. We have to abort."

Inside the reaction cube, Stamets was pulling his hands from the spore-drive pylons, the nanogel encasing his fingers receding from his skin and back into the pylons. Crossing the chamber to the exit, he tapped the door release and the pressure hatch slid aside.

"That's it," he said. "Unless we can reestablish that link, we're dead in the water."

Councilor Hilo, standing near Sen, pointed to Stamets. "What did you do?"

"I didn't do anything." Stamets pointed up. "The link was severed from *Discovery*'s end. There's nothing I could do to stop it, as I had nothing to do with initiating it." He nodded to where Professor Fostra stood at his console, his expression one of utter confusion. "You all have been in control of this process the entire time."

"But you assisted in preparing the initiation sequence," said the professor, "based on your understanding of your ship's navigational systems." He looked to Sen. "I made the necessary changes to our codes for transmission to their ship, under his direction."

Hilo scowled. "Under his direction. You fool. He obviously found a way to send some kind of command or signal to his ship." She gestured to the guards, and Adira watched as they advanced. "Take them. Whatever happens next, we may need them to convince their captain to be agreeable."

"Councilor," said Sen. "We need to remain reasonable. A hostage situation will not be helpful for any of us. Did you not hear their captain? They would have been willing to assist us. Continuing down this path only serves to poison any chance we may have at a peaceful resolution that benefits all Xaheans."

"All Xaheans?" Hilo's voice dripped with contempt. "Do you not understand the crimes we have committed? We may have been acting in the best interests of all our people, but Queen Ki is unlikely to agree with our methods." She waved her hands, gesturing around the chamber. "The queen seeks consensus, mutual cooperation, and understanding from all sides, when it is clear only one side thinks and acts toward keeping our people safe. She would never have agreed to something like this. Introduce such an element of risk to our *home*? To our *entire civilization*?"

Sen shook his head. "It did not have to be this way."

"We had to act, for the good of our people," said Hilo. "No matter the outcome, regardless of whether we succeeded or failed, I always knew we would face punishment. I was prepared for that, as at least with success, I could face punishment knowing we had acted to protect our people from never again having to fear the possibility of oppression."

Shouts of alarm echoed from somewhere in the cavern, followed by the sounds of weapons fire. Adira recognized both Xahean weapons as well as Starfleet phasers, and with this realization they looked to Stamets.

"They found us," said Adira.

Instead of responding to them, Stamets did one of the most uncharacteristic things they had ever seen him do by launching himself toward one of the Xahean guards. The action was so unexpected and so violent it took the guard by surprise and both men tumbled across and over the spore-drive console, taking Fostra with them. The professor was knocked backward, tripping over the guard's feet and sending them and Stamets to the floor. The guard's sidearm was knocked loose and Adira lunged without thinking as the weapon slid across the floor. They were aware of shouts of alarm from the guard's companion, who had begun moving to help with Stamets when they realized they had left Adira an opening.

"No!"

It was Minister Sen, still attempting to maintain the situation with some shred of order. Adira ignored him as their hand closed around the weapon. It felt unfamiliar in their grip, but they still managed to bring it up and around just as the Xahean guard fired. A bolt of hot green energy screamed past their left ear, and they ducked away, adjusting the aim of the strange pistol and firing. The single shot struck the Xahean just below his throat, sending him toppling backward to stumble into a nearby workstation before collapsing to the floor.

Adira flinched at the sight of Stamets being thrown over the console. The commander landed heavily on the floor as his opponent lunged toward him, but Adira fired again. Struck in the shoulder, the guard staggered and collapsed in a heap just as Stamets was pulling himself to his feet. Out of breath and apparently surprised by the fight's abrupt end, he looked around and Adira saw a cut above his right eye and a tear across his already soiled undershirt.

"Thanks," he said.

Swinging to face Sen and Hilo, Adira aimed the weapon at them. "Please don't make me shoot you." They glanced to their left as Stamets stepped forward, now holding the other guard's weapon and directing the still shaken Fostra to stand next to the Xahean leaders. Brushing himself off with his free hand, Stamets looked at the Xaheans and shook his head.

"Captain Burnham was right, you know," he said. "We would've found some way to help you, if you'd just asked."

Her gaze shifting between him and Adira, Hilo glowered at them. "Just like our queen, your captain is naïve. Sometimes, one must be willing to make the unpopular choice to do what is right."

"And when you are queen, you may have the privilege and the burden that comes with such choices."

Looking toward the source of the new voice, Adira saw Queen Ki emerging from a connecting corridor, accompanied by Captain Burnham along with a four-person *Discovery* security team and what Adira guessed was a detail from the queen's personal guards. Dressed in a Starfleet tactical uniform, Burnham carried her phaser in a ready position as the security team and the royal guards fanned out to secure the area.

"Your Highness," said Hilo, and Adira heard the shakiness in her voice.

"Councilor." The queen's demeanor was cold and professional. "Minister Sen. You each have dishonored the oath you swore to serve the Xahean people. Further, your actions, along with everyone involved in this conspiracy, have brought shame to all Xaheans. You are a disgrace to everything we hold dear, and you will pay for your crimes."

She gestured to her guards, who took the three Xaheans into custody. To Adira and Stamets, the queen said, "On behalf of the Xahean people, I deeply apologize for everything that has happened. It saddens me to know this incident will cast a pall over the relationship I sincerely believe the Federation wishes to have with us. I can only beg your forgiveness."

Exchanging looks with Stamets, Adira offered a small bow. "Thank you, Your Highness. I'd like to think that even after all of this, our peoples might forge a new path."

Queen Ki smiled. "Such empathy. Such a desire to forgive. You honor me with your grace, my young friend. May this not be the last time we meet."

Once the queen was escorted from the area, Burnham stepped closer to Adira and Stamets. "You two all right?"

"Nothing a decade of shore leave won't fix," said Stamets. He reached out to place a hand on Adira's shoulder. "Thank you again."

Realizing they still held the Xahean weapon, Adira placed it on the nearby spore-drive console. "I still have no idea what happened."

"Commander Stamets gave us a little assist," said Burnham, her smile wide. "Didn't you?"

Still confused, Adira asked, "How? You had Professor Fostra enter all the instructions to be sent to *Discovery*."

"About half of what I gave him wasn't even necessary." Stamets smiled. "Just a bunch of extra diagnostic checks and status-report triggers." He looked to Burnham. "I figured once we started transmitting, it'd be easier for you to find us, so I was trying to buy some extra time. When I realized all the extra instructions allowed for access checks to the system, I saw a way to leave a variable unpopulated. That was enough to introduce a bug into the code that I hoped someone would find."

Burnham chuckled. "It was a nice trick. Commander Reno saw it and then Zora got ahold of it, and it was game over." She looked around, taking in the massive construct around them. "All of this work. It's incredible."

"It really is," said Stamets. "They just didn't count on me being the missing piece of their puzzle, just as they didn't count on me being the one person who could turn it against them."

Adira asked, "What were you going to do if Captain Burnham didn't find us in time? Go through with the jump?"

His expression turning wistful for a moment, Stamets then revealed a small, wry grin. "No. That part was never going to work."

"It was *never* going to work?" asked Burnham, making no effort to hide her surprise. For their part, Adira could hardly believe their ears.

"Not today." Stamets shrugged. "Maybe one day, but certainly not today. They didn't know that, and neither did anyone else." He turned to Adira, an apologetic look in his eyes. "I just had to sell it long enough for the captain to find us. Sorry."

Next to them, Adira heard Gray laughing, and when they looked, it was to see him standing there, face beaming with amusement and no small amount of pride.

I told you, he said. *I like the way he thinks.*

44

Dull and foreboding, the lifeless gray world was almost lost amid the cloud of ionized gases enveloping it like a thick stifling blanket. Only the cloud bore any semblance of familiarity for Burnham. As for the planet itself, as depicted on the bridge's main viewscreen, it looked nothing like she remembered of what once had been a gleaming, beautiful orb.

"Damn."

Turning to the science station, Burnham saw Sylvia Tilly glancing around the bridge, her sheepish expression making it seem as if she was only just realizing she had spoken aloud. A few of her crewmates, notably Ronald Bryce and Eva Nilsson, exchanged sympathetic looks with the young lieutenant. Seated at their forward stations, Keyla Detmer and Joanna Owosekun also offered unspoken support. Standing next to Tilly, Paul Stamets placed an arm around her shoulders for a brief hug.

"I have seen archived imagery of Xahea," said Queen Ki from where she stood before the viewscreen, in front of Detmer and Owosekun. "I've never seen the planet itself with my own eyes. No Xahean has, for nearly thirty generations. Based on the journals left by those who were among the last to depart the planet, I thought I had an idea of what to expect." The queen shook her head. "The reality is so much worse."

Sensing the weight of revelation and bitter, unforgiving truth weighing on Ki's shoulders, Burnham wanted to reach out, to connect with her on some level more heartfelt than the straightforward association they had forged as a matter of diplomacy. The progress they had made thanks to their respective positions was, she hoped, only the beginning of a long and mutually rewarding friendship, and this moment called for so much more.

After clearing her throat, Ki straightened her posture as if remembering her status. "Can you tell me anything about our homeworld I do not already know?"

Struggling to keep her own feelings at bay, Burnham looked to Tilly and nodded.

"Your Highness," said the science officer, picking up the cue. "Our scans show a thin debris field encircling Xahea. We think this is whatever remained of the ore-processing stations we know once orbited your planet. They must have exploded during the Burn, and their relatively low orbits saw to it Xahea's atmosphere was contaminated beyond all hope. Based on our sensor scans, we believe the entire planet was rendered uninhabitable."

"And before that?" asked the queen.

Tilly cast an uncertain glance toward Burnham before replying, "We're honestly not sure, Your Highness. At least, not after the early twenty-fifth century. Our sensors show nearly eighty percent of the planet's dilithium was excavated. The remainder is still there. Having not been refined, it survived the Burn. As for the population, we know the bulk of those who survived the Cardassian Occupation and the Dominion War evacuated the planet. You also mentioned other ships that set out on their own."

Nodding, Ki replied, "That is correct. We have no way of knowing if any of those other ships ever returned. However, in the archived journals recorded before the exodus, the environmental situation on Xahea was becoming untenable, and the planet would be unable to support life within just a few generations. Despite this, and while there are no historical archives of such figures, a percentage of Xaheans elected to remain behind. There is no record of their ultimate fate."

What had those people endured? Burnham wondered. Deteriorating environmental conditions at the very least, but would other races have followed in the footsteps of the Cardassians and the Dominion, moving in to stake a claim? It was a point of embarrassment for her that she did not have these answers for Ki. For the entirety of her life, the Federation represented a shining example of diverse cultures coming together in the spirit of joint cooperation, support, and achievement. That it could remove itself from the interstellar stage long enough to see its influence diminish so dramatically was still unfathomable to her. Such actions after the Burn could be justified to an extent, given those circumstances and the fact that the entire galaxy had suffered in the wake of that cataclysm. Centuries before that, however, at a time recorded as one of the most active and influential eras for the respective histories of so many cultures? That level of short-sightedness was overwhelming.

But we can fix it, Burnham thought. *We have the opportunity, and the will. We can absolutely do this. I hope.*

"It could be terraformed," said Tilly, drawing the gaze of everyone on the bridge. Now the focus of attention, the lieutenant straightened her posture and once more faced Ki. "What I'm saying, Your Highness, is that Xahea could be terraformed. It would take decades even with the technology we have now, but it's possible."

She caught herself just before saying something else, as though trying to anticipate the reaction from her impromptu audience. "I guess what I mean to say is it's possible if you let us—let the *Federation*—help you. We would do that . . . would *want* to do that. For you. *All* of you. All of *your people.*" Stopping herself, she drew a calming breath. "I'm sorry, Your Highness. It's just that I know how much Xahea meant to your people."

Ki smiled. "You are pure of heart, Lieutenant. I can see why Queen Po trusted you and so easily accepted your friendship." To Burnham's surprise, Tilly managed to weather the praise with aplomb, even though she reached up to wipe the corner of her left eye.

Turning back to Burnham, the queen said, "It is an intriguing and, dare I say it, romantic notion that we might return there. I do not know what it means to be so connected to a world, to bond with the planet of our birth the way our forebears did. Their belief that they shared existence with the planet itself was as remarkable as it was steadfast. I have no reason to question their convictions, but I also fear Xahea's time has passed."

Her voice growing softer as she spoke, she moved to gaze once more upon the pitiful world that was but a shadow of the planet she knew only from stories. "Like the people she protected, our world suffered greatly at the whims of oppressors. Her spirit was crushed alongside that of every Xahean who slaved under the boots of tyrants. While those who survived managed to forge a new life, the scars of what they endured never truly healed. Instead, they were passed on to us, their descendants, so that we might remember everything our ancestors and Xahea itself lost."

Ki turned to face Burnham and the rest of the bridge crew. "Your offer to assist in such a tremendous undertaking moves me, Captain. Terraforming might succeed at bringing the planet itself back to a measure of new life, the unique elements that bonded Xahea to her people. It is this bond—that essence— that I believe is gone. Our sister is dead, and what you propose would leave us with a pale imitation of her. I do not believe any of my people would want that."

Her gaze shifted to Tilly, and she offered a respectful nod. "What this unfortunate affair has done is make me realize the mistakes we have made. If we had simply been honest with ourselves and perhaps not so consumed by fears rooted in our tragic past, perhaps we would not have been so resistant to change."

She paused, casting her eyes toward the deck. Burnham sensed how the queen, driven as she was by an authentic desire to serve her people with integrity and compassion, remained troubled. "In my attempts to find common ground and peace between opposing viewpoints, I forgot my duty to act in the best interests of my people, even if that action is not always understood or appreciated. That responsibility includes helping guide them toward such understanding, not through coercion or simple brute force, but by fostering open dialogue, mutual respect, and trust. By doing what I thought was protecting my people, I failed them. I held them back, rather than pushed them to grow." Once again, she looked to Tilly. "Queen Po was a visionary in that regard. I should have more closely followed the example she set so long ago."

Tilly glanced around the bridge again before replying, "Po couldn't have anticipated everything your people faced, Your Highness. She ruled Xahea in a very different, more prosperous time. I don't doubt she was amazing at it." Her eyes shifted to Burnham for a fleeting moment before she added, "But in my admittedly limited experience, the true test of leadership comes during times of great adversity. I'd think if she were here today, she'd be on your side."

"I will try to remember that." Ki smiled. "Just as I will remember how you and your captain have shown support for us, even after all that has happened. I feel as though this may be a turning point in the course of our history, though there remains much work to be done. Unity to restore, along with not simply a common purpose but an embracing of the universe around us. Xahea would have wanted that for us, I think."

Burnham said, "You don't have to do this alone, Your Highness. Colonization is still an option. There are many star systems out there we've only charted but never explored. Somewhere out there is a world you can make your own, a place that would give everyone a chance to build the life they want for themselves while still preserving all it means to be Xahean." She stepped closer to the queen. "We can help with that. *Discovery*'s spore drive makes surveying some of these systems an easy proposition. We can help you find a world that's far enough away to offer your people the sense of security they seek, but perhaps not so far away as to be completely out of touch."

"Out of touch with the Federation, you mean," said Ki. "Even after everything that has happened, after the attacks and affronts to your crew, you would still help us."

"That's right. We owe you this much, but also so much more." Burnham gestured to her bridge crew. "It would allow us to correct the mistakes from so long ago, and perhaps we might build a better future for both our peoples, together."

The queen clasped her hands before her. "You give me much to think about, Captain, but suppose we do find this world you believe awaits us. It might take generations just to move Sanctuary there. We may not even have the resources to complete such a journey."

Burnham replied, "We would help with that as well."

Stepping around the science console, Stamets held up a hand. "Your Highness, if I may, there is another possibility. The spore drive created by your people isn't without merit, but I believe it actually is feasible to use *Discovery* the way I suggested."

"I thought you said it wouldn't work," replied Tilly.

"It wasn't going to work then, under those conditions." The commander shrugged. "But with enough power and the necessary preparations to ensure Sanctuary's safety? It's feasible, and it's not like we won't have time to work up the right computer models to help us."

"We?" Tilly smiled. "Cool."

Stamets said, "It's not something I'd want to do *a lot*, but if and when the Xaheans find a world suited to their needs, I think we can help them get there."

"We move Sanctuary to this new world, and it becomes a moon of sorts," said Ki. "Those who wish to remain within the habitat could do so, and those wanting a life on the planet could pursue that path."

As if taking all of this in, she looked around the bridge. "I can see from your faces that your desire to help us is genuine, and I know many of my people believe it as well." She turned back to the main viewscreen, her eyes lingering on the dead world of her ancestors. "Our people did what was necessary to survive and to preserve what remained of our heritage. For better or worse, we redefined what it means to be Xahean. Can we do it again? Is it possible for us to find a new path to contentment by attempting to re-create even in passing fashion all we were forced to abandon? It seems like a daunting challenge."

"Your Highness," said Burnham, "there's a saying among my people: 'You can't go home again.' For us, it usually means we accept the past is the past, and it's detrimental to focus on it when the future is there, waiting for us."

Stamets added, "I don't believe you or your people truly want to go home. You just want wherever you are to *feel* like home. A large part of making that real is the people you choose to surround you." He looked to Burnham, holding her gaze an extra moment. In that interval, Burnham saw his remaining bitterness melting away. He placed his hand on his heart, and though his next words remained unspoken, she knew what they were and that they were meant solely for her.

I'm sorry.

Looking away from the viewscreen, Ki turned to face Burnham once more. "Very well, Captain. Let us see what the future holds, together."

45

"I've already explained everything to the Evoran leadership. They're expecting your arrival in three days."

Standing in her ready room before a holographic projection of Admiral Vance, Burnham nodded in acknowledgment. "Understood, Admiral."

"Don't take too long, though. An official delegation is already assembled and en route to Sanctuary. Diplomats, engineers, sociologists: the usual assortment of experts and advisors. There's a preliminary plan in development for a mission to help the Xaheans scout for a world they might colonize. Once a suitable candidate is located, we'll proceed with Commander Stamets's idea for using Discovery *to transport their Sanctuary to its new home. Whether the Xaheans decide to continue using the sphere as an artificial satellite where some of their population can live is up to them. On the other hand, there's also been an initial discussion about it possibly being transitioned to serve as a starbase for us, perhaps even crewed by Xaheans."*

Despite herself, Burnham blinked at the news. "That's extraordinary, sir."

"It's certainly encouraging, but let's not get ahead of ourselves. Queen Ki is pushing the message of collaboration for all it's worth. She's getting help from some of the planets where we've reestablished communication, who've offered to assist in the relocation and colonization effort and have made invitations to visit their worlds."

It was almost overwhelming to hear. Burnham knew there was still a long way to go before the Xaheans truly felt comfortable integrating into an interstellar community rather than existing on its fringes. Still, the progress made in such a short time was promising.

"I'm just glad we could help, sir."

"There are several steps to navigate before we're there." Vance's expression softened. *"Regardless, it's a solid start to our renewed relationship with the Xaheans, and that's all due to you and your crew, Captain. Well done."*

Burnham nodded. "Thank you, Admiral."

"The opportunity to right an all-but-forgotten wrong is a wondrous display of Federation ideals. I have to tell you that since Discovery*'s arrival and seeing what you bring to the table? It's been a very long time since I've felt this level of optimism. Please pass on my sincere thanks to your people, Captain."*

Vance's hologram disappeared, leaving the ready room to Burnham. Closing her eyes, she savored the momentary solitude, the silence around her interrupted only by the low, omnipresent hum of *Discovery*'s engines as the ship traveled at warp.

Followed by the door chime.

Smiling to herself, Burnham said, "Come." She turned to the door as it opened to admit Sylvia Tilly. The lieutenant appeared nervous, but also a bit eager. While this certainly was not unusual for her, Burnham could only wonder what might have prompted it just now.

"Good evening, Captain," said Tilly. "I hope I'm not interrupting?"

"Of course not." Burnham gestured for her to enter. "What can I do for you?"

Stepping inside the ready room, Tilly replied, "We received a transmission from Sanctuary." She motioned with her hands. "I mean, I received a transmission. They sent it to me. Just me. It was from Queen Ki, and she sent it directly to me."

"Okay?"

Her anxiety now evident, Tilly said, "She sent me a message from Po."

Burnham blinked several times, processing the unexpected response. "Really?"

"Really." Walking farther into the room, Tilly looked at the floor. "Ki said it's something Po recorded not long after we left, and it's been held in a protected archive since then. According to Ki, every leader after Po was entrusted with its safekeeping, without ever knowing its contents or why it was being kept." She paused, tossing more hand gestures. "You know, I'm guessing with other important stuff. State secrets, launch codes, whatever."

"Sure." Burnham suppressed the urge to giggle. "Have you opened the message?"

Tilly shook her head. "Not yet. Ki said it's been sealed since Po recorded it, under royal decree. Her instructions were for it to remain unopened until it could be given to me, no matter how many years passed or whatever might happen before it could be delivered. Ki told me it was among the most sacred duties she and her predecessors undertook, and she was honored it was she who was able to give it to me. I guess they take royal decrees pretty seriously." She wiped a single tear from the corner of her left eye. "I wanted to share it. With you. Just in case, you know, there was some sort of planetary-leader highbrow stuff I should probably be passing on to Admiral Vance or something."

"Sylvia," replied Burnham. "Po made the message for you, hoping you'd see it nine hundred years later. She made sure whoever ruled Xahea after her safeguarded it until it could be given to you. Even though she could never have anticipated everything that happened to her people and how their views about the Federation would change over centuries, her successors still made sure that message was kept. That says a lot, not just about Queen Ki but also those who came before her."

Forcing a smile, Tilly sniffed and wiped at her nose. "So, we should probably watch it."

"That's what I'm thinking," said Burnham, waiting while Tilly activated her holo-padd and tapped a few controls before making a swiping gesture away from her.

In response to the action, a holographic projection appeared before them, solidifying into the form of Me Hani Ika Hali

Ka Po. The Xahean queen was of course just as Burnham re-membered her, young and exuding a supreme confidence some might find extraordinary for someone with such limited life experience. Burnham was certain the demands of leadership Po had taken from her mother had required an accelerated matura-tion on the queen's part.

"*Tilly!*" said the Po hologram. "*At least, I hope it's you watching this, Tilly. If not, then somebody somewhere has some ex-plaining to do about disobeying my royal orders. What's the point of being queen if you can't issue inviolable proclamations with death sentences for those who flout them?*"

Despite her reddened eyes, Tilly laughed at her friend. Burnham stepped closer, putting her arm around her.

"*Right before I recorded this, I received a message from Cap-tain Pike. He told me they'd detected the last Red Angel burst, the one from Commander Burnham letting him and the* Enterprise *crew know you'd made it safely to the future. He didn't know which exact year you ended up dropping into, so I'm guessing it's more or less where Burnham figured you needed to be. I hope you and your friends are okay.*"

Po's expression turned more thoughtful, and she extended a hand. Burnham noted Tilly started to move toward the queen before catching herself, and she suppressed another smile while tightening her embrace around the lieutenant's shoulder.

"*First off, be sure to tell Commander Burnham that I think she's amazing. Doing what she did, knowing it was a one-way trip with no guarantees?*" Po shook her head. "*Incredible, but what you and the rest of your crew did? Everyone and everything you gave up, to keep the rest of us safe? You left your home and everyone in it to ensure a future for everyone else. I hope whatever future you've found is a good one, and if it isn't, then I hope you do everything you can to make it your home. You deserve that much. I know there are only a handful of people who will ever know the truth about what you did and why you did it, and I'm honored to be one of them. I'll miss you, Sylvia Tilly, and there won't be a day*"

for the rest of my life that I don't think about you. To you and your
friends, I wish you well."

Po capped her final words with a smile that lingered until
the hologram vanished. Stepping away from Tilly, Burnham
watched as her friend wiped once more at her eyes.

"Wow," said the lieutenant. "Can't say I was expecting
that."

Burnham replied, "Thank you for sharing it with me. One
of the nice things about reestablishing contact with the Xaheans
is that maybe we'll get to learn more about their history, including details about Po's reign."

"Part of me wants that, but then I start thinking about what
came after." Tilly sniffed, still gathering herself. "She didn't live
to see everything that happened. For all we know, her time as
queen was the last prosperous period her people had."

"But that's not entirely true," said Burnham. "Even after
everything they went through, they didn't give up. They found
a way, reinventing themselves and figuring out how to forge a
new life, and they never lost sight of who they are and where
they come from. We're just helping them with the next part of
their journey."

Drawing herself up, Tilly smiled. "It took us long enough,
but I'm glad we could finally return the favor."

46

Burnham was happy to see the hangar bay filling up. Already attended by a sizable portion of the ship's off-duty personnel, this evening seemed to have an additional energy level attached to it. Dozens of crewmembers had taken up space on the deck, with others bringing chairs and smaller cargo containers as had become the informal custom for events of this sort. The buzz of numerous low-volume, overlapping conversations filled the vast chamber.

"There are more people than the last time I was here," she said.

Standing next to her near the bay's rear bulkhead, Hugh Culber replied, "It might have something to do with you declaring all personnel off duty for the next twenty-four hours."

"Yes, that's probably it."

Culber said, "It was a nice touch, encouraging civilian attire for events like this."

That nearly everyone in attendance was out of uniform, following her invitation to opt for more comfortable clothing, made her smile. She looked down at the simple jade dress she had chosen for the evening. "Are you really off duty if you're still dressed for duty?"

Not all that long ago, Burnham would have fretted over the idea of a starship's entire complement being "off duty" at the same time. It certainly had not been the norm aboard the ships on which she had served earlier in her career. As a young officer, she had been taught by those senior to her that vigilance and attention were intangible yet critical duties required of every crewmember. The nature of the missions in which she participated seldom allowed for extended periods of leisure time outside scheduled shore leave. Aboard a ship in deep space, separated by days or weeks from any assistance, a moment's negligence might spell disaster and automated, computer-controlled systems could go only so far.

That was then, Burnham mused. *And this is now.* Starfleet had evolved since *Discovery*'s day, and so had a great many other things. Her ability to trust automation and software had grown by leaps and bounds. She also had come to realize that taking time for one's own mental health and well-being was an invaluable personal care regimen that needed to be embraced. There was much work to be done, for sure, but they could not accomplish the tasks Starfleet demanded of them if they were not at their best. Burnham pledged not to forget that, for herself or her crew.

"Everything all right, Zora?" she asked.

"All systems functioning normally, Captain," responded *Discovery*'s computer. *"I will alert you immediately if that changes in any way. I hope you have a pleasant evening."*

Culber asked, "Zora, what's tonight's movie?"

"Doctor Arbusala actually helped me with my selection, Doctor Culber, and he asked me not to announce the title ahead of time."

"Keeping it a surprise?" Burnham cocked an eyebrow. "That certainly doesn't sound suspicious at all."

"I assure you, Captain, nothing sinister is afoot."

Burnham turned to see that Doctor Arbusala had entered the hangar bay with another group of *Discovery* crewmembers and was now moving to join them.

"Doctor," said Culber. "You're conspiring with Zora now?"

The Denobulan smiled. "Conspire? I do not believe it is quite so ominous." He clasped his hands behind his back. "I was talking with Zora, and she mentioned that with the vast library of options available to her, she found it challenging to make a selection the entire crew might enjoy, or at least those who choose to participate in your movie nights. I suggested whatever film or holovid she selects should somehow convey or reinforce with positivity a theme that could be interpreted as featuring strong ties to what the crew may have recently experienced or endured, or is currently facing."

Burnham cocked an eyebrow as she pondered this unexpected development. It was certainly an interesting notion, and consistent with Zora's still nascent attempts to find her footing both with *Discovery*'s computer as well as its crew. With what else might the artificial intelligence experiment as she became more comfortable with her environment?

"And what did she find?" asked Burnham.

"Thanks to her, I now know that years before humanity made first contact with a nonterrestrial species, your entertainment featured numerous stories of such encounters. These dramatizations ran the gamut from peaceful interactions to full-scale invasions by aliens bent on conquest. However, there was one interesting film about a rather large group of extraterrestrials who crash on Earth and are left with no choice but to integrate into human society. Zora tells me the story of how these new arrivals face all manner of challenges before they come to accept their circumstances and turn to building a new life is really quite inspiring."

"Easier said than done," said Culber.

Arbusala replied, "Quite correct, Doctor, but the path to such a worthy goal is likely rich with interesting stories." He paused, glancing around the crowded hangar bay. "I daresay the same is true with another group of outsiders attempting to make their way in a new world."

"And Zora picked this film?" asked Burnham.

"Indeed I did, Captain," replied Zora. *"I hope you enjoy it."*

When no further information seemed to be forthcoming, Burnham raised her hands in mock surrender. Resigned to the fact her rank appeared to afford her no privileges in this situation, she asked, "Doctor, I guess it's almost time for you to leave us."

"That's correct." The doctor bowed his head. "I have asked

Admiral Vance to assign me to the official delegation returning to Sanctuary. I feel I might be useful as the Federation works to reestablish our relationship with the Xaheans."

"If you can do for them even a fraction of what you did for us," said Burnham, "I suspect you'll be just fine."

"I certainly hope so, Captain." Arbusala smiled. "After all, my work here is certainly very much done."

"And what did you learn?" asked Culber. "Or do we have to wait for your report to Starfleet?"

Once again, Arbusala smiled. "Contrary to what many of your crew believed, Doctor, Admiral Vance didn't send me here to find what, if anything, might be 'wrong' with you or your crew. Quite the opposite, actually. My task was to observe you—all of you—as you continue adapting to your new circumstances and carrying out your duties with such a high degree of performance. What I've witnessed has been rather remarkable."

"In what way?" asked Burnham.

Pausing to once more look out across the hangar bay and the people assembled there, Arbusala replied, "This isn't simply a starship's crew, Captain. It's a *family*, one of the quintessential facets of one's identity. Like Janeway's *Voyager*, you pulled together during a period of extreme trial, and in those times when you thought yourself all alone in the universe, you safeguarded and cared for one another with the same fierce determination one displays when protecting a child, a relative, or a partner."

"We didn't really have much of a choice," said Culber. "When we first got here, we were all we had." He looked to Burnham. "Some of us didn't even have that, at least at first."

Arbusala nodded in acknowledgment. "And that's what's even more noteworthy, Doctor. You did have a choice. For your own personal reasons, each of you elected to follow this path, to commit yourselves to a calling far greater than even the one demanded by swearing a Starfleet oath. One might argue that it wasn't an actual choice given the stakes and your feelings for one another, but I think it's important to remember the distinction. Each of you sacrificed everything to be here, together." He gestured toward the crew on the hangar bay. "There is no stronger family than the family you choose."

"It's certainly gotten us this far," said Burnham.

"There will be difficulty, of course, but the resilience this crew has demonstrated is astonishing." Stepping closer, Arbusala lowered his voice. "It is a tremendous credit to you both. You've each successfully navigated this challenge in ways for which you are ideally suited, caring for your crew and responding to their needs, and never letting them lose sight of who they are. Starfleet officers with duties and responsibilities, yes, but also a *family* with an obligation and a fervent desire to watch over one another. The example you and your crew provide every day is worthy not just of study but emulation." To Culber, he added, "Doctor, your guardianship of Adira and Gray Tal is quite simply extraordinary. I sincerely hope you find a way for Gray to manifest in physical form. While it would be an immense technological achievement, what it might mean for him and Adira is an even greater triumph."

Exchanging glances with Burnham, Culber cleared his throat. "Thank you, Doctor. I appreciate everything you've done while you've been with us."

"As do I," added Burnham. "Please feel free to visit us again."

Once again, Arbusala's broad smile returned. "I may very well do that. You were already where you need to be, going forward. After a prolonged period of darkness, the Federation and Starfleet have finally begun returning to the light. *Discovery*'s arrival is a principal reason for that. Perhaps you feel lost, given how the galaxy passed you by during all those centuries you skipped, but it's also true the Federation and Starfleet lost their way for a time. Yes, they have modern technology and so much else to lean on for support, but I also believe they have much to learn from how things used to be done. You and your crew will be their guides. Just keep doing what you do so well."

Taking his leave, Arbusala turned as though intending to

head toward the middle of the hangar bay, but then he stopped. He turned and held out his hands to Burnham and Culber.

"I do have one last piece of advice specifically for the two of you. Don't get so caught up in looking after everyone else that you forget to take care of yourselves." The three of them exchanged final smiles. "Good luck to you both, and your crew."

After he was gone, Culber turned to Burnham. "Well, that was unexpected."

"Indeed." She put a hand on his arm. "And he was right. You're a wonderful doctor, Hugh, but you're an even greater friend. I can't imagine what I'd do without you."

Culber placed his hand on hers. "I've seen what you'll do for us, Captain. I'm honored to serve with you, and proud to call you *my* friend."

The hangar bay's main lighting dimmed and the conversations began to fade. With a final appreciative look, Culber headed off to where Paul Stamets, Joann Owosekun, and Keyla Detmer sat on a grouping of cargo containers. Just as Burnham began looking for a place to watch the movie, Cleveland Booker entered the hangar bay. Already a civilian, he was ahead of everyone else so far as choice of clothing and had opted for an open-collared dark shirt over maroon trousers, a far nicer ensemble than he normally sported.

"You dressed up for me?" she asked.

Noting her attire, Booker offered a mock grimace. "Not enough, I think."

"You'll do."

They moved to a group of unoccupied chairs, settling into their seats as a holoprojection appeared at the front of the hangar bay. Framed against the open aperture and the streaking stars of warped space behind *Discovery* was the image of a bright sun ejecting a plume of plasma as a space vessel soared past.

"Are you all right?" asked Booker in a low voice, and only then did Burnham realize she was letting her attention and gaze wander from the film to the crew scattered around her.

"I'm fine." She rested a hand on his thigh. "I was just thinking."

Leaning closer, Booker draped his arm around her shoulders. "About what?"

"Despite everything we've been through and how close we are as a crew—as a *family*—for the longest time I wondered if that would be enough to see us through here. If it would be enough for us to fit in here, in this century." Burnham pressed against him, relaxing for the first time in a while. "But I think we've made it. We're home."

ACKNOWLEDGMENTS

As always, my first round of thanks is reserved for my editors at Gallery Books, Ed Schlesinger and Margaret Clark. *Somewhere to Belong* is my twenty-fourth *Star Trek* novel and the twentieth while working under guidance from either or both of these individuals going back nearly twenty years. They've tolerated entirely too much of my irreverent goofiness over that span of time, far more than should perhaps be required given their respective compensation packages, and each of the books I've written under their watchful eye is better for their involvement.

Thanks also to Kirsten Beyer, fan-favorite *Star Trek* novelist who later found herself creating *Star Trek* for the screen, and a friend for longer than either of those wonderful accomplishments. As she did for my previous *Discovery* novel, 2018's *Drastic Measures*, she gifted me with those most precious of commodities: her time, her counsel, and her patience. We had fabulous conversations about this story before Margaret and Ed turned me loose to write it, and she was always a phone call or text message away whenever I had the odd question. To say this book would not have been possible without her assistance is more than a colossal understatement. It's simply an immutable fact.

326 ACKNOWLEDGMENTS

Last but not least, thanks to my hetero life mate, frequent writing partner, and perpetual sounding board, Kevin Dilmore: We don't actually have to be working together for him to be collaborating with me, even if he doesn't know it at the time. Over the course of nearly twenty-five years, countless chickens have given their wings in service to our brainstorming, assorted shenanigans, and friendship.

ABOUT THE AUTHOR

Dayton Ward has been modified to fit this medium,
to write in the space allotted, and has been edited for content.
Reader discretion is advised.

Visit him at
www.daytonward.com